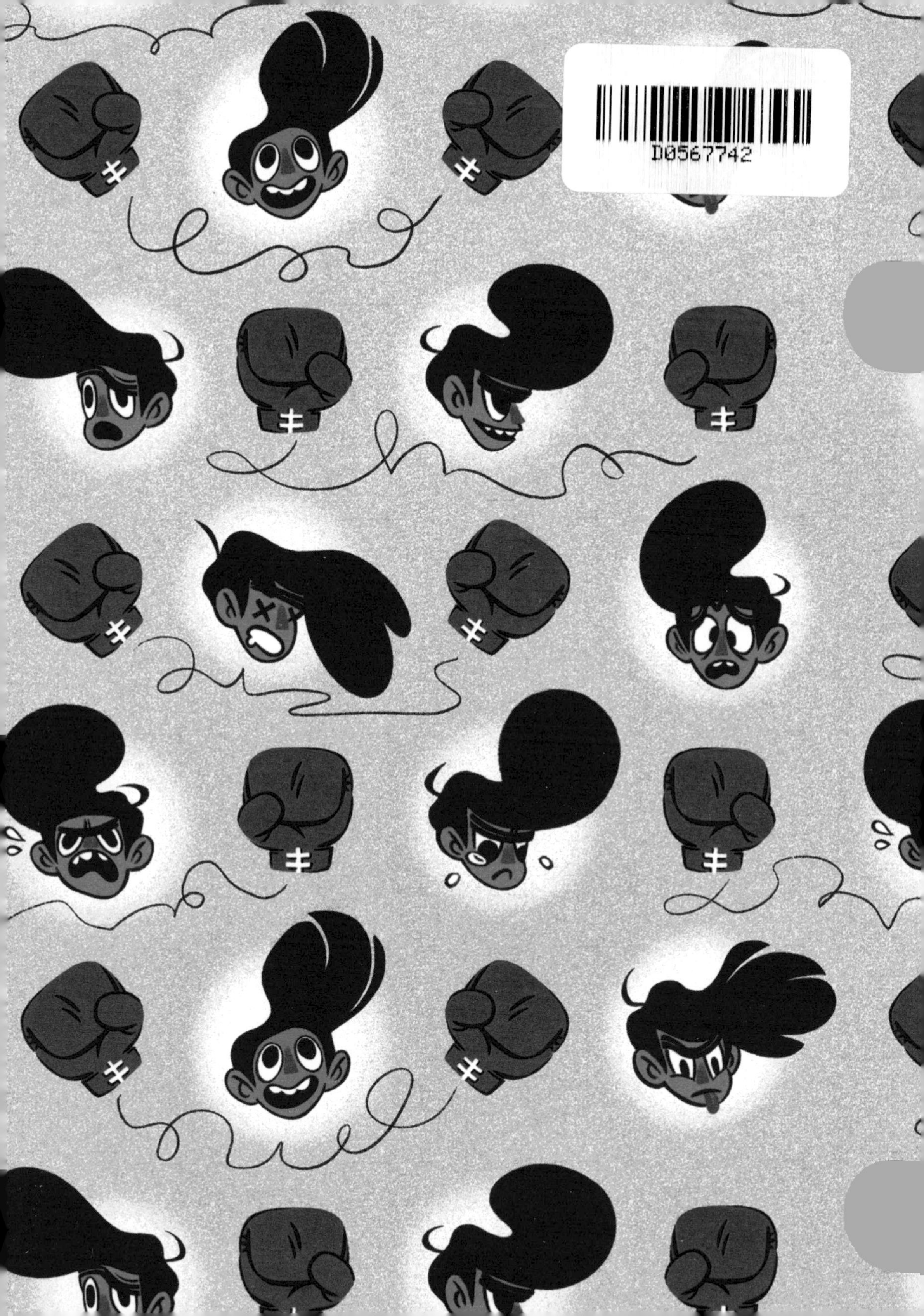

FOR THE SMALL-FISTED AND PERSISTENT

AND FOR MY FAMILY:
SK, PK, AK AND, OF COURSE, TR.

First edition published in 2021 by Nobrow Ltd.
27 Westgate Street, London E8 3RL.

Text and illustrations © Lara Kaminoff 2021.

Lara Kaminoff has asserted her right under the Copyright, Designs and
Patents Act, 1988, to be identified as the Author and Illustrator of this Work.

1 3 5 7 9 10 8 6 4 2

Published in the US by Nobrow (US) Inc.
Printed in Poland on FSC® certified paper.

MIX
Paper from
responsible sources
FSC® C163799

ISBN: 978-1-910620-78-6
www.nobrow.net

LARA KAMINOFF

HOW TO PICK A FIGHT

NOBROW

LONDON | LOS ANGELES

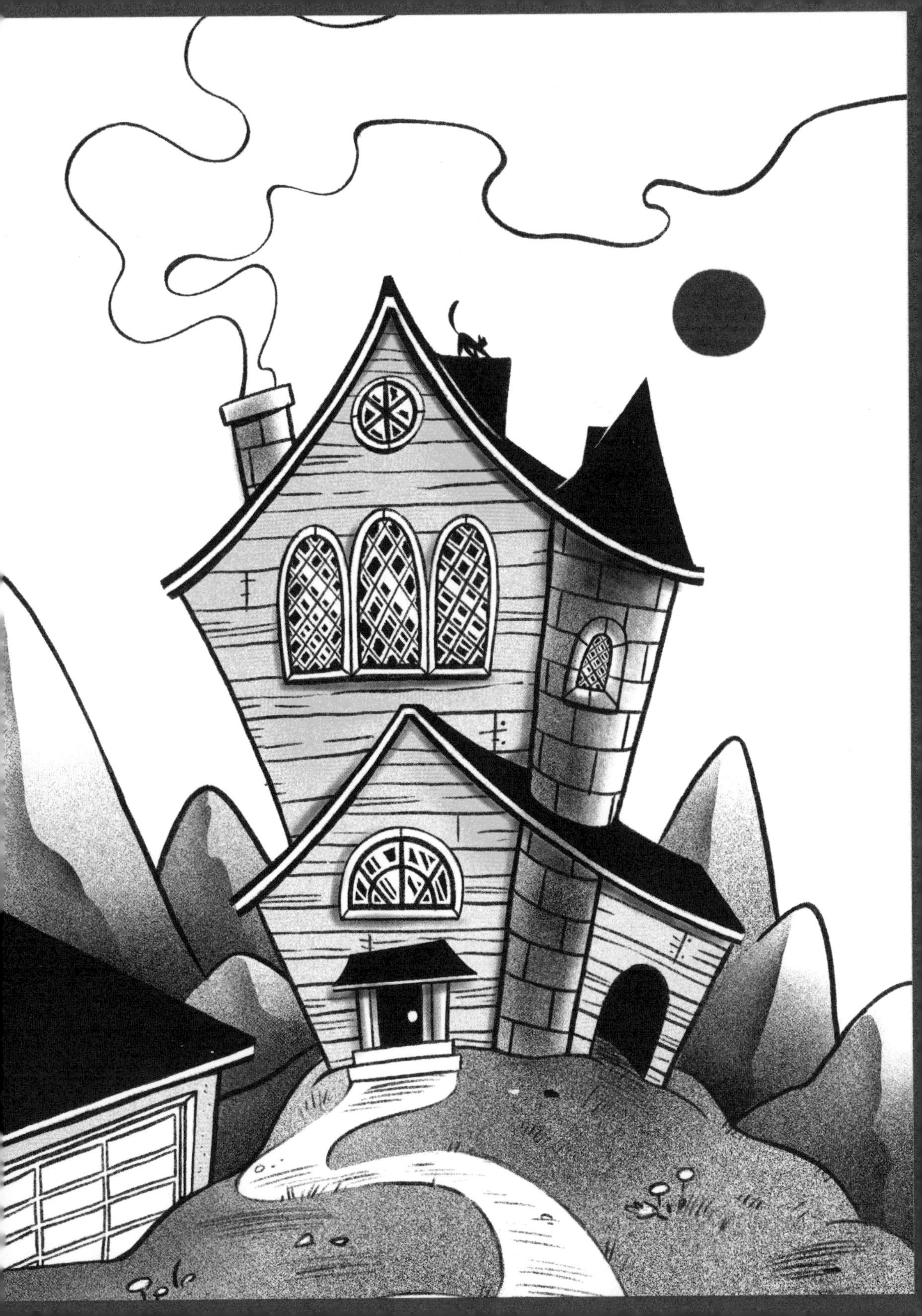

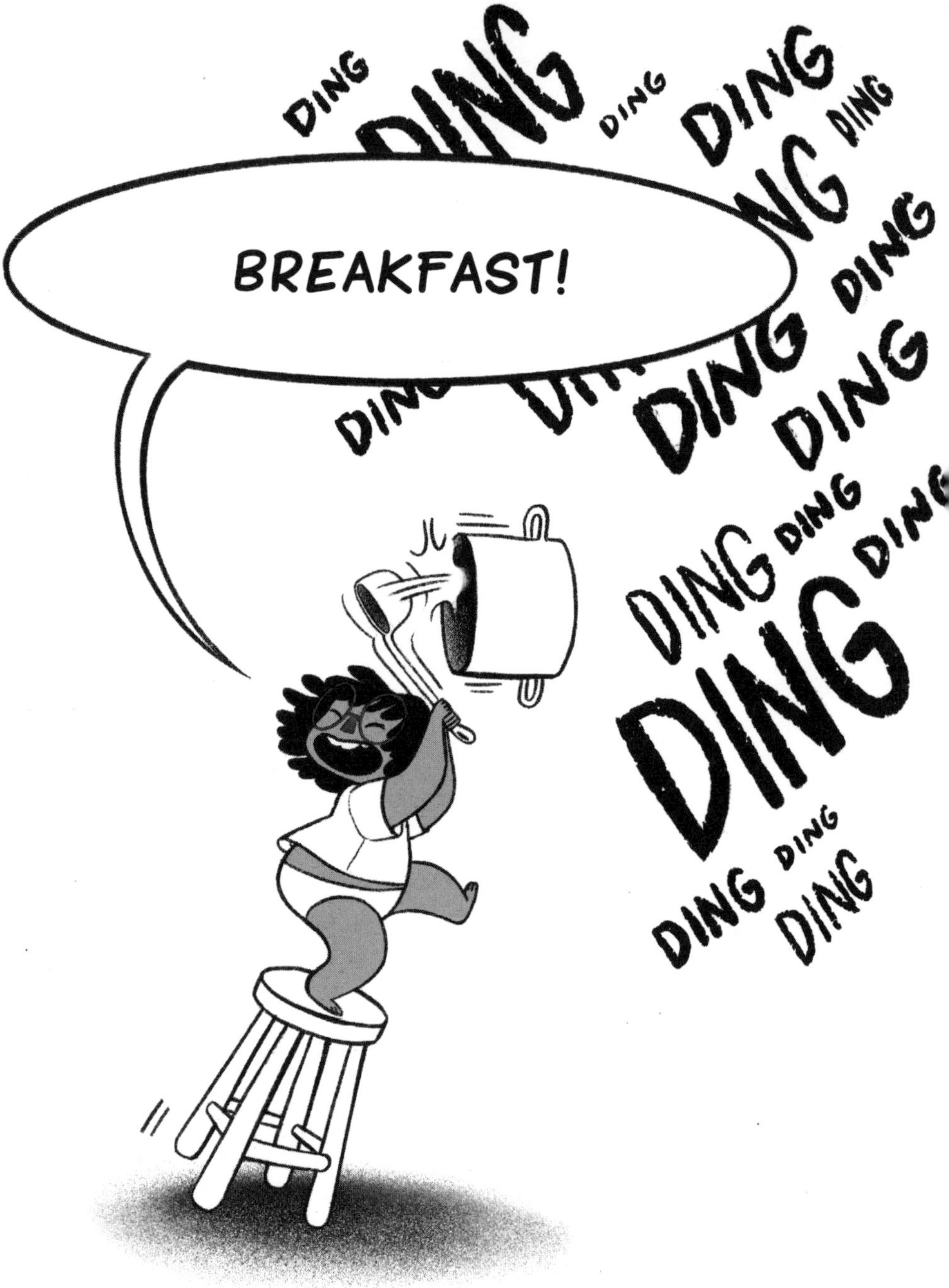
BREAKFAST!
DING
DING
DING
DING
DING
DING
DING
DING
DING
DING
DING
DING
DING
DING
DING
DING
DING

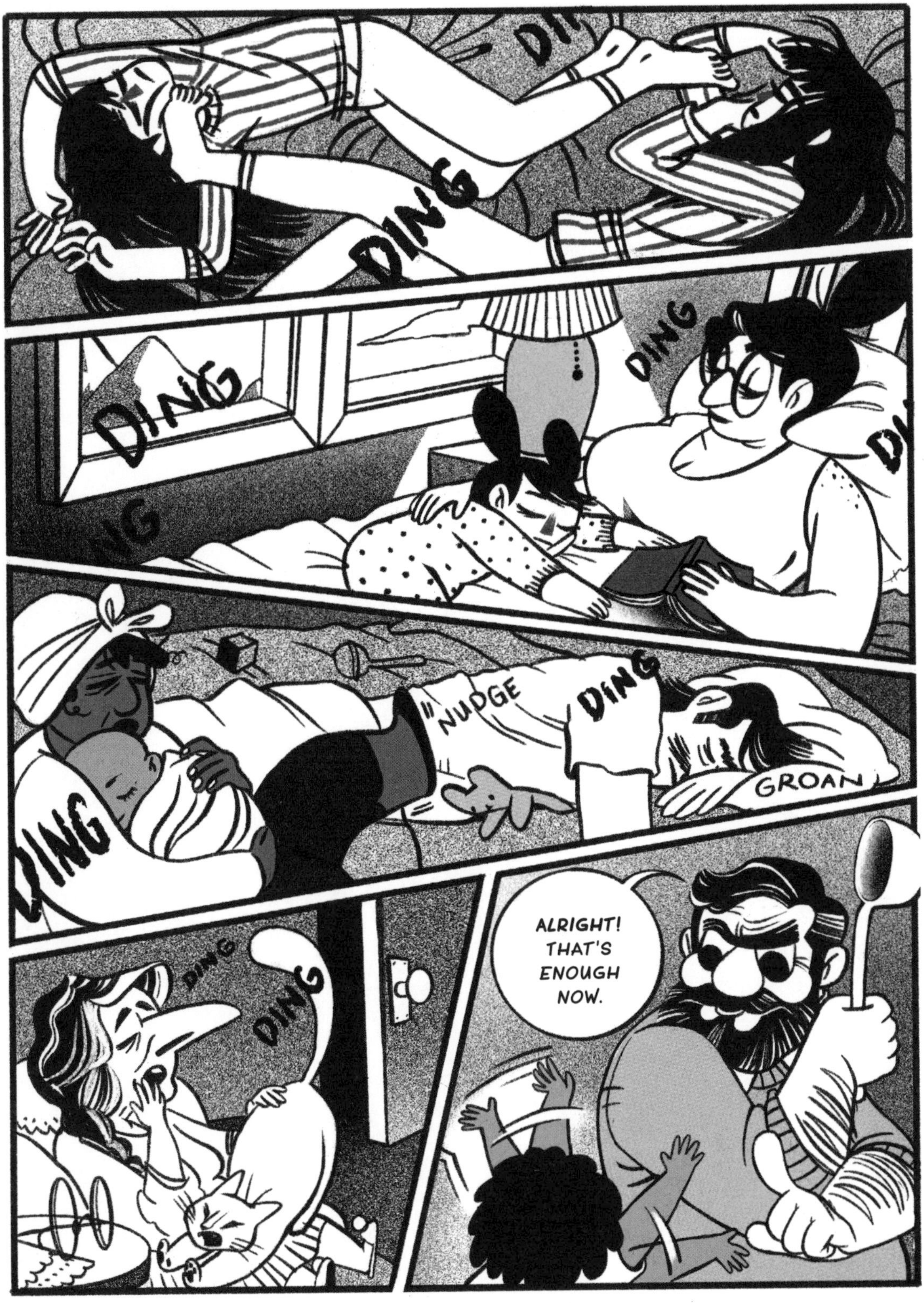

DING
DING
DING
DING
DING
NUDGE
DING
GROAN
DING
DING
DING
ALRIGHT! THAT'S ENOUGH NOW.

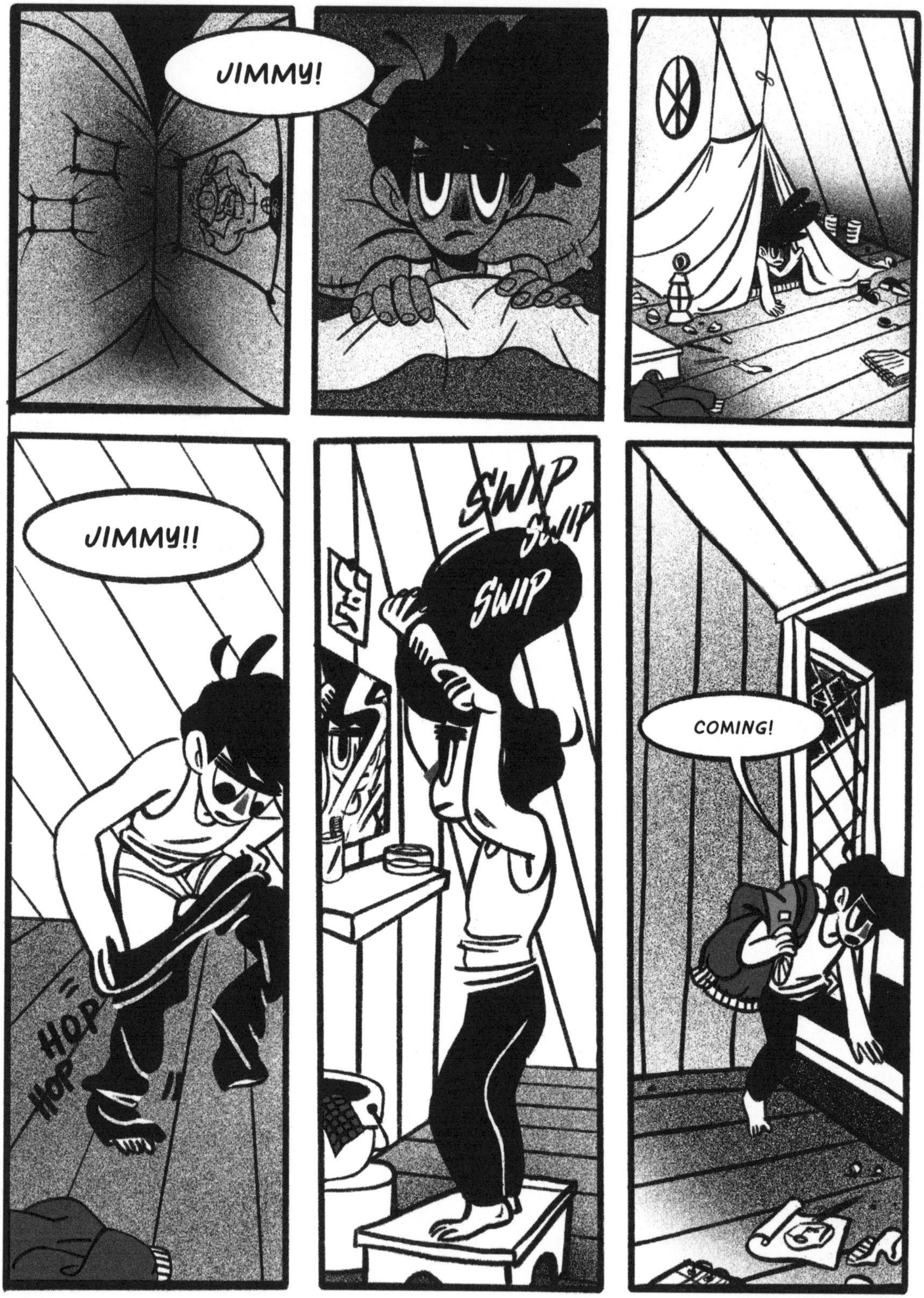
JIMMY!
JIMMY!!
HOP
HOP
SWIP
SWIP
SWIP
COMING!

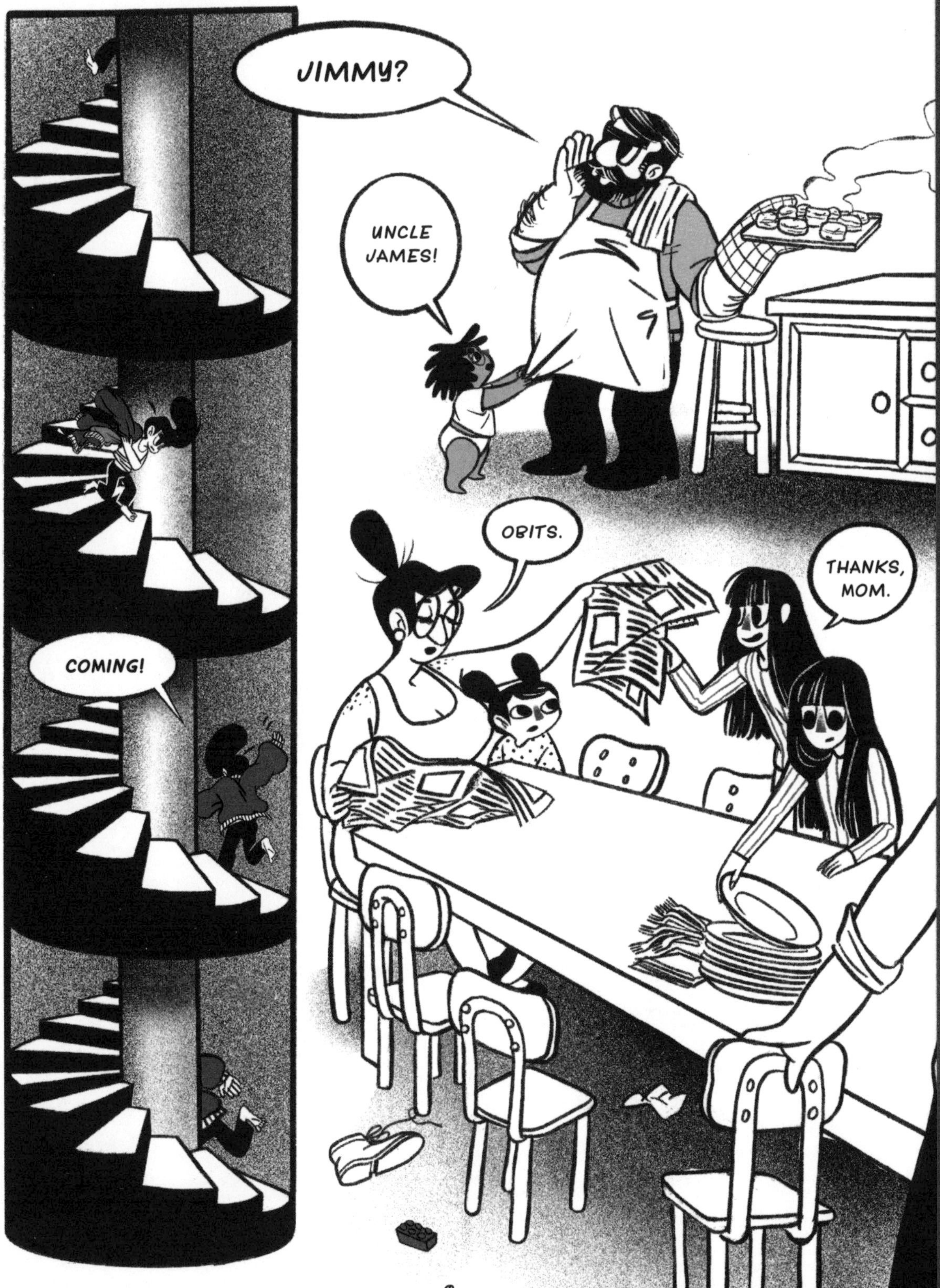
JIMMY?
COMING!
UNCLE JAMES!
OBITS.
THANKS, MOM.

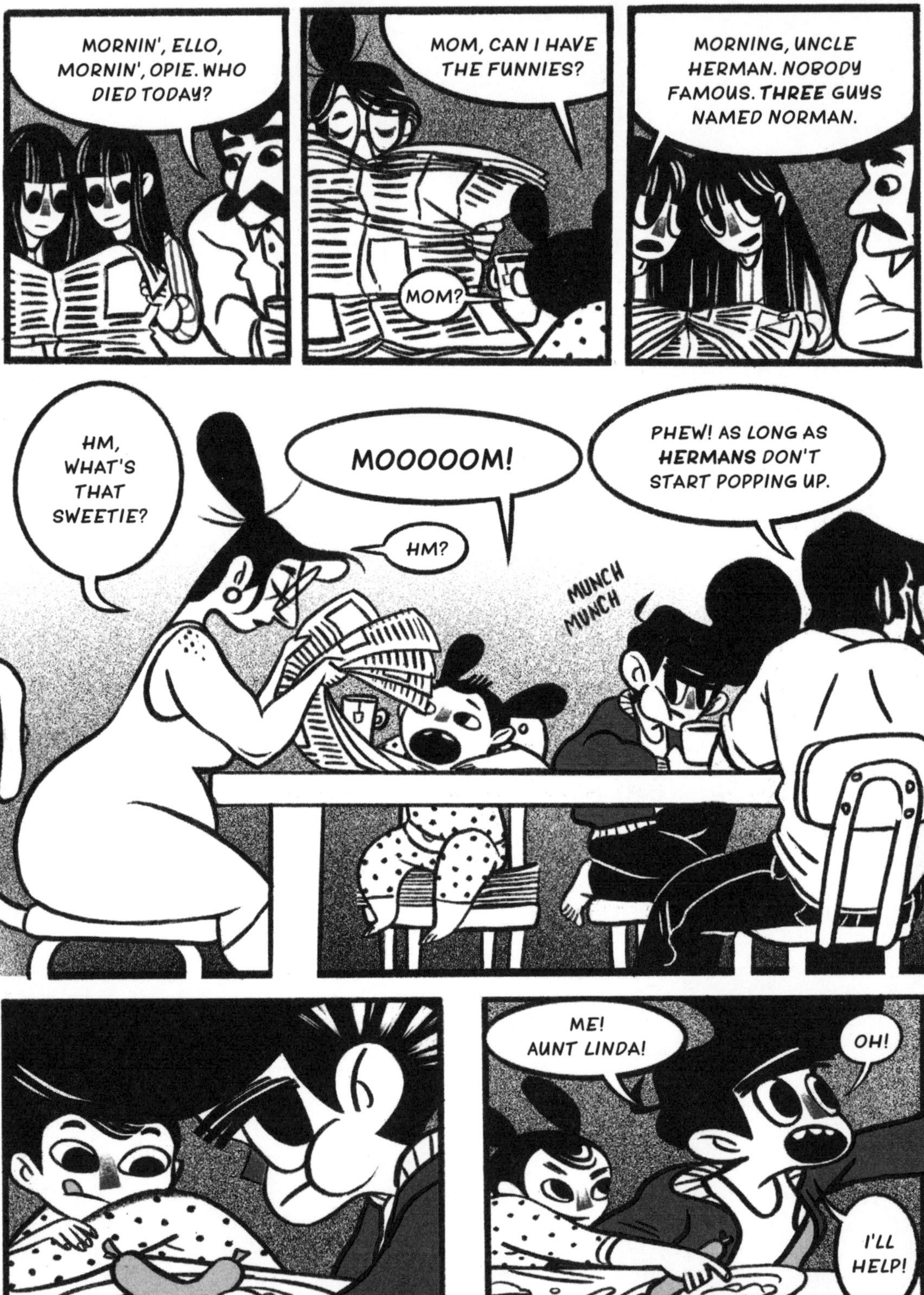
MORNIN', ELLO, MORNIN', OPIE. WHO DIED TODAY?
MOM, CAN I HAVE THE FUNNIES?
MOM?
MORNING, UNCLE HERMAN. NOBODY FAMOUS. THREE GUYS NAMED NORMAN.
HM, WHAT'S THAT SWEETIE?
MOOOOOM!
HM?
PHEW! AS LONG AS HERMANS DON'T START POPPING UP.
MUNCH MUNCH
ME! AUNT LINDA!
OH!
I'LL HELP!

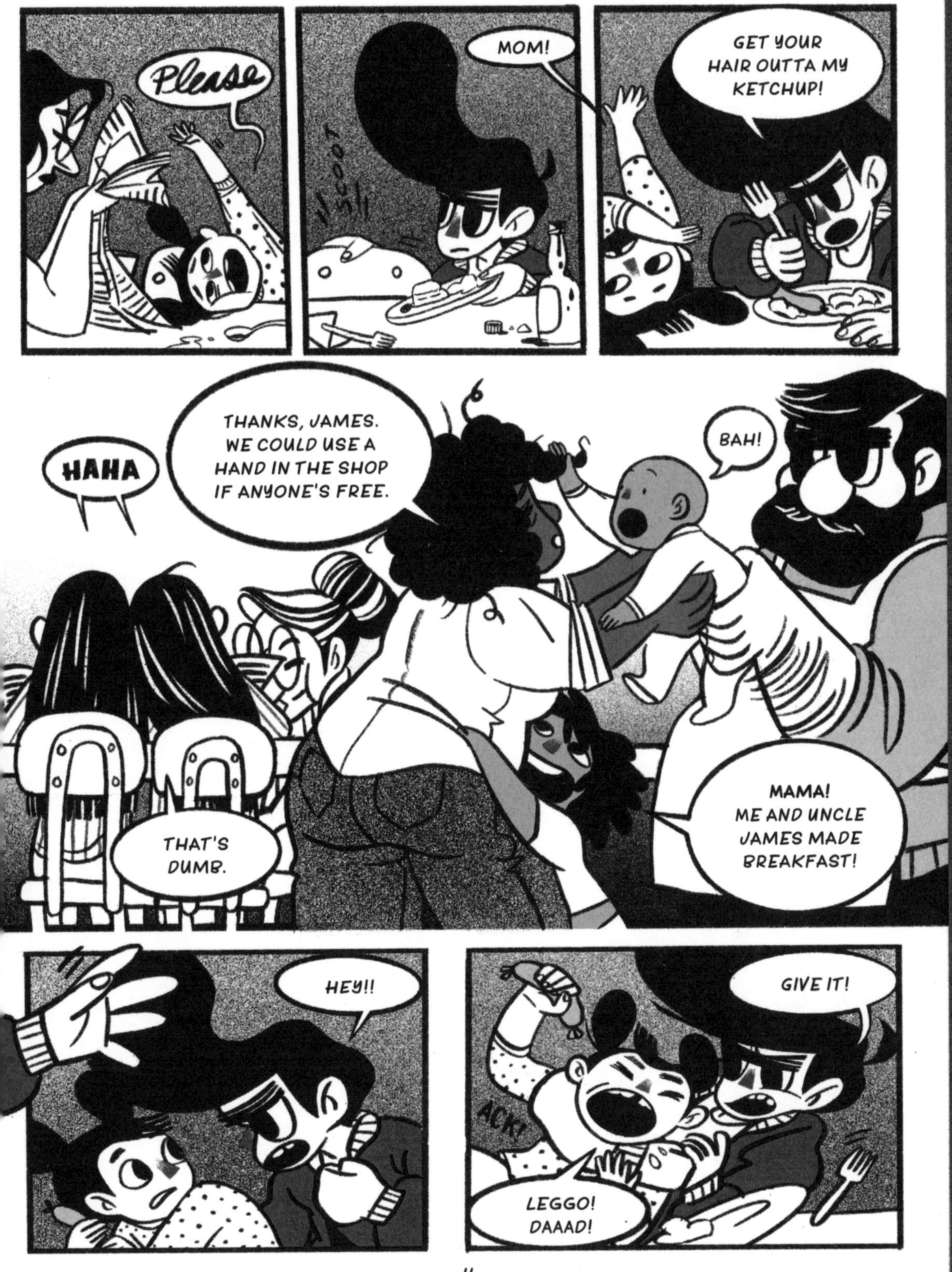
Please
SCOOT
MOM!
GET YOUR HAIR OUTTA MY KETCHUP!
HAHA
THANKS, JAMES. WE COULD USE A HAND IN THE SHOP IF ANYONE'S FREE.
BAH!
THAT'S DUMB.
MAMA! ME AND UNCLE JAMES MADE BREAKFAST!
HEY!!
GIVE IT!
ACK!
LEGGO! DAAAD!

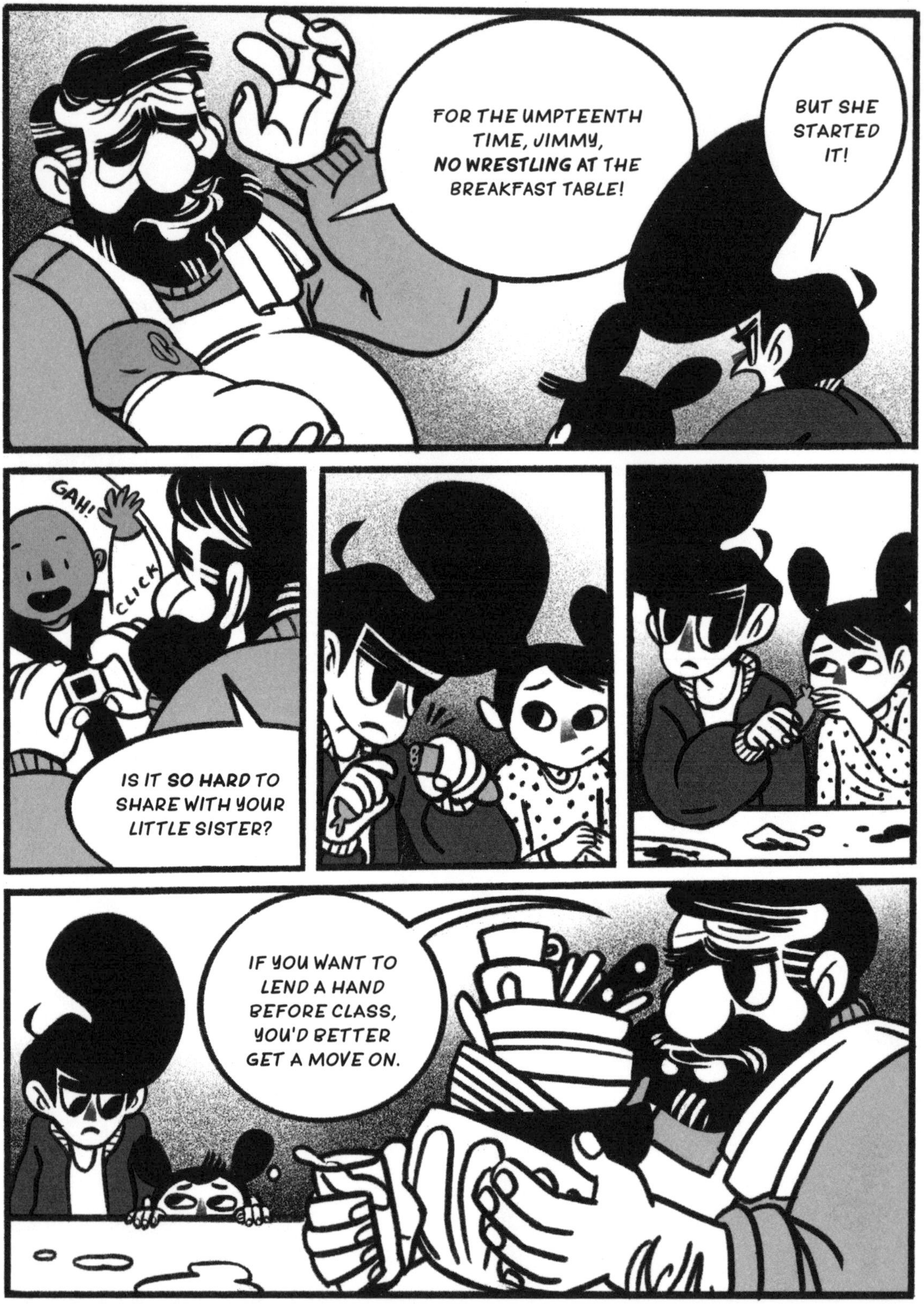
FOR THE UMPTEENTH TIME, JIMMY, **NO WRESTLING** AT THE BREAKFAST TABLE!
BUT SHE STARTED IT!
GAH!
CLICK
IS IT **SO HARD** TO SHARE WITH YOUR LITTLE SISTER?
IF YOU WANT TO LEND A HAND BEFORE CLASS, YOU'D BETTER GET A MOVE ON.

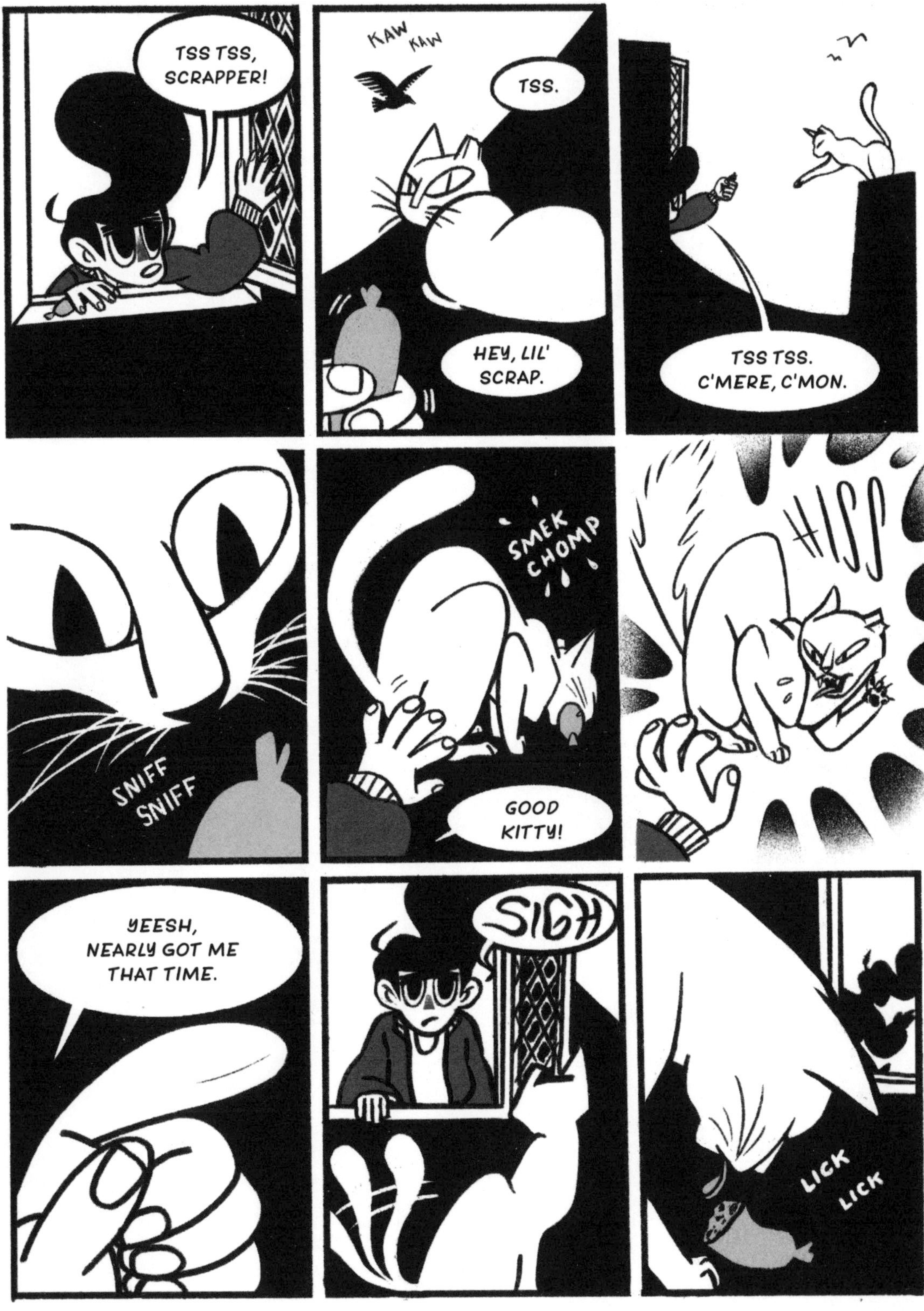
TSS TSS, SCRAPPER!
KAW KAW
TSS.
HEY, LIL' SCRAP.
TSS TSS. C'MERE, C'MON.
SNIFF SNIFF
SMEK CHOMP
GOOD KITTY!
HISS
YEESH, NEARLY GOT ME THAT TIME.
SIGH
LICK LICK

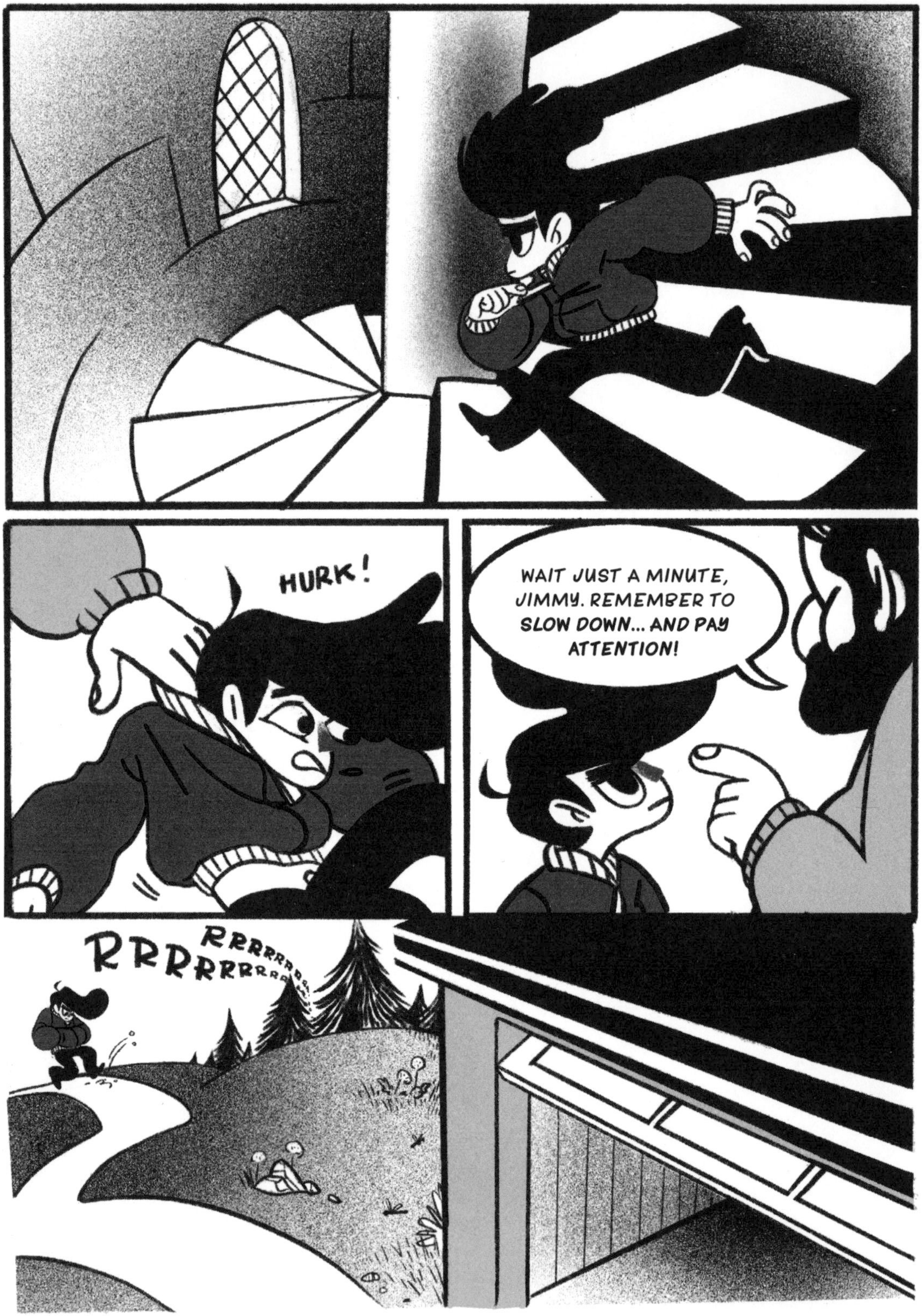
HURK!
WAIT JUST A MINUTE, JIMMY. REMEMBER TO SLOW DOWN... AND PAY ATTENTION!
RRRRRRRRRRRR
RRRRRRRRR

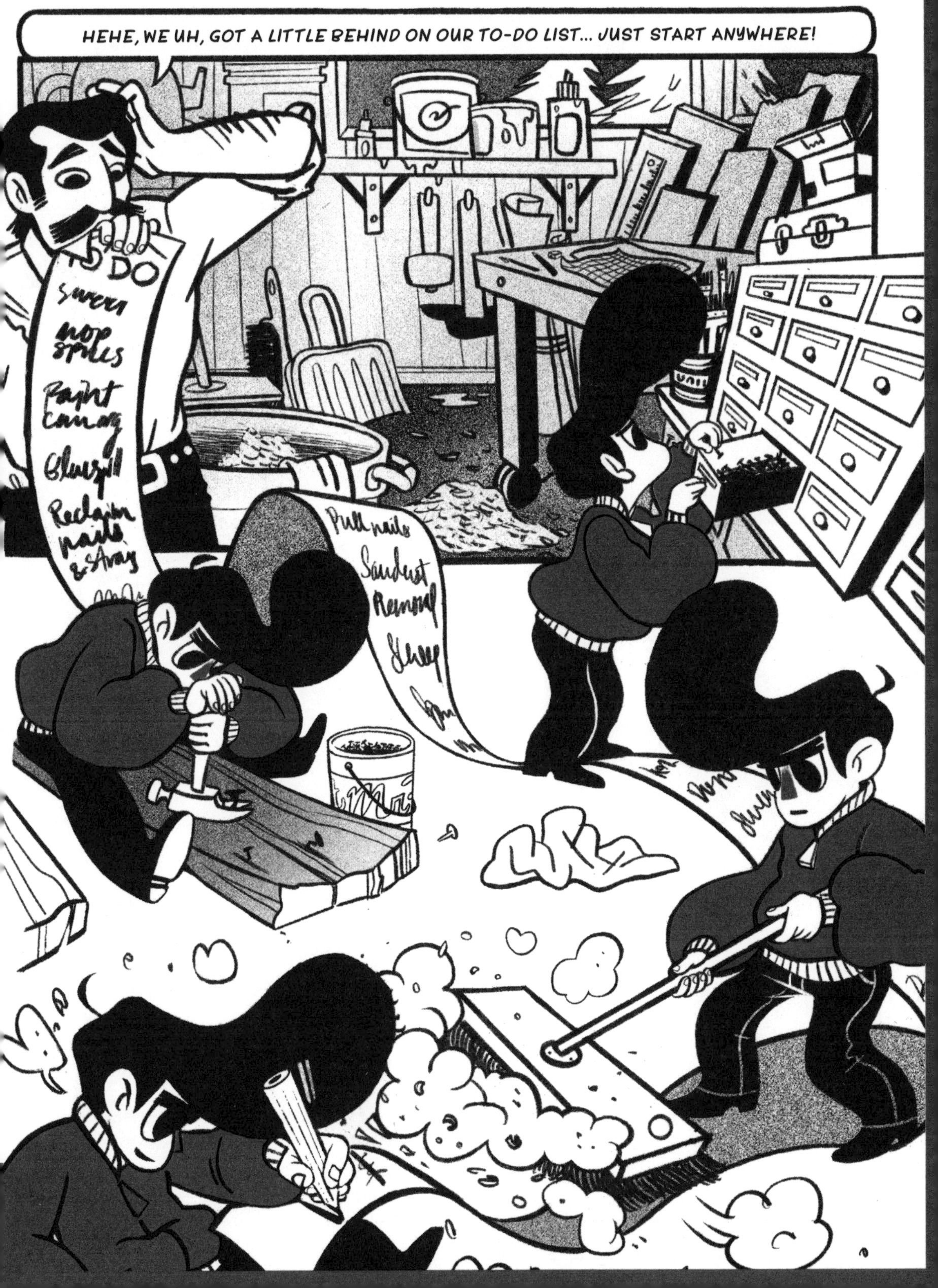
HEHE, WE UH, GOT A LITTLE BEHIND ON OUR TO-DO LIST... JUST START ANYWHERE!
TO DO
Pull nails

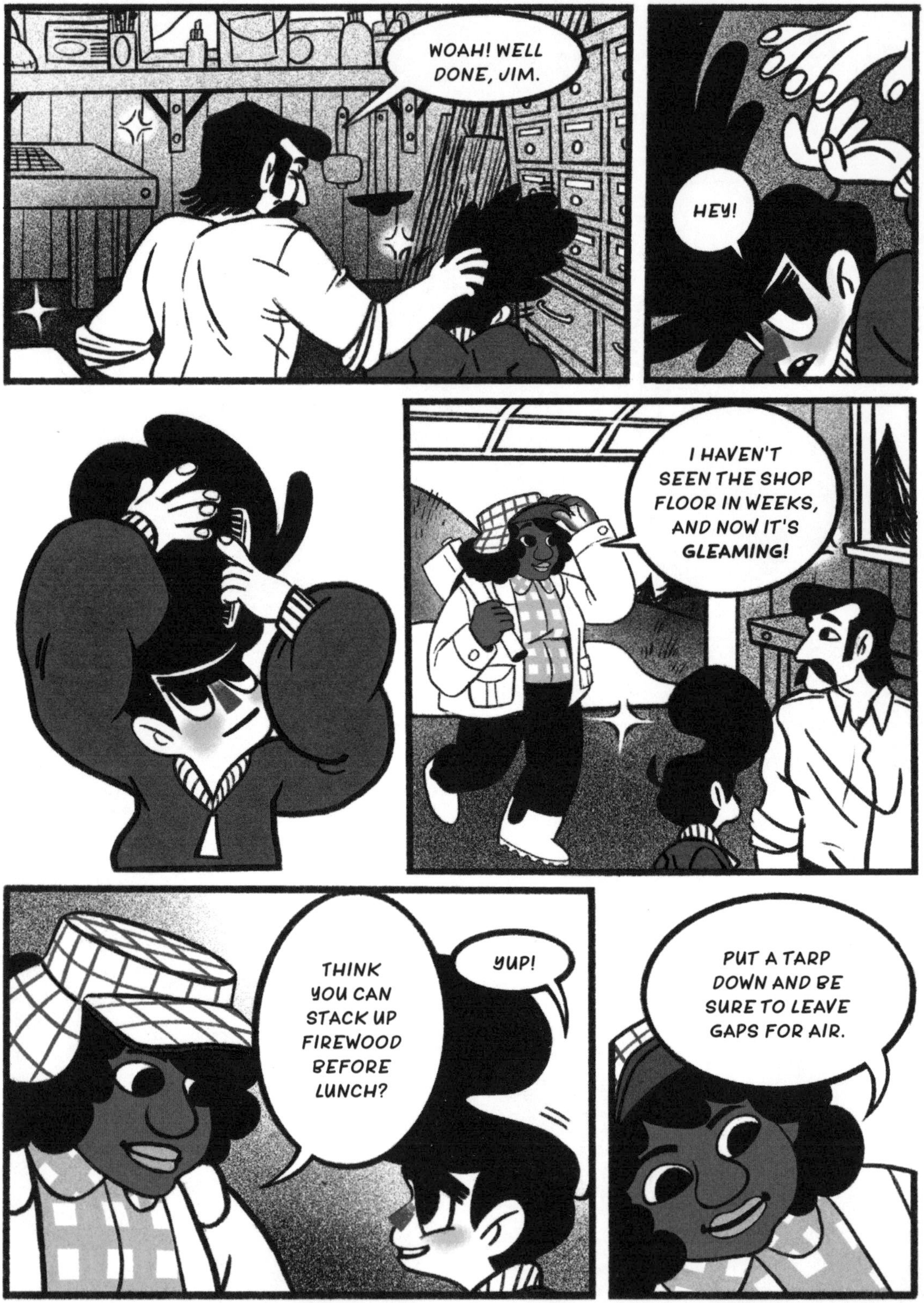
WOAH! WELL DONE, JIM.
HEY!
I HAVEN'T SEEN THE SHOP FLOOR IN WEEKS, AND NOW IT'S **GLEAMING!**
THINK YOU CAN STACK UP FIREWOOD BEFORE LUNCH?
YUP!
PUT A TARP DOWN AND BE SURE TO LEAVE GAPS FOR AIR.

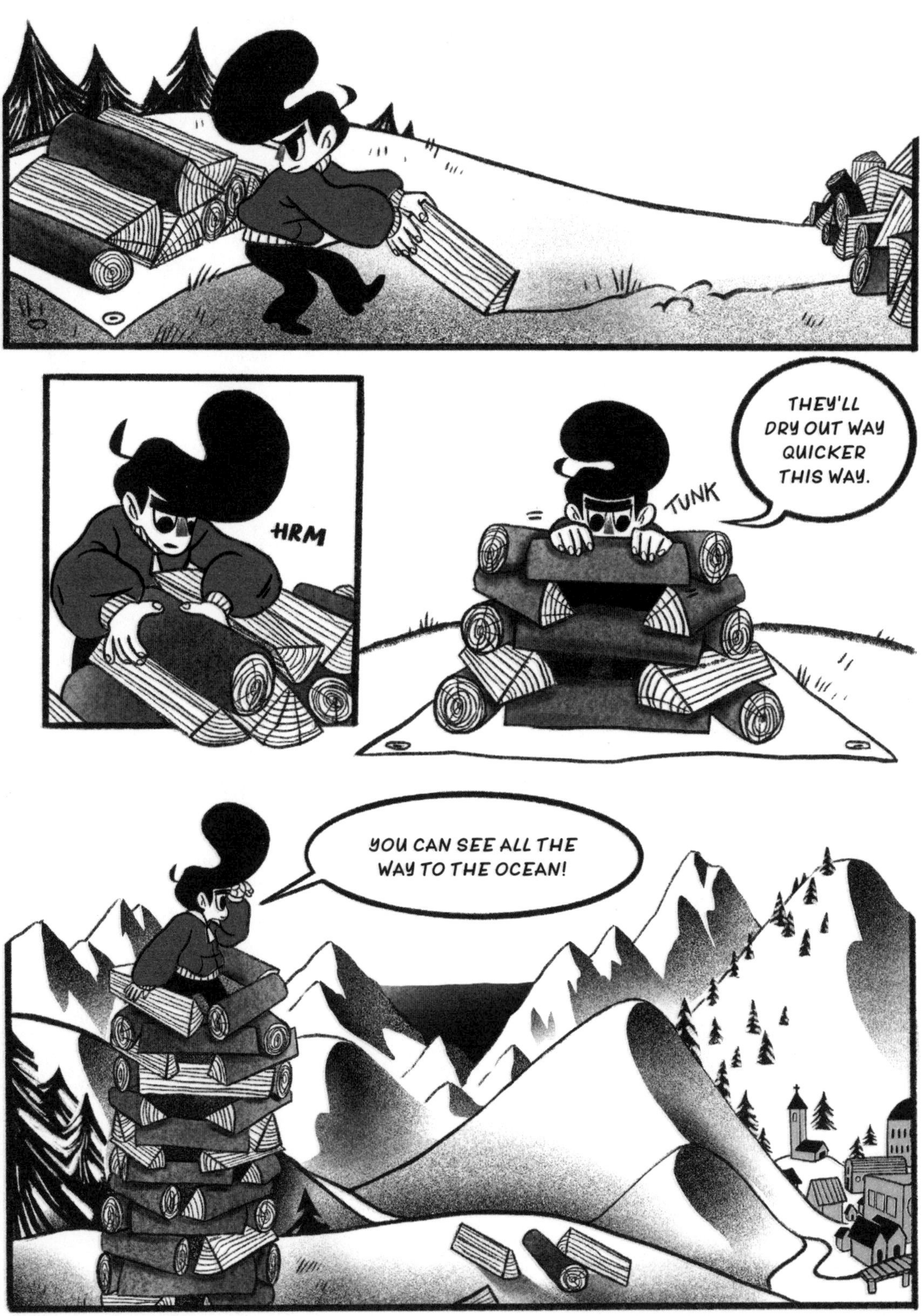
HRM
TUNK
THEY'LL DRY OUT WAY QUICKER THIS WAY.
YOU CAN SEE ALL THE WAY TO THE OCEAN!

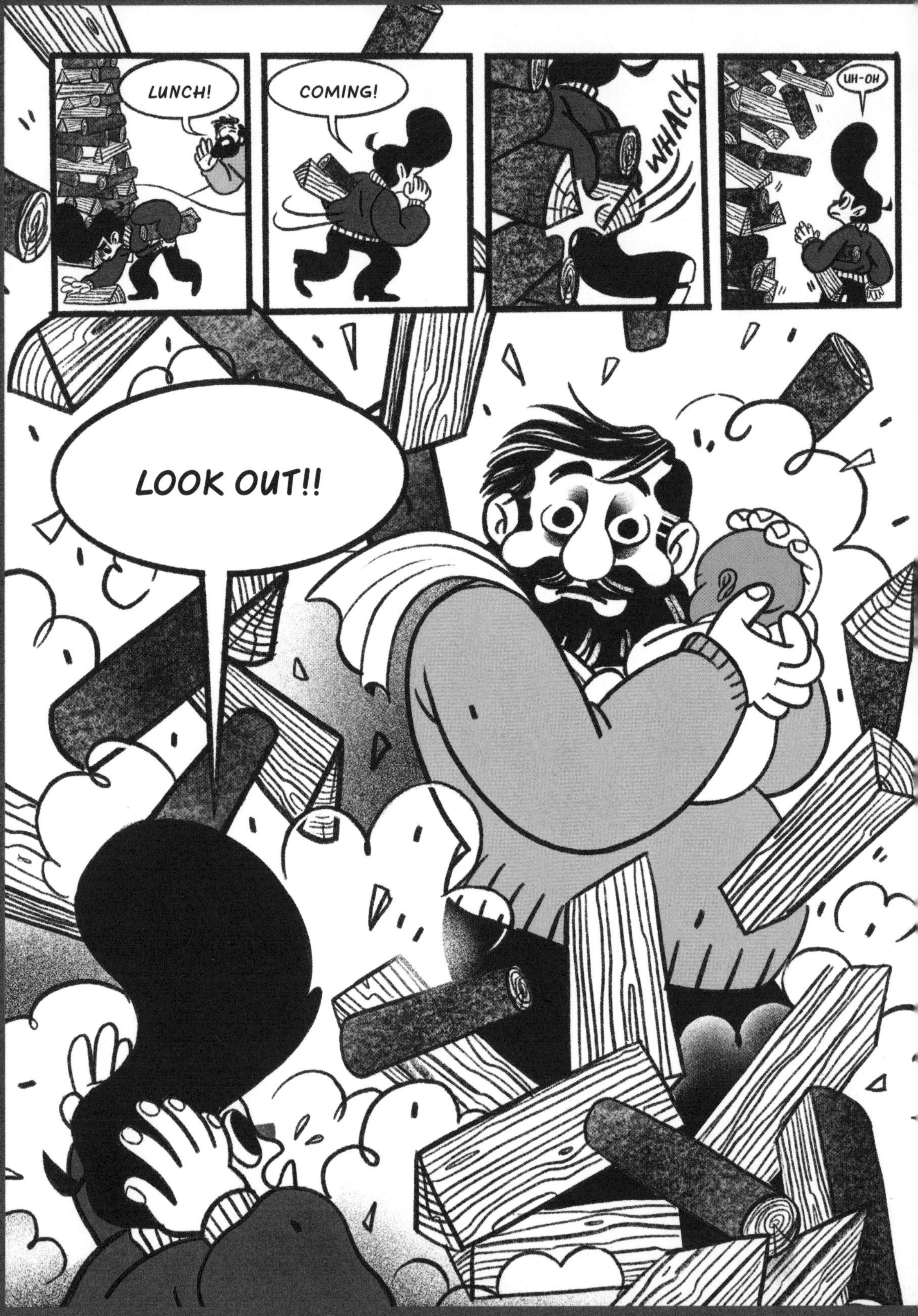
LUNCH!
COMING!
WHACK
UH-OH
LOOK OUT!!

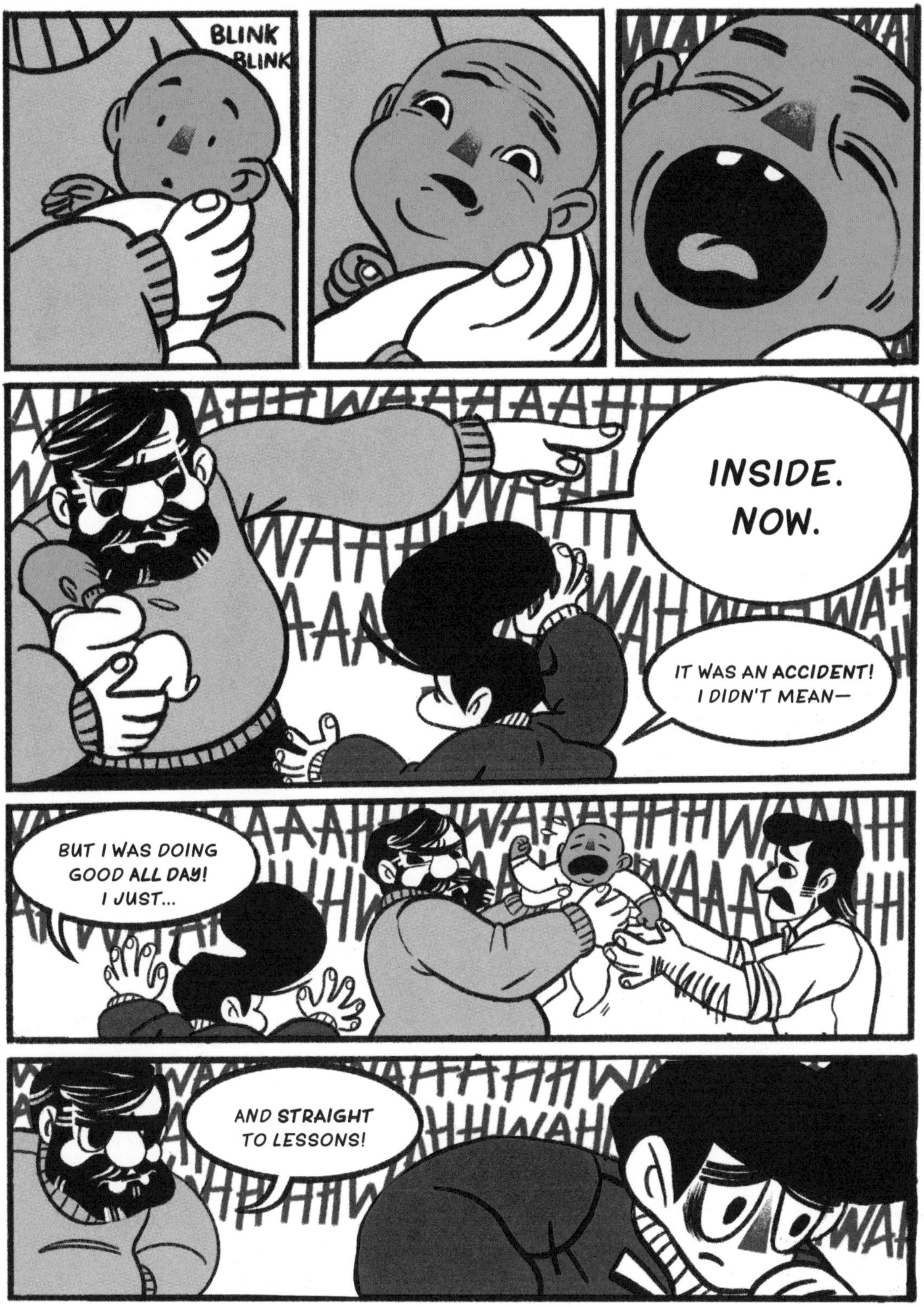
BLINK
BLINK
INSIDE. NOW.
IT WAS AN ACCIDENT! I DIDN'T MEAN—
BUT I WAS DOING GOOD ALL DAY! I JUST...
AND STRAIGHT TO LESSONS!

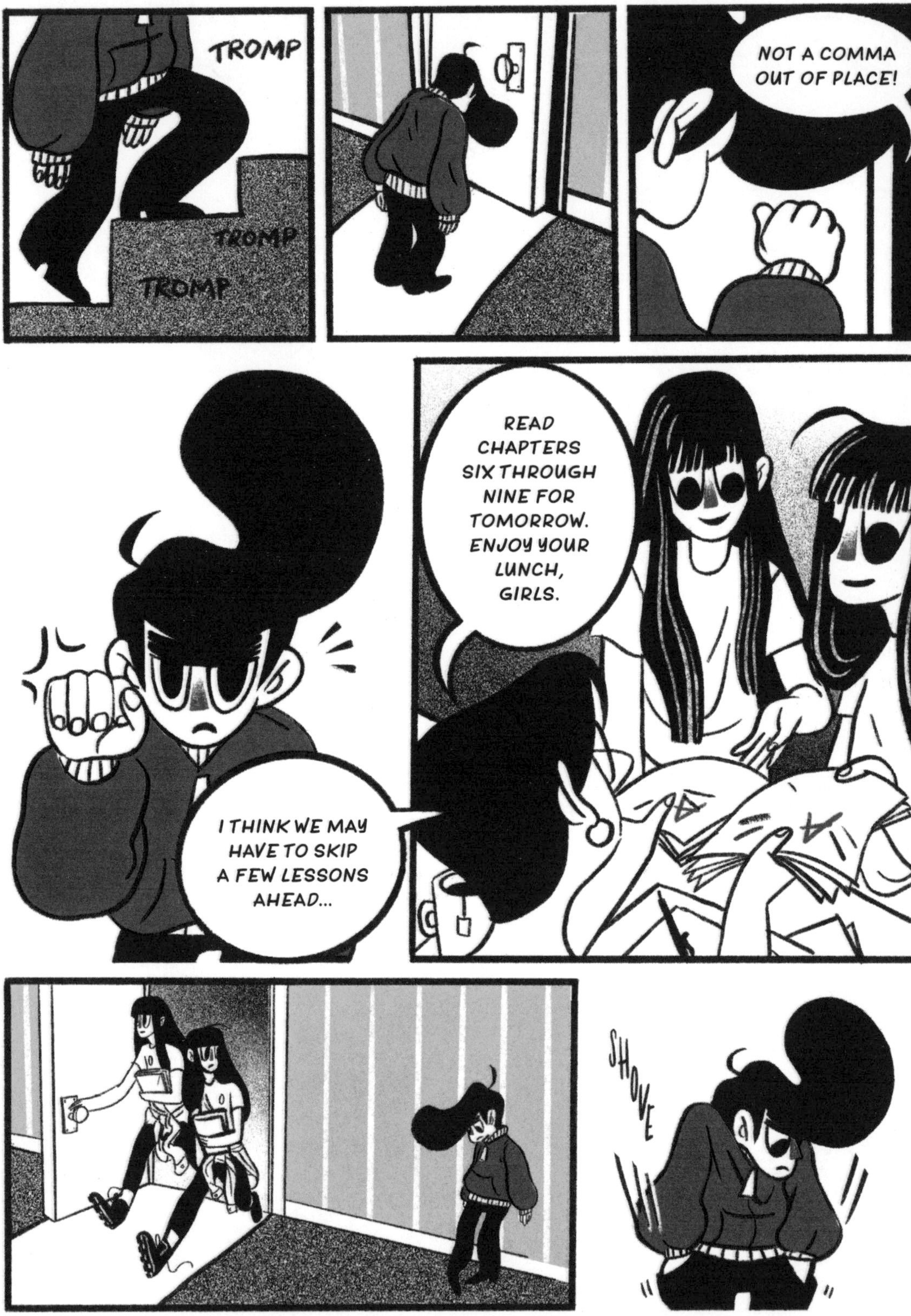
TROMP
TROMP
TROMP
NOT A COMMA OUT OF PLACE!
READ CHAPTERS SIX THROUGH NINE FOR TOMORROW. ENJOY YOUR LUNCH, GIRLS.
I THINK WE MAY HAVE TO SKIP A FEW LESSONS AHEAD...
SHOVE

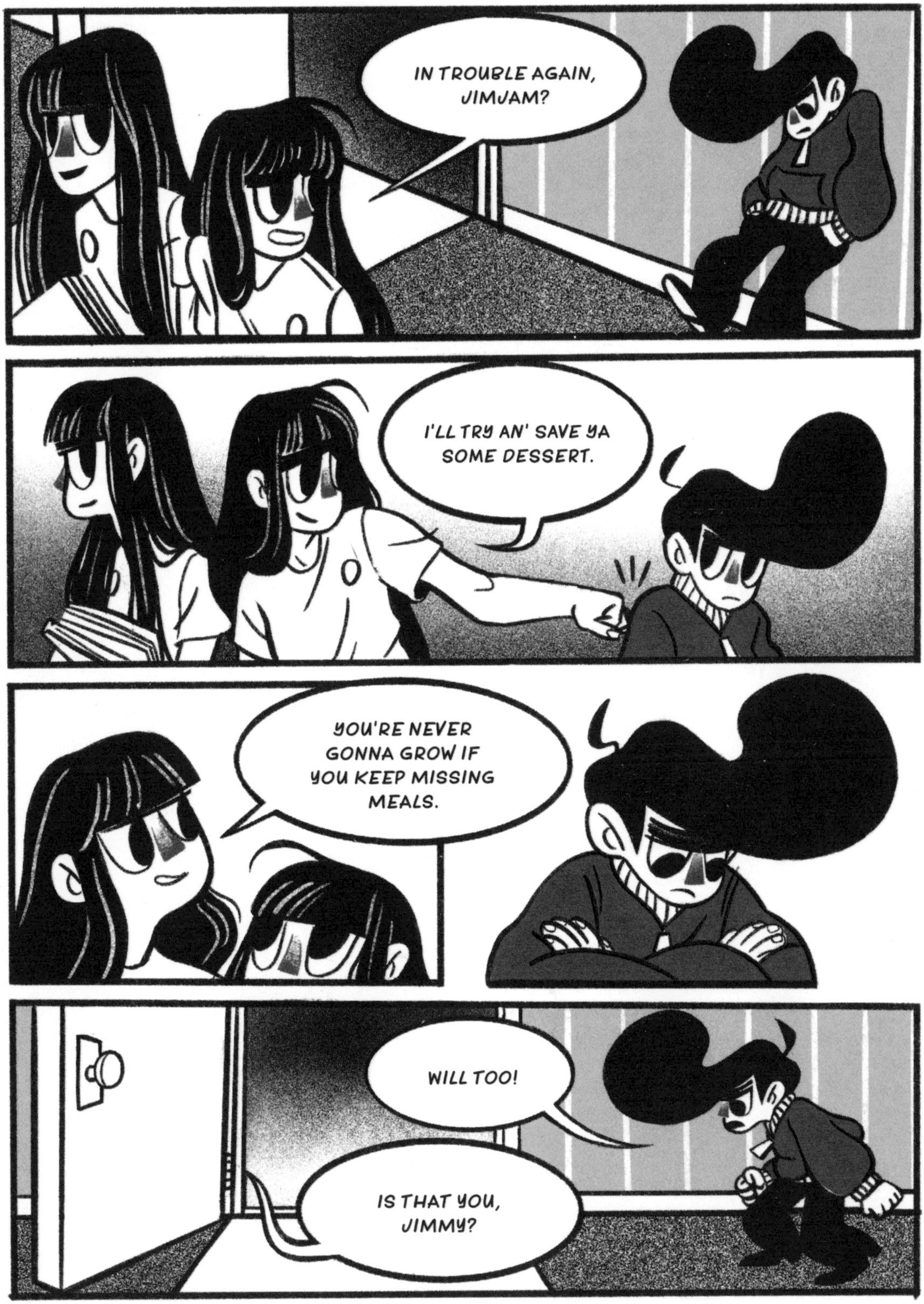
IN TROUBLE AGAIN, JIMJAM?
I'LL TRY AN' SAVE YA SOME DESSERT.
YOU'RE NEVER GONNA GROW IF YOU KEEP MISSING MEALS.
WILL TOO!
IS THAT YOU, JIMMY?

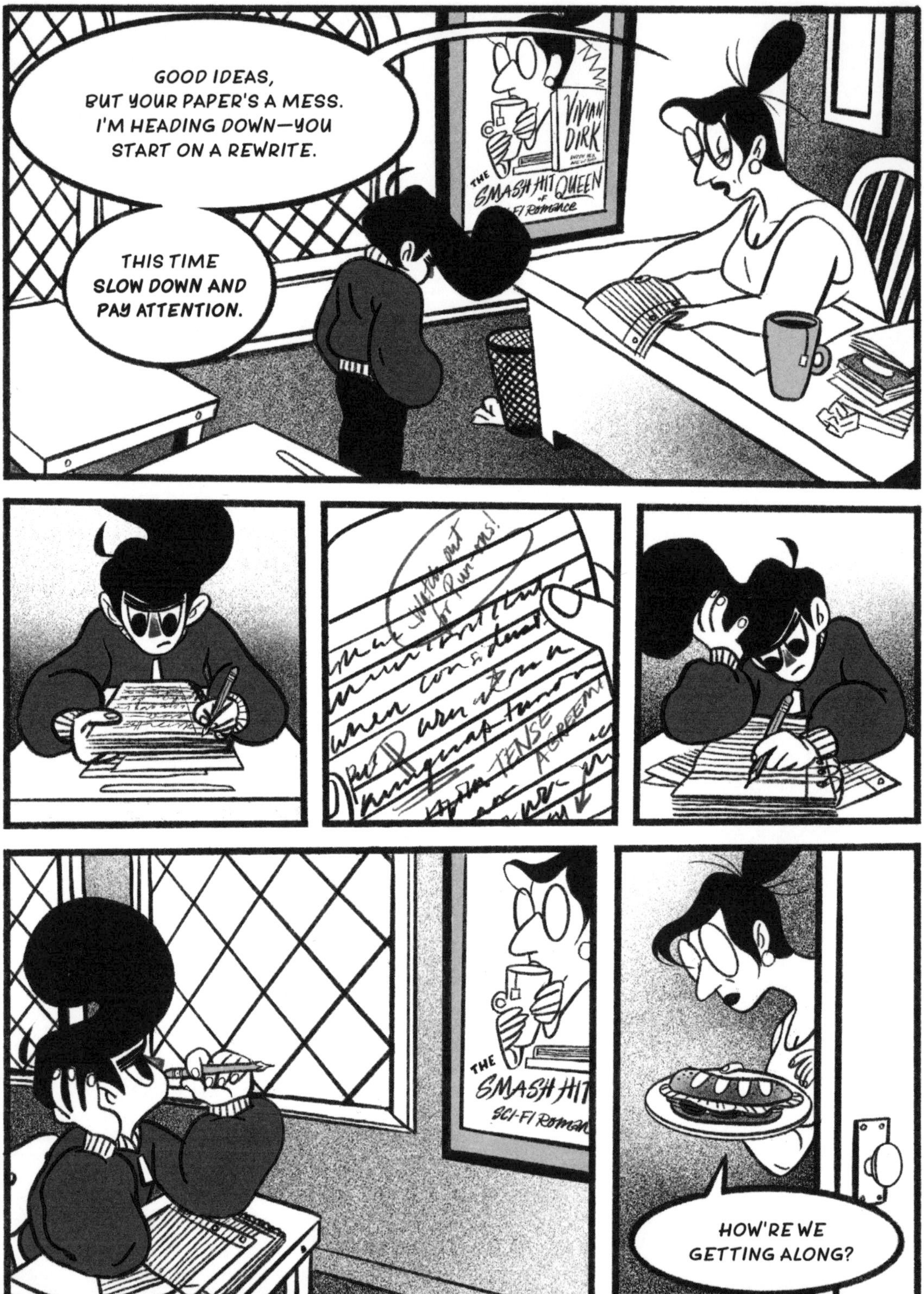
GOOD IDEAS, BUT YOUR PAPER'S A MESS. I'M HEADING DOWN—YOU START ON A REWRITE.
THIS TIME SLOW DOWN AND PAY ATTENTION.
HOW'RE WE GETTING ALONG?

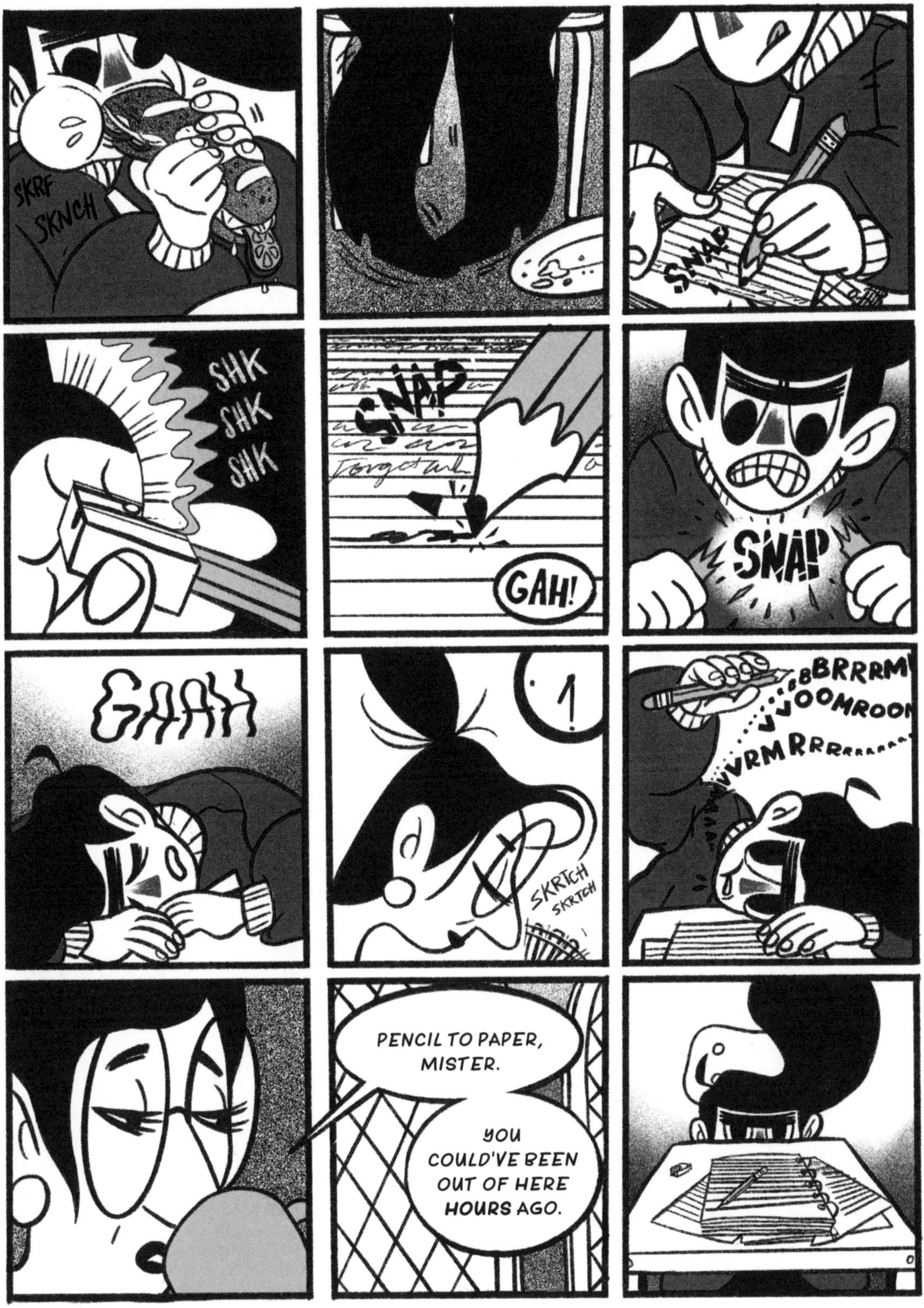
SKRF
SKNCH
SNAP
SHK
SHK
SHK
SNAP
GAH!
SNAP
GAAH
SKRTCH
SKRTCH
BRRRM
VVOOMROOM
VVRM RRRRR
PENCIL TO PAPER, MISTER.
YOU COULD'VE BEEN OUT OF HERE HOURS AGO.

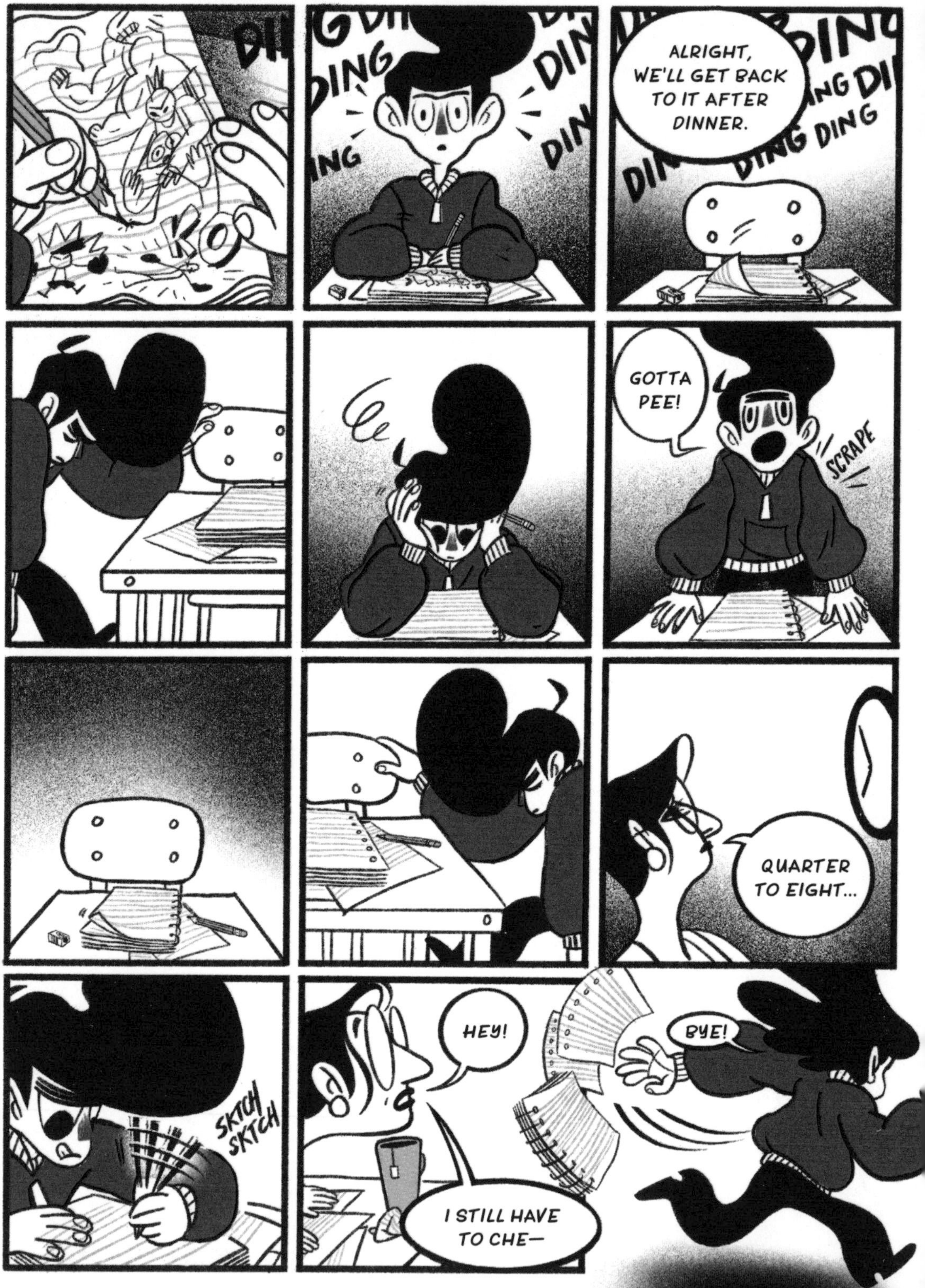
KO
DING DING DING DING
ALRIGHT, WE'LL GET BACK TO IT AFTER DINNER.
DING DING DING DING
GOTTA PEE!
SCRAPE
QUARTER TO EIGHT...
SKTCH SKTCH
HEY!
I STILL HAVE TO CHE—
BYE!

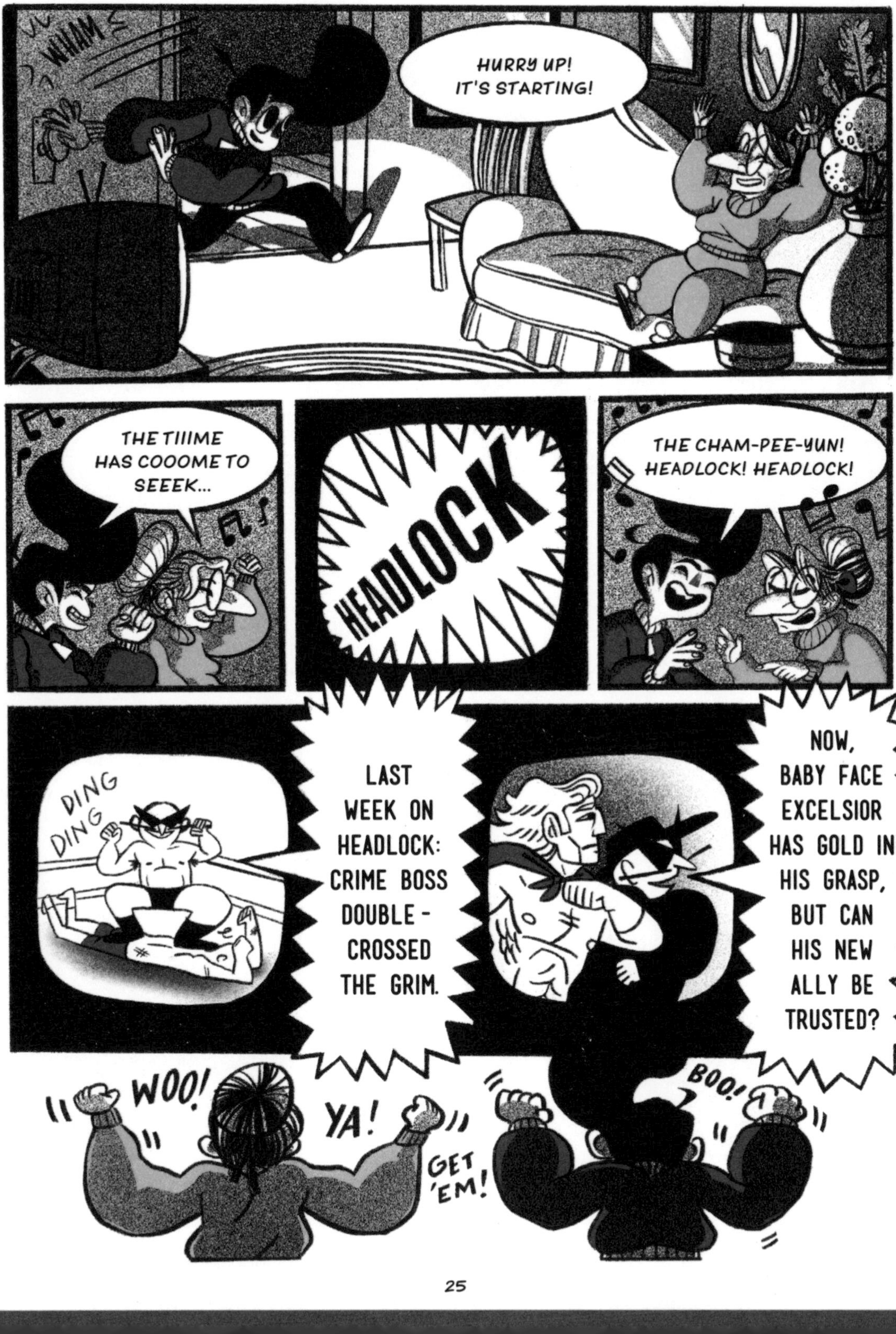
WHAM
HURRY UP! IT'S STARTING!
THE TIIIME HAS COOOME TO SEEEK...
HEADLOCK
THE CHAM-PEE-YUN! HEADLOCK! HEADLOCK!
DING DING
LAST WEEK ON HEADLOCK: CRIME BOSS DOUBLE-CROSSED THE GRIM.
NOW, BABY FACE EXCELSIOR HAS GOLD IN HIS GRASP, BUT CAN HIS NEW ALLY BE TRUSTED?
WOO!
YA!
GET 'EM!
BOO!

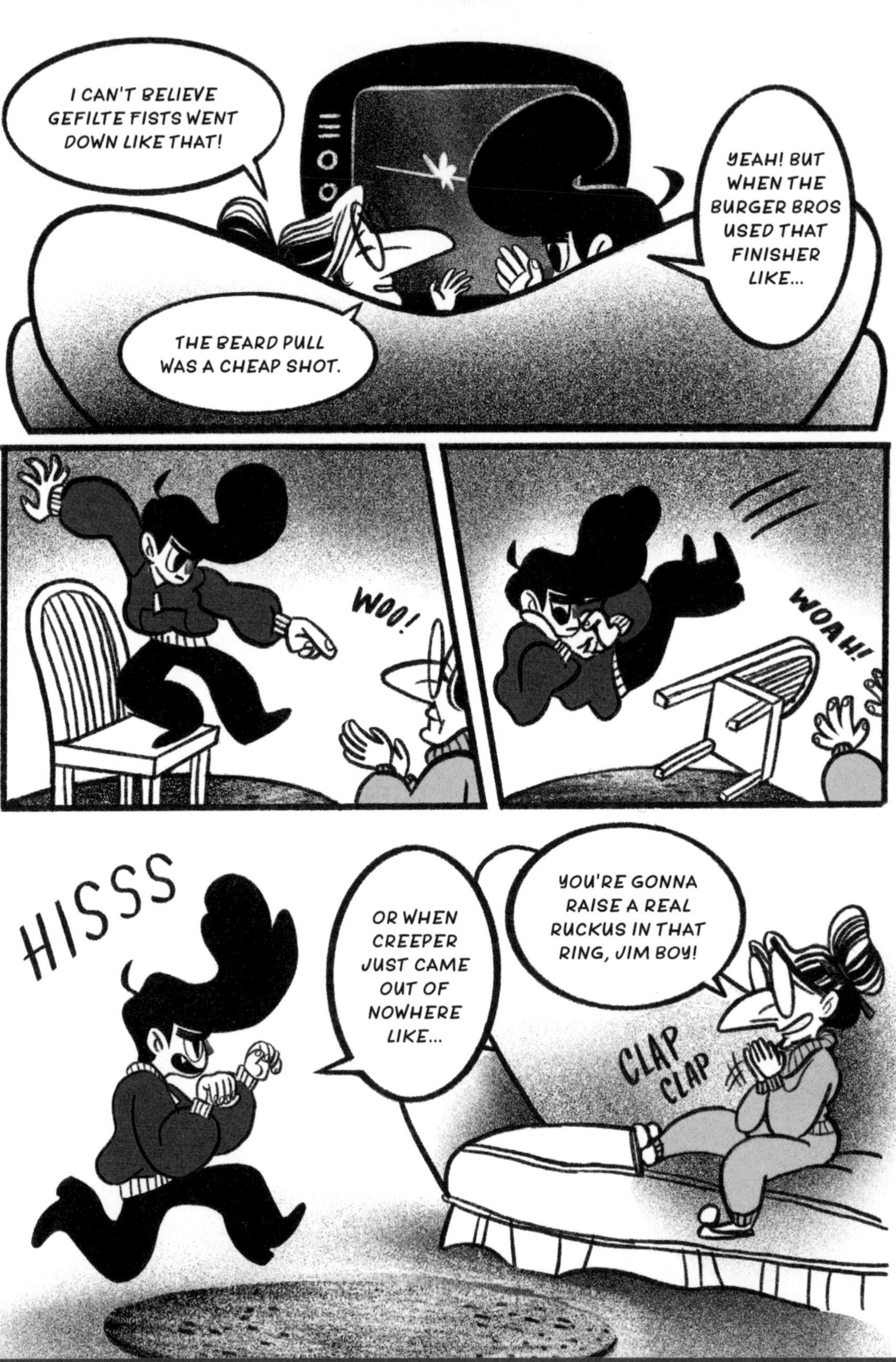

I CAN'T BELIEVE GEFILTE FISTS WENT DOWN LIKE THAT!
YEAH! BUT WHEN THE BURGER BROS USED THAT FINISHER LIKE...
THE BEARD PULL WAS A CHEAP SHOT.
WOO!
WOAH!
HISSS
OR WHEN CREEPER JUST CAME OUT OF NOWHERE LIKE...
YOU'RE GONNA RAISE A REAL RUCKUS IN THAT RING, JIM BOY!
CLAP CLAP

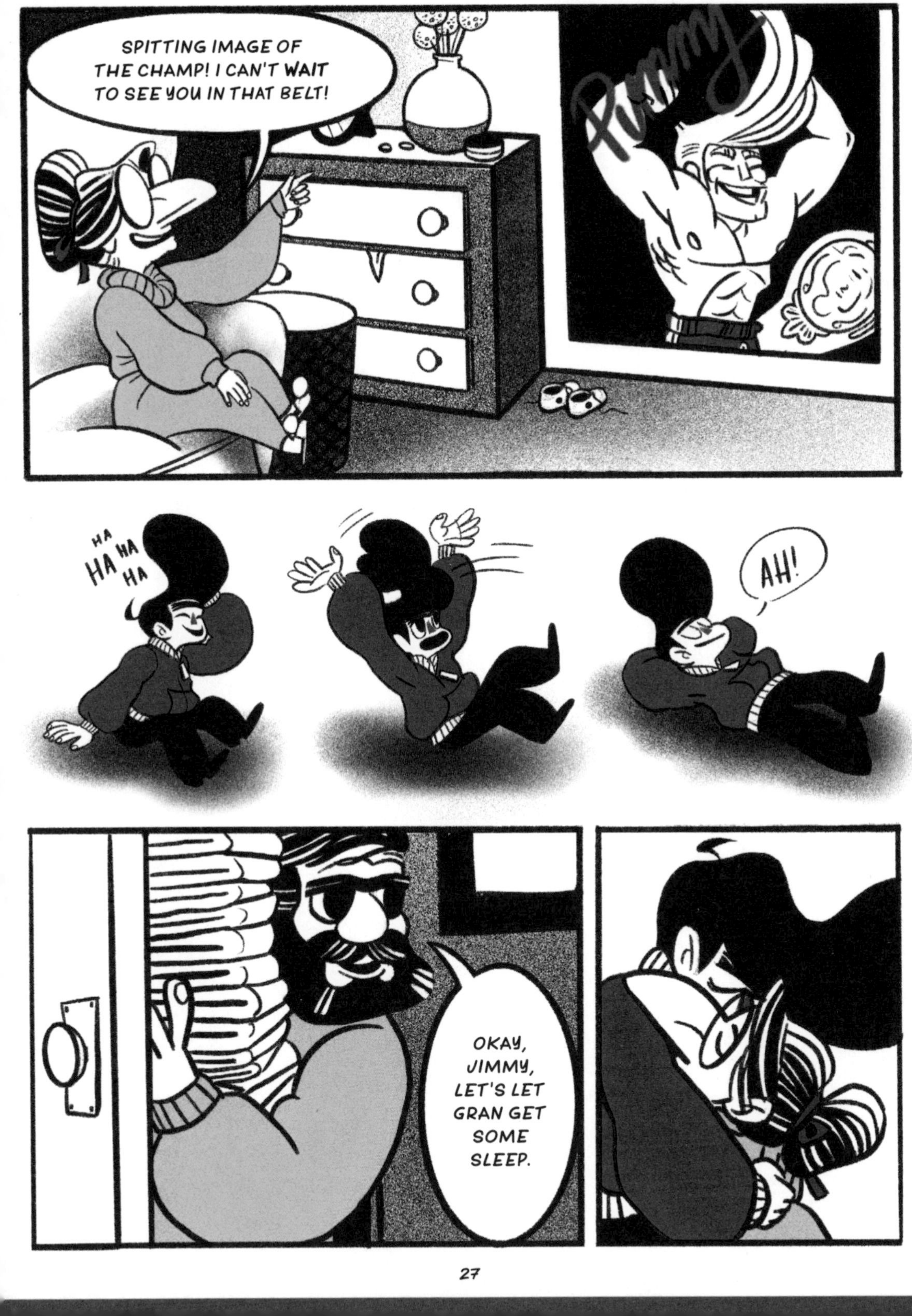
SPITTING IMAGE OF THE CHAMP! I CAN'T WAIT TO SEE YOU IN THAT BELT!
HA HA HA HA
AH!
OKAY, JIMMY, LET'S LET GRAN GET SOME SLEEP.

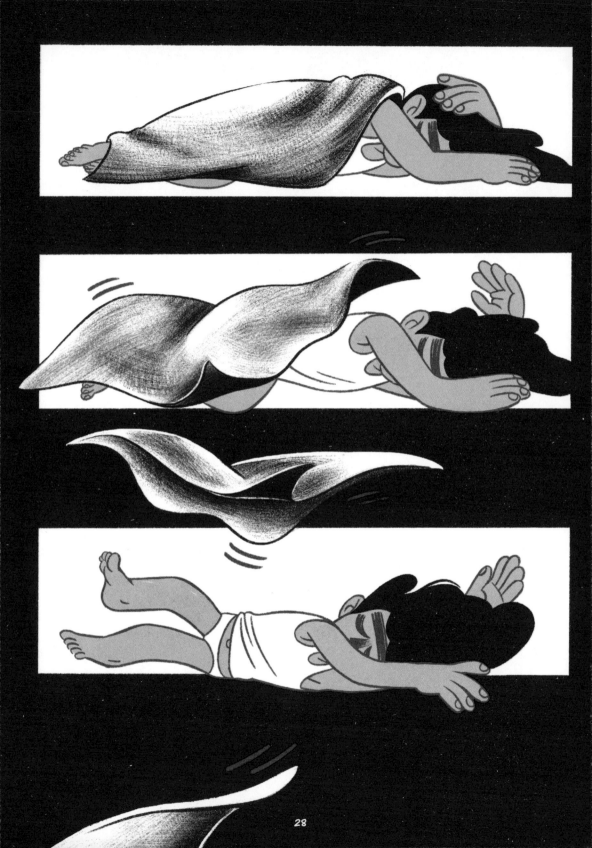

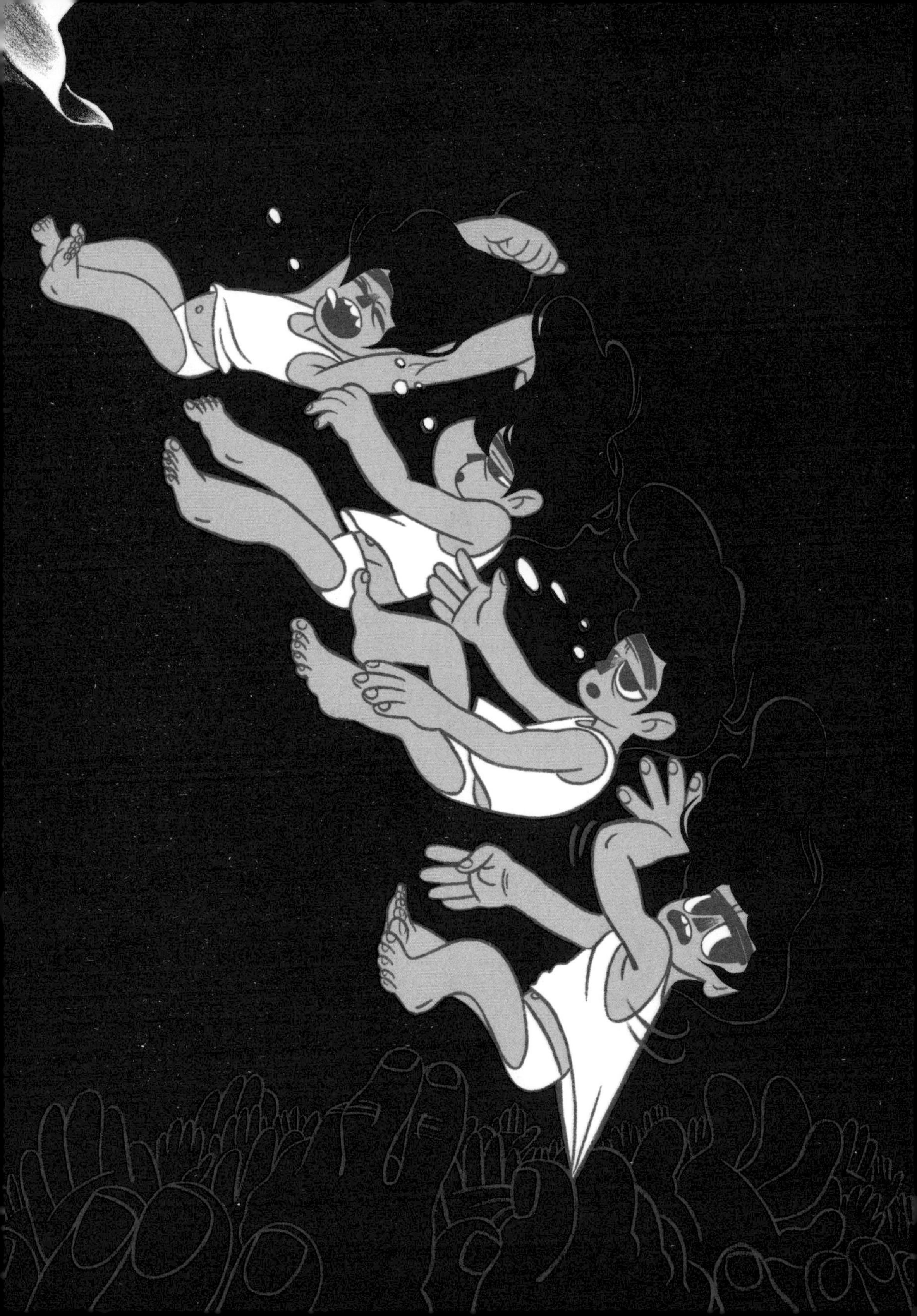

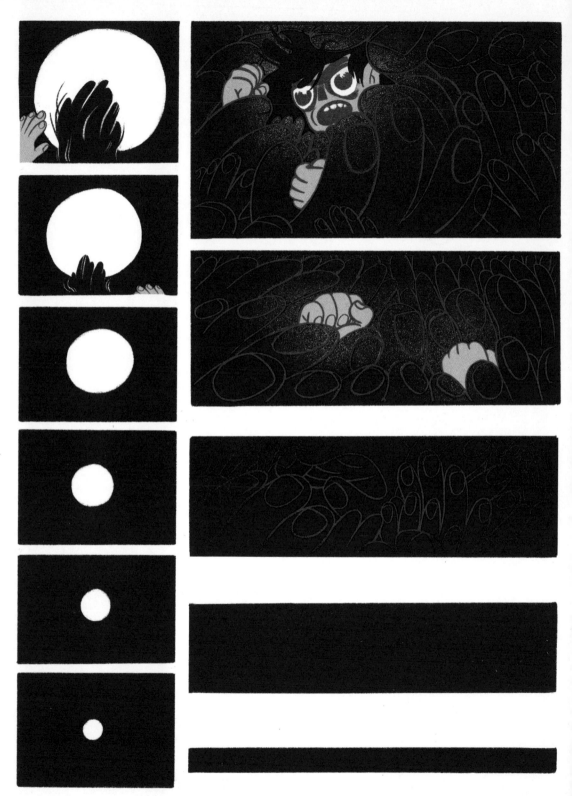

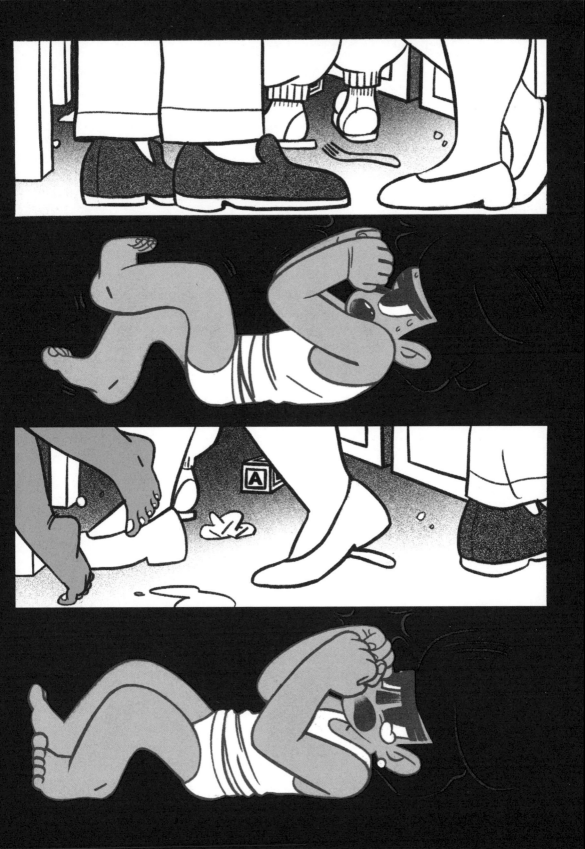

CHAPTER 1

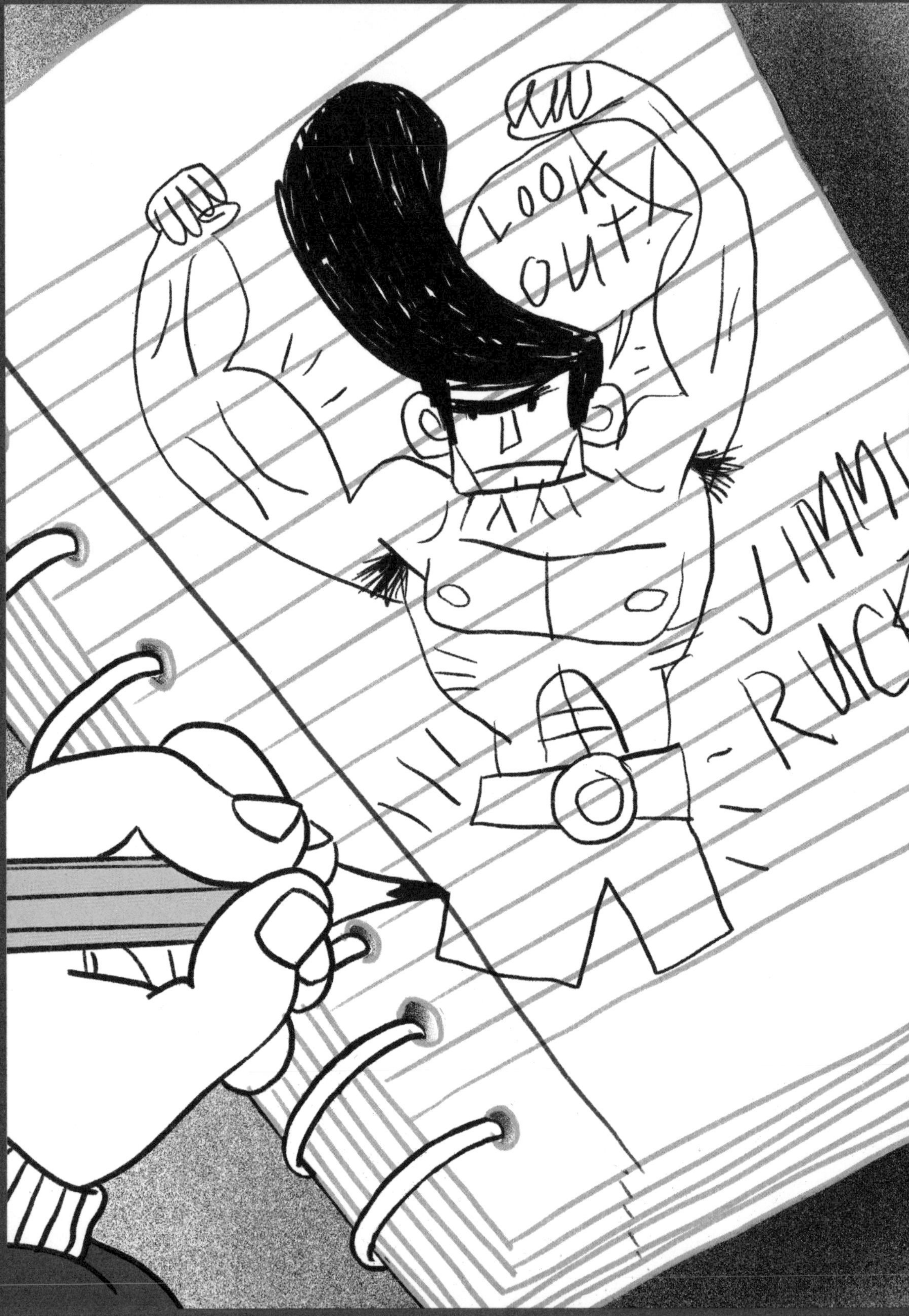
LOOK OUT!

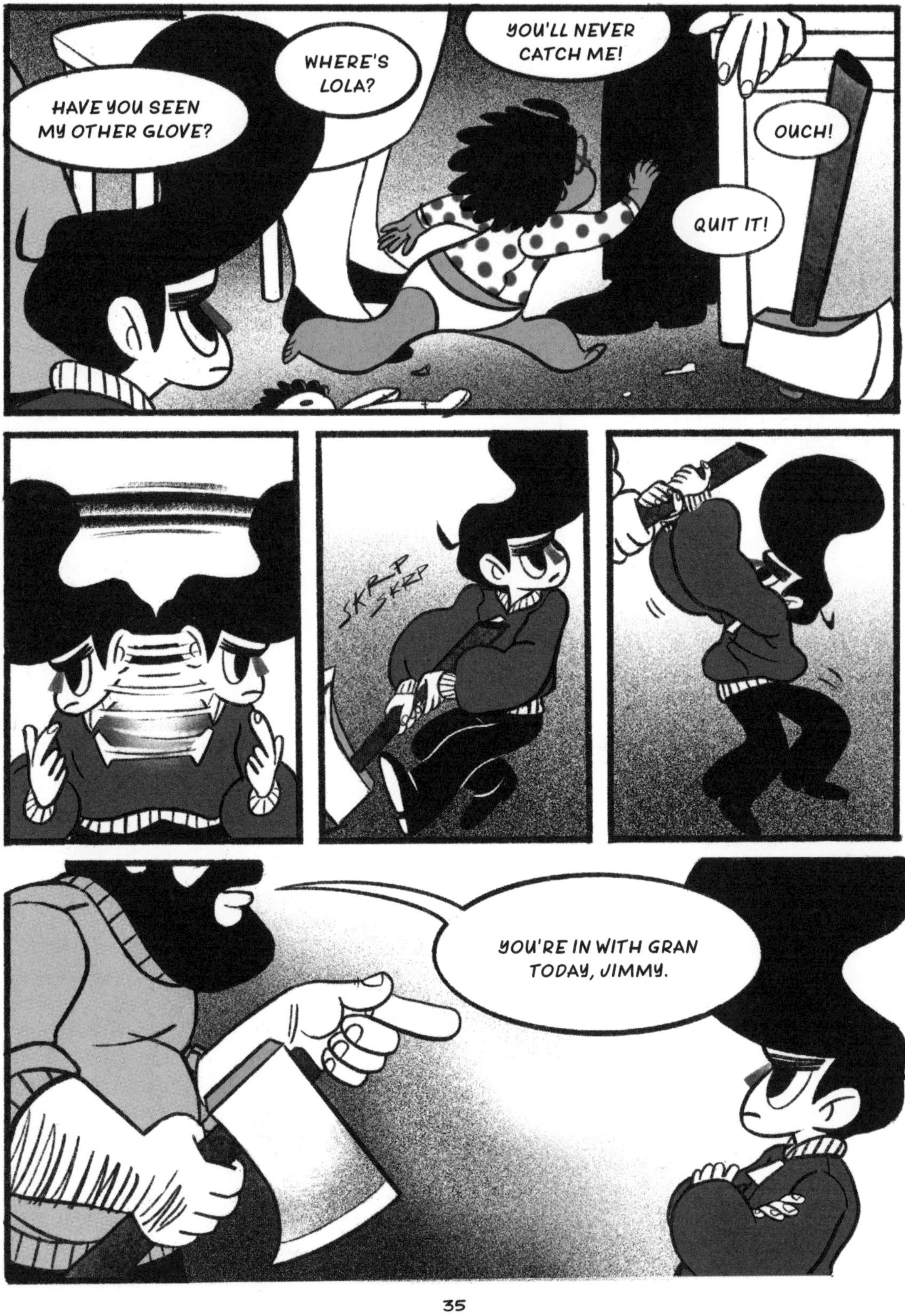
HAVE YOU SEEN MY OTHER GLOVE?
WHERE'S LOLA?
YOU'LL NEVER CATCH ME!
OUCH!
QUIT IT!
SKRP SKRP
YOU'RE IN WITH GRAN TODAY, JIMMY.

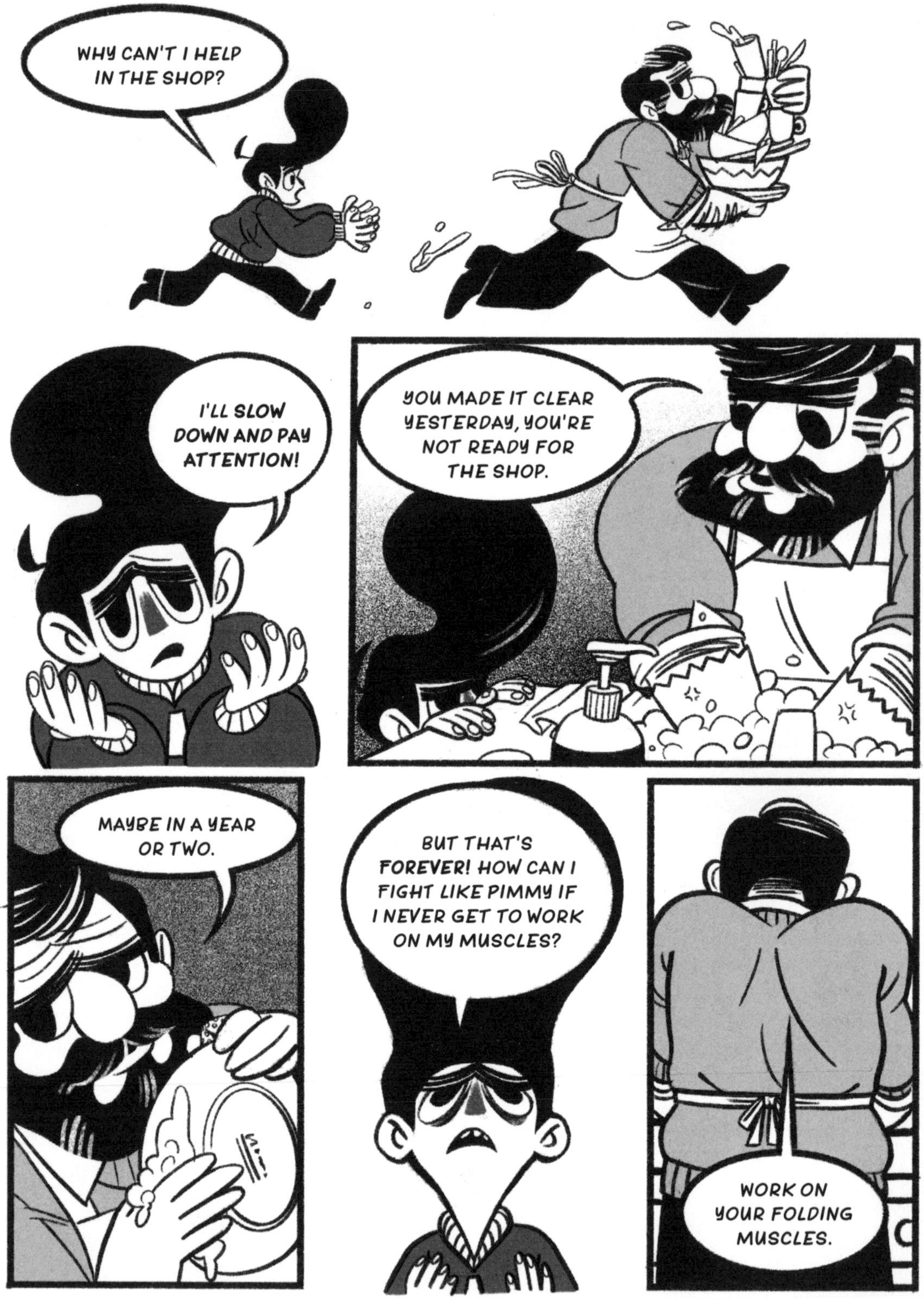
WHY CAN'T I HELP IN THE SHOP?
I'LL SLOW DOWN AND PAY ATTENTION!
YOU MADE IT CLEAR YESTERDAY, YOU'RE NOT READY FOR THE SHOP.
MAYBE IN A YEAR OR TWO.
BUT THAT'S FOREVER! HOW CAN I FIGHT LIKE PIMMY IF I NEVER GET TO WORK ON MY MUSCLES?
WORK ON YOUR FOLDING MUSCLES.

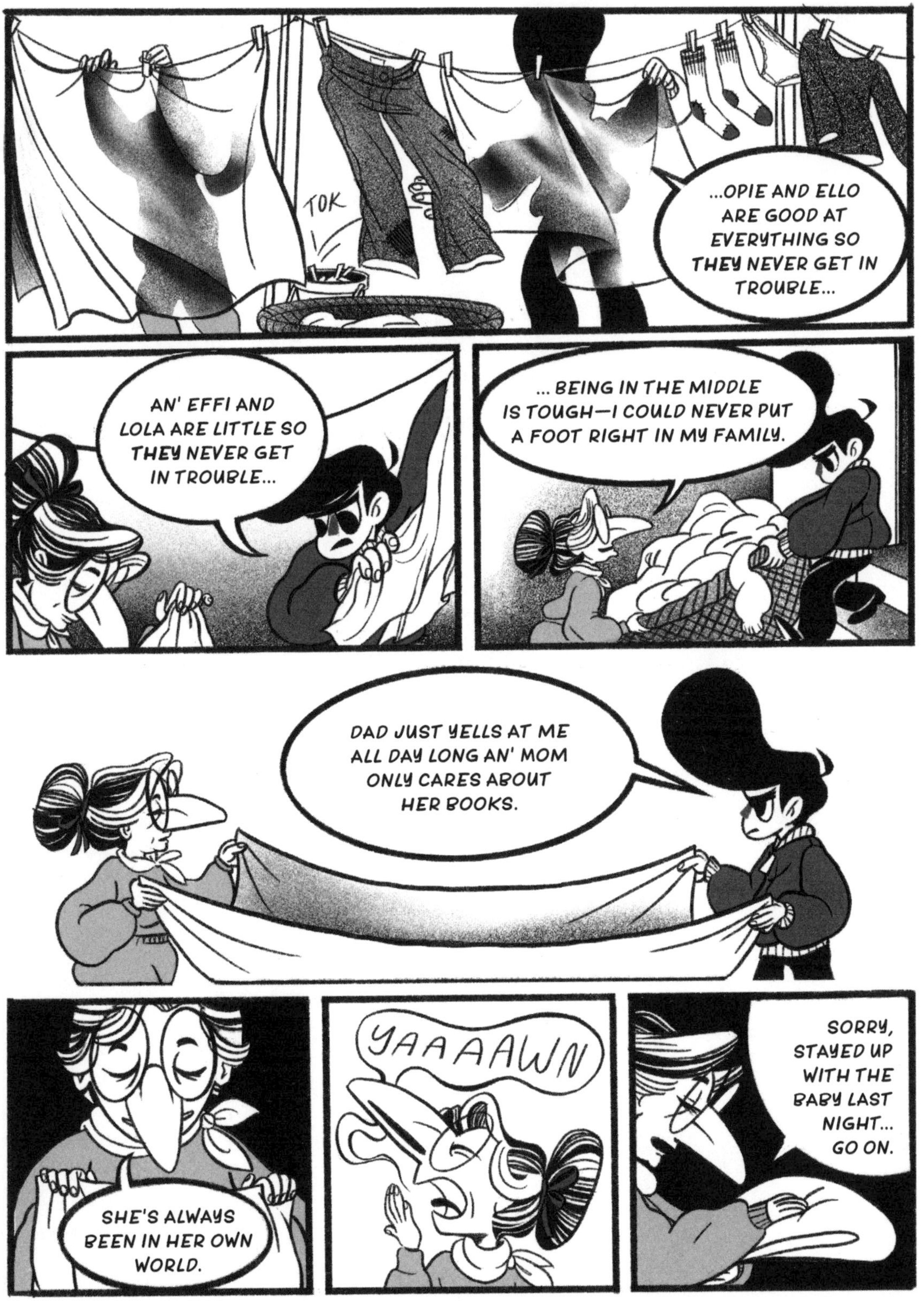
TOK
...OPIE AND ELLO ARE GOOD AT EVERYTHING SO THEY NEVER GET IN TROUBLE...
AN' EFFI AND LOLA ARE LITTLE SO THEY NEVER GET IN TROUBLE...
... BEING IN THE MIDDLE IS TOUGH—I COULD NEVER PUT A FOOT RIGHT IN MY FAMILY.
DAD JUST YELLS AT ME ALL DAY LONG AN' MOM ONLY CARES ABOUT HER BOOKS.
SHE'S ALWAYS BEEN IN HER OWN WORLD.
YAAAAAWN
SORRY, STAYED UP WITH THE BABY LAST NIGHT... GO ON.

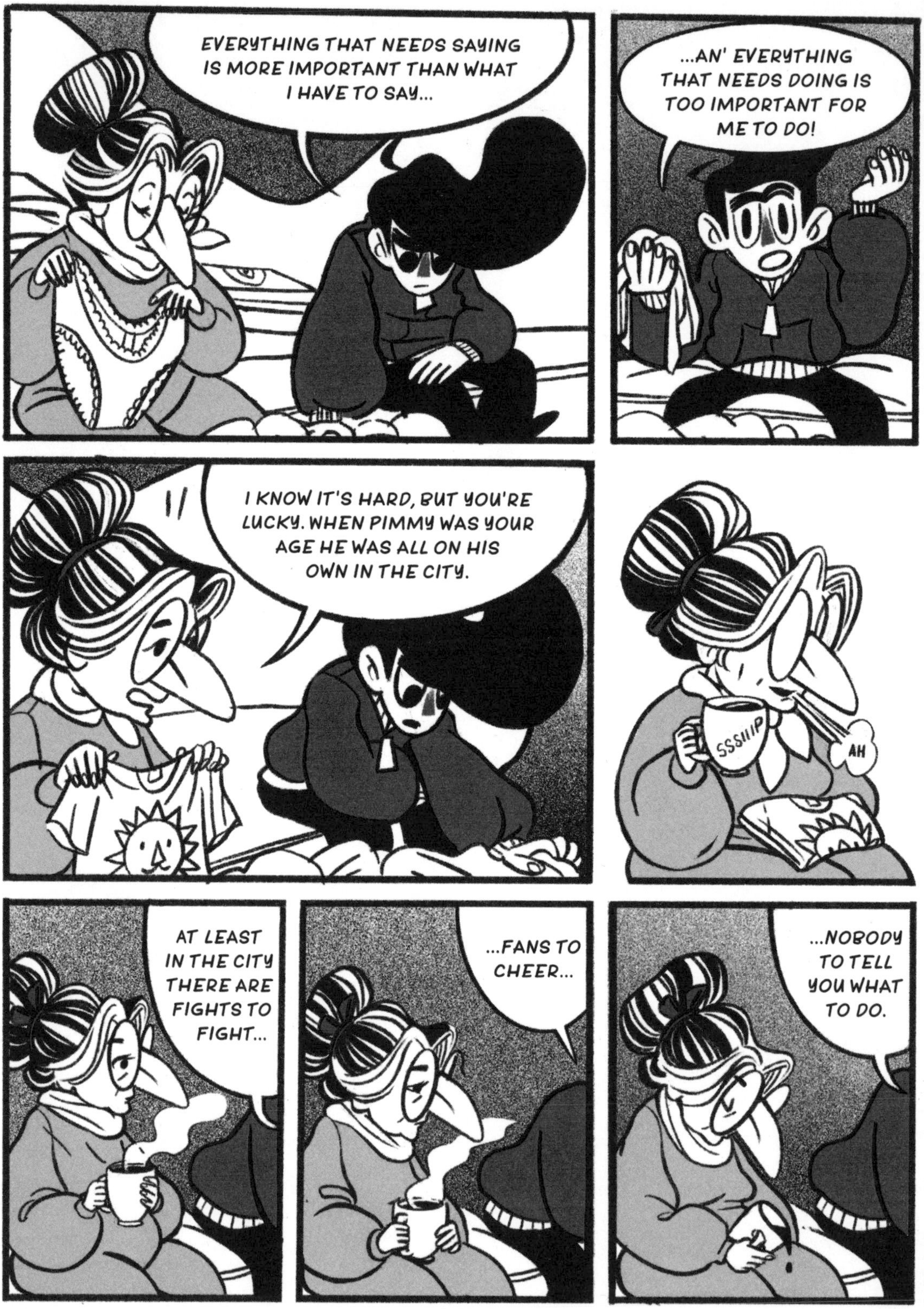
EVERYTHING THAT NEEDS SAYING IS MORE IMPORTANT THAN WHAT I HAVE TO SAY...
...AN' EVERYTHING THAT NEEDS DOING IS TOO IMPORTANT FOR ME TO DO!
!!
I KNOW IT'S HARD, BUT YOU'RE LUCKY. WHEN PIMMY WAS YOUR AGE HE WAS ALL ON HIS OWN IN THE CITY.
SSSIIIP
AH
AT LEAST IN THE CITY THERE ARE FIGHTS TO FIGHT...
...FANS TO CHEER...
...NOBODY TO TELL YOU WHAT TO DO.

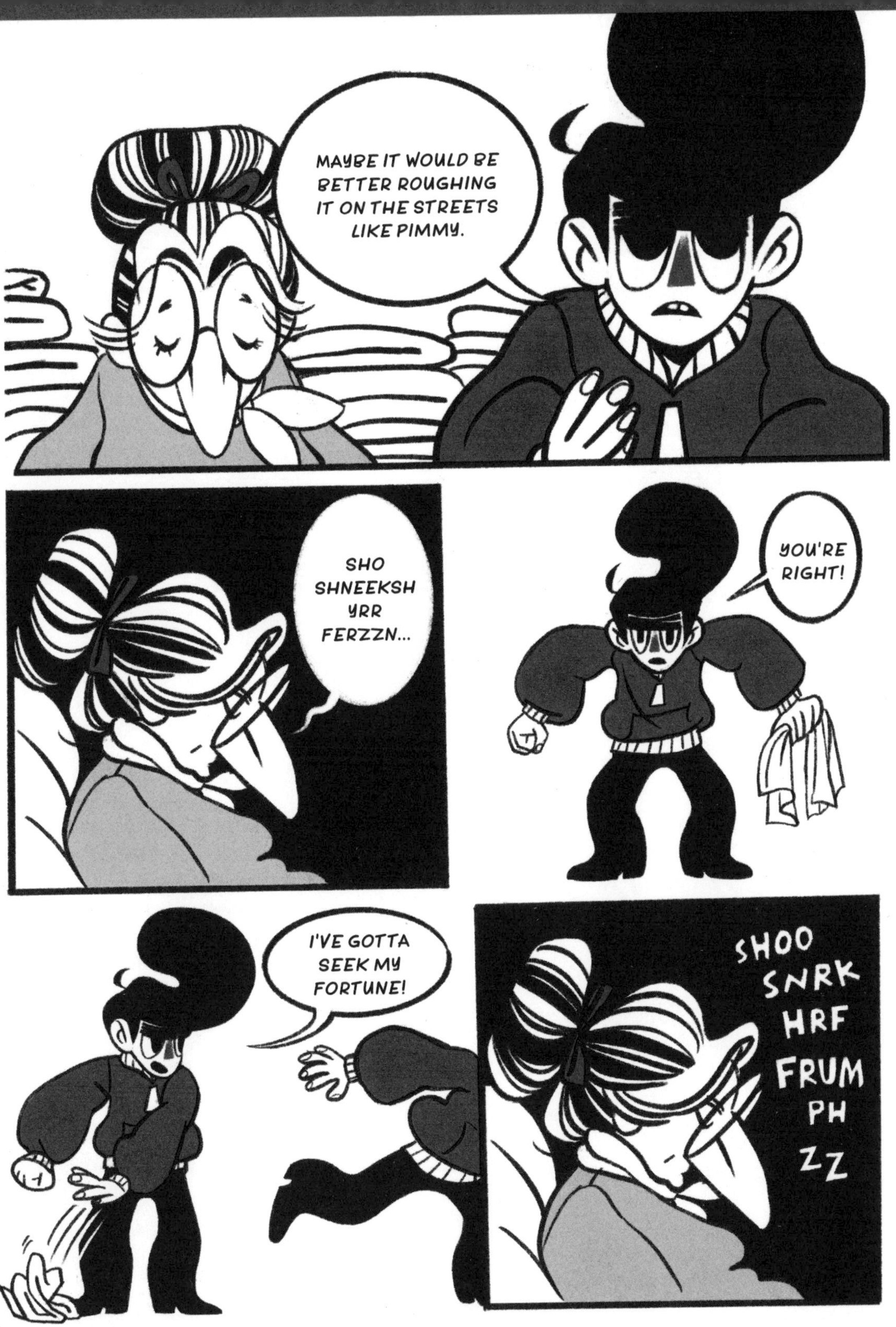
MAYBE IT WOULD BE BETTER ROUGHING IT ON THE STREETS LIKE PIMMY.
SHO SHNEEKSH YRR FERZZN...
YOU'RE RIGHT!
I'VE GOTTA SEEK MY FORTUNE!
SHOO SNRK HRF FRUM PH ZZ

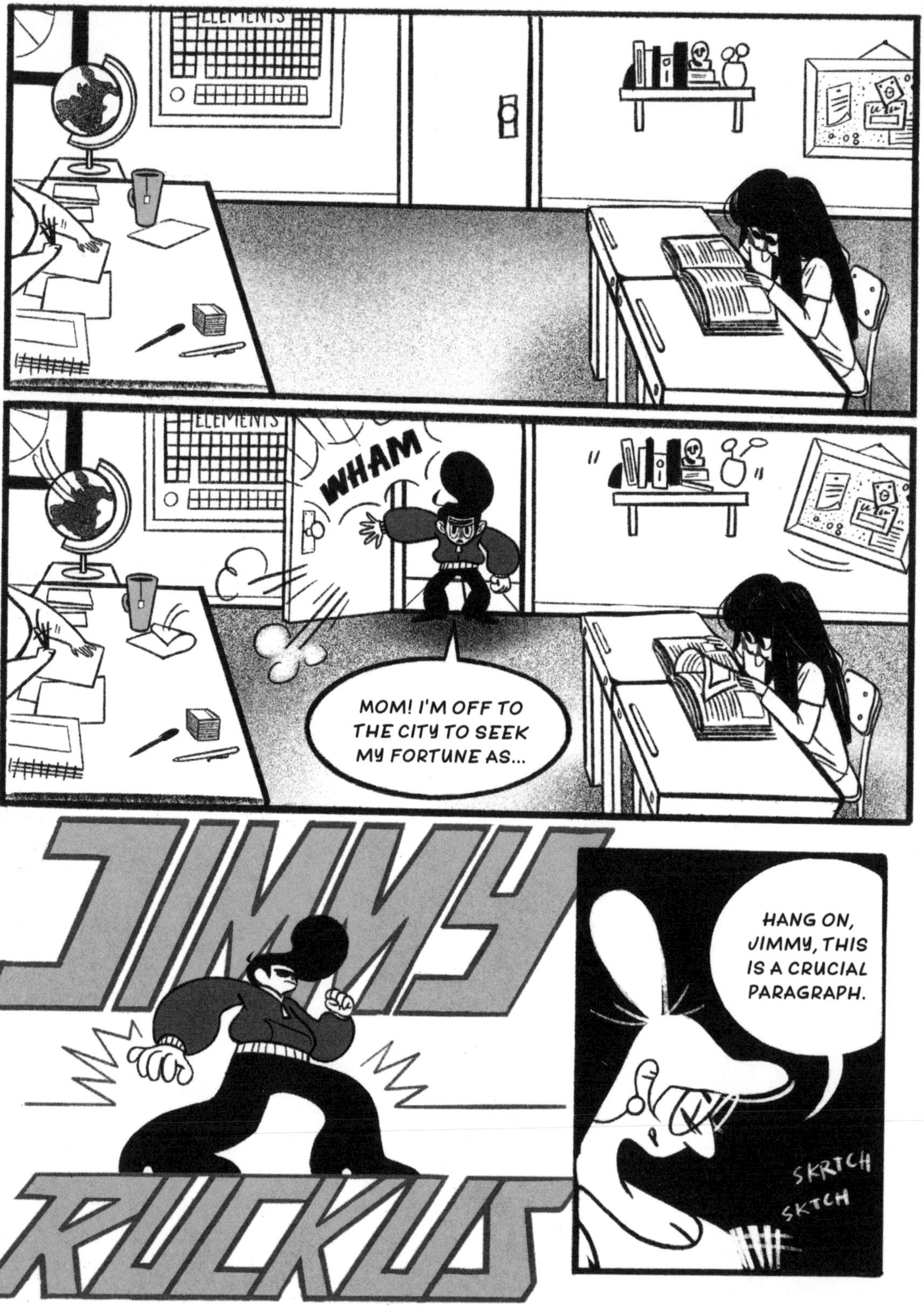
ELEMENTS
ELEMENTS
WHAM
MOM! I'M OFF TO THE CITY TO SEEK MY FORTUNE AS...
JIMMY RUCKUS
HANG ON, JIMMY, THIS IS A CRUCIAL PARAGRAPH.
SKRTCH
SKTCH

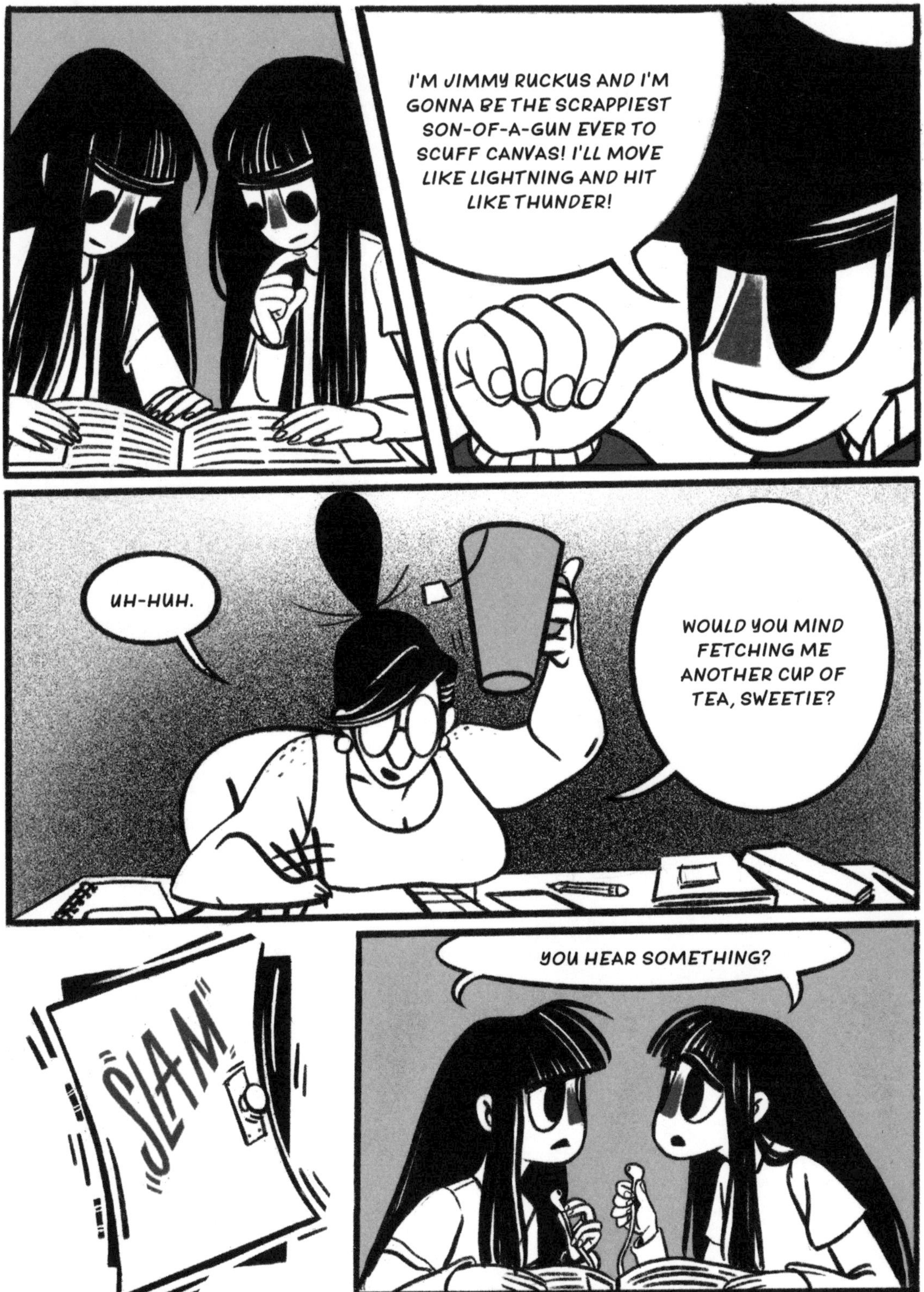
I'M JIMMY RUCKUS AND I'M GONNA BE THE SCRAPPIEST SON-OF-A-GUN EVER TO SCUFF CANVAS! I'LL MOVE LIKE LIGHTNING AND HIT LIKE THUNDER!
UH-HUH.
WOULD YOU MIND FETCHING ME ANOTHER CUP OF TEA, SWEETIE?
SLAM
YOU HEAR SOMETHING?

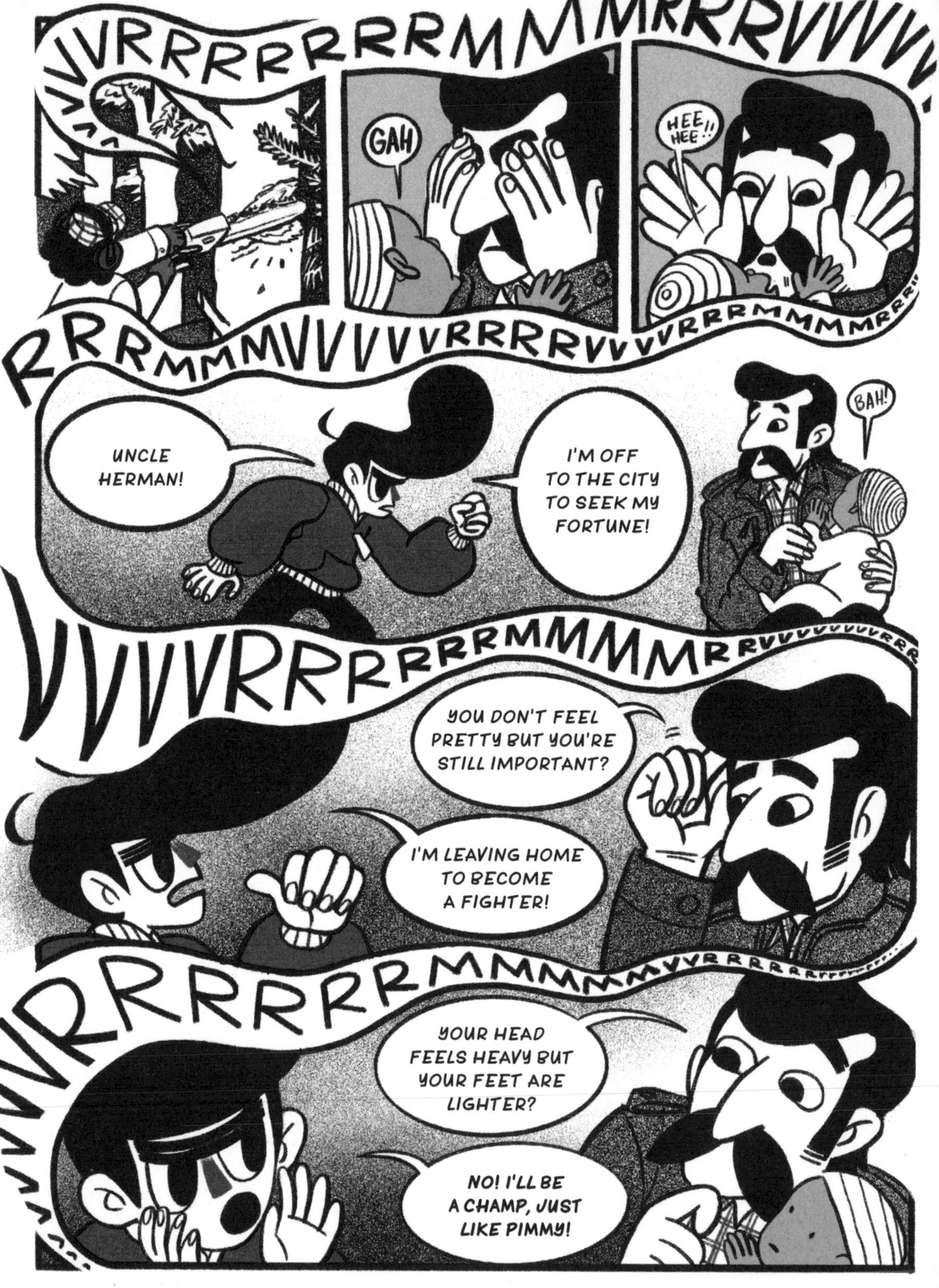
VVVVRRRRRRRMMMRRRVVVVVV
GAH
HEE HEE!!
RRRMMVVVVVVRRRRRVVVVVRRRMMMMRRR
UNCLE HERMAN!
I'M OFF TO THE CITY TO SEEK MY FORTUNE!
BAH!
VVVVRRRRRRMMMMRRVVVVVVVVVRRR
YOU DON'T FEEL PRETTY BUT YOU'RE STILL IMPORTANT?
I'M LEAVING HOME TO BECOME A FIGHTER!
VVVVRRRRRRRMMMMMMVVRRRRRRrrrrr
YOUR HEAD FEELS HEAVY BUT YOUR FEET ARE LIGHTER?
NO! I'LL BE A CHAMP, JUST LIKE PIMMY!

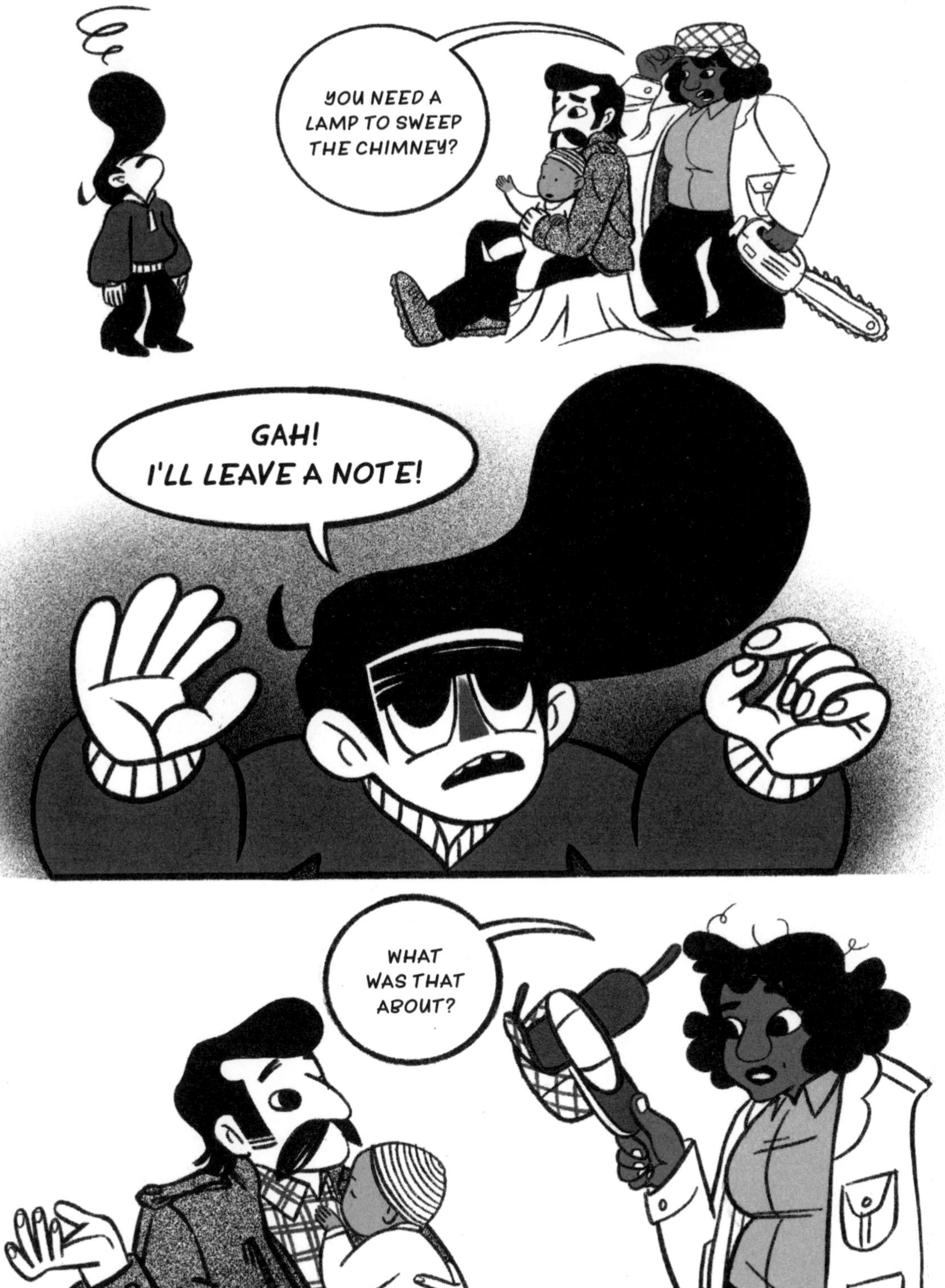
YOU NEED A LAMP TO SWEEP THE CHIMNEY?
GAH! I'LL LEAVE A NOTE!
WHAT WAS THAT ABOUT?

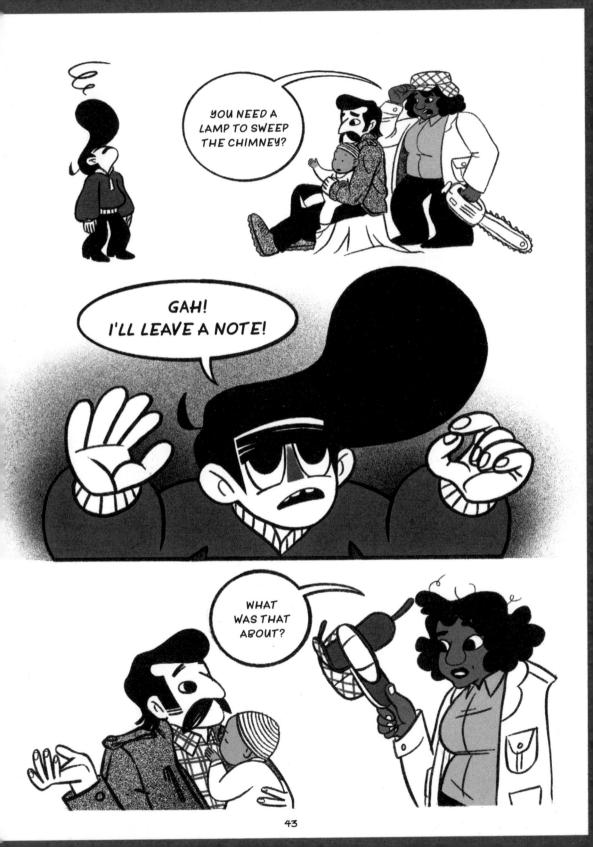

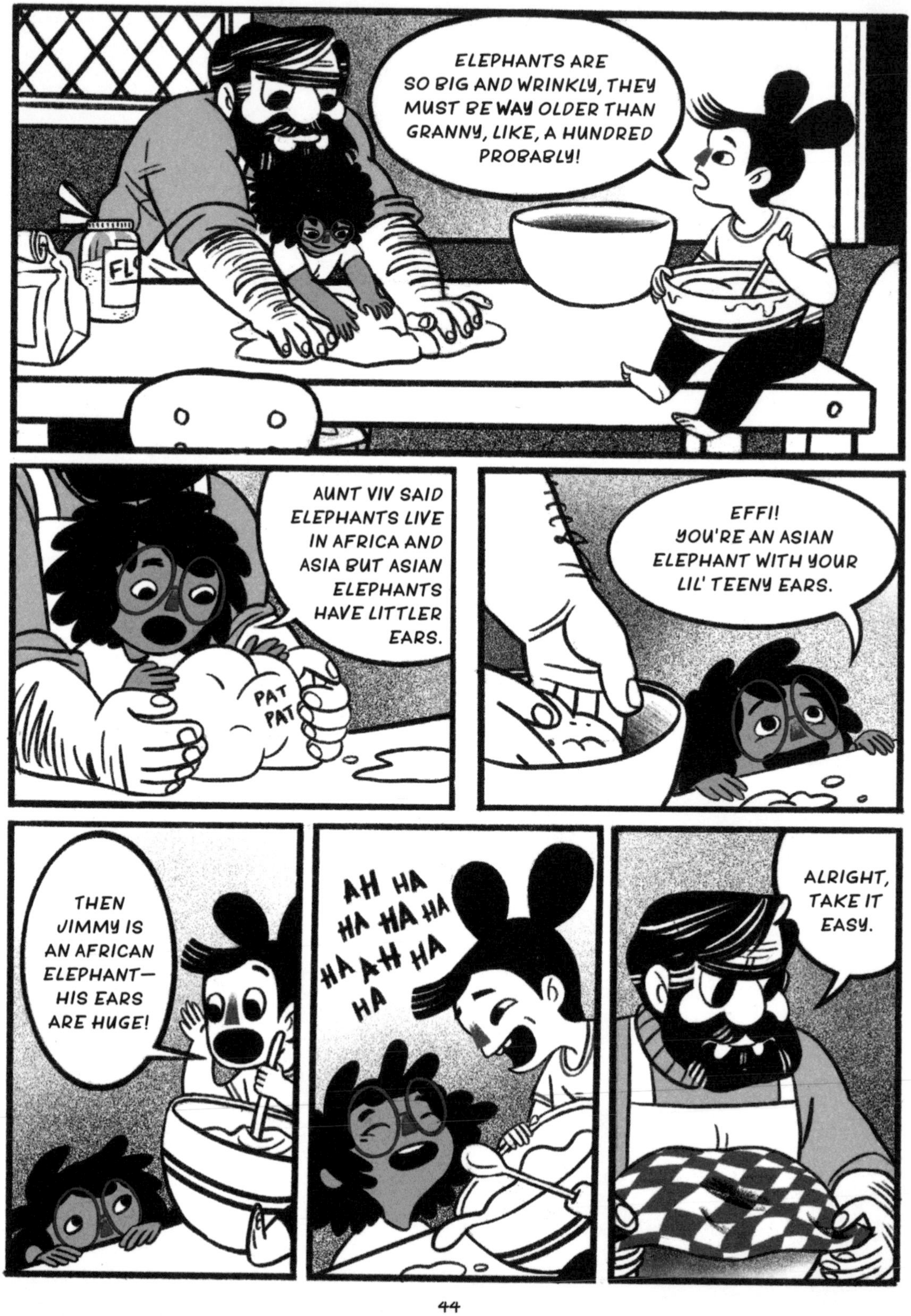
ELEPHANTS ARE SO BIG AND WRINKLY, THEY MUST BE WAY OLDER THAN GRANNY, LIKE, A HUNDRED PROBABLY!
AUNT VIV SAID ELEPHANTS LIVE IN AFRICA AND ASIA BUT ASIAN ELEPHANTS HAVE LITTLER EARS.
PAT PAT
EFFI! YOU'RE AN ASIAN ELEPHANT WITH YOUR LIL' TEENY EARS.
THEN JIMMY IS AN AFRICAN ELEPHANT— HIS EARS ARE HUGE!
AH HA HA HA HA HA HA AH HA HA
ALRIGHT, TAKE IT EASY.

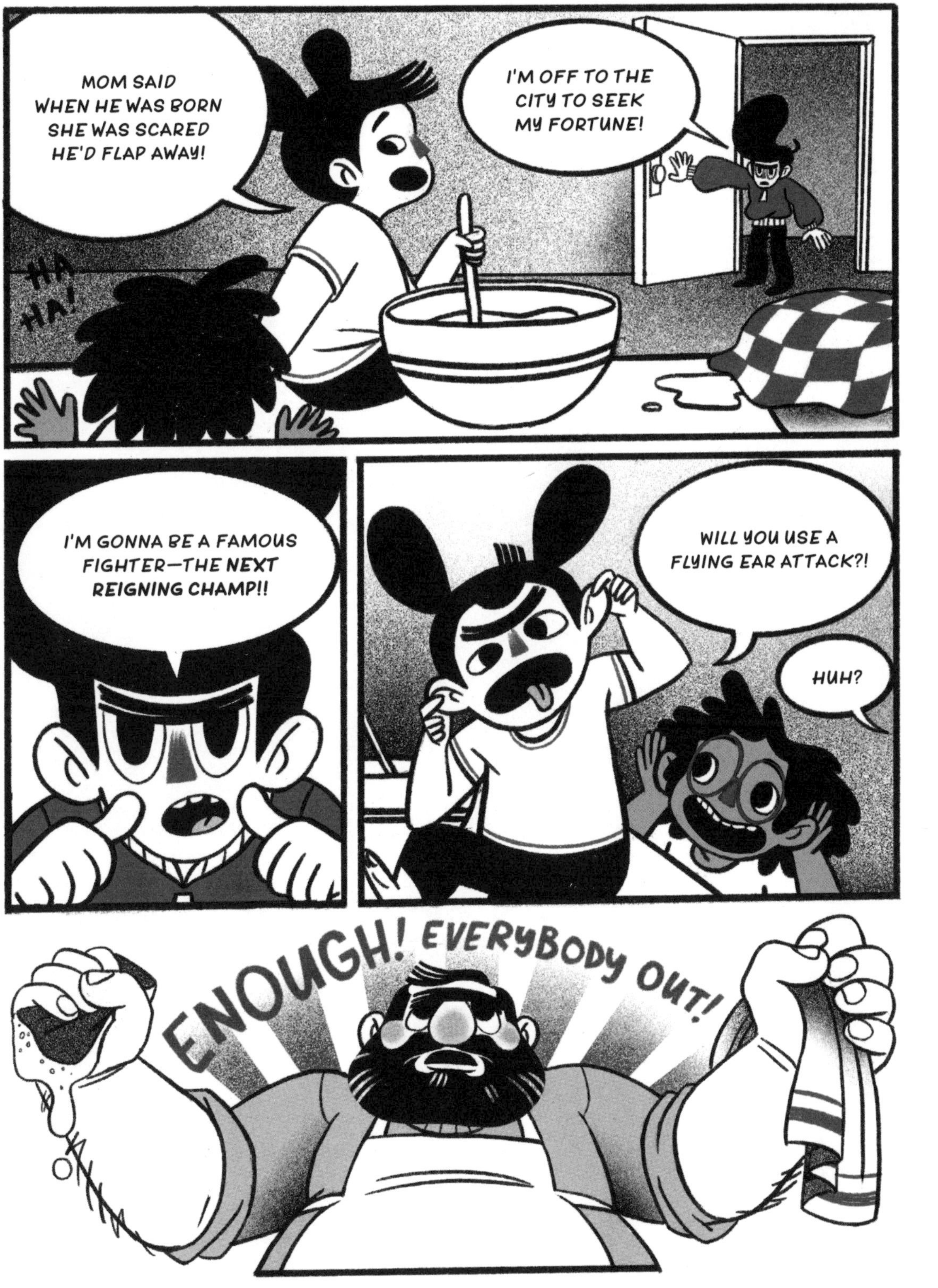
MOM SAID WHEN HE WAS BORN SHE WAS SCARED HE'D FLAP AWAY!
I'M OFF TO THE CITY TO SEEK MY FORTUNE!
HA HA!
I'M GONNA BE A FAMOUS FIGHTER—THE NEXT REIGNING CHAMP!!
WILL YOU USE A FLYING EAR ATTACK?!
HUH?
ENOUGH! EVERYBODY OUT!

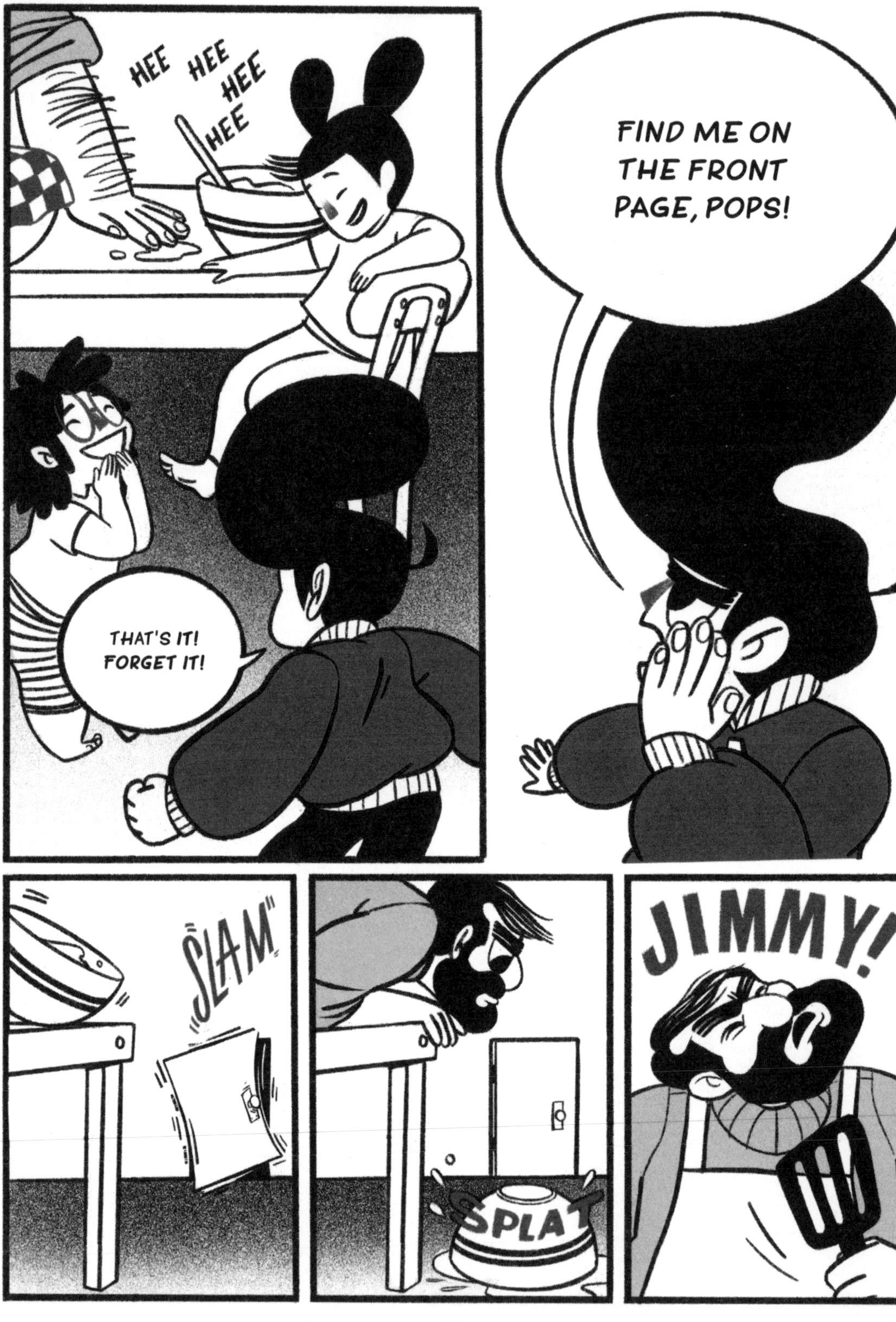
HEE HEE HEE HEE
FIND ME ON THE FRONT PAGE, POPS!
THAT'S IT! FORGET IT!
SLAM
SPLAT
JIMMY!

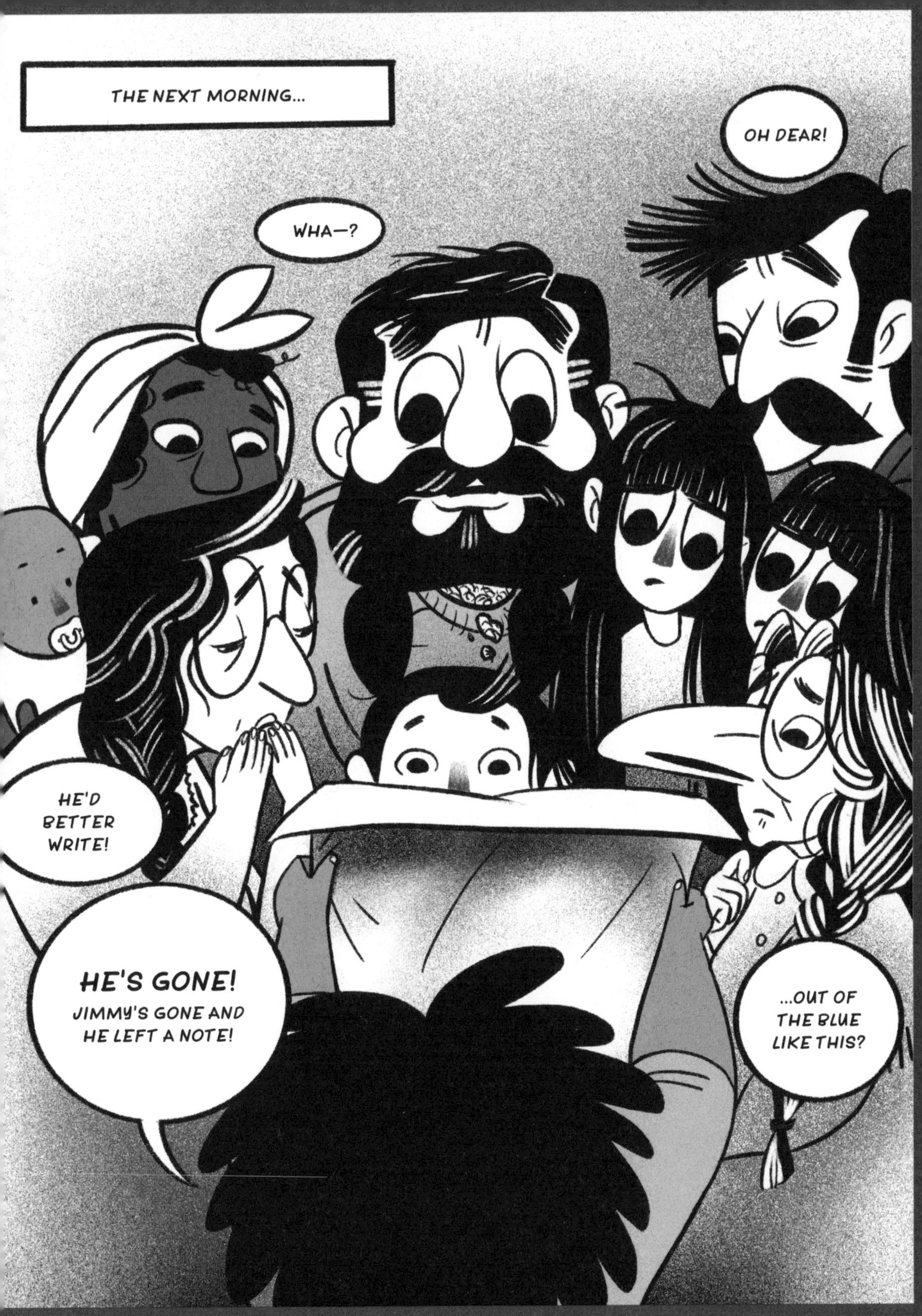
THE NEXT MORNING...
OH DEAR!
WHA—?
HE'D BETTER WRITE!
HE'S GONE! JIMMY'S GONE AND HE LEFT A NOTE!
...OUT OF THE BLUE LIKE THIS?

CHAPTER 2

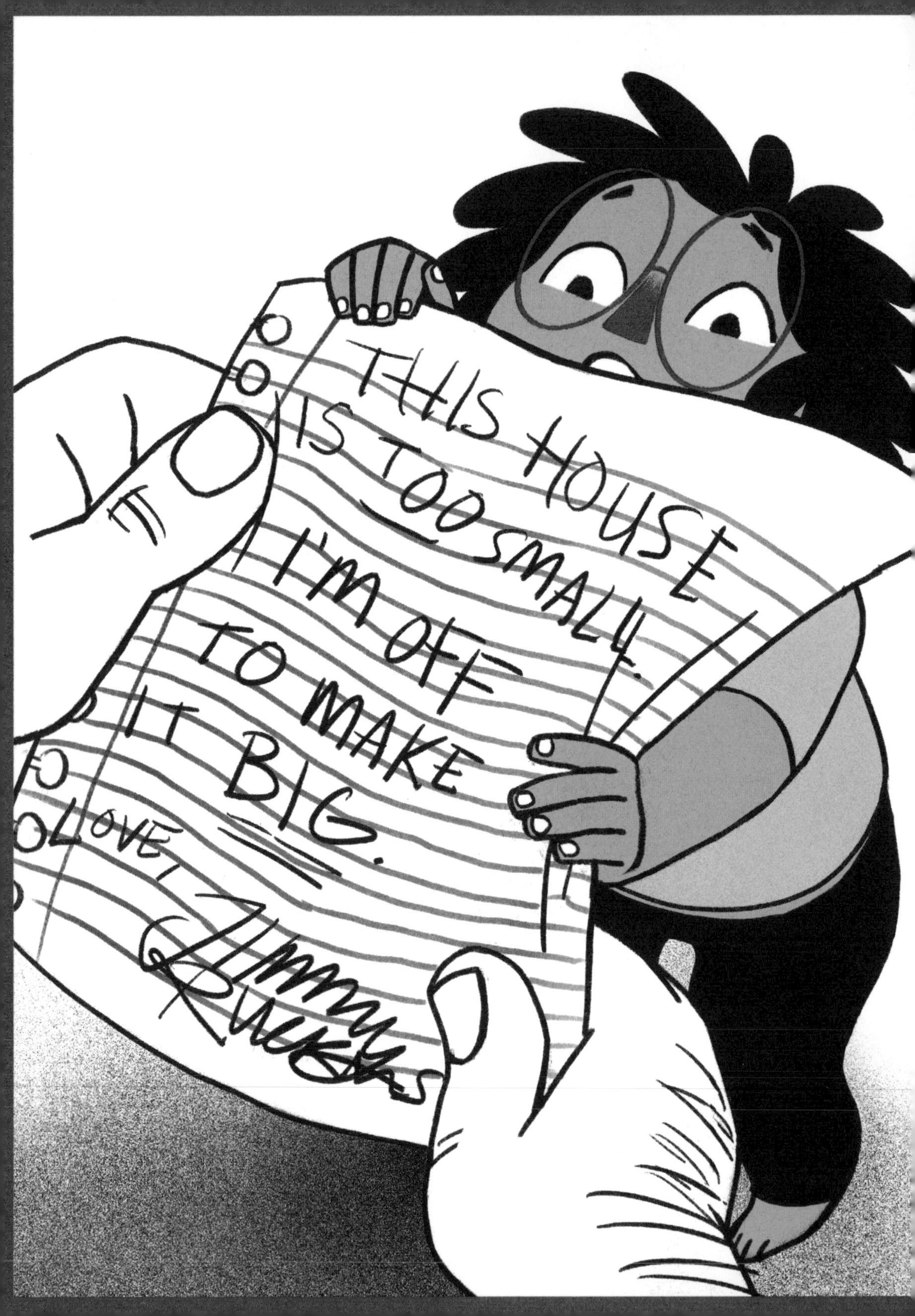
THIS HOUSE
IS TOO SMALL.
I'M OFF
TO MAKE
IT BIG.
LOVE,

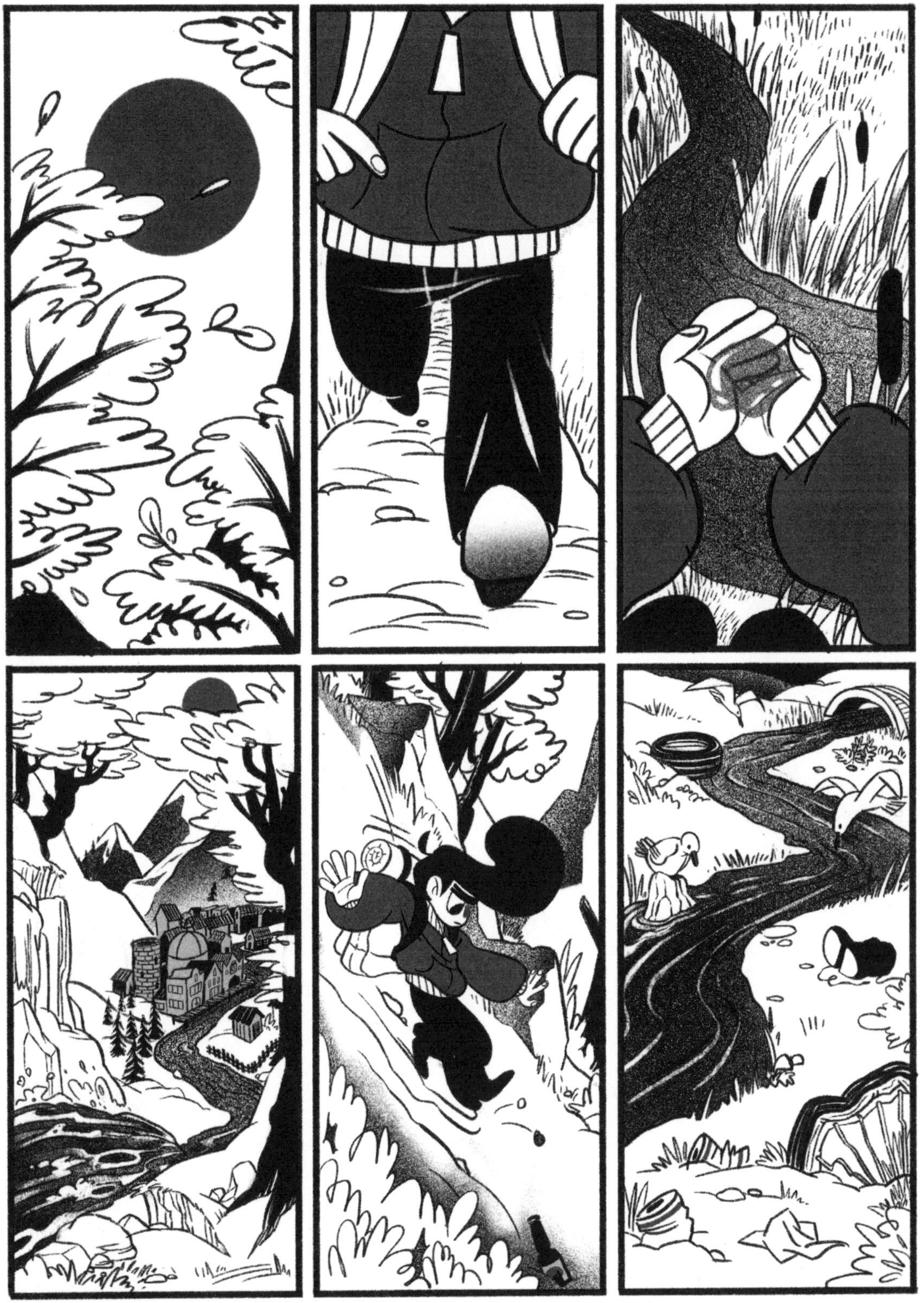

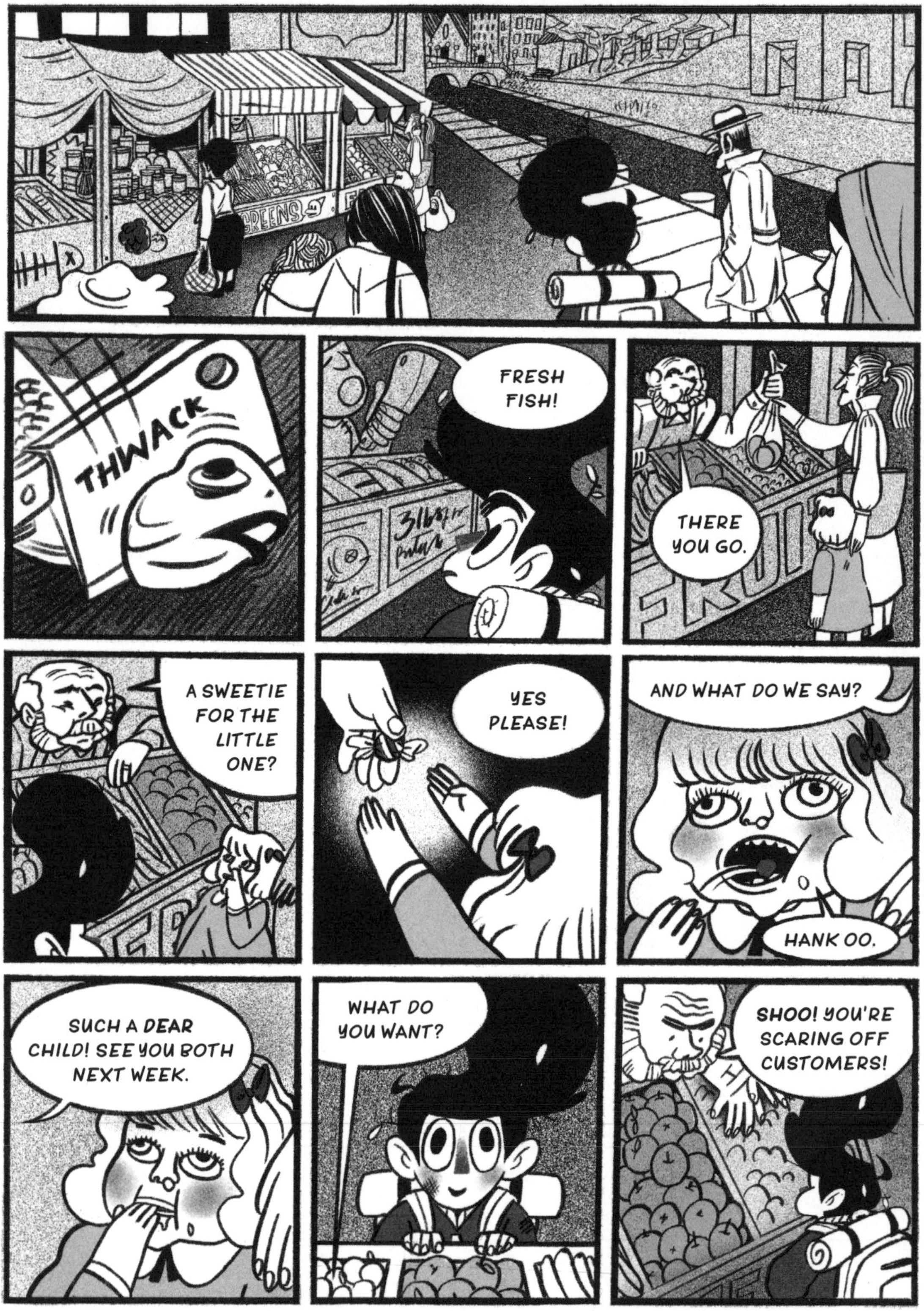
GREENS
THWACK
FRESH FISH!
THERE YOU GO.
A SWEETIE FOR THE LITTLE ONE?
YES PLEASE!
AND WHAT DO WE SAY?
HANK OO.
SUCH A DEAR CHILD! SEE YOU BOTH NEXT WEEK.
WHAT DO YOU WANT?
SHOO! YOU'RE SCARING OFF CUSTOMERS!

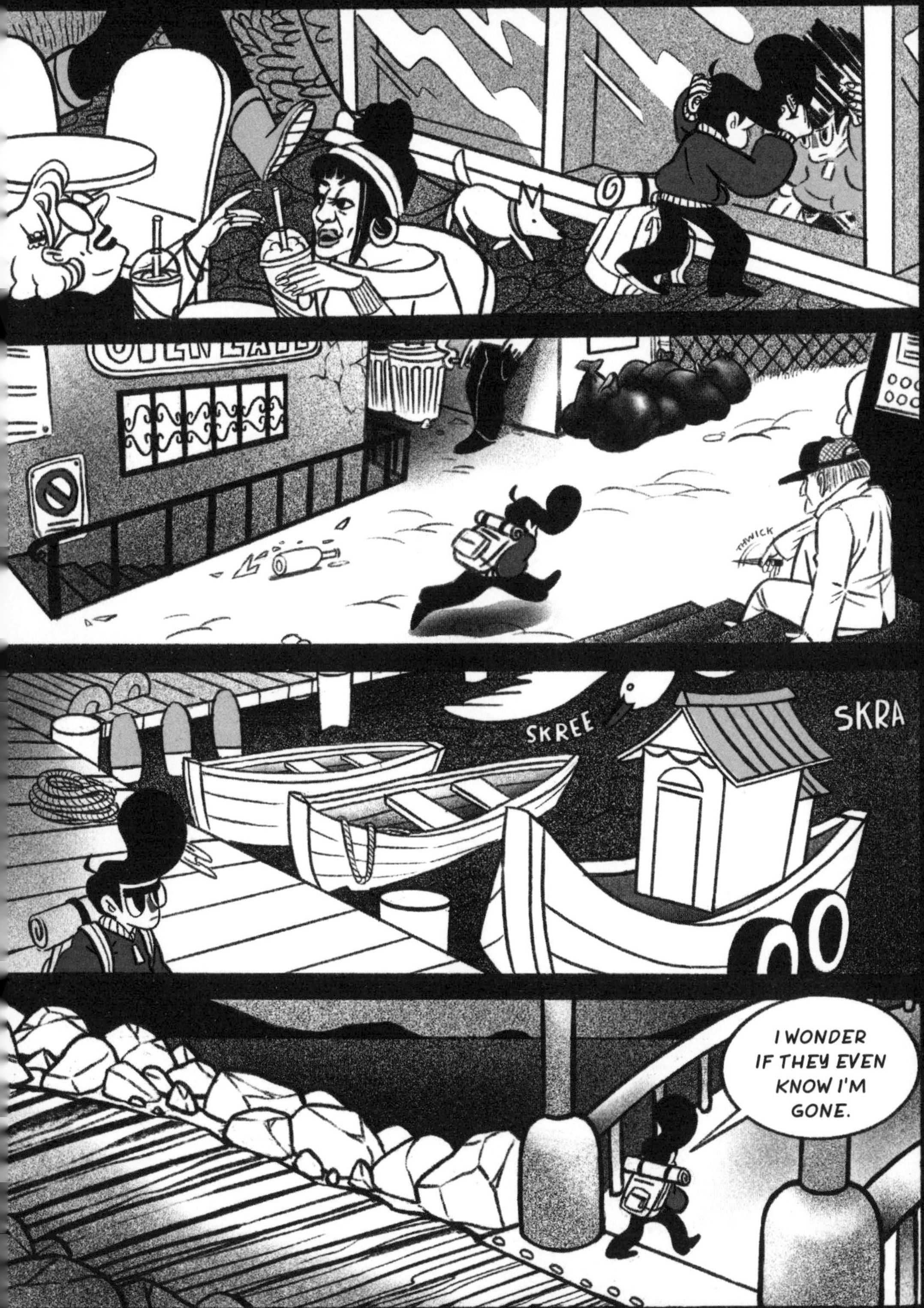
THWICK
SKREE
SKRA
I WONDER IF THEY EVEN KNOW I'M GONE.

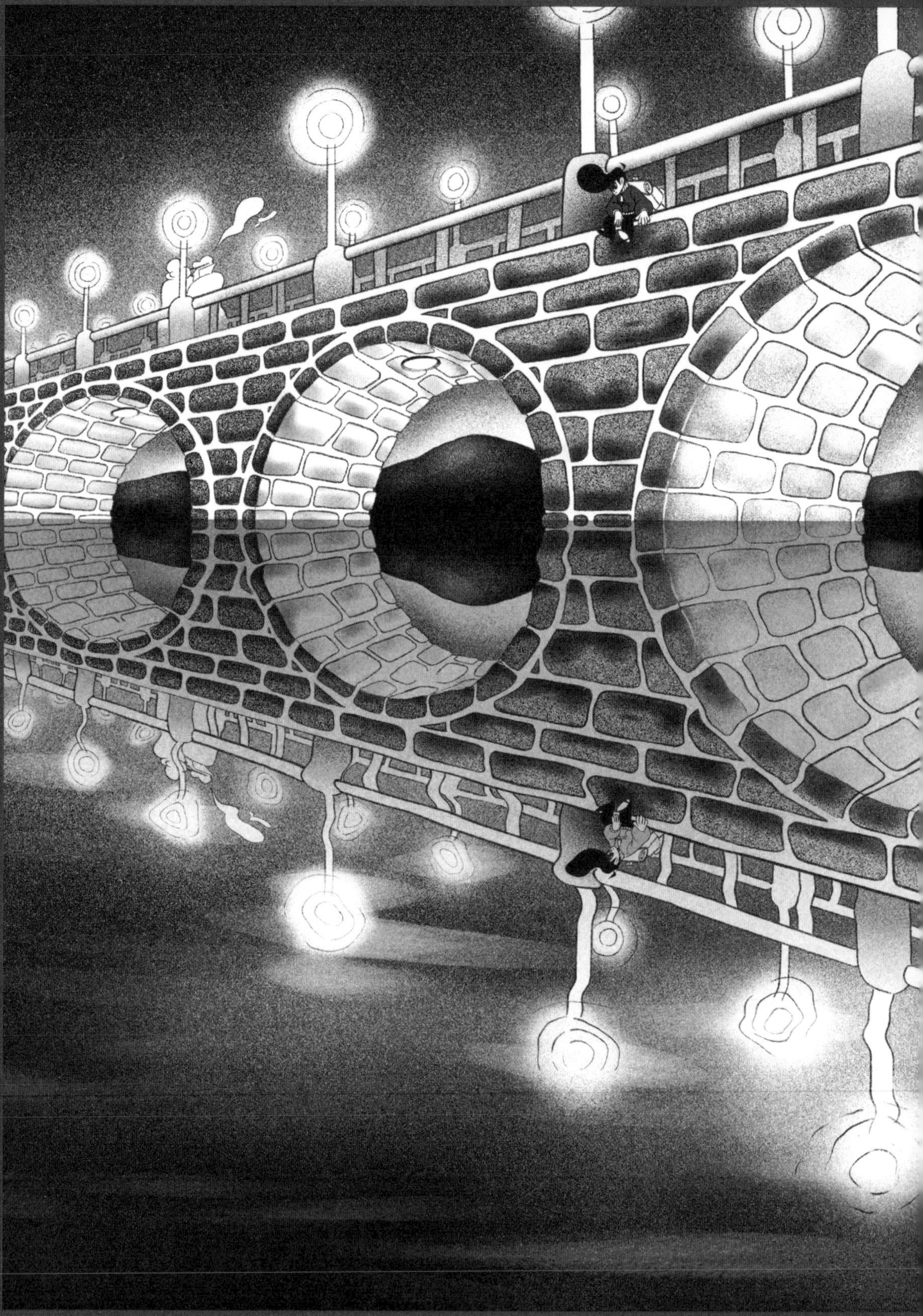

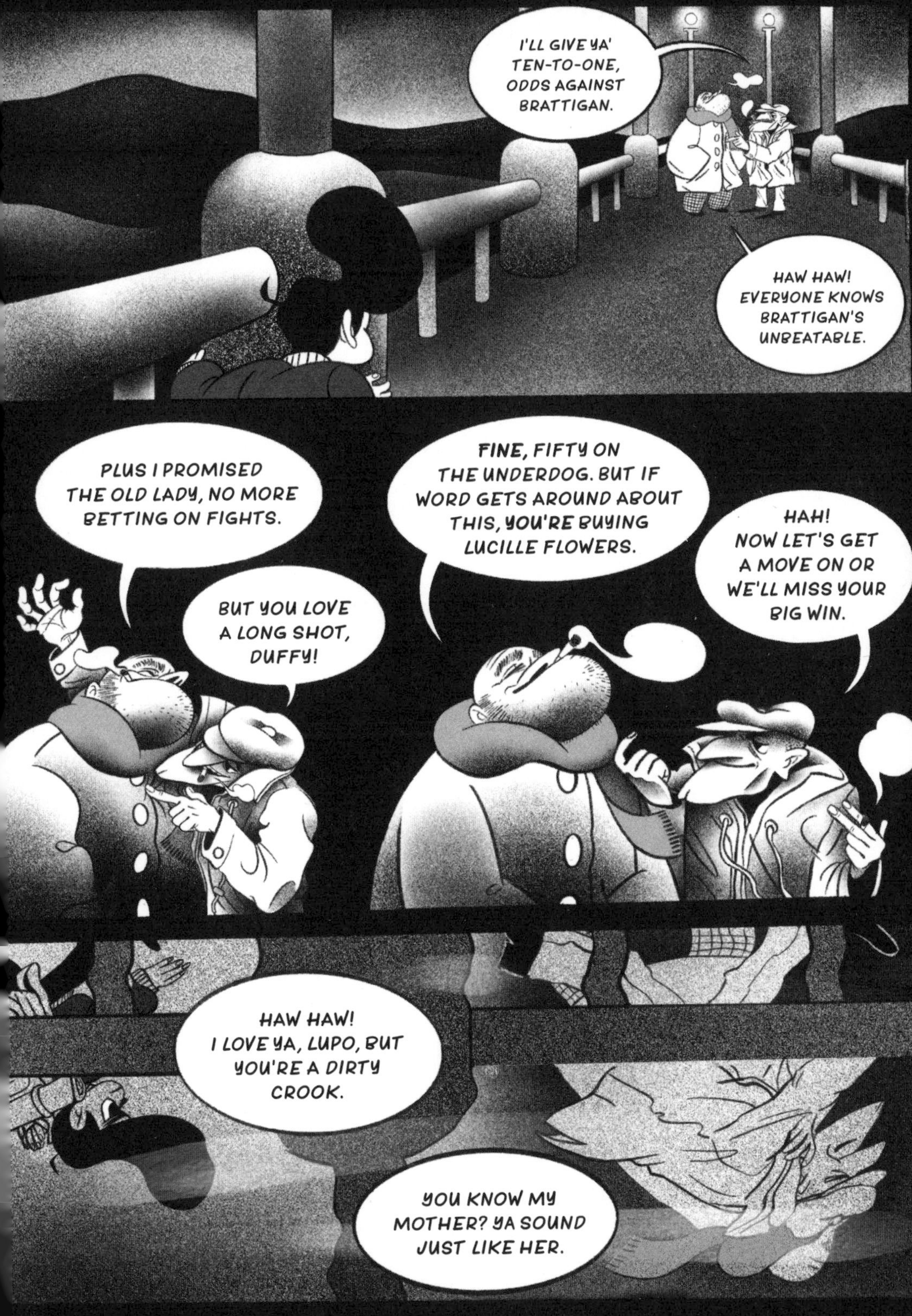
I'LL GIVE YA' TEN-TO-ONE, ODDS AGAINST BRATTIGAN.
HAW HAW! EVERYONE KNOWS BRATTIGAN'S UNBEATABLE.
PLUS I PROMISED THE OLD LADY, NO MORE BETTING ON FIGHTS.
BUT YOU LOVE A LONG SHOT, DUFFY!
FINE, FIFTY ON THE UNDERDOG. BUT IF WORD GETS AROUND ABOUT THIS, YOU'RE BUYING LUCILLE FLOWERS.
HAH! NOW LET'S GET A MOVE ON OR WE'LL MISS YOUR BIG WIN.
HAW HAW! I LOVE YA, LUPO, BUT YOU'RE A DIRTY CROOK.
YOU KNOW MY MOTHER? YA SOUND JUST LIKE HER.

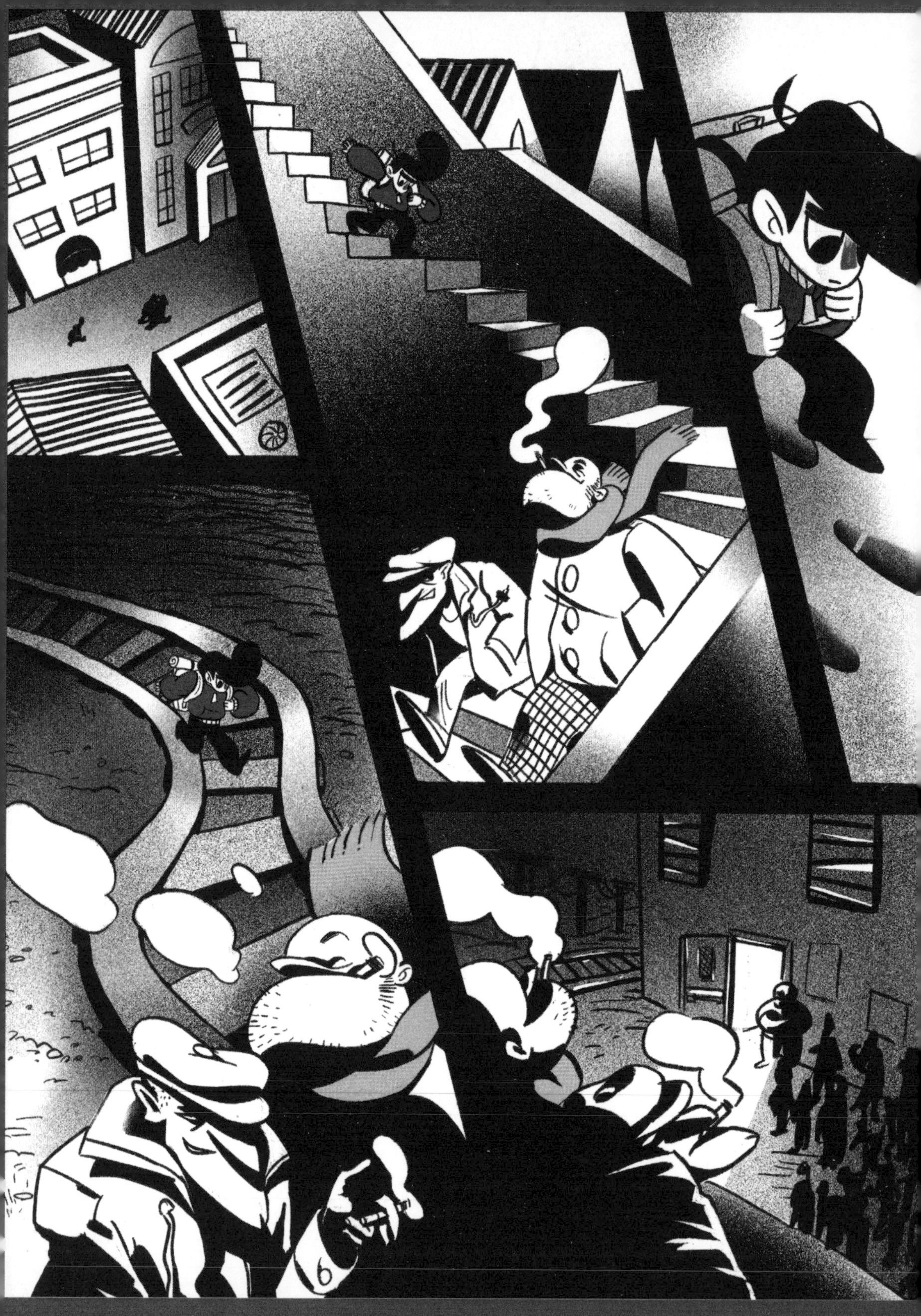

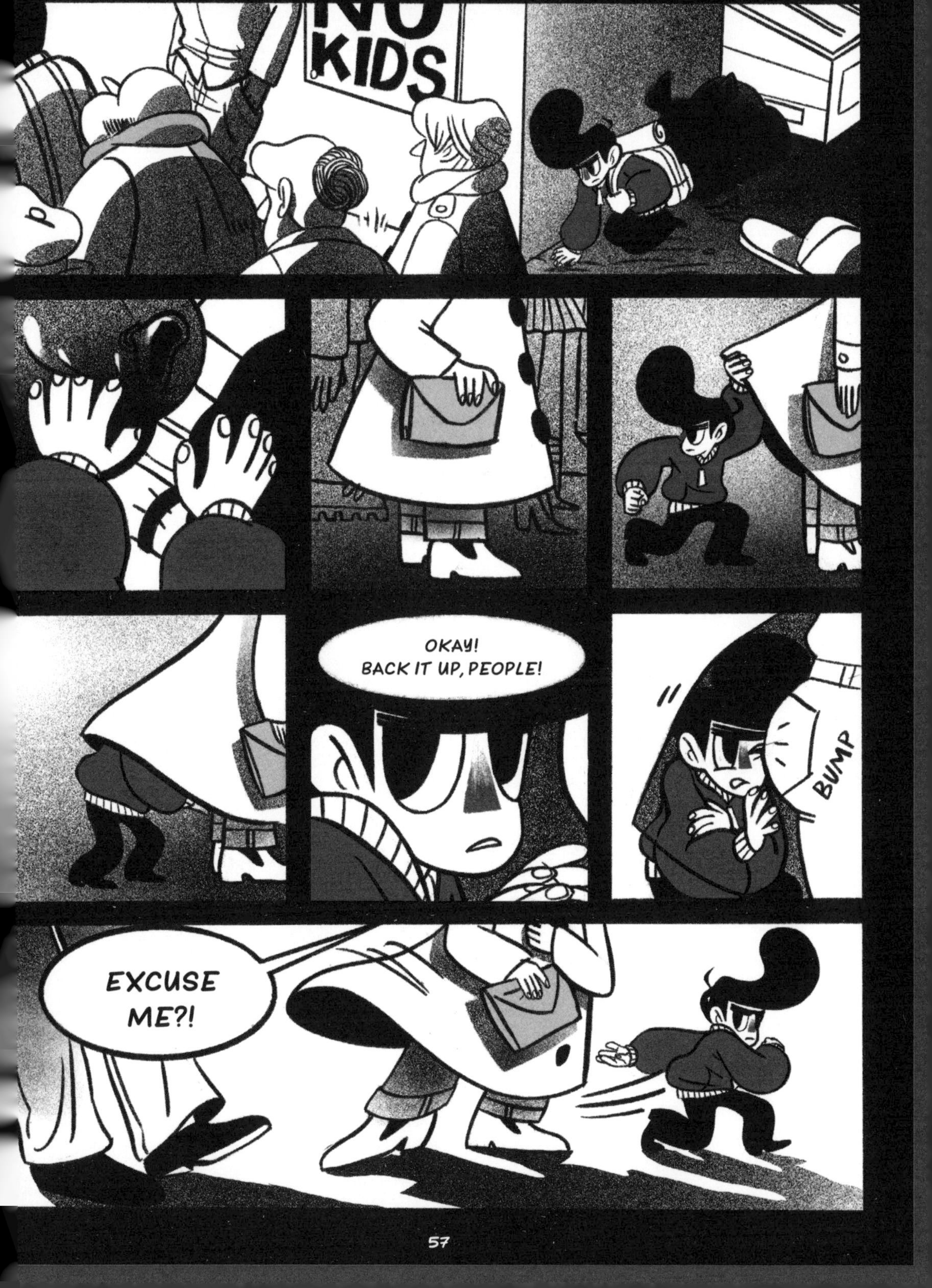
NO
KIDS
OKAY!
BACK IT UP, PEOPLE!
BUMP
EXCUSE ME?!

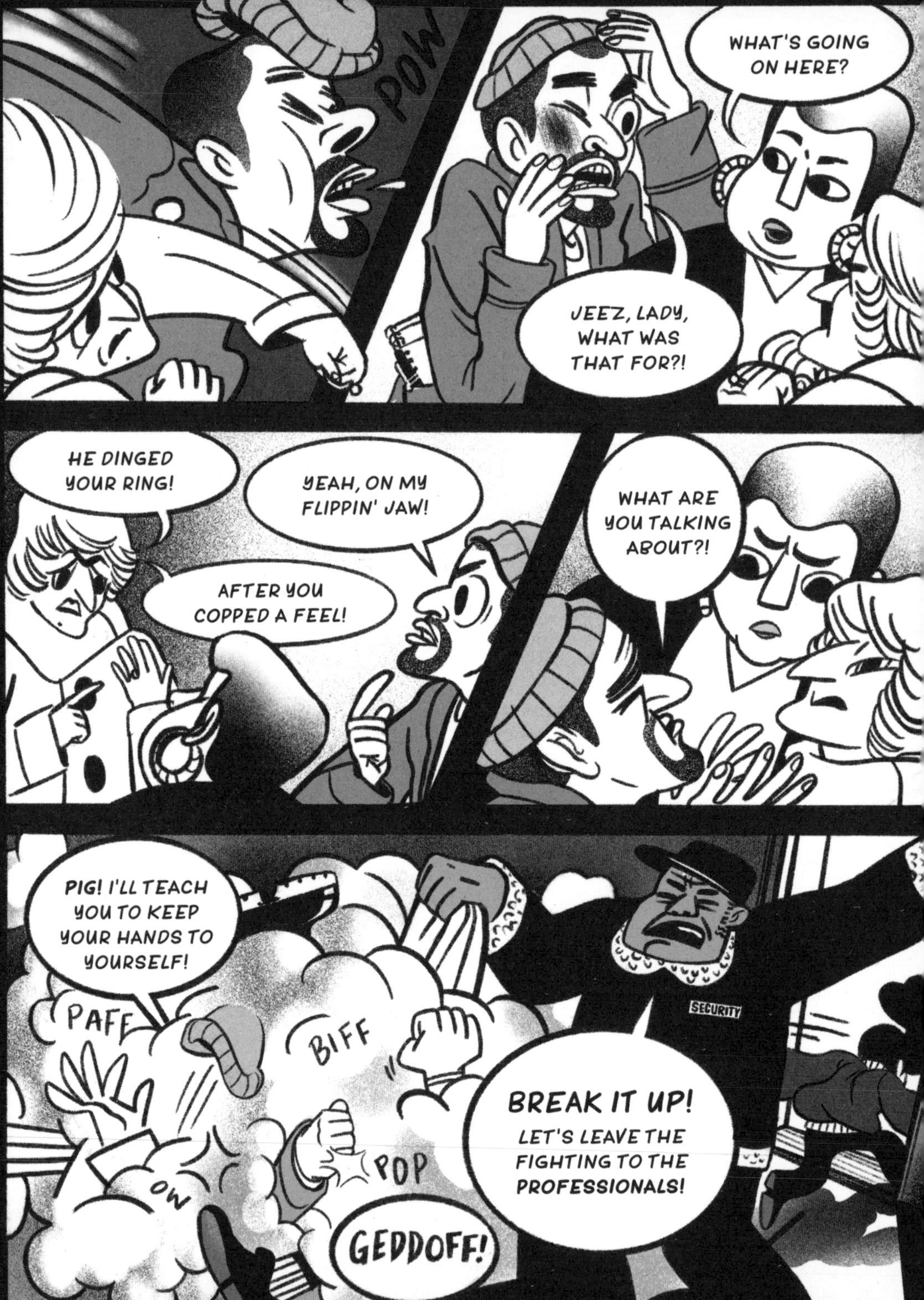
POW
WHAT'S GOING ON HERE?
JEEZ, LADY, WHAT WAS THAT FOR?!
HE DINGED YOUR RING!
YEAH, ON MY FLIPPIN' JAW!
AFTER YOU COPPED A FEEL!
WHAT ARE YOU TALKING ABOUT?!
PIG! I'LL TEACH YOU TO KEEP YOUR HANDS TO YOURSELF!
PAFF
BIFF
OW
POP
GEDDOFF!
SECURITY
BREAK IT UP!
LET'S LEAVE THE FIGHTING TO THE PROFESSIONALS!

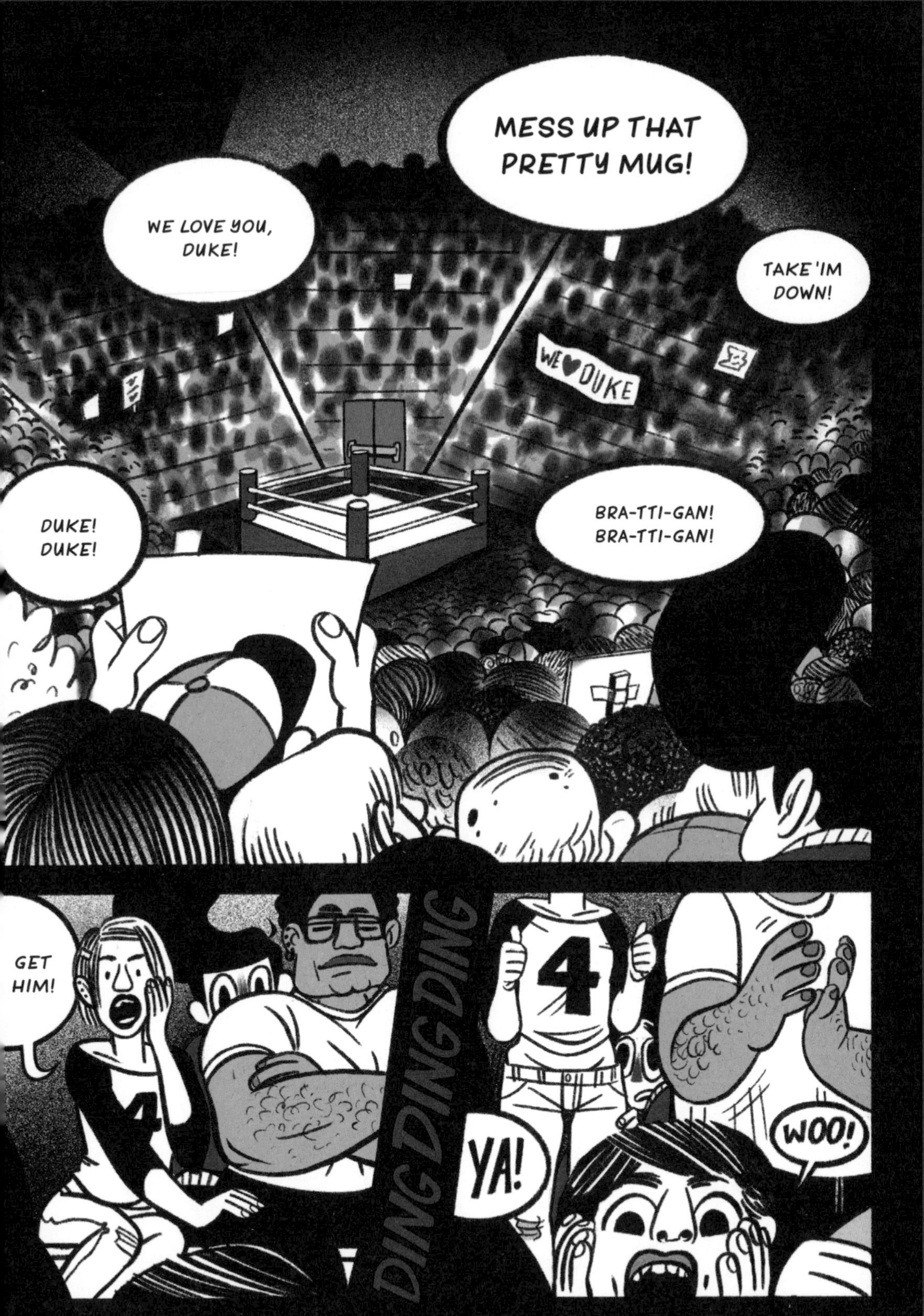
WE LOVE YOU, DUKE!
MESS UP THAT PRETTY MUG!
TAKE 'IM DOWN!
WE ♥ DUKE
DUKE! DUKE!
BRA-TTI-GAN! BRA-TTI-GAN!
GET HIM!
DING DING DING
4
YA!
WOO!

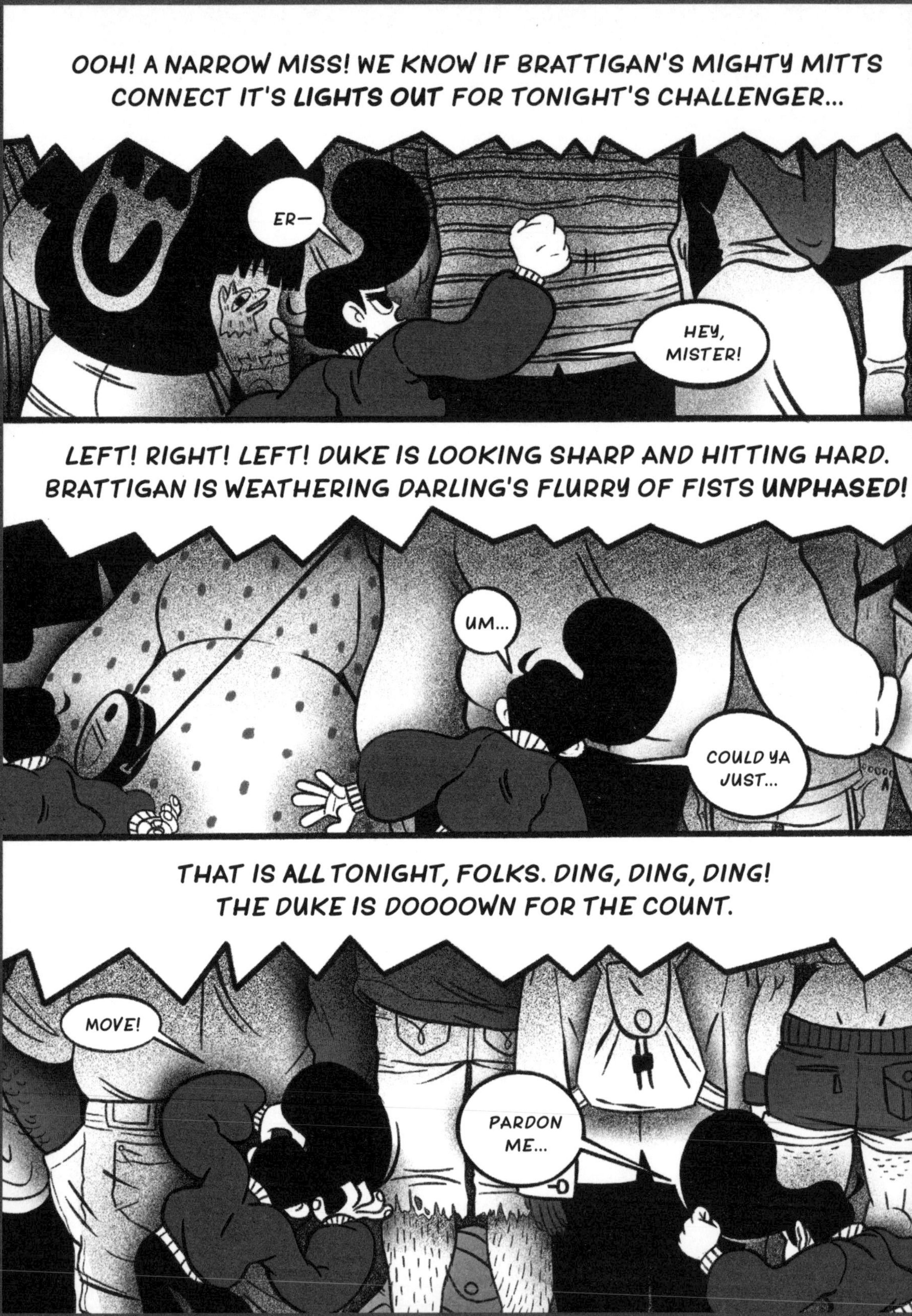
OOH! A NARROW MISS! WE KNOW IF BRATTIGAN'S MIGHTY MITTS CONNECT IT'S LIGHTS OUT FOR TONIGHT'S CHALLENGER...
ER—
HEY, MISTER!
LEFT! RIGHT! LEFT! DUKE IS LOOKING SHARP AND HITTING HARD. BRATTIGAN IS WEATHERING DARLING'S FLURRY OF FISTS UNPHASED!
UM...
COULD YA JUST...
THAT IS ALL TONIGHT, FOLKS. DING, DING, DING! THE DUKE IS DOOOOWN FOR THE COUNT.
MOVE!
PARDON ME...

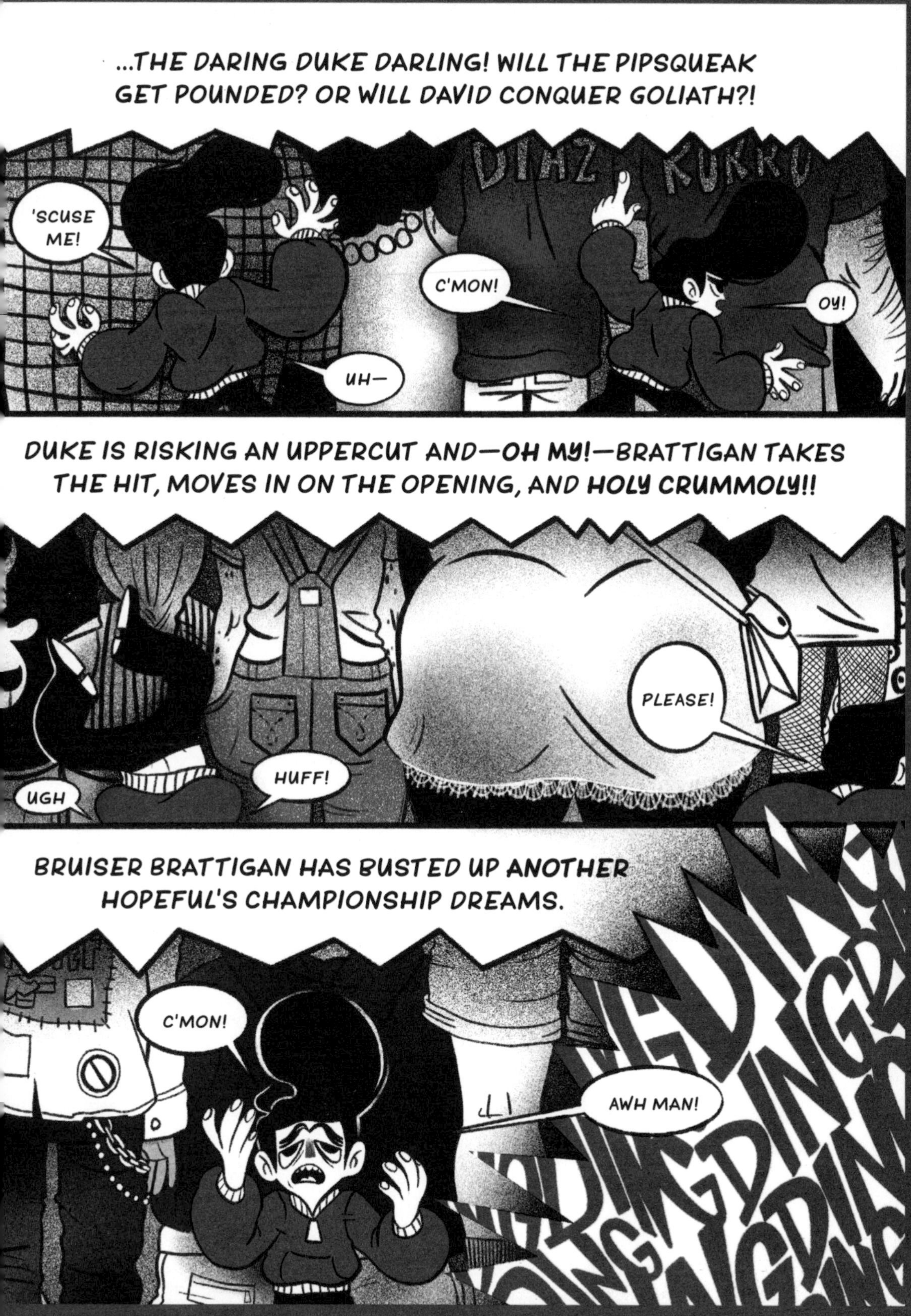
...THE DARING DUKE DARLING! WILL THE PIPSQUEAK GET POUNDED? OR WILL DAVID CONQUER GOLIATH?!
'SCUSE ME!
UH—
C'MON!
OY!
DUKE IS RISKING AN UPPERCUT AND—OH MY!—BRATTIGAN TAKES THE HIT, MOVES IN ON THE OPENING, AND HOLY CRUMMOLY!!
UGH
HUFF!
PLEASE!
BRUISER BRATTIGAN HAS BUSTED UP ANOTHER HOPEFUL'S CHAMPIONSHIP DREAMS.
C'MON!
AWH MAN!

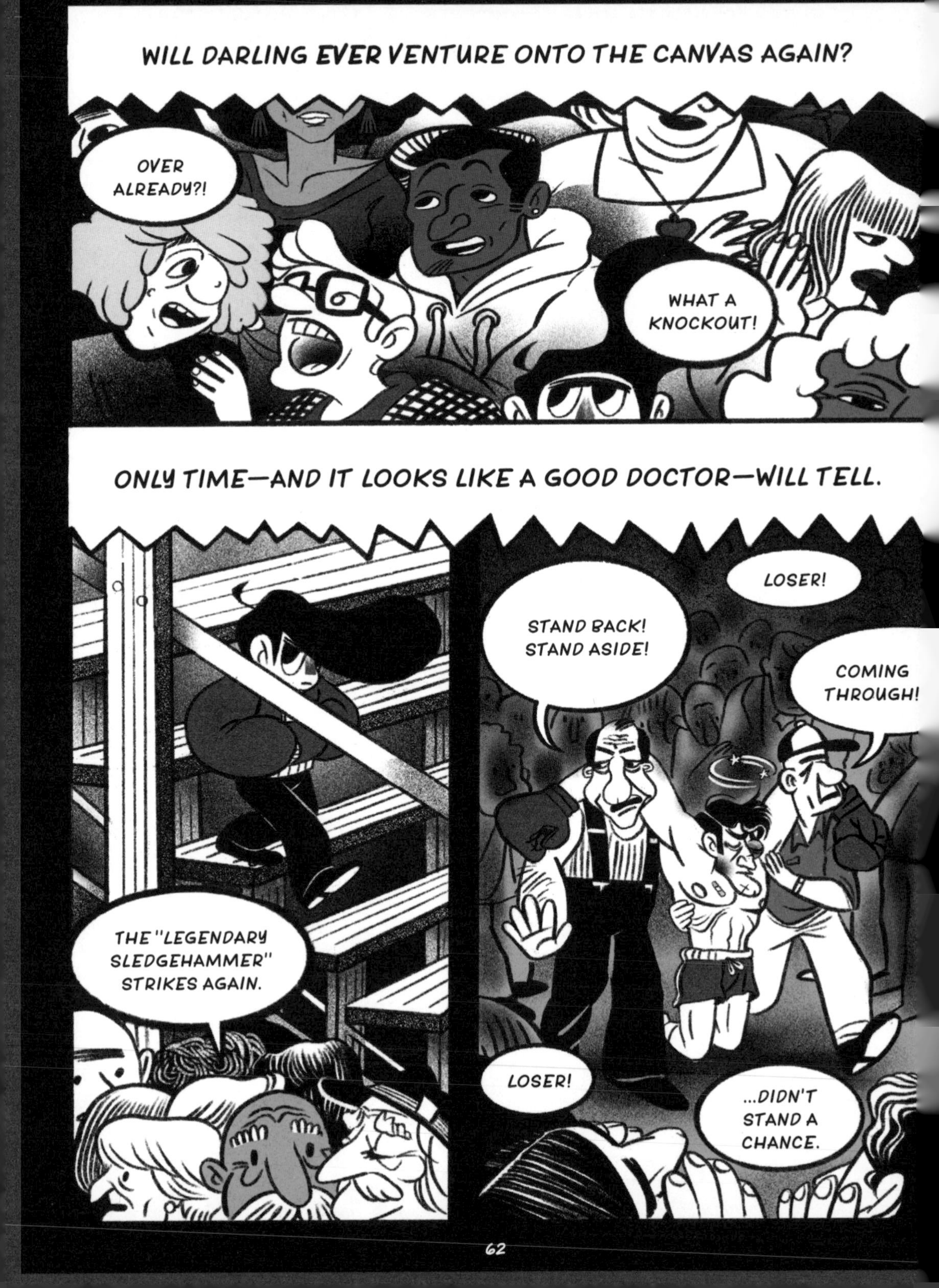
WILL DARLING EVER VENTURE ONTO THE CANVAS AGAIN?
OVER ALREADY?!
WHAT A KNOCKOUT!
ONLY TIME—AND IT LOOKS LIKE A GOOD DOCTOR—WILL TELL.
THE "LEGENDARY SLEDGEHAMMER" STRIKES AGAIN.
LOSER!
STAND BACK! STAND ASIDE!
COMING THROUGH!
LOSER!
...DIDN'T STAND A CHANCE.

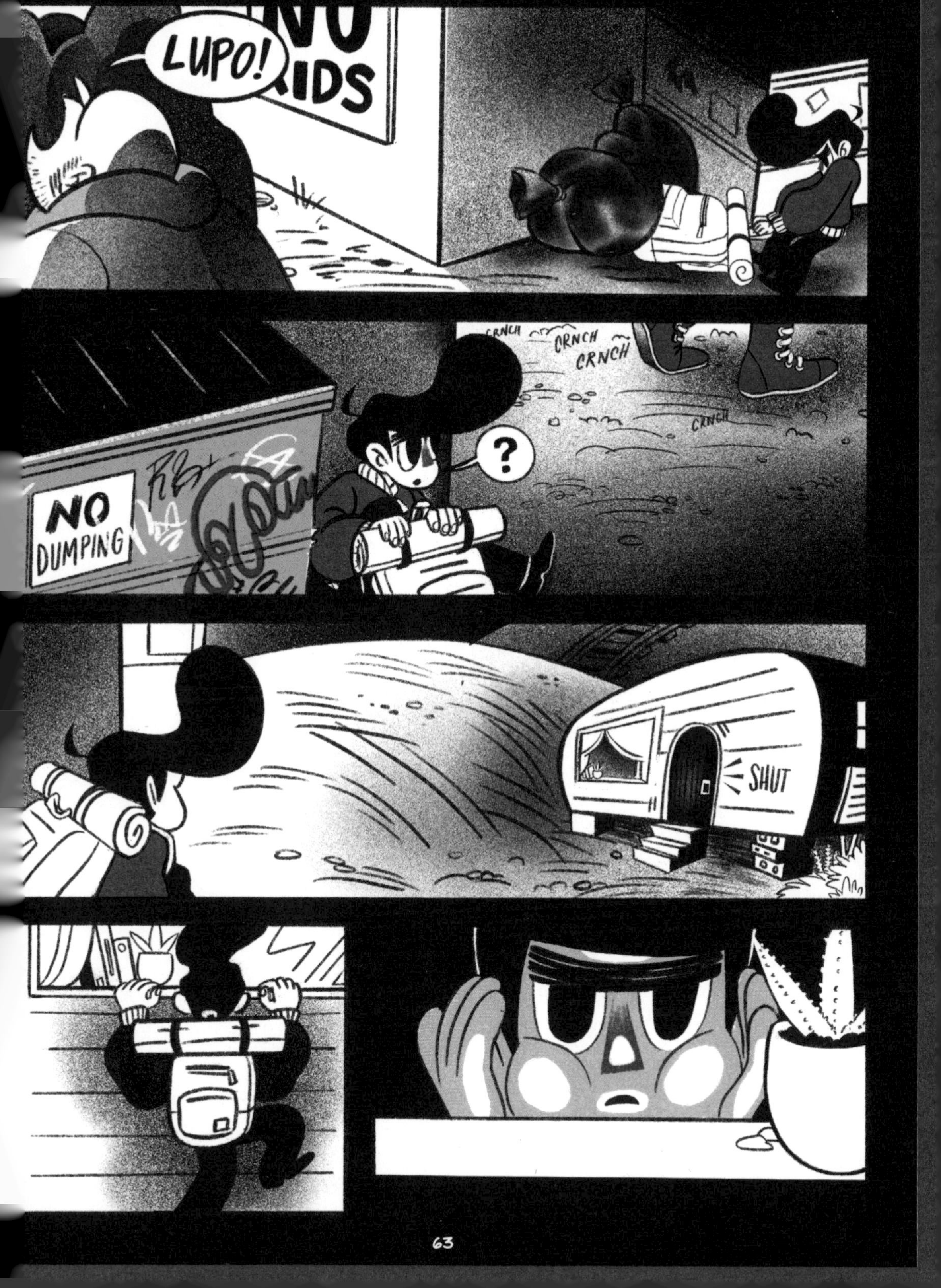
LUPO!
CRNCH
CRNCH
CRNCH
CRNCH
?
NO DUMPING
SHUT

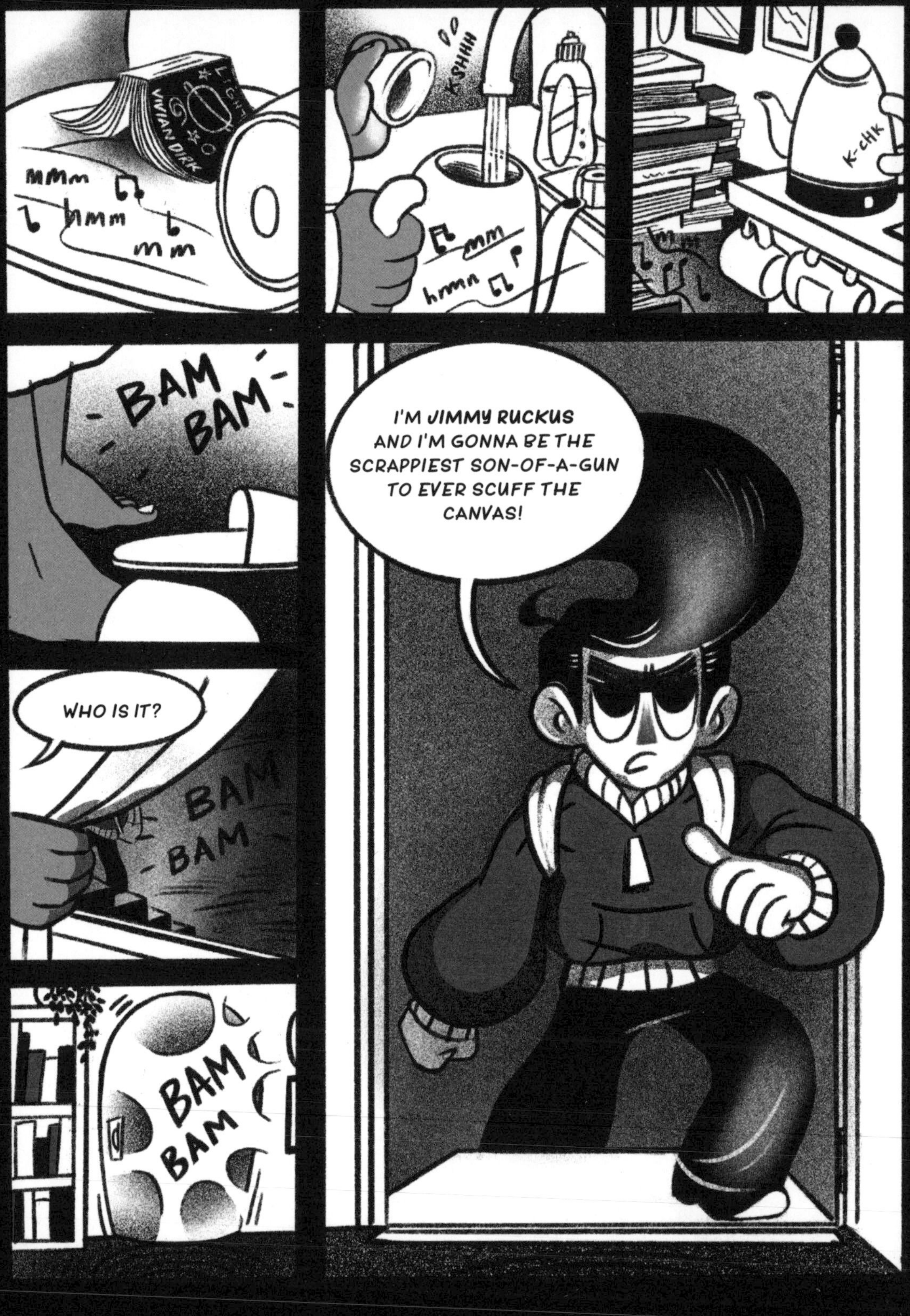
LIGHT
VIVIAN DIRK
MMM
hmm
mm
KSHHH
mm
hmm
K-CHK
BAM
BAM
WHO IS IT?
BAM
BAM
BAM
BAM
I'M JIMMY RUCKUS AND I'M GONNA BE THE SCRAPPIEST SON-OF-A-GUN TO EVER SCUFF THE CANVAS!

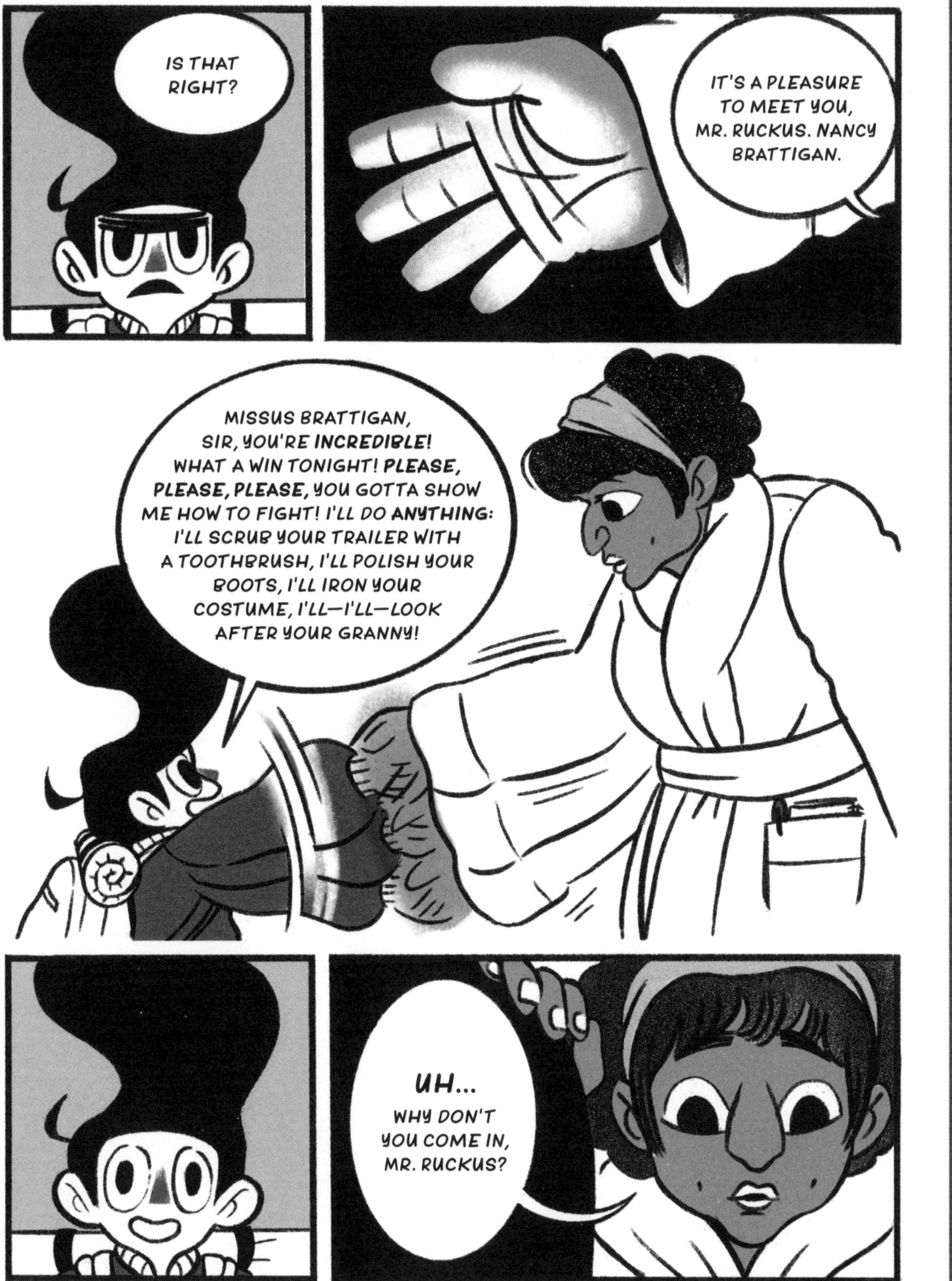
IS THAT RIGHT?
IT'S A PLEASURE TO MEET YOU, MR. RUCKUS. NANCY BRATTIGAN.
MISSUS BRATTIGAN, SIR, YOU'RE **INCREDIBLE**! WHAT A WIN TONIGHT! **PLEASE, PLEASE, PLEASE,** YOU GOTTA SHOW ME HOW TO FIGHT! I'LL DO **ANYTHING**: I'LL SCRUB YOUR TRAILER WITH A TOOTHBRUSH, I'LL POLISH YOUR BOOTS, I'LL IRON YOUR COSTUME, I'LL—I'LL—LOOK AFTER YOUR GRANNY!
UH... WHY DON'T YOU COME IN, MR. RUCKUS?

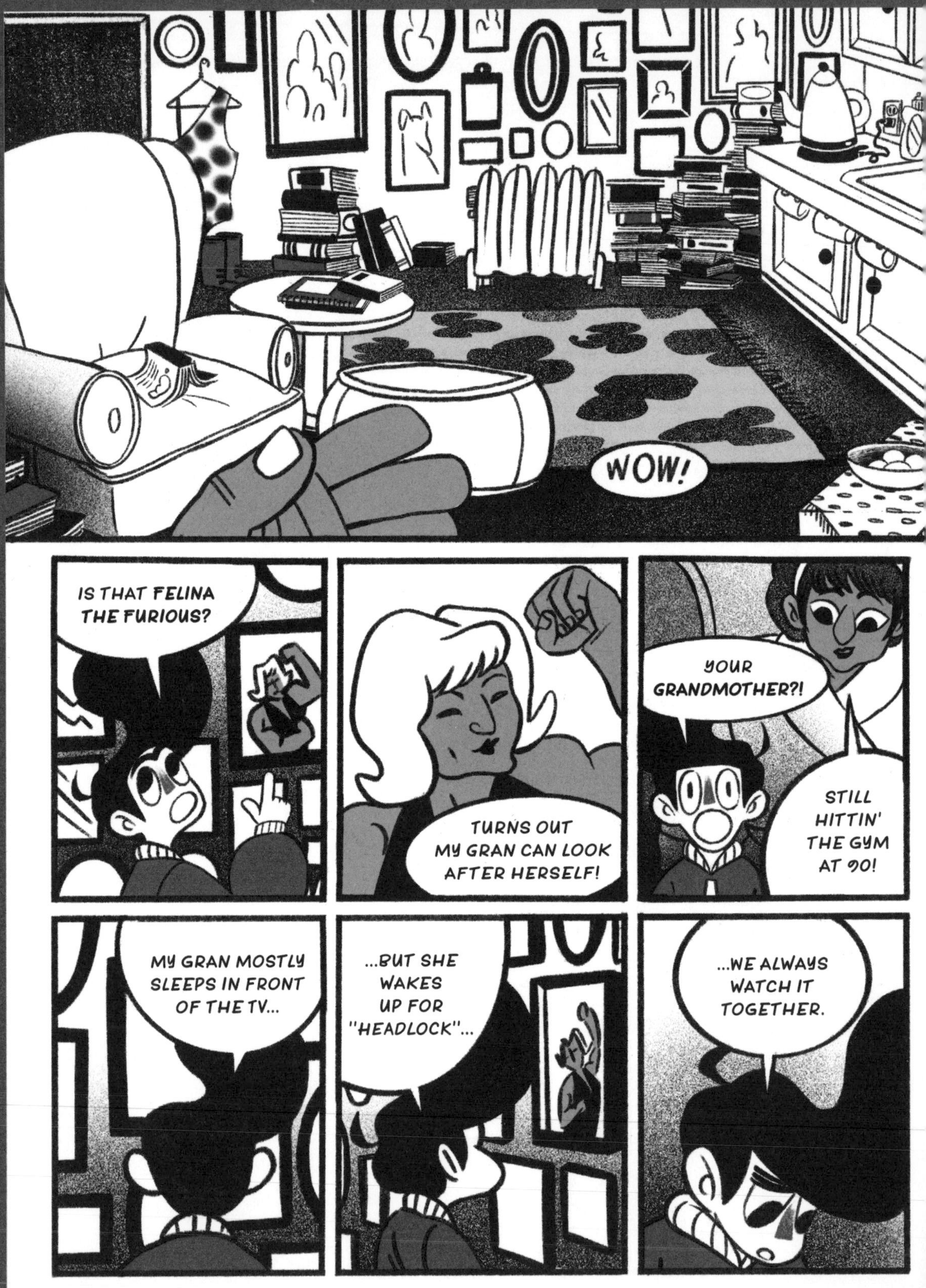
WOW!
IS THAT FELINA THE FURIOUS?
TURNS OUT MY GRAN CAN LOOK AFTER HERSELF!
YOUR GRANDMOTHER?!
STILL HITTIN' THE GYM AT 90!
MY GRAN MOSTLY SLEEPS IN FRONT OF THE TV...
...BUT SHE WAKES UP FOR "HEADLOCK"...
...WE ALWAYS WATCH IT TOGETHER.

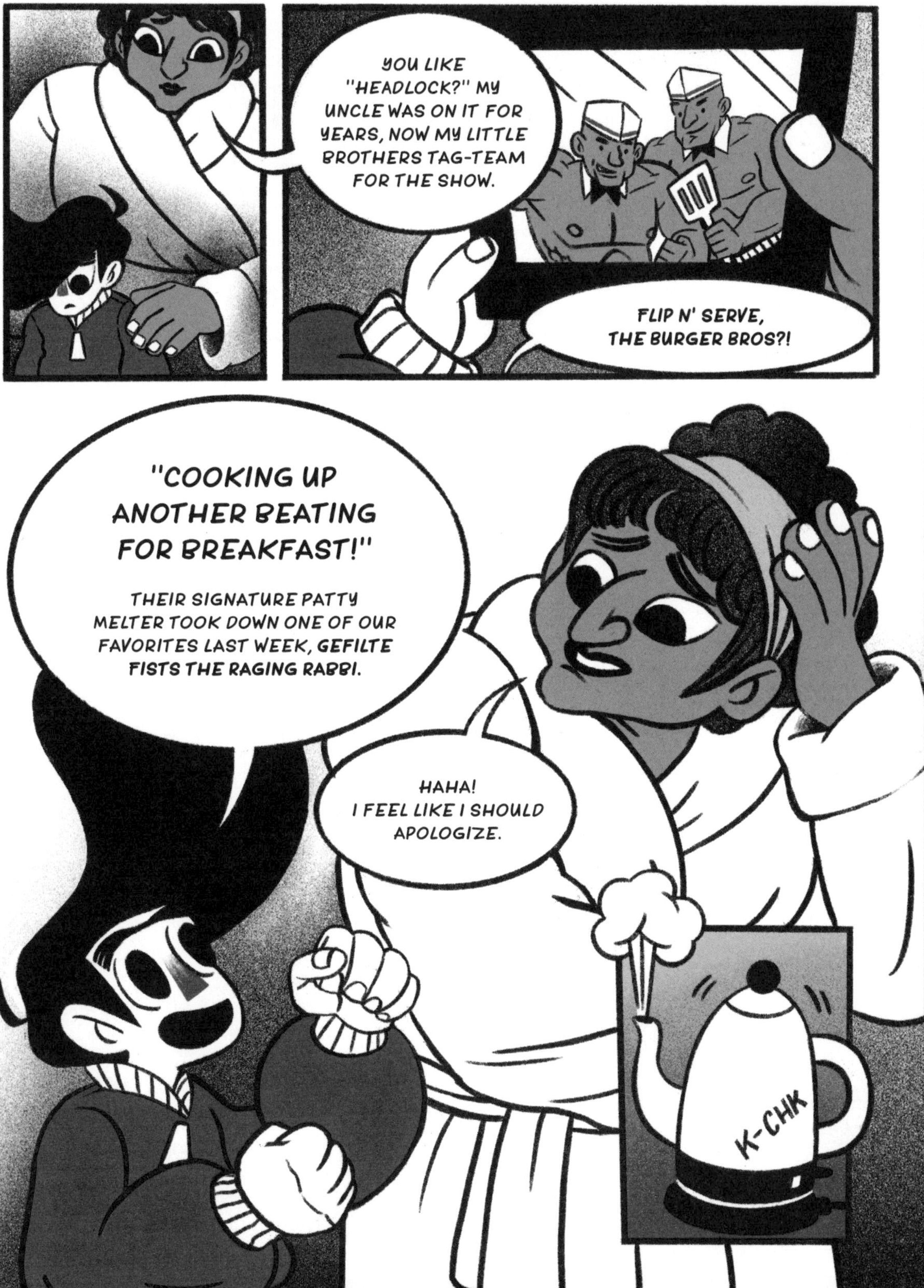
YOU LIKE "HEADLOCK?" MY UNCLE WAS ON IT FOR YEARS, NOW MY LITTLE BROTHERS TAG-TEAM FOR THE SHOW.
FLIP N' SERVE, THE BURGER BROS?!
"COOKING UP ANOTHER BEATING FOR BREAKFAST!"
THEIR SIGNATURE PATTY MELTER TOOK DOWN ONE OF OUR FAVORITES LAST WEEK, GEFILTE FISTS THE RAGING RABBI.
HAHA! I FEEL LIKE I SHOULD APOLOGIZE.
K-CHK

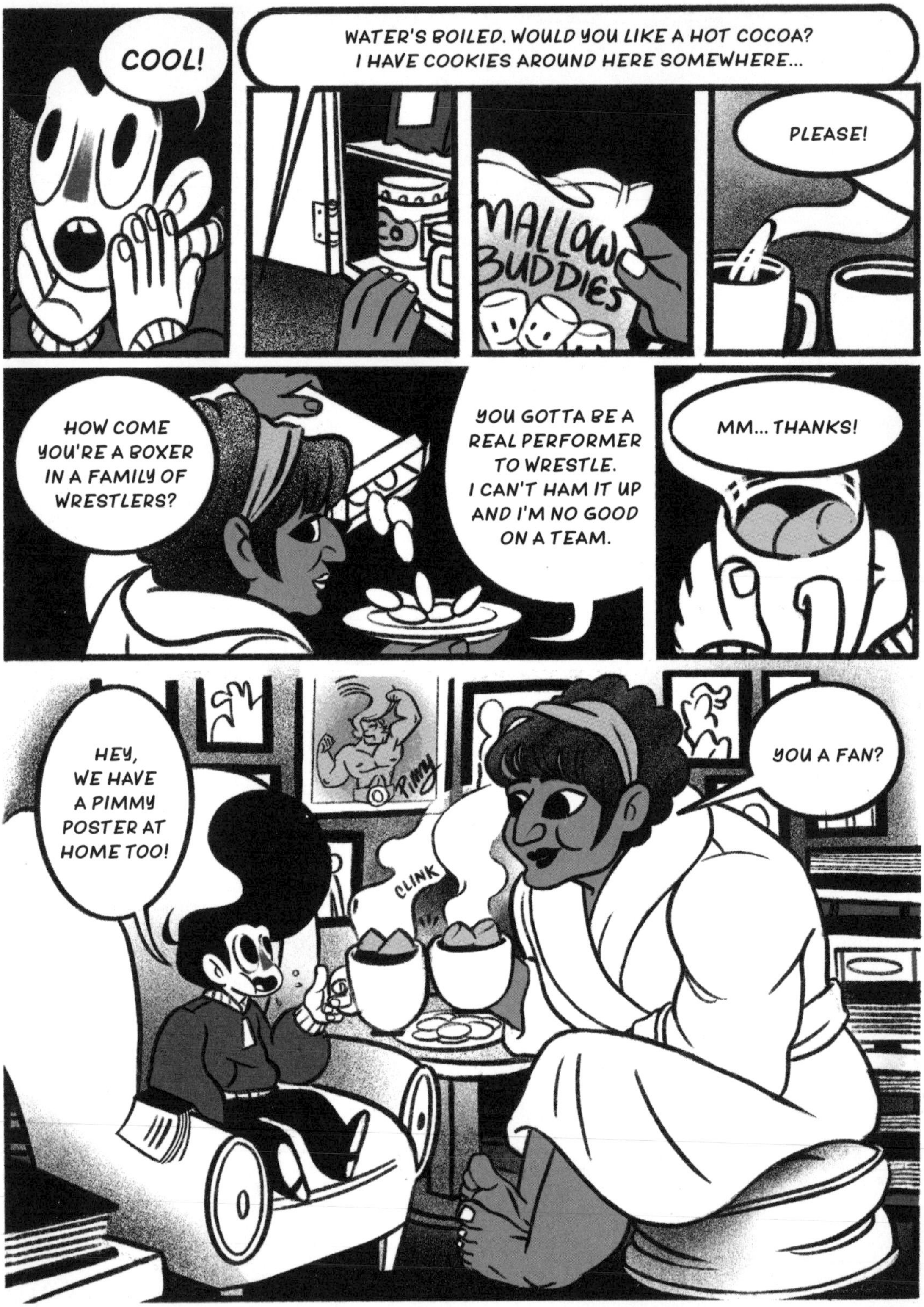
COOL!
WATER'S BOILED. WOULD YOU LIKE A HOT COCOA? I HAVE COOKIES AROUND HERE SOMEWHERE...
MALLOW BUDDIES
PLEASE!
HOW COME YOU'RE A BOXER IN A FAMILY OF WRESTLERS?
YOU GOTTA BE A REAL PERFORMER TO WRESTLE. I CAN'T HAM IT UP AND I'M NO GOOD ON A TEAM.
MM... THANKS!
HEY, WE HAVE A PIMMY POSTER AT HOME TOO!
PIMMY
CLINK
YOU A FAN?

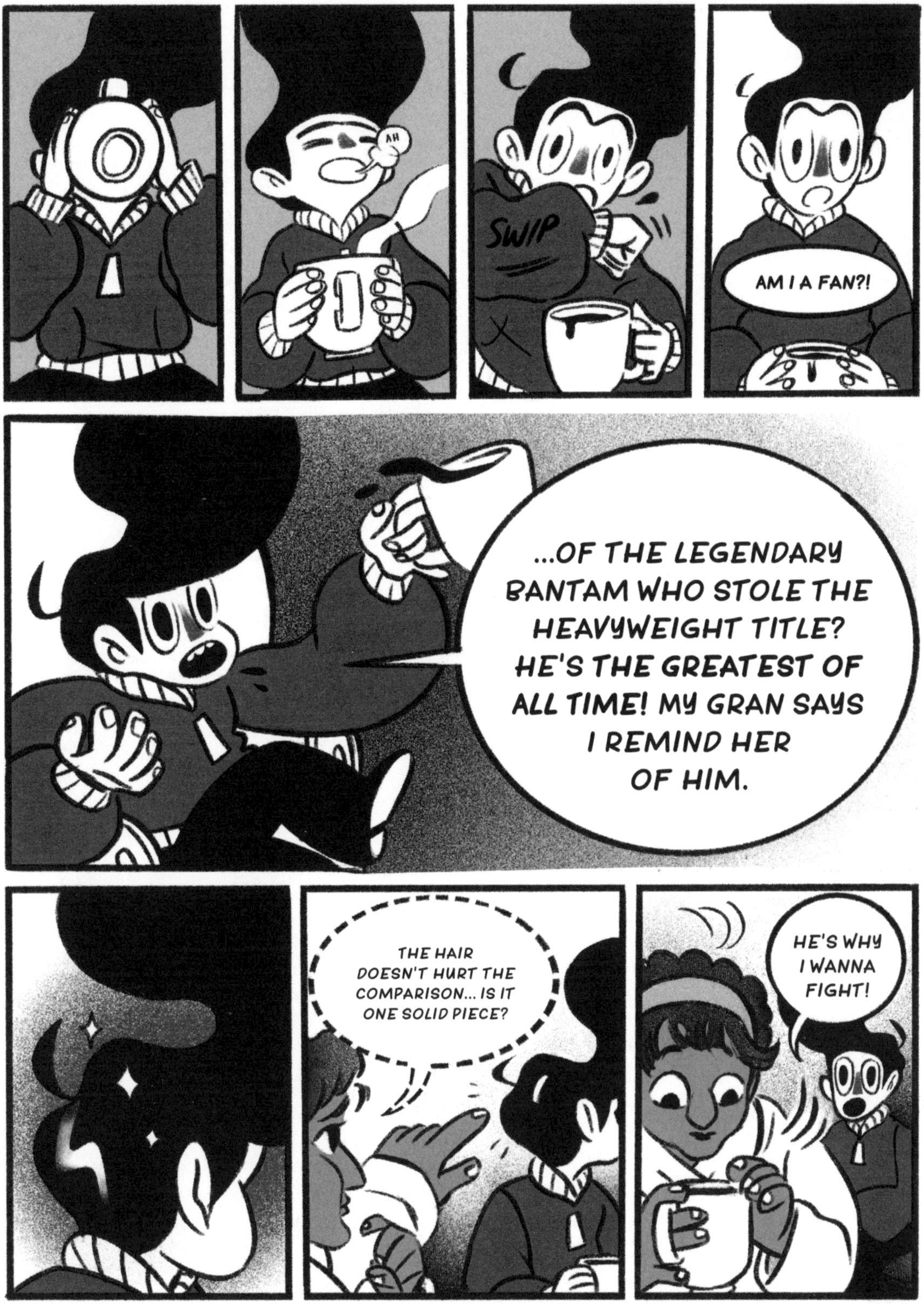

AH
SWIP
AM I A FAN?!
...OF THE LEGENDARY BANTAM WHO STOLE THE HEAVYWEIGHT TITLE? HE'S THE GREATEST OF ALL TIME! MY GRAN SAYS I REMIND HER OF HIM.
THE HAIR DOESN'T HURT THE COMPARISON... IS IT ONE SOLID PIECE?
HE'S WHY I WANNA FIGHT!

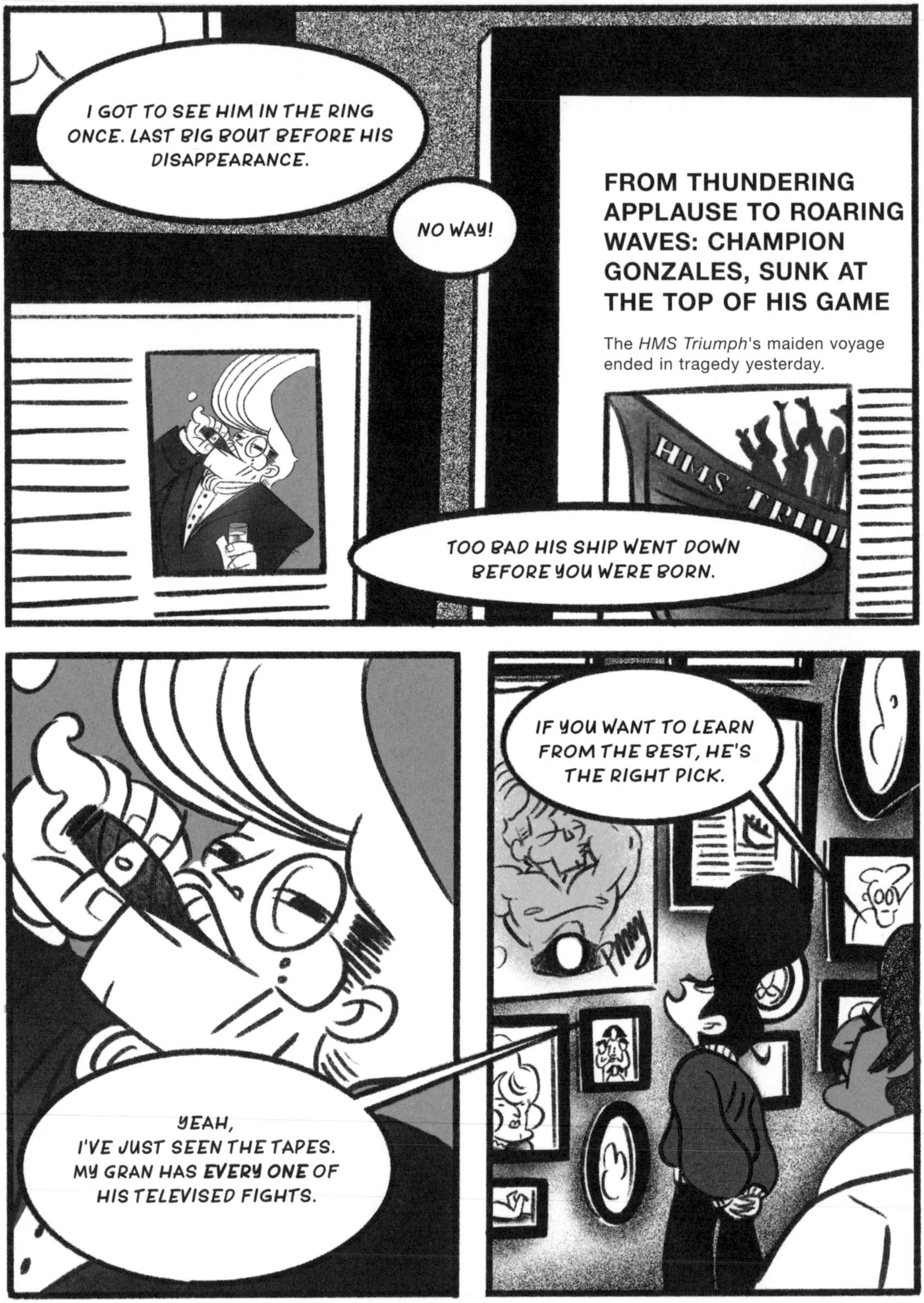
I GOT TO SEE HIM IN THE RING ONCE. LAST BIG BOUT BEFORE HIS DISAPPEARANCE.
NO WAY!
FROM THUNDERING APPLAUSE TO ROARING WAVES: CHAMPION GONZALES, SUNK AT THE TOP OF HIS GAME
The *HMS Triumph*'s maiden voyage ended in tragedy yesterday.
HMS TRIU
TOO BAD HIS SHIP WENT DOWN BEFORE YOU WERE BORN.
YEAH, I'VE JUST SEEN THE TAPES. MY GRAN HAS **EVERY ONE** OF HIS TELEVISED FIGHTS.
IF YOU WANT TO LEARN FROM THE BEST, HE'S THE RIGHT PICK.

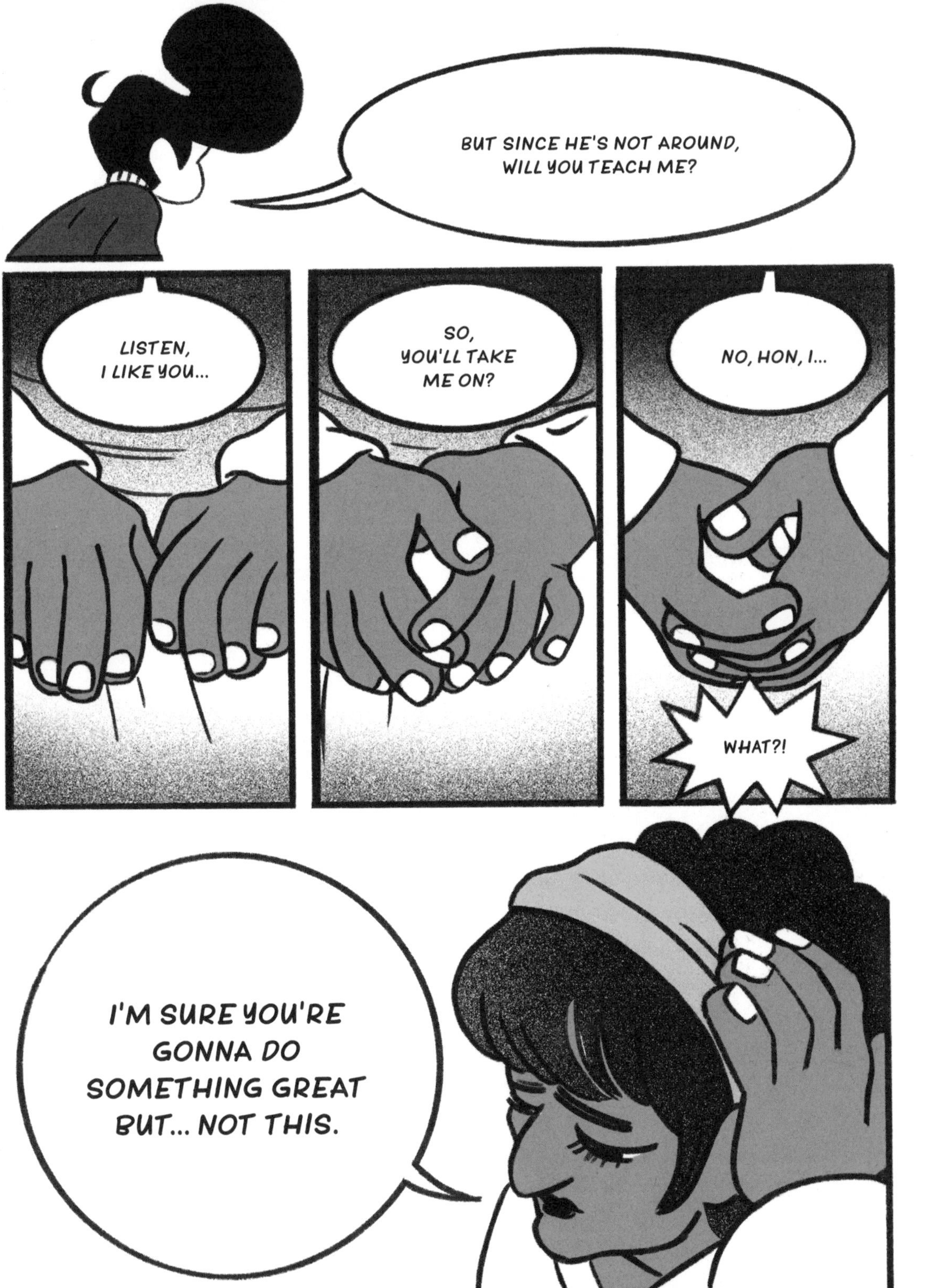
BUT SINCE HE'S NOT AROUND, WILL YOU TEACH ME?
LISTEN, I LIKE YOU...
SO, YOU'LL TAKE ME ON?
NO, HON, I...
WHAT?!
I'M SURE YOU'RE GONNA DO SOMETHING GREAT BUT... NOT THIS.

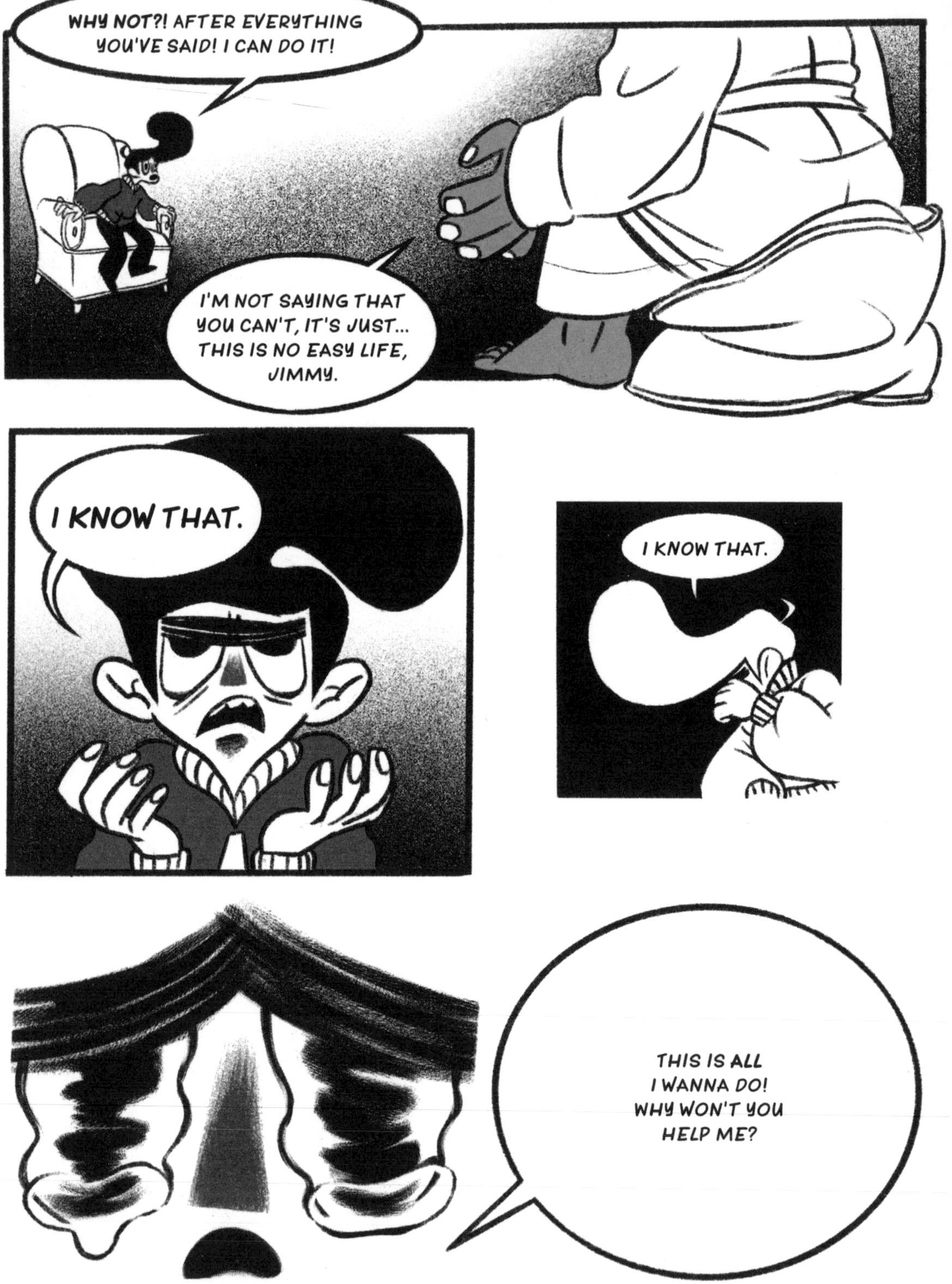
WHY NOT?! AFTER EVERYTHING YOU'VE SAID! I CAN DO IT!
I'M NOT SAYING THAT YOU CAN'T, IT'S JUST... THIS IS NO EASY LIFE, JIMMY.
I KNOW THAT.
I KNOW THAT.
THIS IS ALL I WANNA DO! WHY WON'T YOU HELP ME?

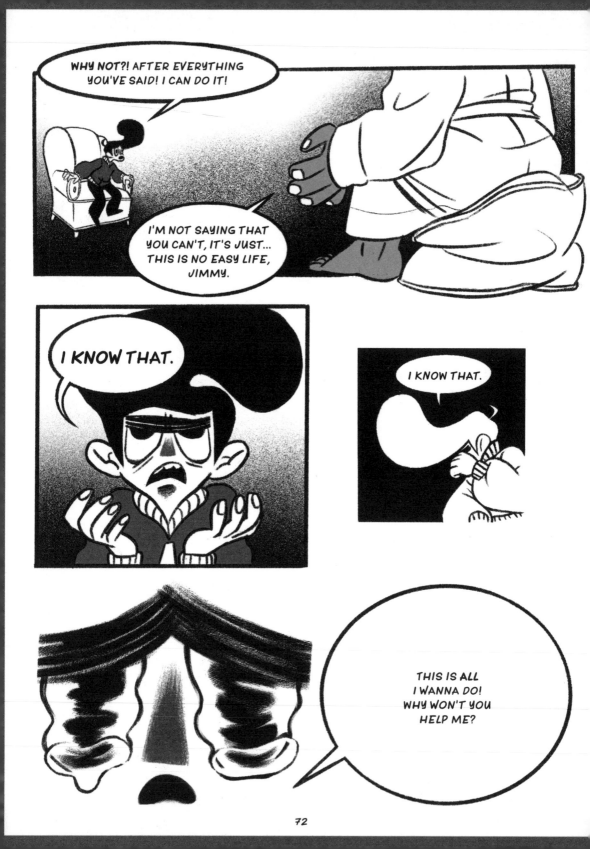

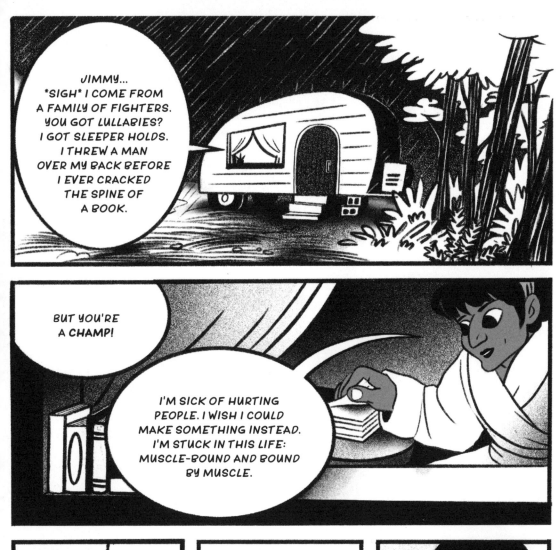

JIMMY... *SIGH* I COME FROM A FAMILY OF FIGHTERS. YOU GOT LULLABIES? I GOT SLEEPER HOLDS. I THREW A MAN OVER MY BACK BEFORE I EVER CRACKED THE SPINE OF A BOOK.

BUT YOU'RE A CHAMP!

I'M SICK OF HURTING PEOPLE. I WISH I COULD MAKE SOMETHING INSTEAD. I'M STUCK IN THIS LIFE: MUSCLE-BOUND AND BOUND BY MUSCLE.

...HEY, THAT'S NOT BAD...

SKTCH
SKTCH

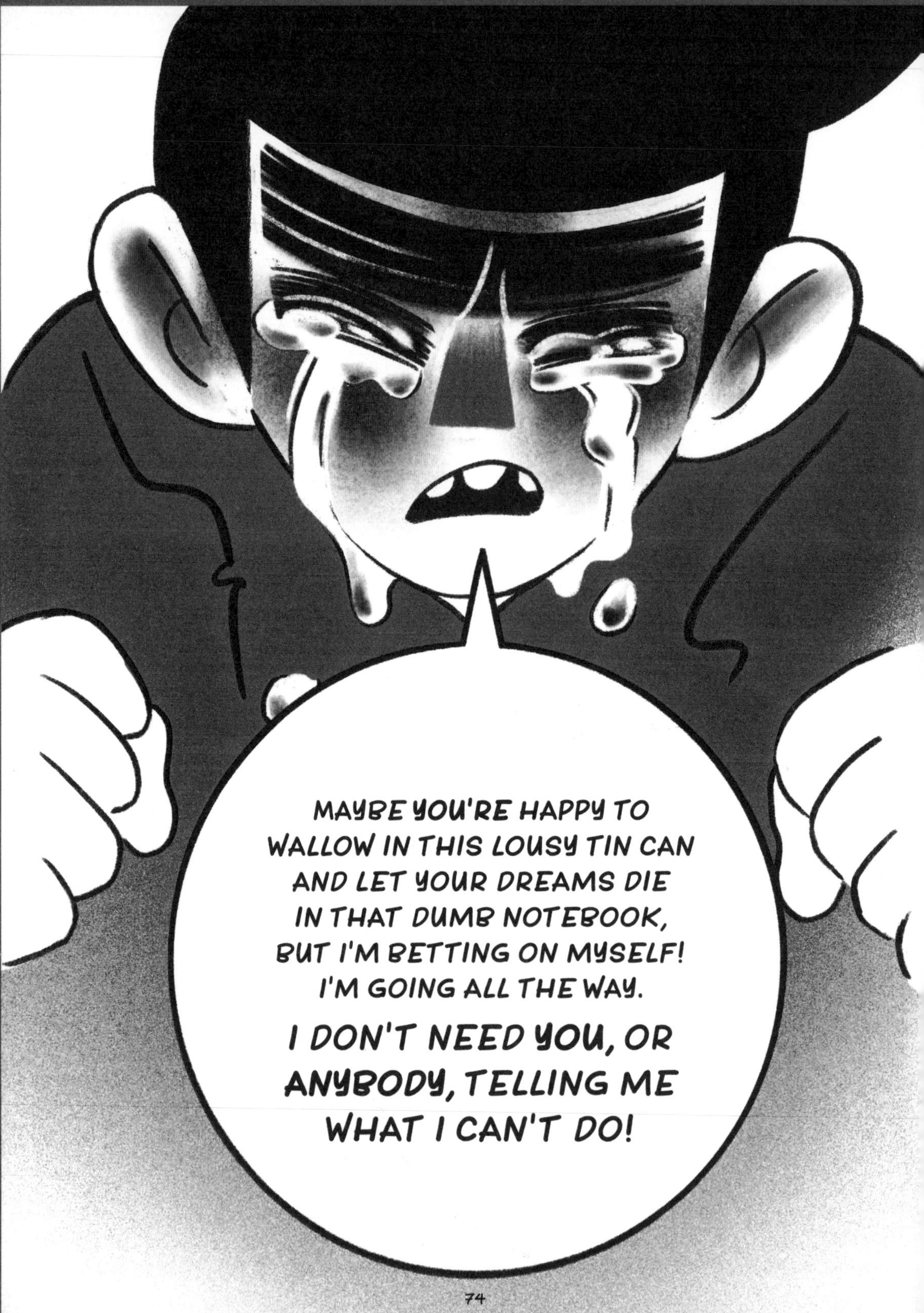
MAYBE YOU'RE HAPPY TO WALLOW IN THIS LOUSY TIN CAN AND LET YOUR DREAMS DIE IN THAT DUMB NOTEBOOK, BUT I'M BETTING ON MYSELF! I'M GOING ALL THE WAY. I DON'T NEED YOU, OR ANYBODY, TELLING ME WHAT I CAN'T DO!

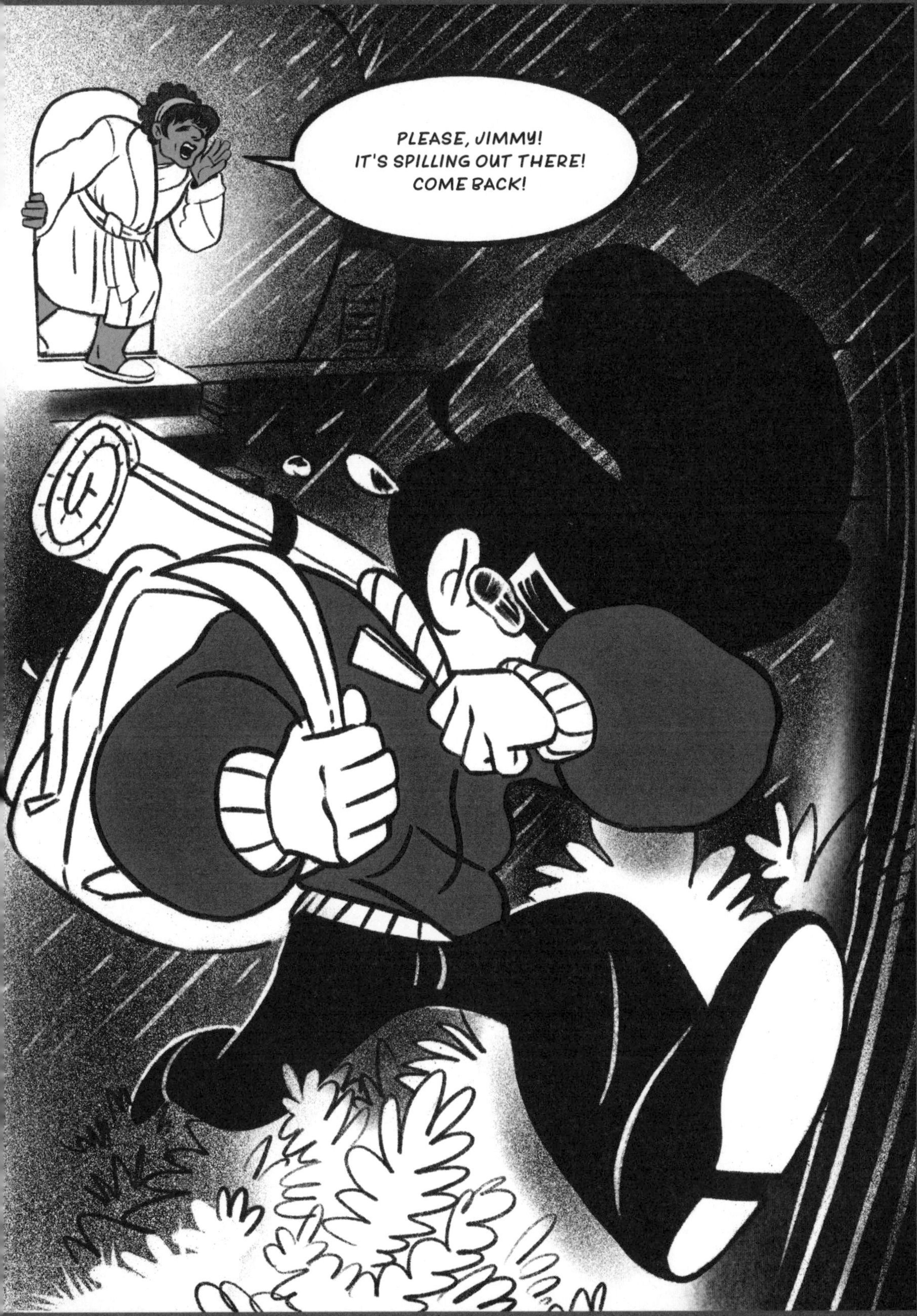
PLEASE, JIMMY! IT'S SPILLING OUT THERE! COME BACK!

CHAPTER 3

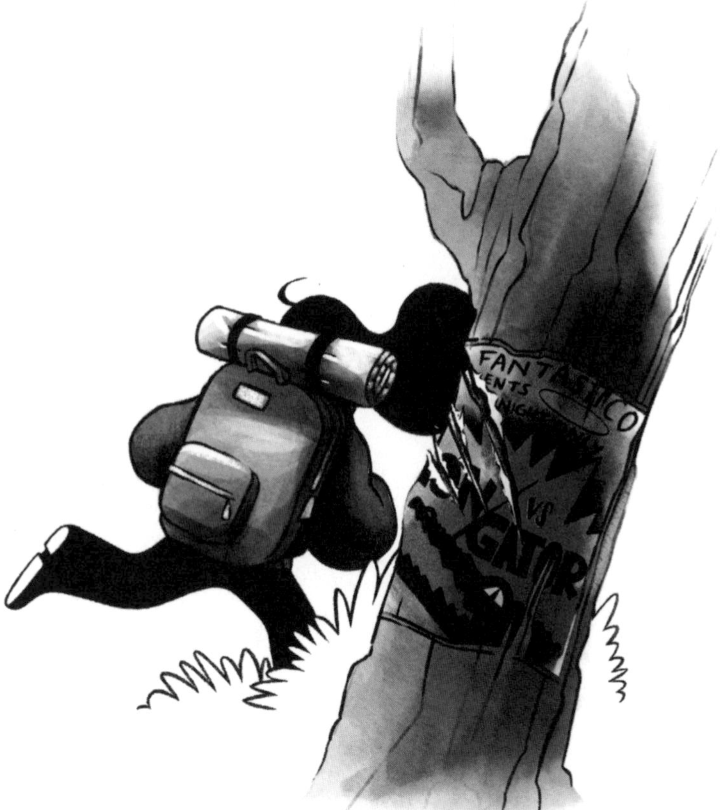
FANTASTICO
VS
GATOR

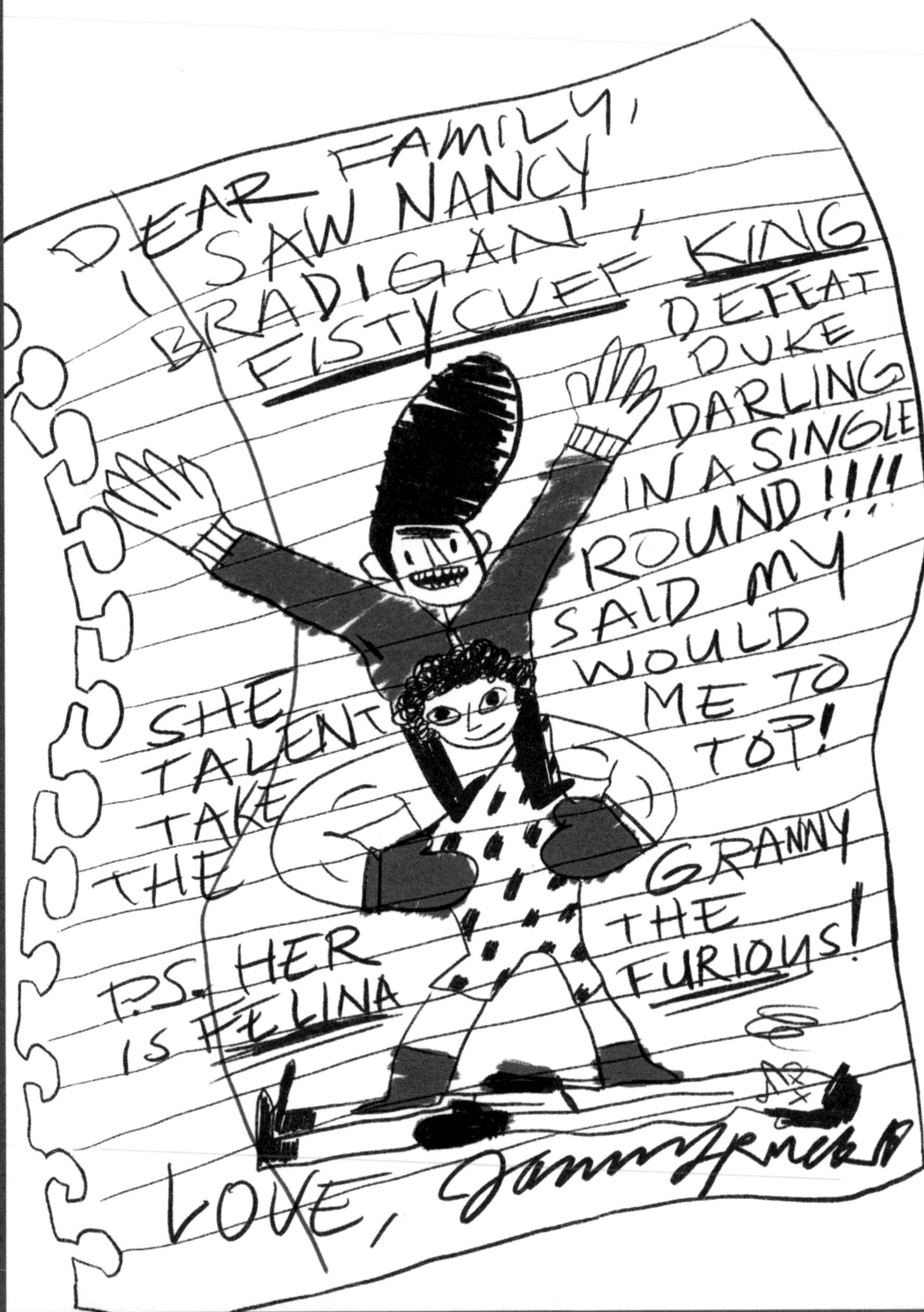
DEAR FAMILY,
I SAW NANCY BRADIGAN, FISTYCUFF KING DEFEAT DUKE DARLING IN A SINGLE ROUND!!!!
SHE SAID MY TALENT WOULD TAKE ME TO THE TOP!
P.S. HER GRANNY IS FELINA THE FURIOUS!
LOVE,

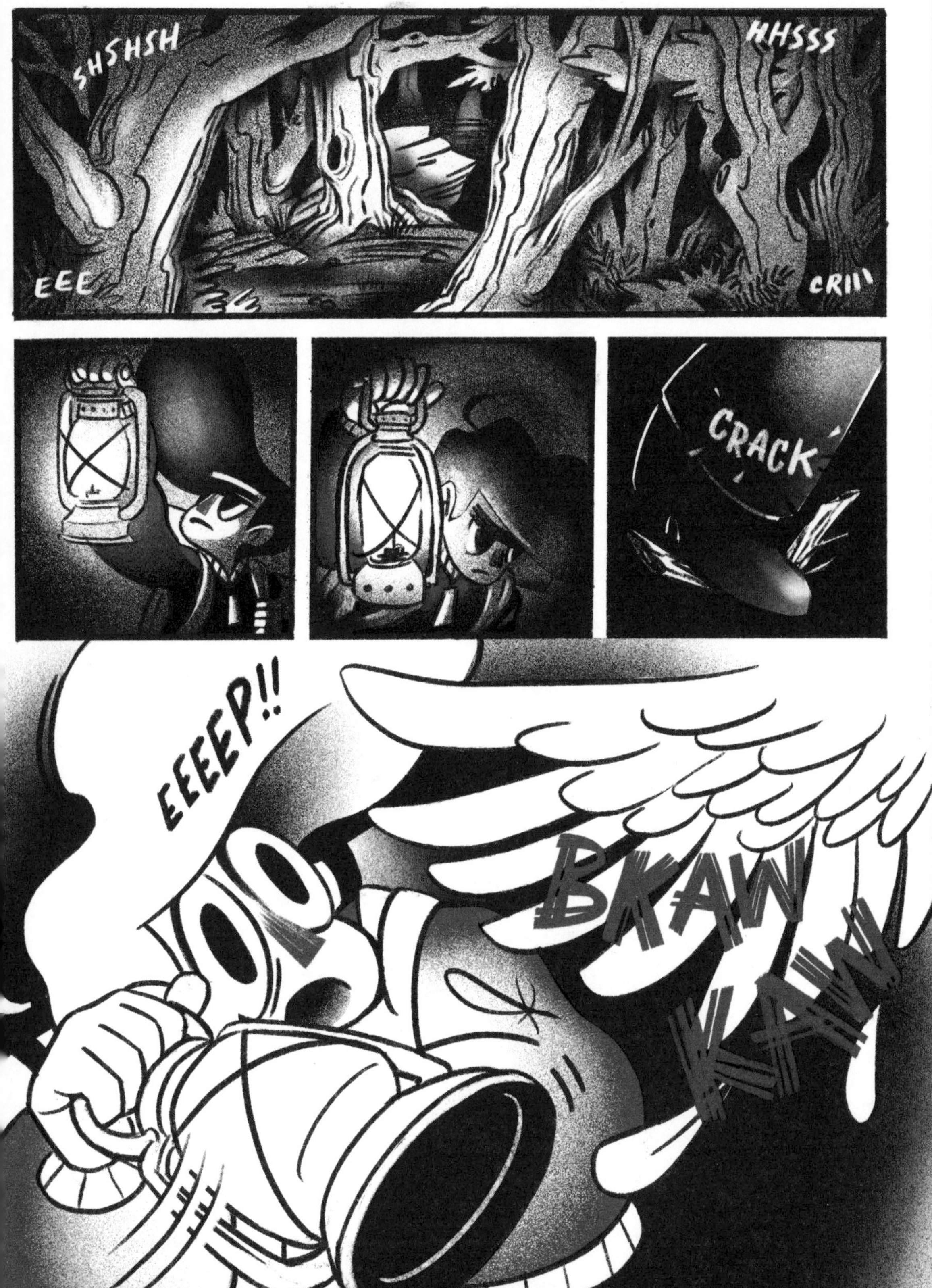
SHSHSH
HHSSS
EEE
CRIII
CRACK
EEEEP!!
BKAW
KAW

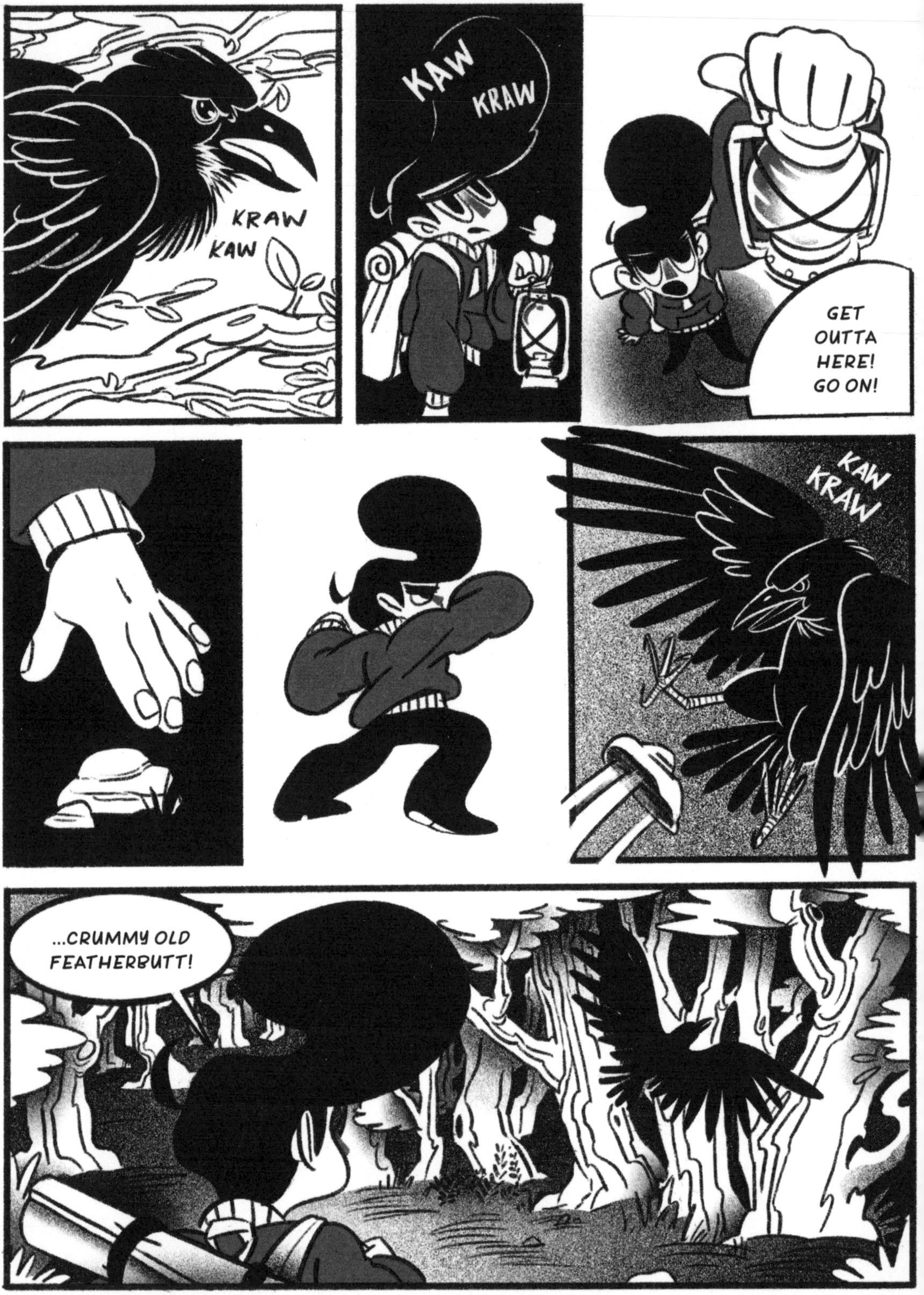
KRAW
KAW
KAW
KRAW
GET OUTTA HERE! GO ON!
KAW
KRAW
...CRUMMY OLD FEATHERBUTT!

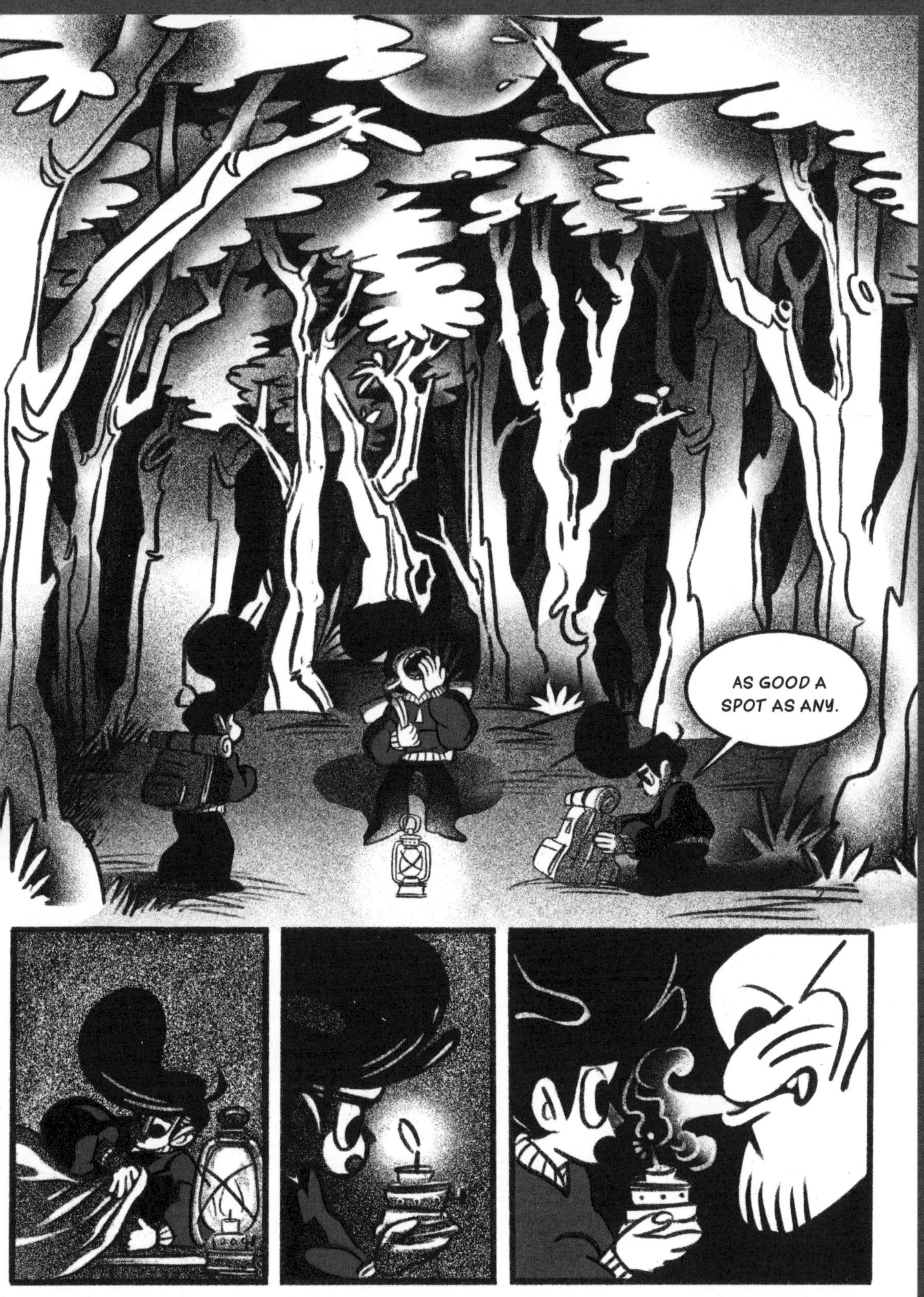
AS GOOD A SPOT AS ANY.

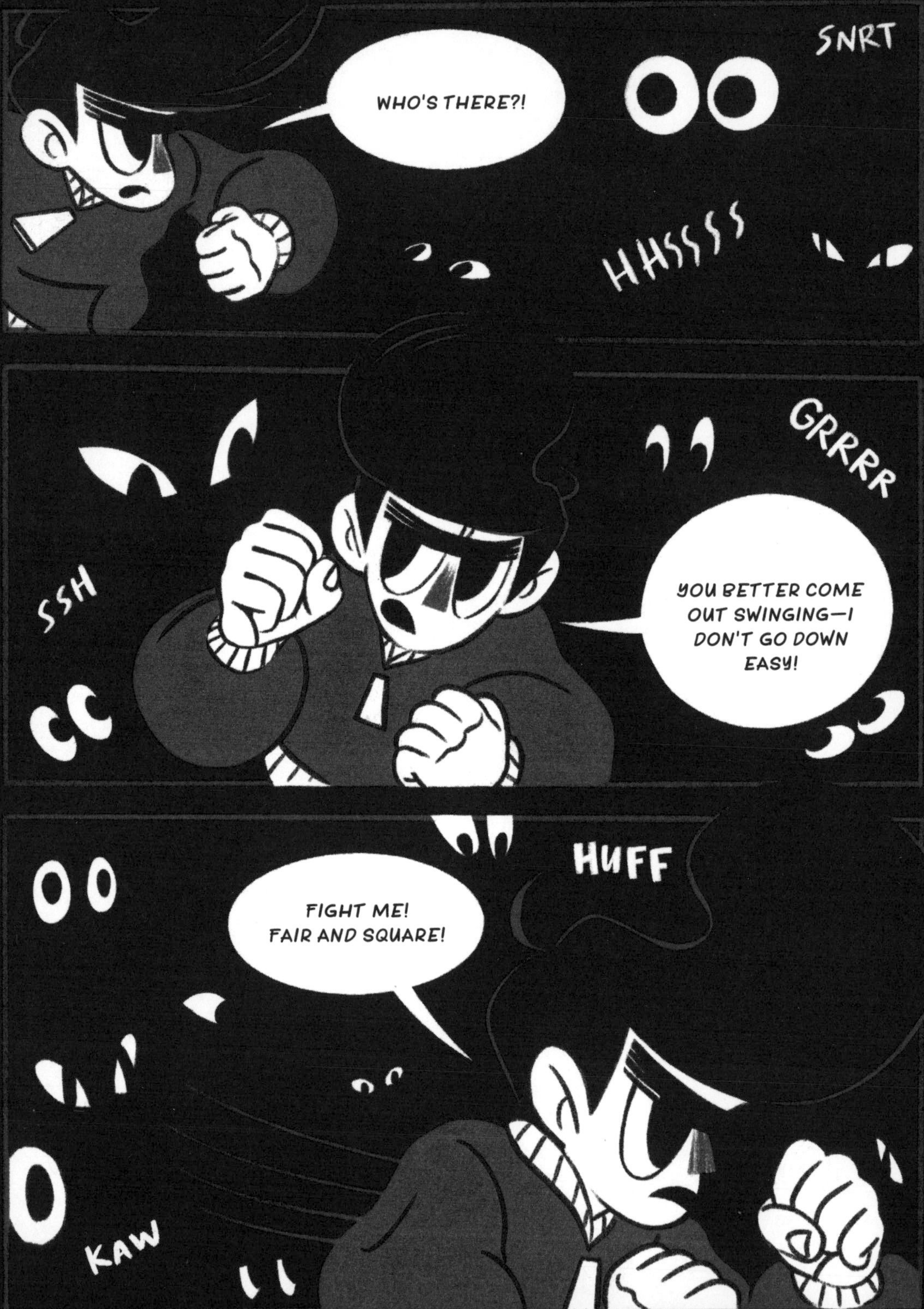
SNRT
WHO'S THERE?!
HHSSSS
GRRRR
SSH
YOU BETTER COME OUT SWINGING—I DON'T GO DOWN EASY!
HUFF
FIGHT ME! FAIR AND SQUARE!
KAW

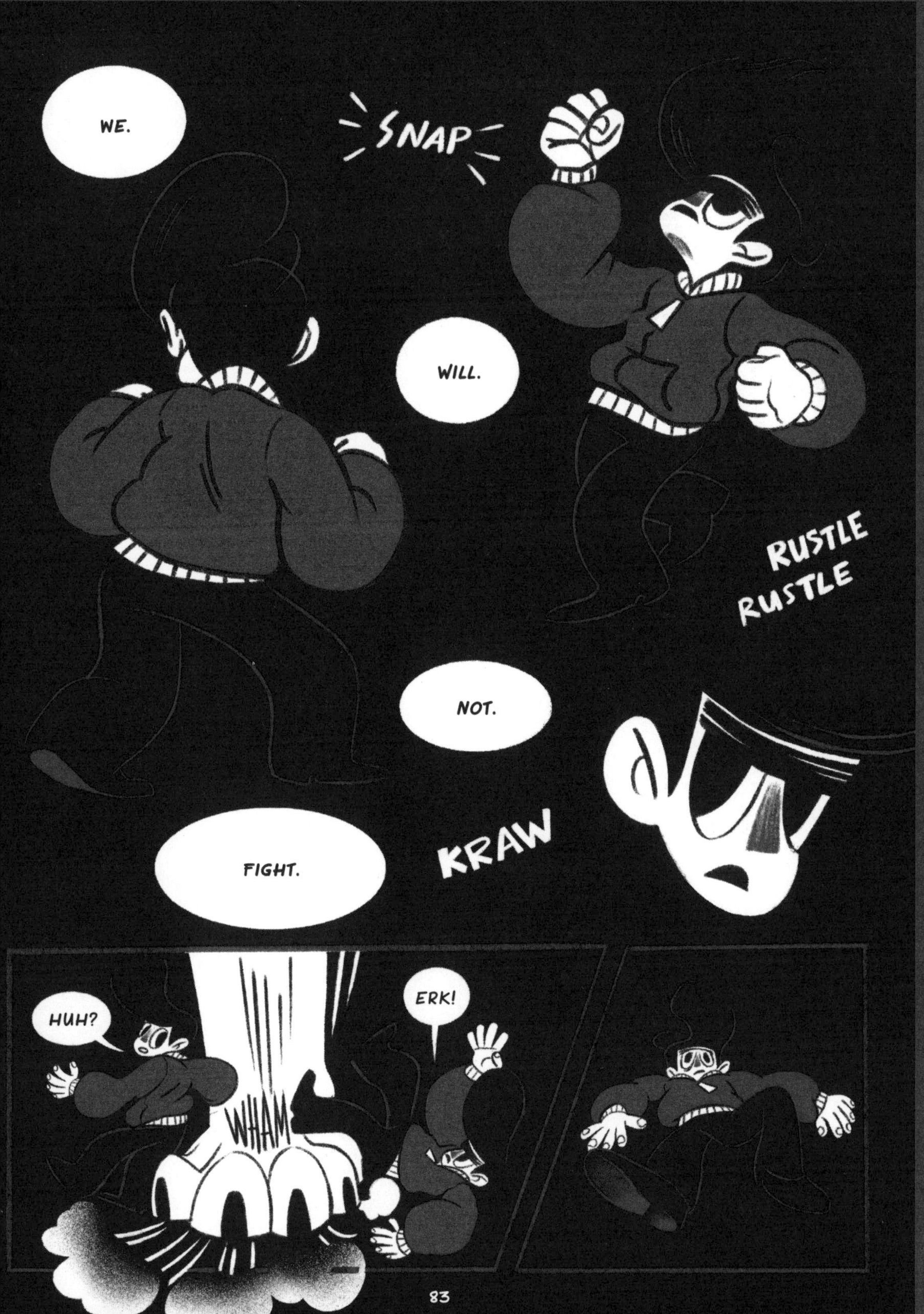
WE.
SNAP
WILL.
RUSTLE
RUSTLE
NOT.
FIGHT.
KRAW
HUH?
ERK!
WHAM

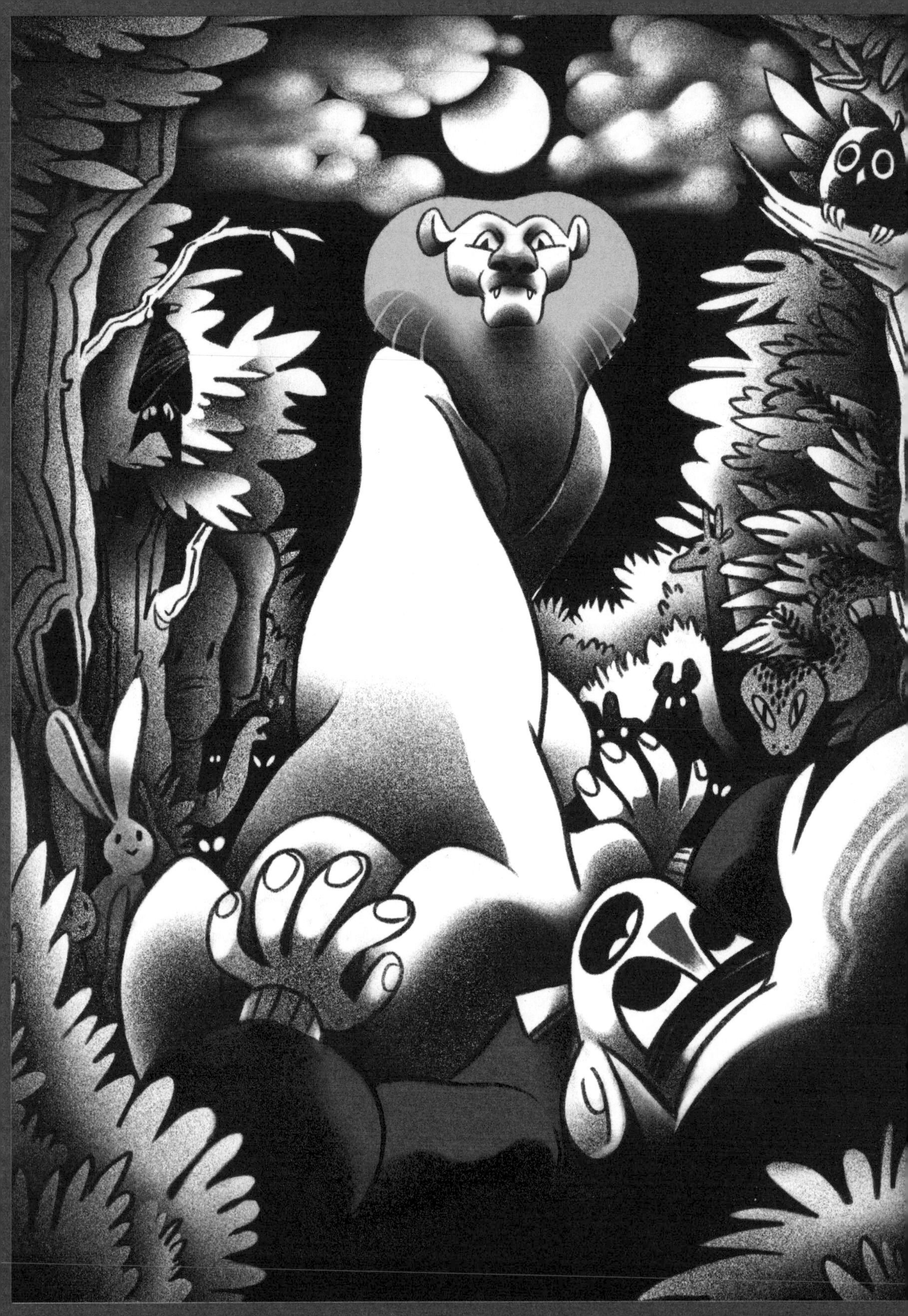

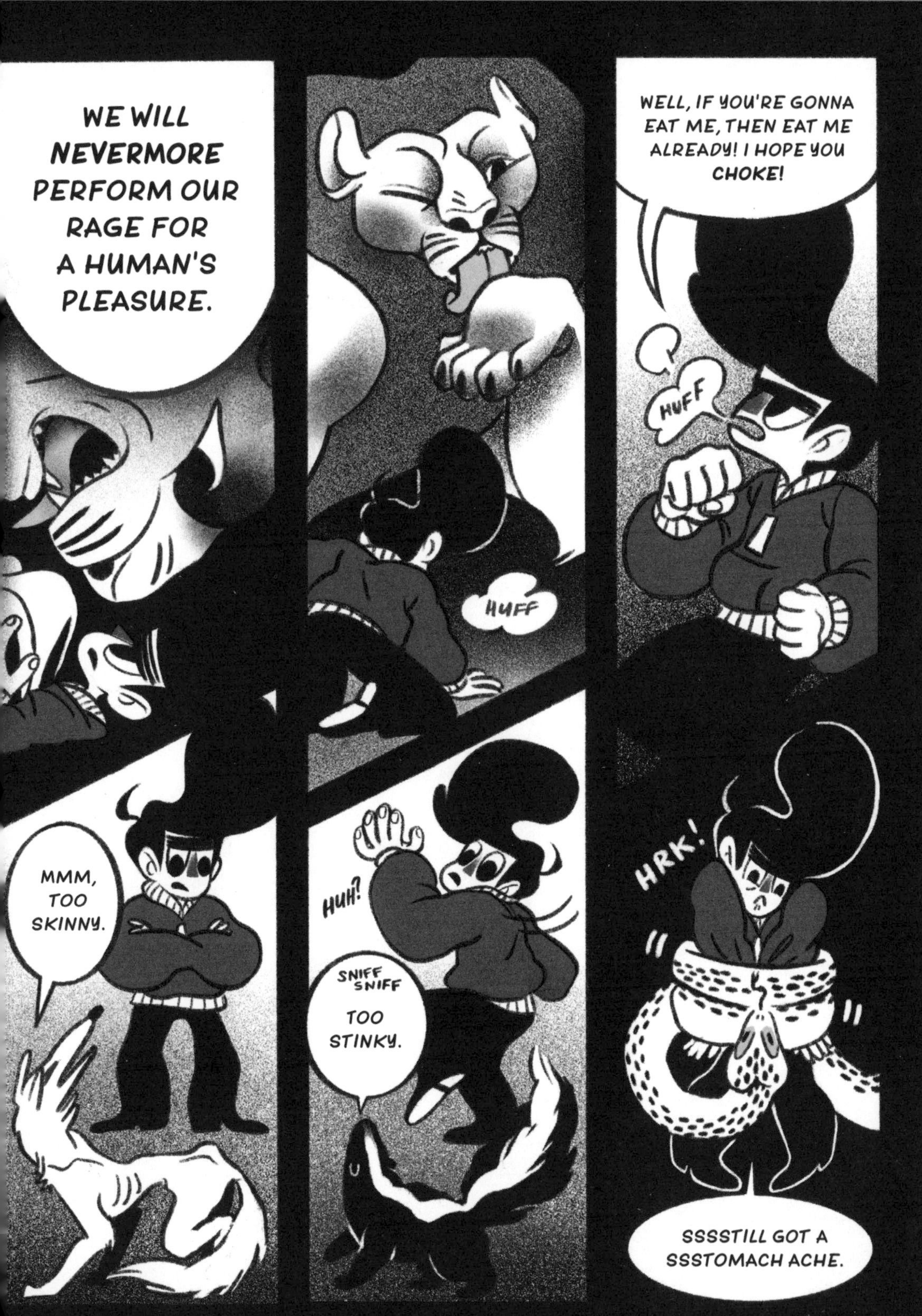
WE WILL NEVERMORE PERFORM OUR RAGE FOR A HUMAN'S PLEASURE.
HUFF
WELL, IF YOU'RE GONNA EAT ME, THEN EAT ME ALREADY! I HOPE YOU CHOKE!
HUFF
MMM, TOO SKINNY.
HUH?
SNIFF SNIFF
TOO STINKY.
HRK!
SSSSTILL GOT A SSSTOMACH ACHE.

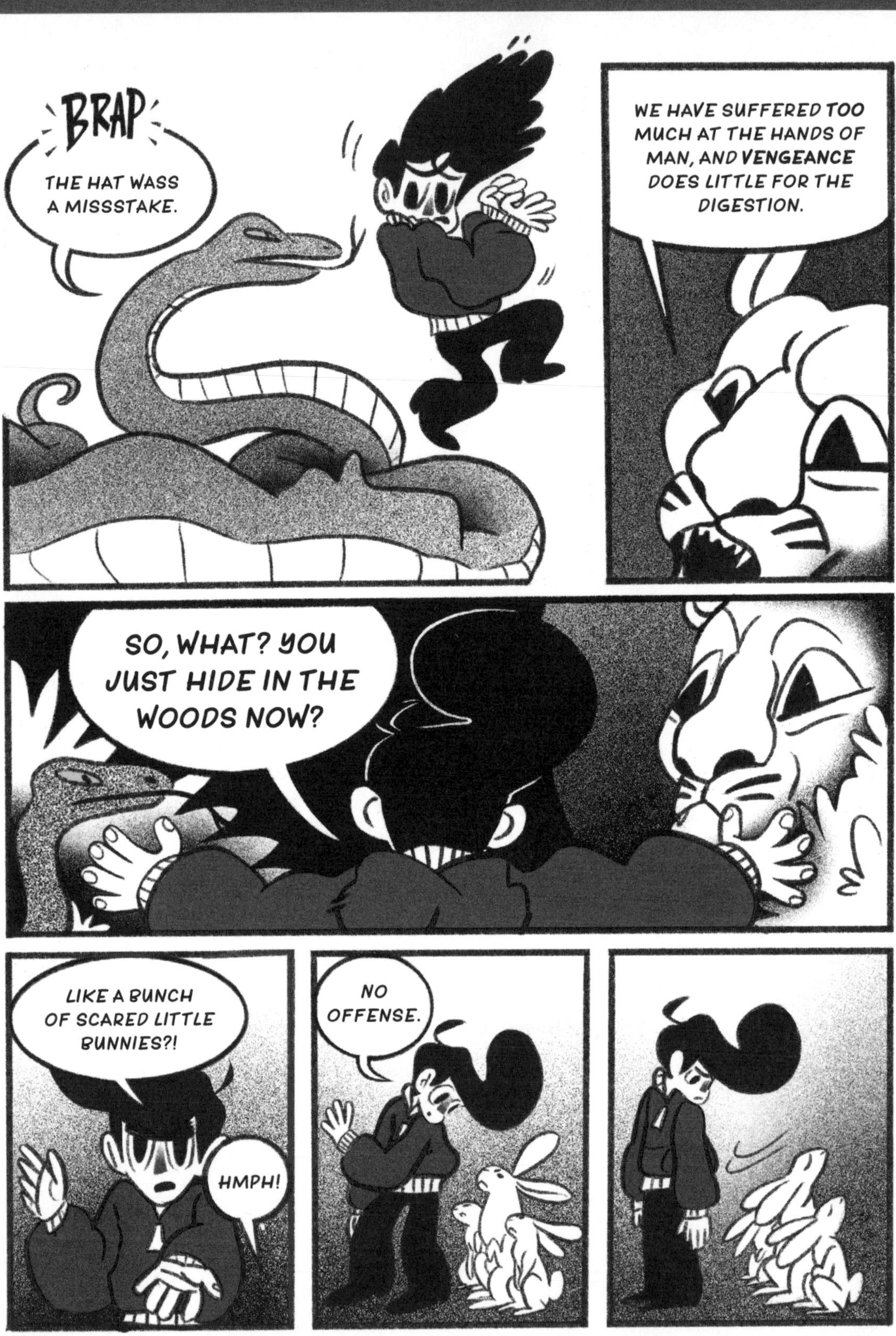
BRAP
THE HAT WASS A MISSSTAKE.
WE HAVE SUFFERED TOO MUCH AT THE HANDS OF MAN, AND VENGEANCE DOES LITTLE FOR THE DIGESTION.
SO, WHAT? YOU JUST HIDE IN THE WOODS NOW?
LIKE A BUNCH OF SCARED LITTLE BUNNIES?!
HMPH!
NO OFFENSE.

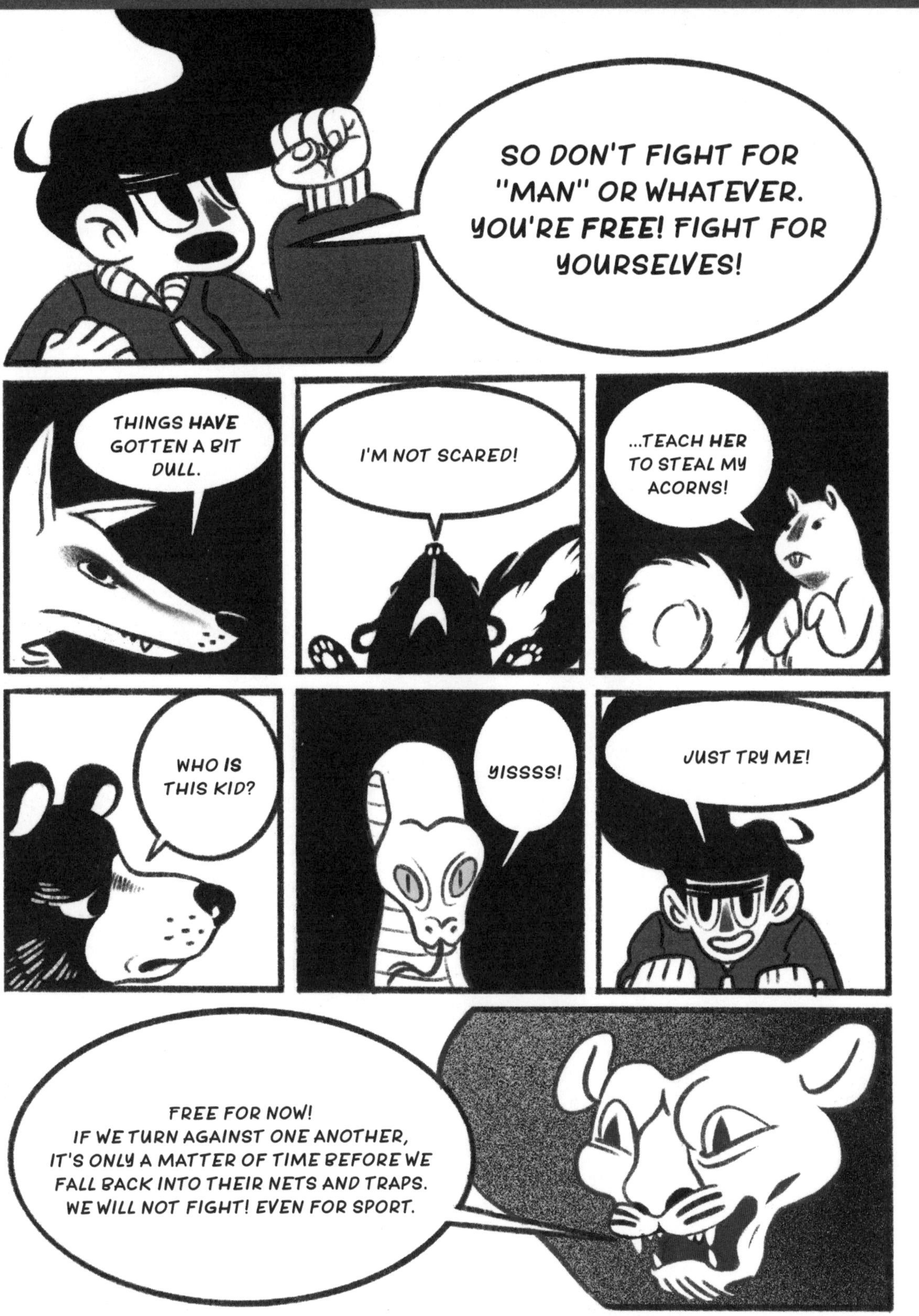
SO DON'T FIGHT FOR "MAN" OR WHATEVER. YOU'RE FREE! FIGHT FOR YOURSELVES!
THINGS HAVE GOTTEN A BIT DULL.
I'M NOT SCARED!
...TEACH HER TO STEAL MY ACORNS!
WHO IS THIS KID?
YISSSS!
JUST TRY ME!
FREE FOR NOW! IF WE TURN AGAINST ONE ANOTHER, IT'S ONLY A MATTER OF TIME BEFORE WE FALL BACK INTO THEIR NETS AND TRAPS. WE WILL NOT FIGHT! EVEN FOR SPORT.

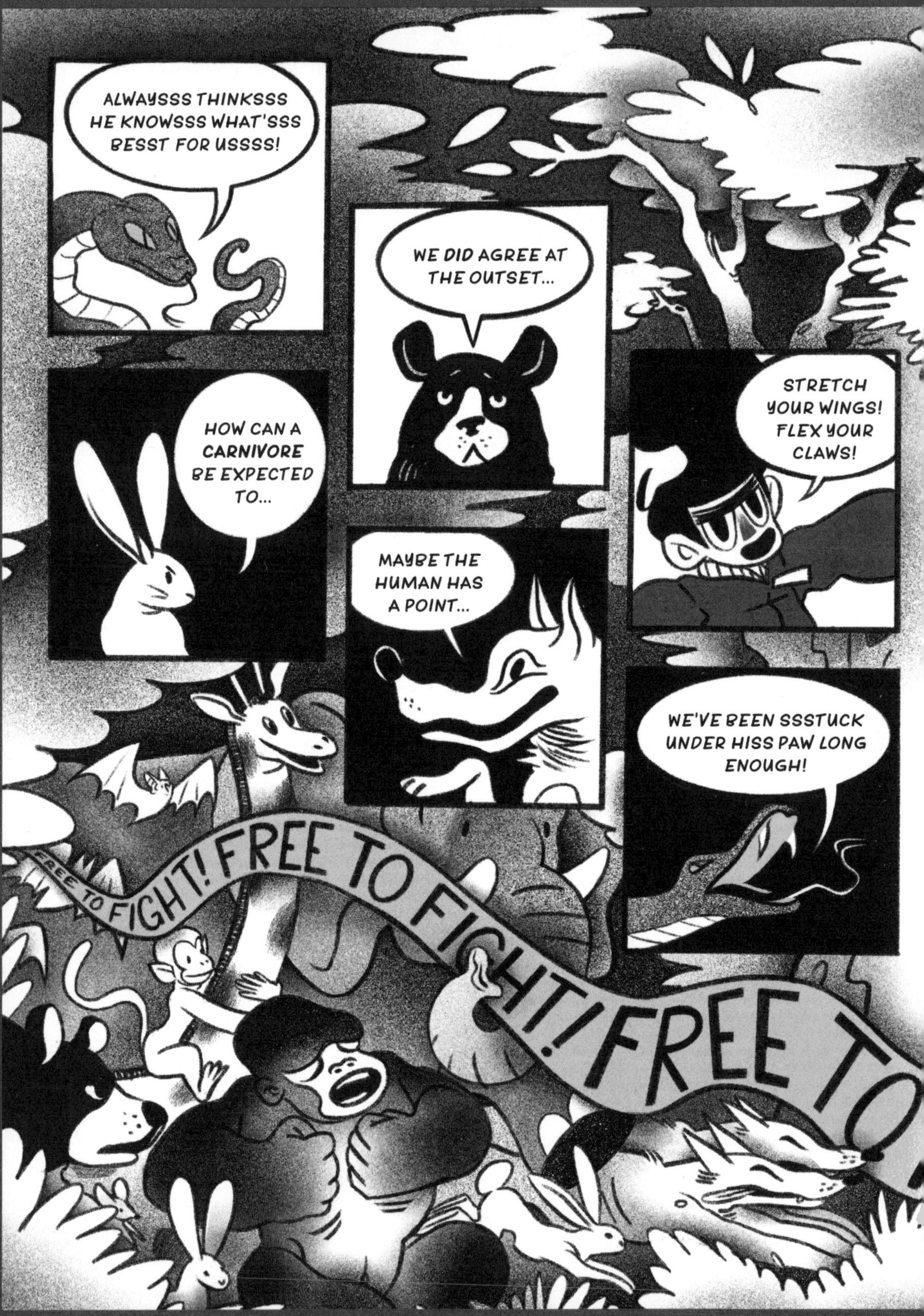
ALWAYSSS THINKSSS HE KNOWSSS WHAT'SSS BESST FOR USSSS!
WE DID AGREE AT THE OUTSET...
HOW CAN A CARNIVORE BE EXPECTED TO...
MAYBE THE HUMAN HAS A POINT...
STRETCH YOUR WINGS! FLEX YOUR CLAWS!
WE'VE BEEN SSSTUCK UNDER HISS PAW LONG ENOUGH!
FREE TO FIGHT! FREE TO FIGHT! FREE TO

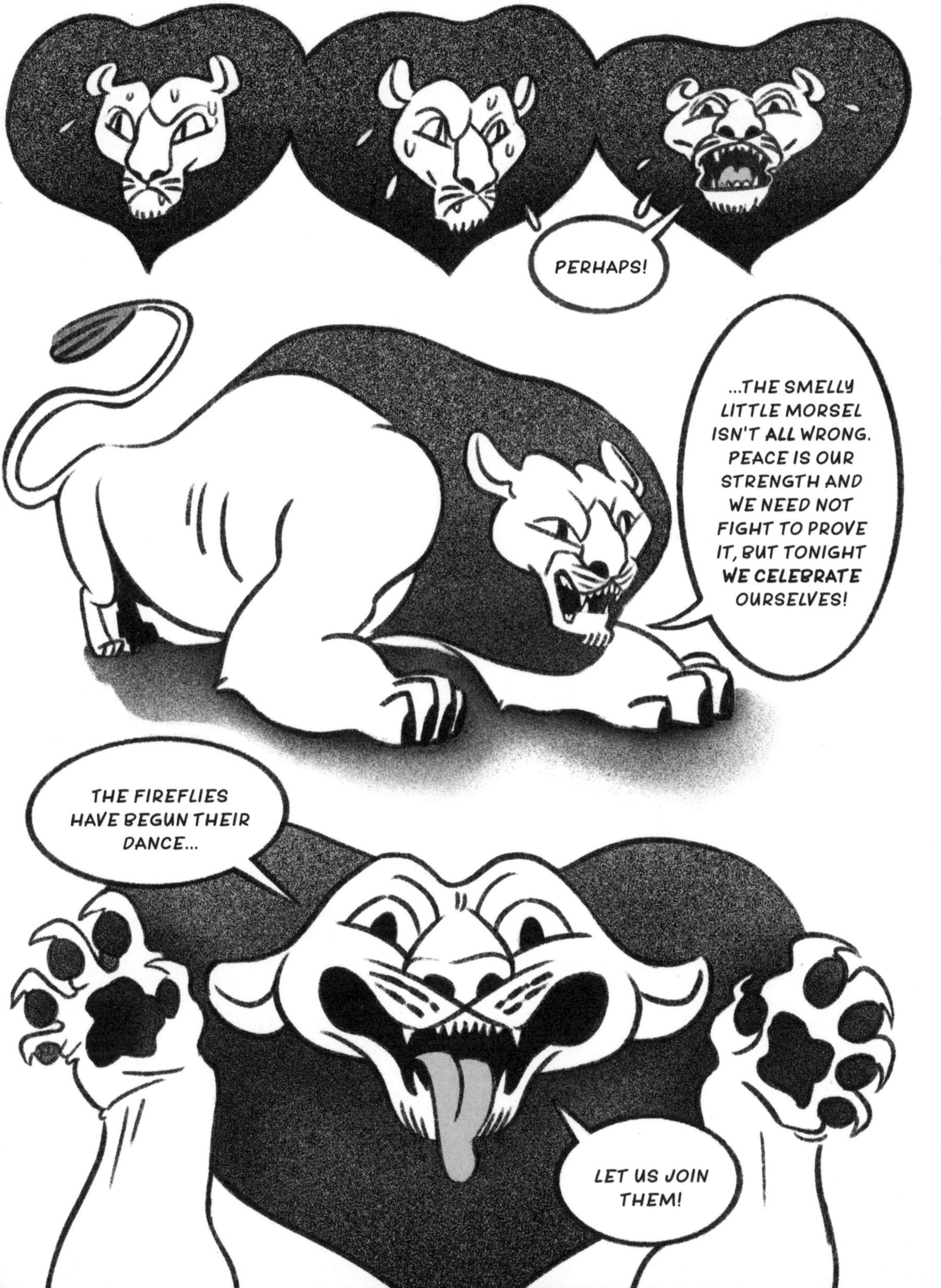
PERHAPS!
...THE SMELLY LITTLE MORSEL ISN'T ALL WRONG. PEACE IS OUR STRENGTH AND WE NEED NOT FIGHT TO PROVE IT, BUT TONIGHT WE CELEBRATE OURSELVES!
THE FIREFLIES HAVE BEGUN THEIR DANCE...
LET US JOIN THEM!

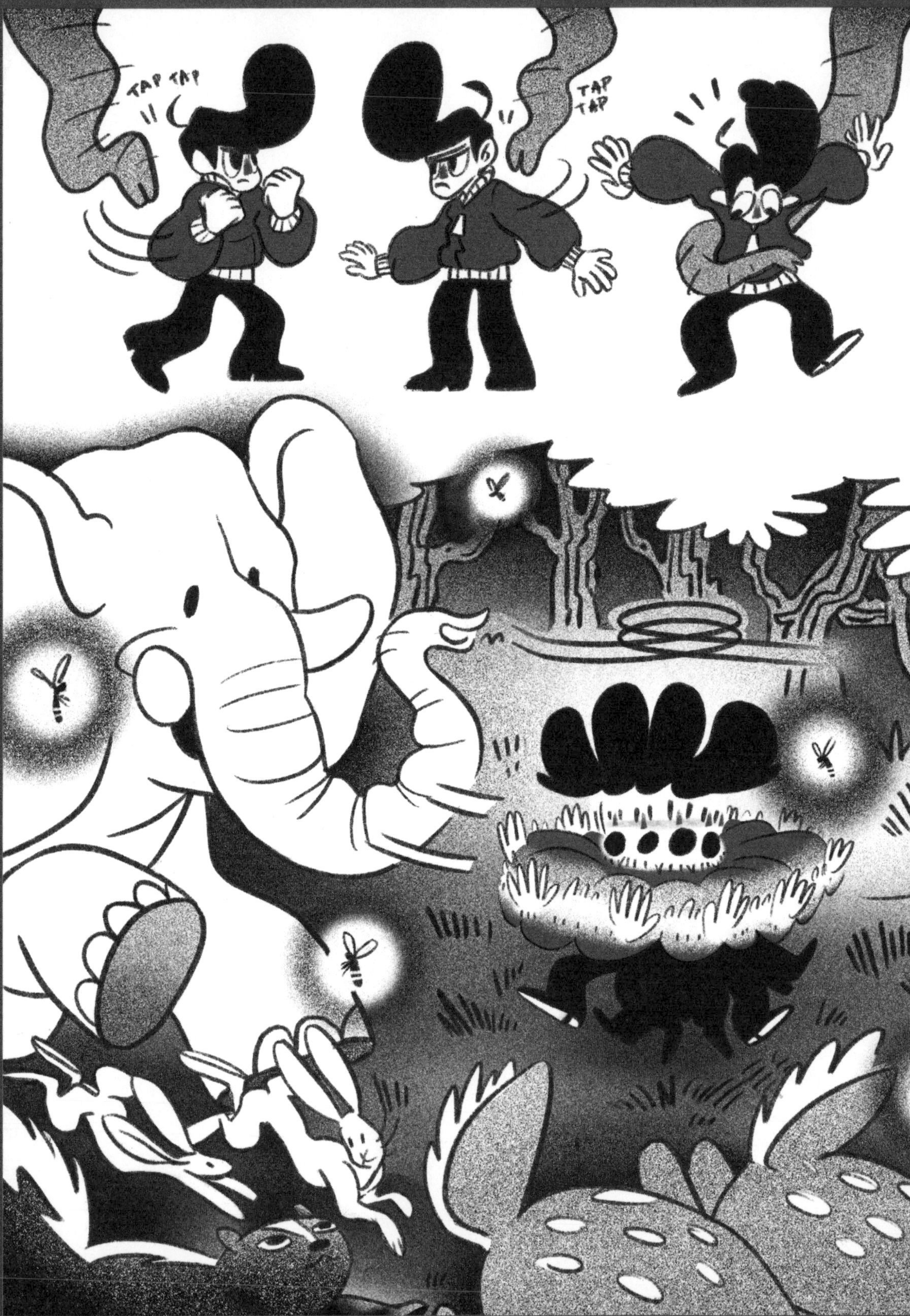
TAP TAP
TAP TAP

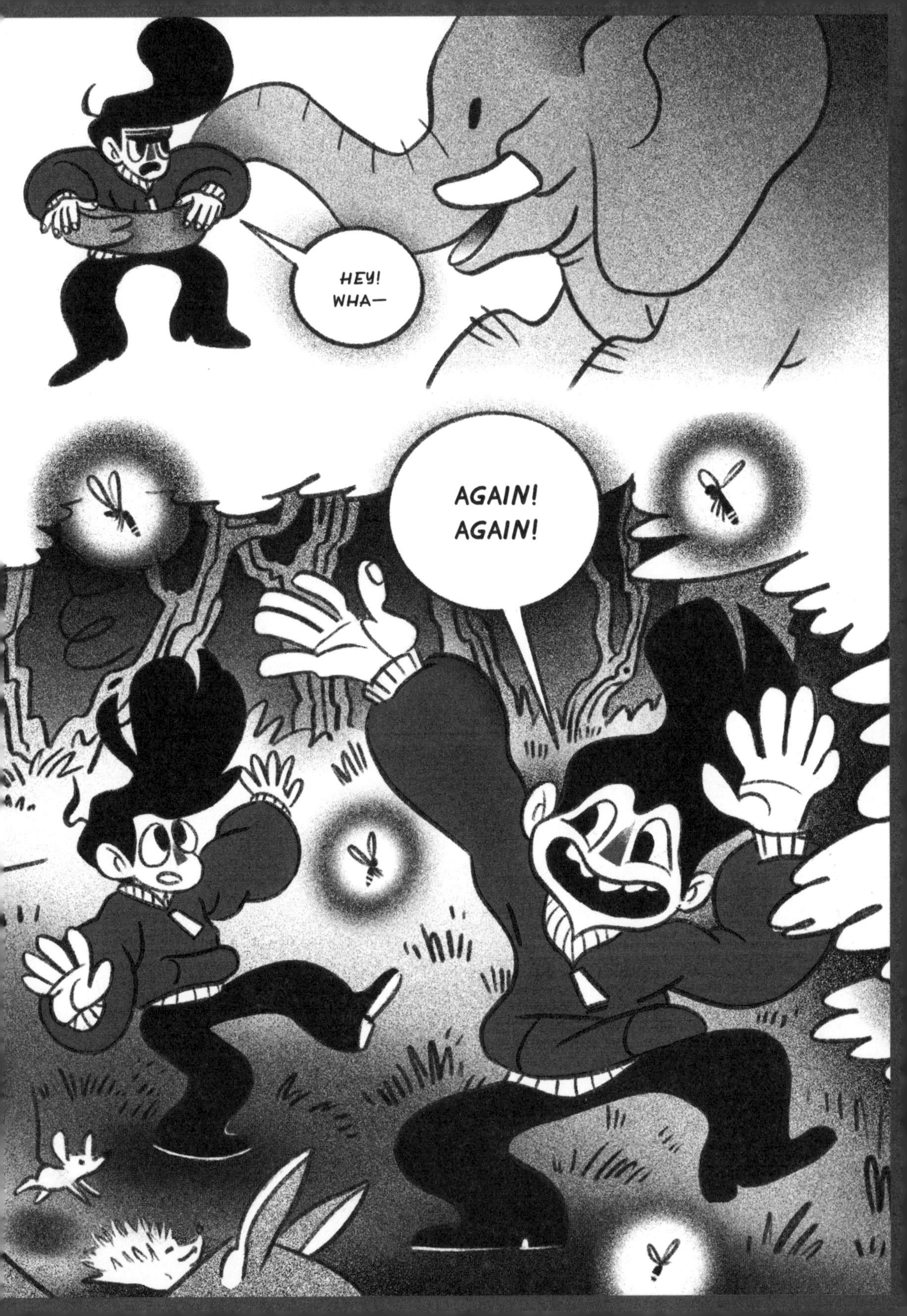
HEY!
WHA—
AGAIN!
AGAIN!

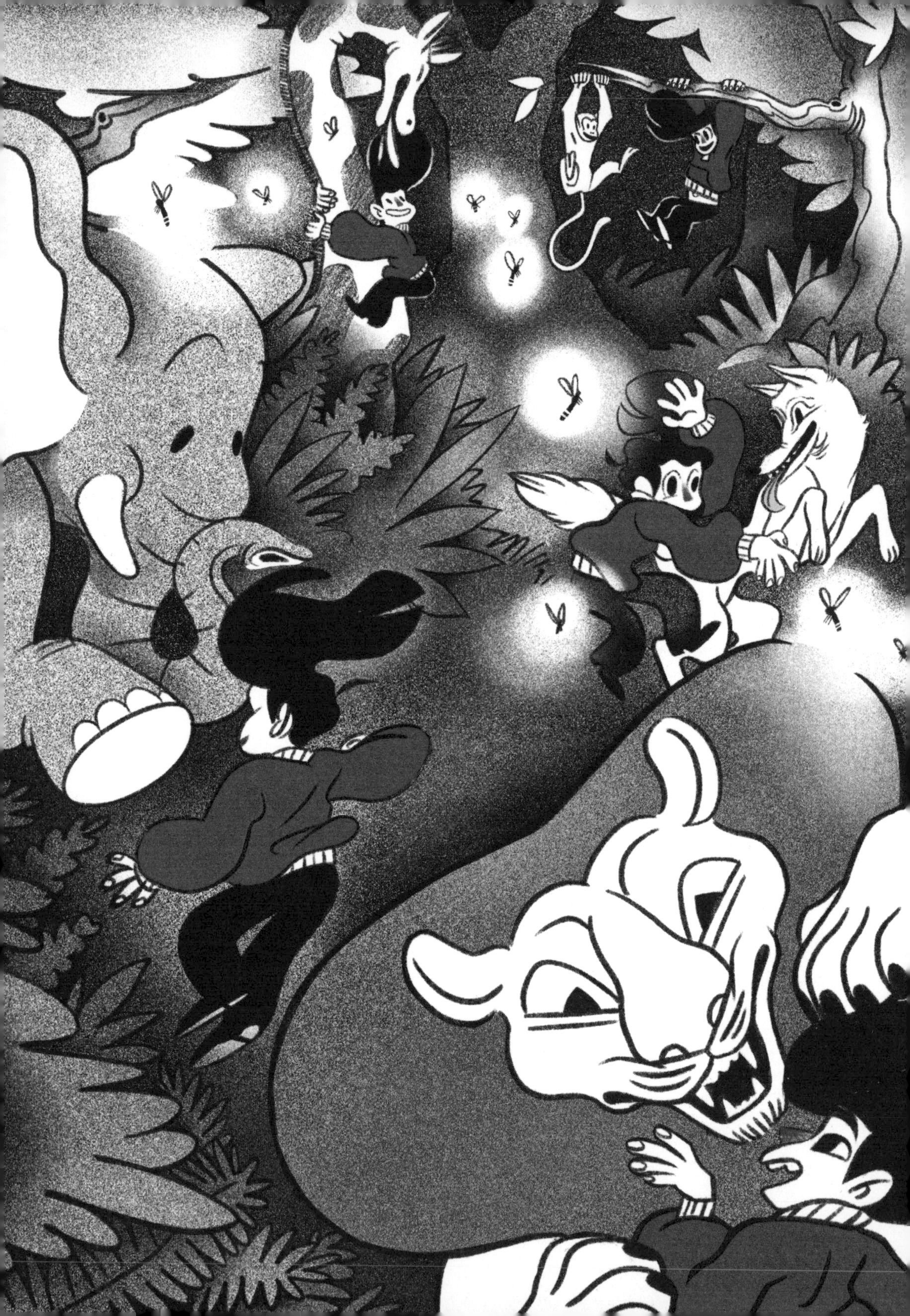

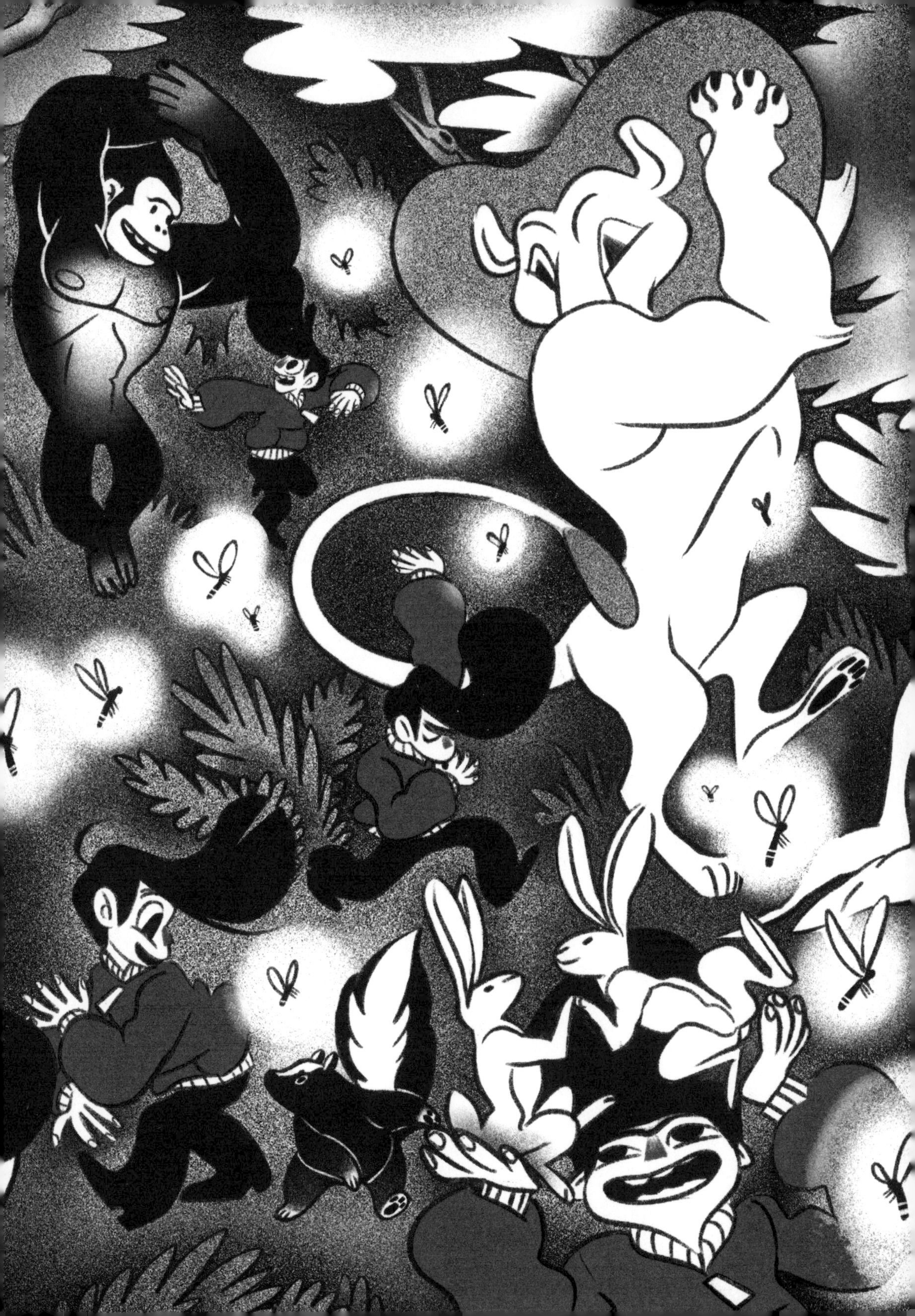

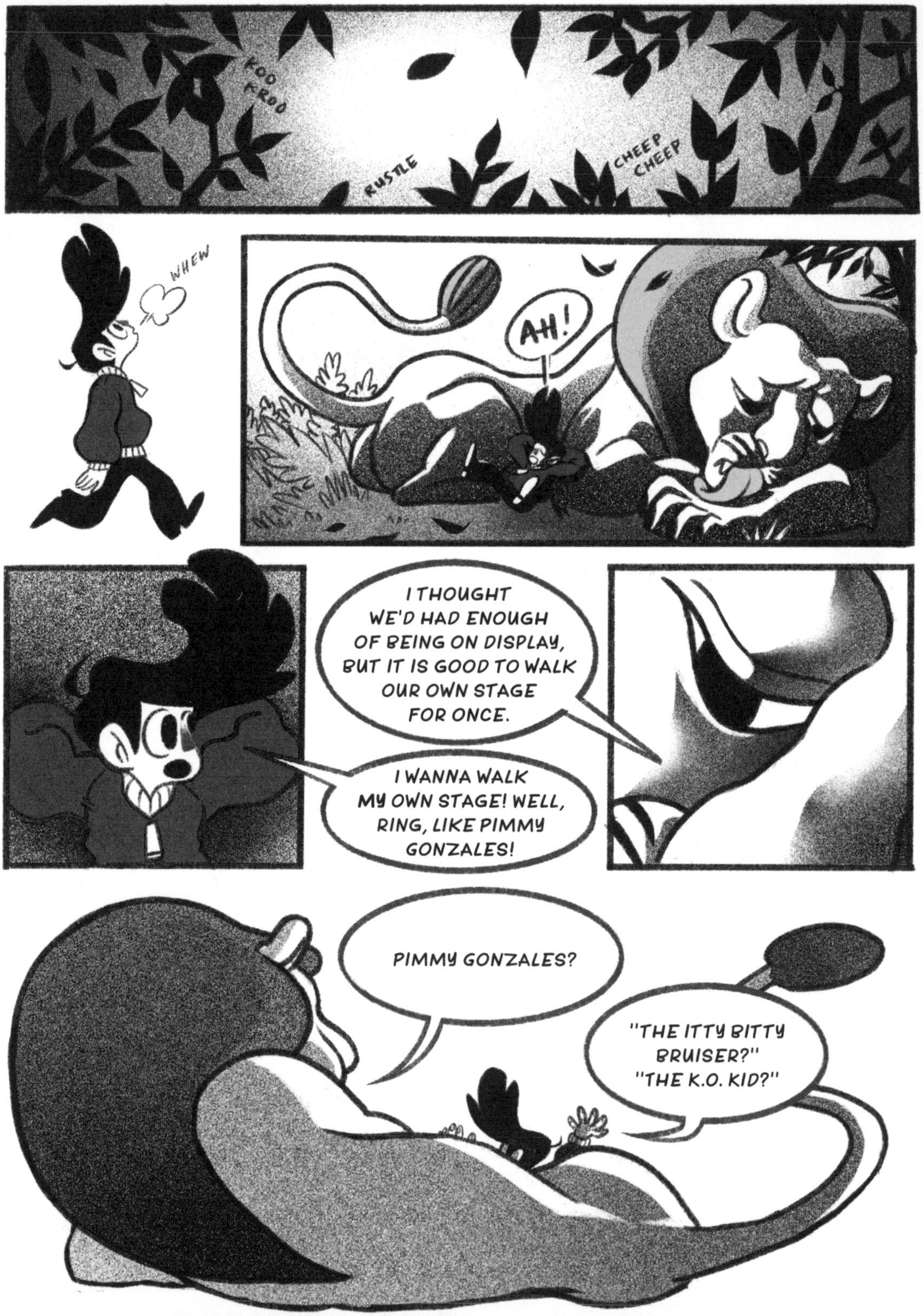
KOO KROO
RUSTLE
CHEEP CHEEP
WHEW
AH!
I THOUGHT WE'D HAD ENOUGH OF BEING ON DISPLAY, BUT IT IS GOOD TO WALK OUR OWN STAGE FOR ONCE.
I WANNA WALK MY OWN STAGE! WELL, RING, LIKE PIMMY GONZALES!
PIMMY GONZALES?
"THE ITTY BITTY BRUISER?" "THE K.O. KID?"

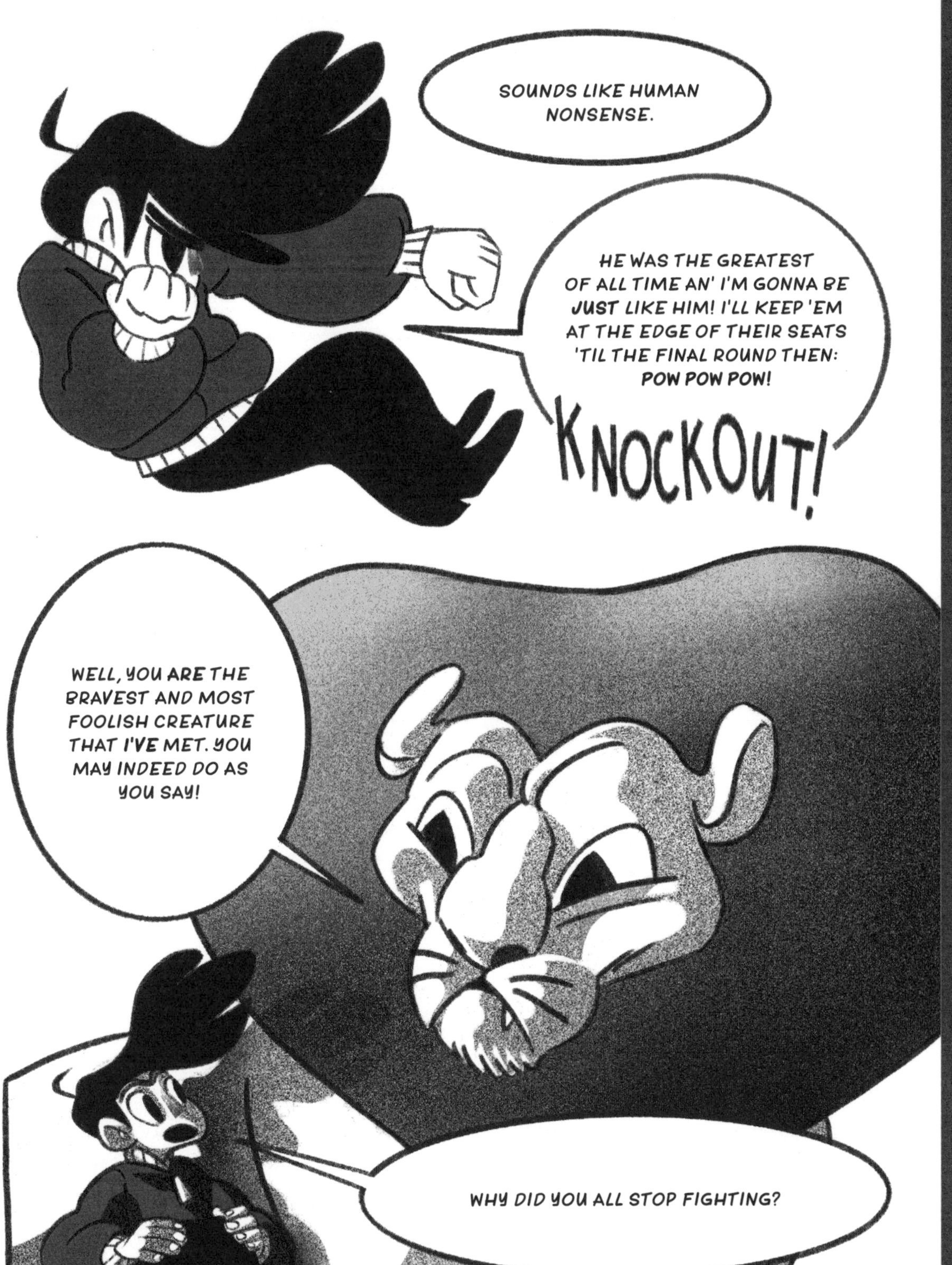
SOUNDS LIKE HUMAN NONSENSE.
HE WAS THE GREATEST OF ALL TIME AN' I'M GONNA BE JUST LIKE HIM! I'LL KEEP 'EM AT THE EDGE OF THEIR SEATS 'TIL THE FINAL ROUND THEN: POW POW POW!
KNOCKOUT!
WELL, YOU ARE THE BRAVEST AND MOST FOOLISH CREATURE THAT I'VE MET. YOU MAY INDEED DO AS YOU SAY!
WHY DID YOU ALL STOP FIGHTING?

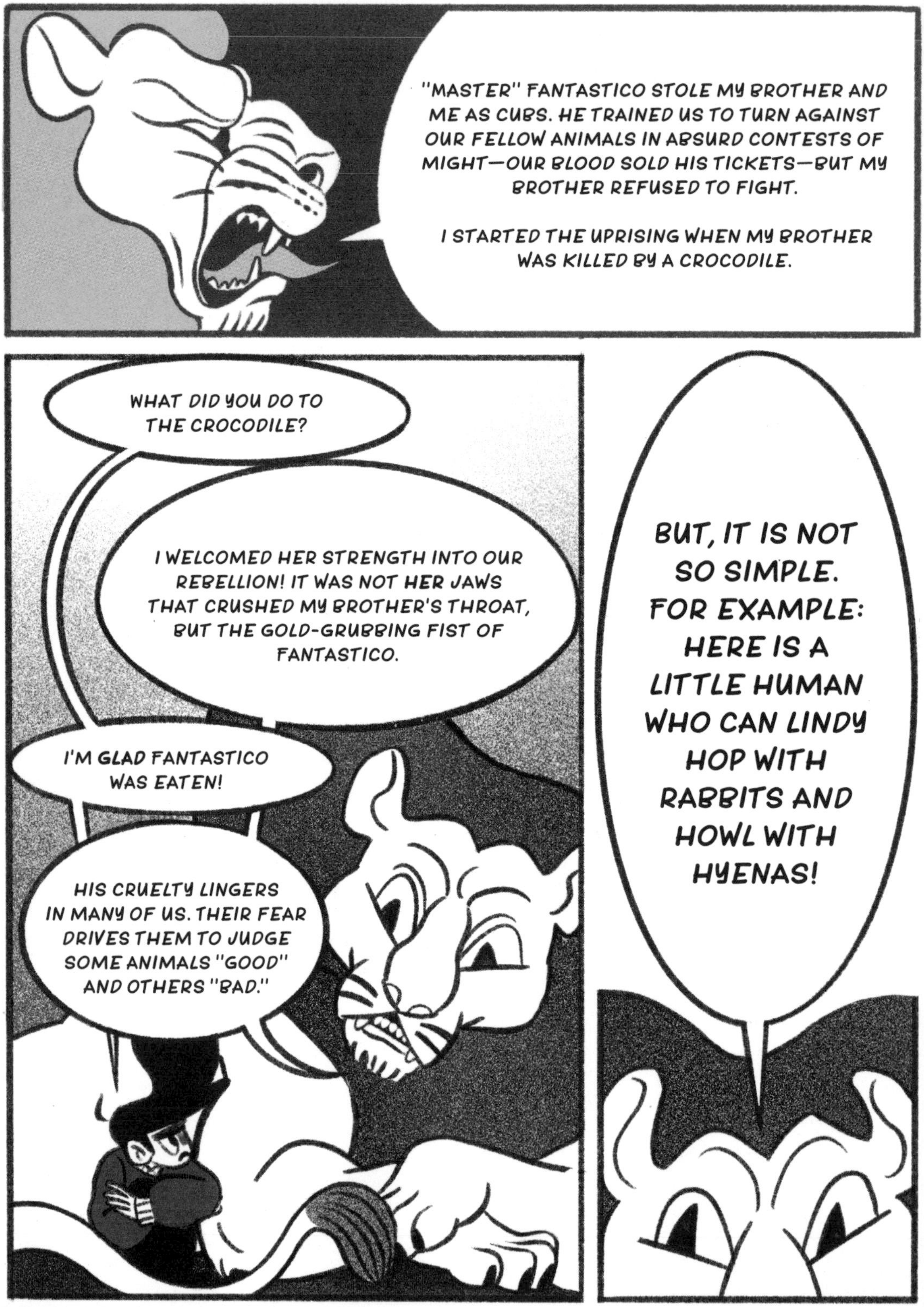
"MASTER" FANTASTICO STOLE MY BROTHER AND ME AS CUBS. HE TRAINED US TO TURN AGAINST OUR FELLOW ANIMALS IN ABSURD CONTESTS OF MIGHT—OUR BLOOD SOLD HIS TICKETS—BUT MY BROTHER REFUSED TO FIGHT.
I STARTED THE UPRISING WHEN MY BROTHER WAS KILLED BY A CROCODILE.
WHAT *DID* YOU DO TO THE CROCODILE?
I WELCOMED HER STRENGTH INTO OUR REBELLION! IT WAS NOT **HER** JAWS THAT CRUSHED MY BROTHER'S THROAT, BUT THE GOLD-GRUBBING FIST OF FANTASTICO.
I'M **GLAD** FANTASTICO WAS EATEN!
HIS CRUELTY LINGERS IN MANY OF US. THEIR FEAR DRIVES THEM TO JUDGE SOME ANIMALS "GOOD" AND OTHERS "BAD."
BUT, IT IS NOT SO SIMPLE. FOR EXAMPLE: HERE IS A LITTLE HUMAN WHO CAN LINDY HOP WITH RABBITS AND HOWL WITH HYENAS!

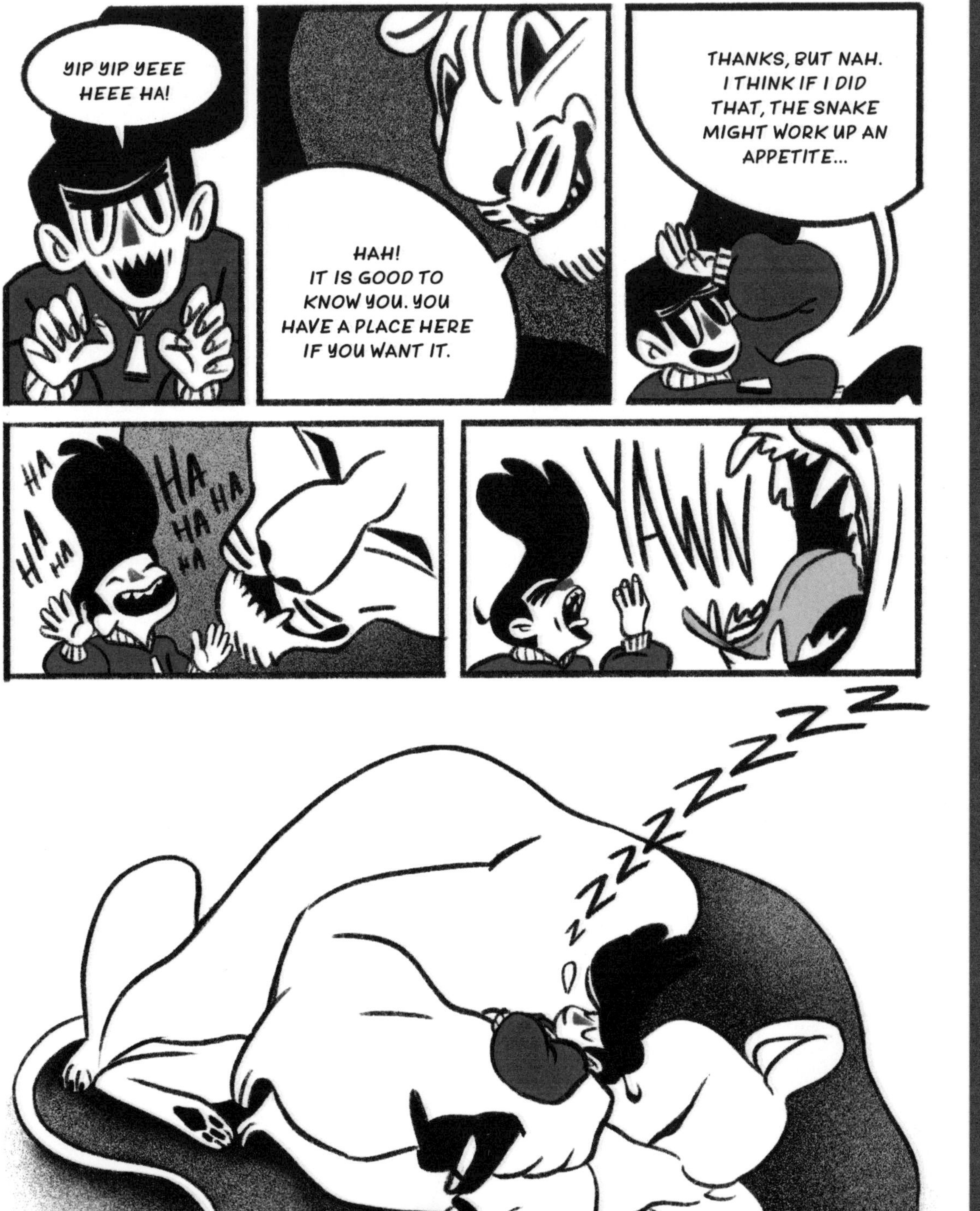
YIP YIP YEEE HEEE HA!
HAH! IT IS GOOD TO KNOW YOU. YOU HAVE A PLACE HERE IF YOU WANT IT.
THANKS, BUT NAH. I THINK IF I DID THAT, THE SNAKE MIGHT WORK UP AN APPETITE...
HA HA HA HA
HA HA HA HA
YAWN
ZZZZZZZZZZZZZZ

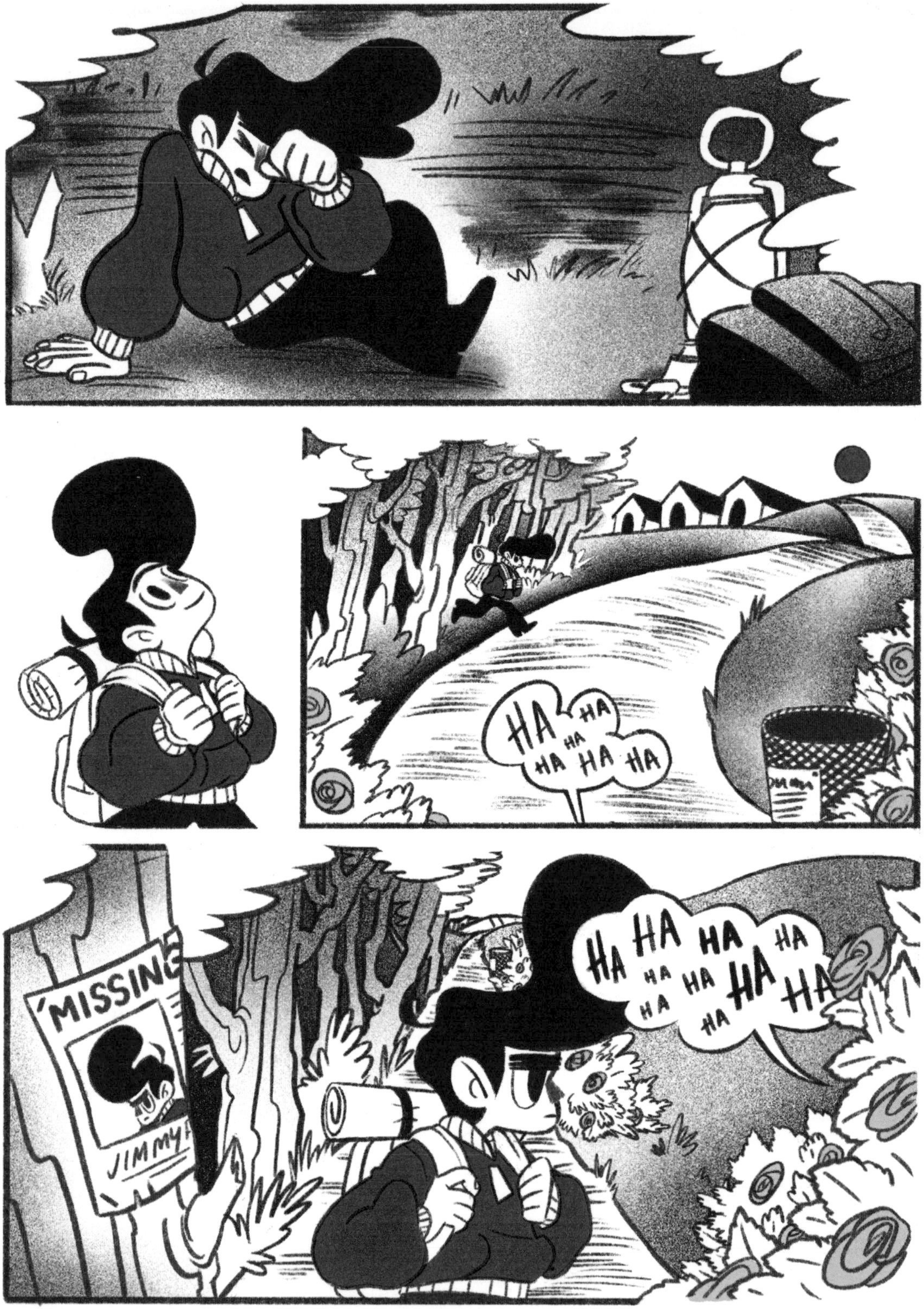
HA HA HA HA HA HA
MISSING
JIMMY
HA HA HA HA HA HA HA HA HA HA

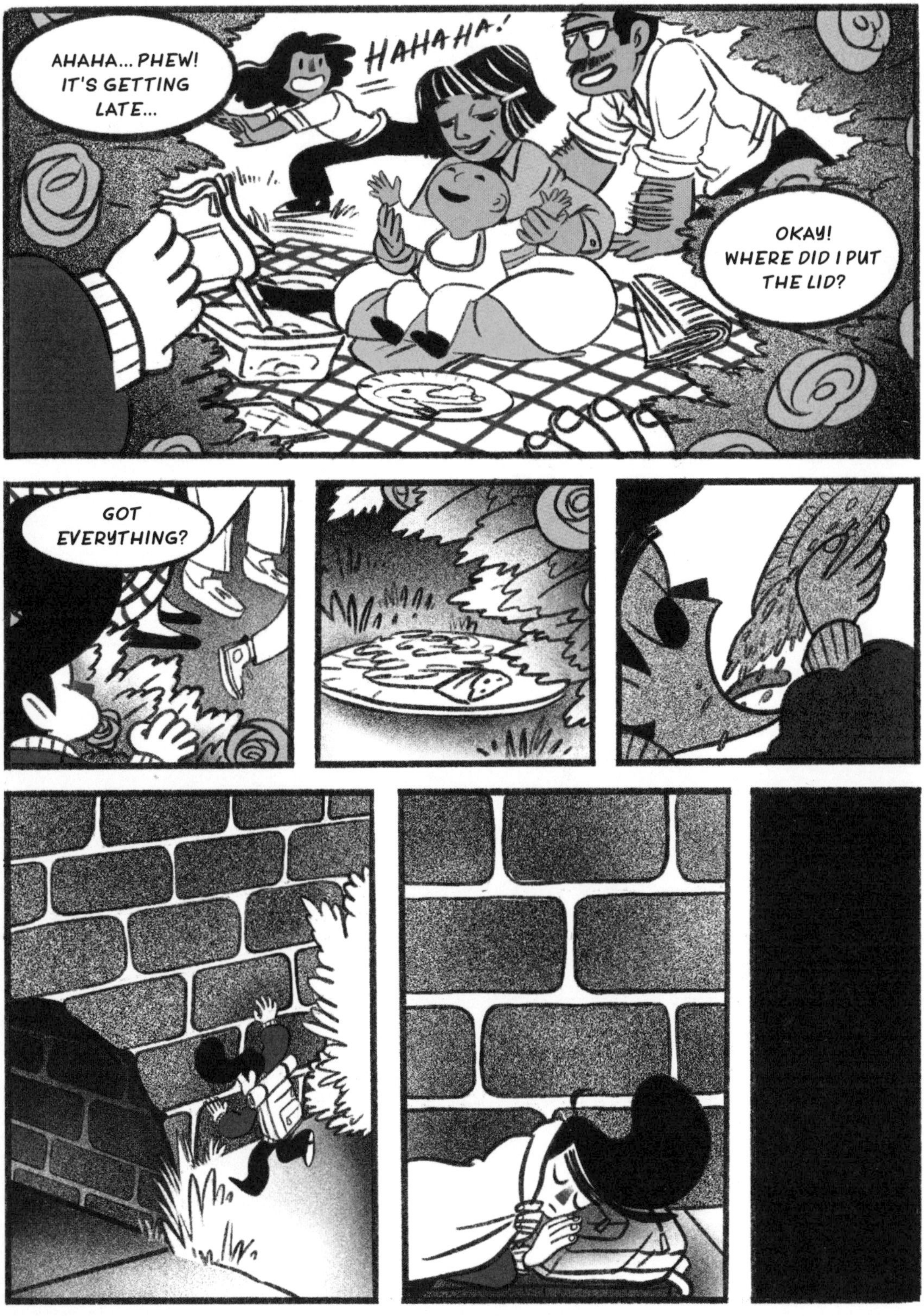
AHAHA... PHEW! IT'S GETTING LATE...
HAHAHA!
OKAY! WHERE DID I PUT THE LID?
GOT EVERYTHING?

CHAPTER 4

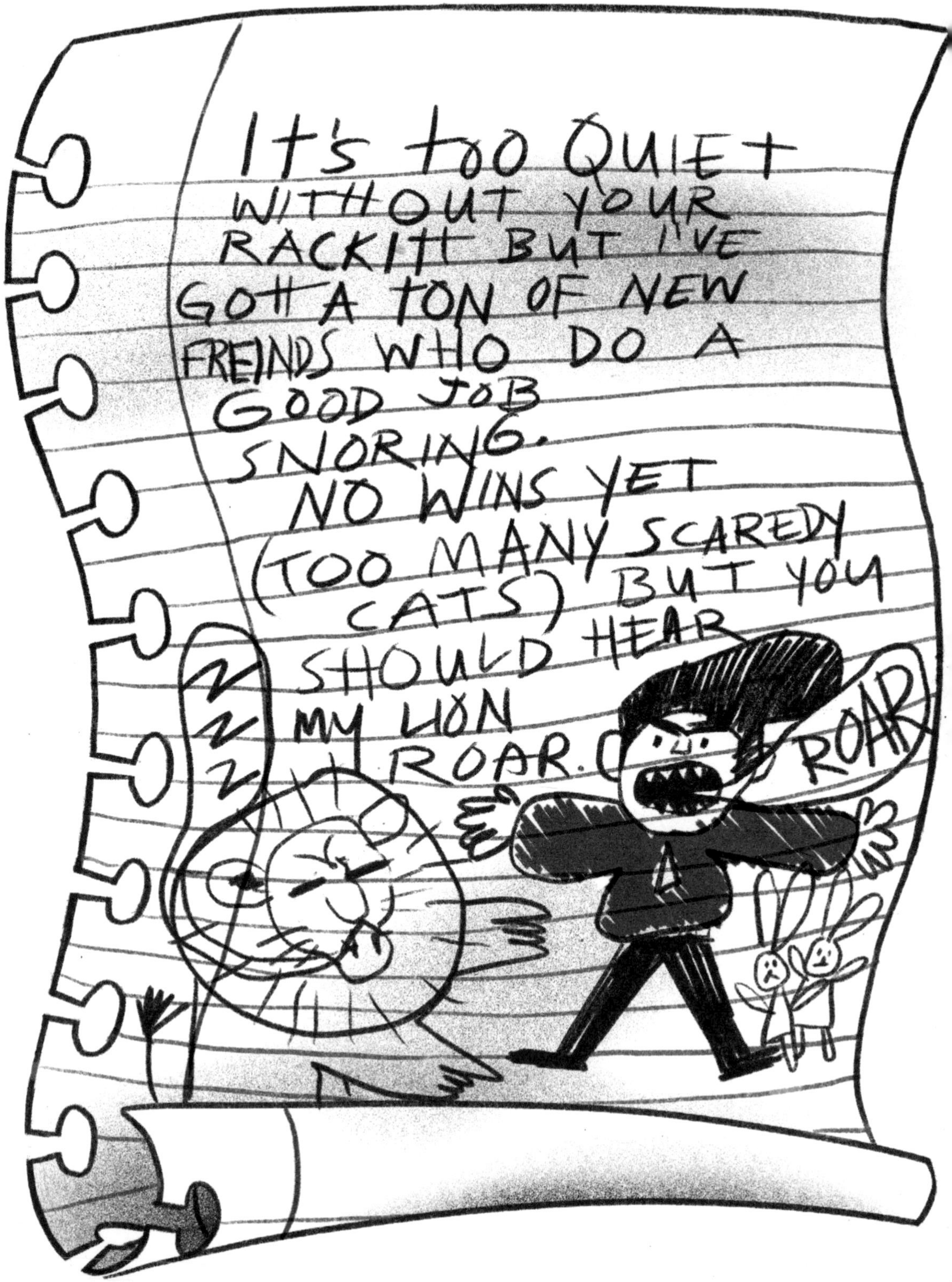
It's too QUIET WITHOUT YOUR RACKITT BUT I'VE GOTT A TON OF NEW FREINDS WHO DO A GOOD JOB SNORING. NO WINS YET (TOO MANY SCAREDY CATS) BUT YOU SHOULD HEAR MY LION ROAR.
ZZZ
ROAR

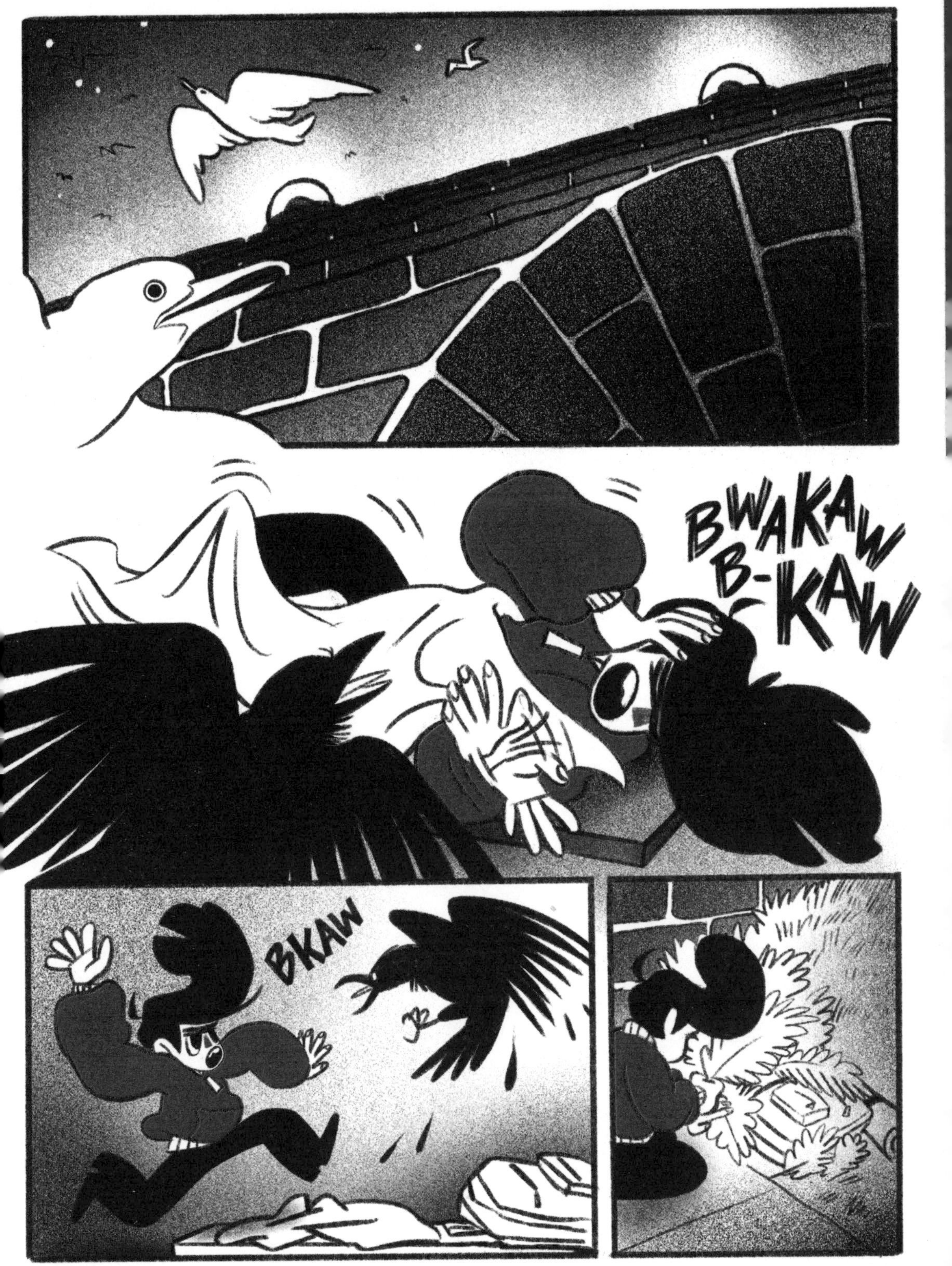
BWAKAW
B-KAW
BKAW

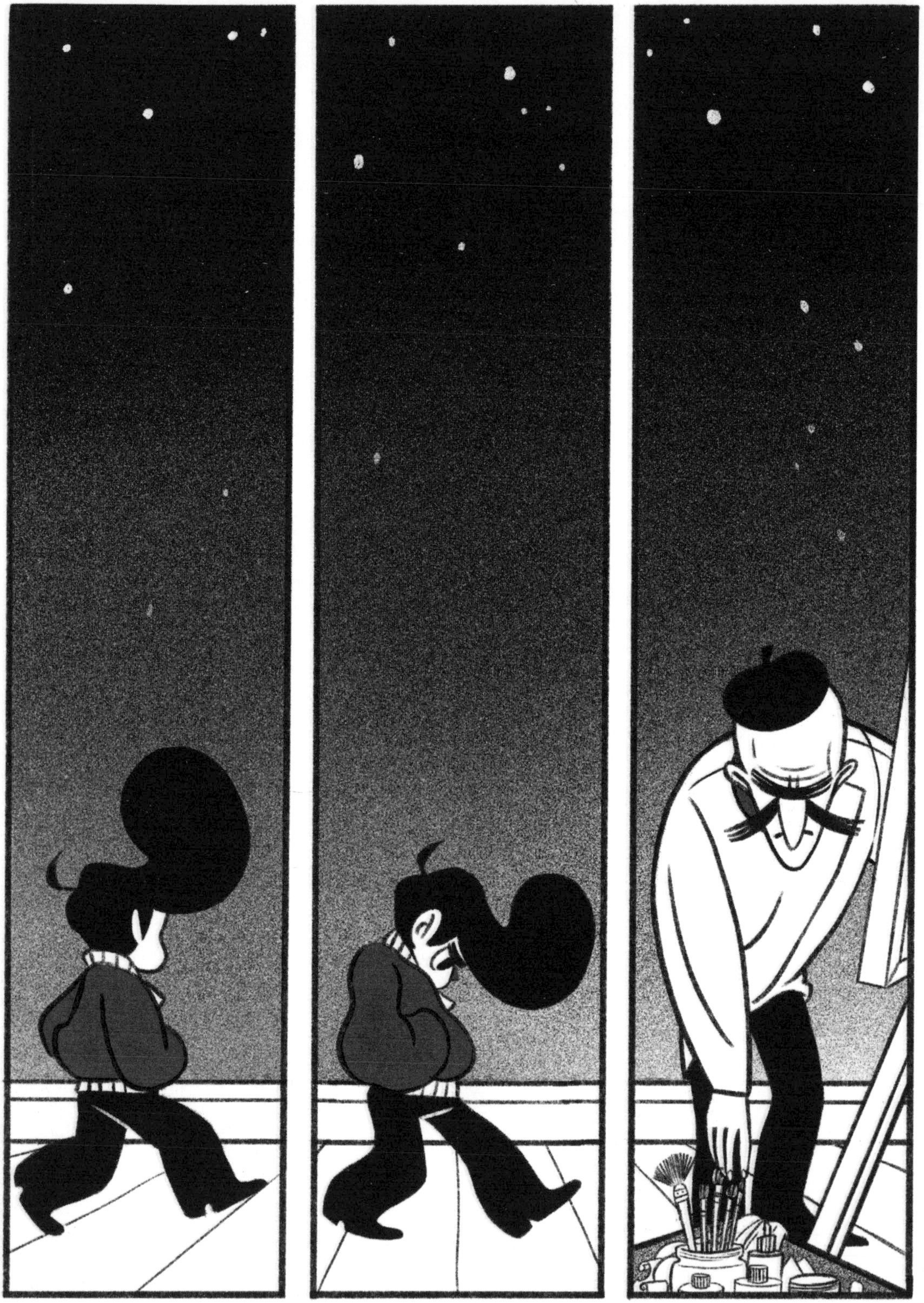

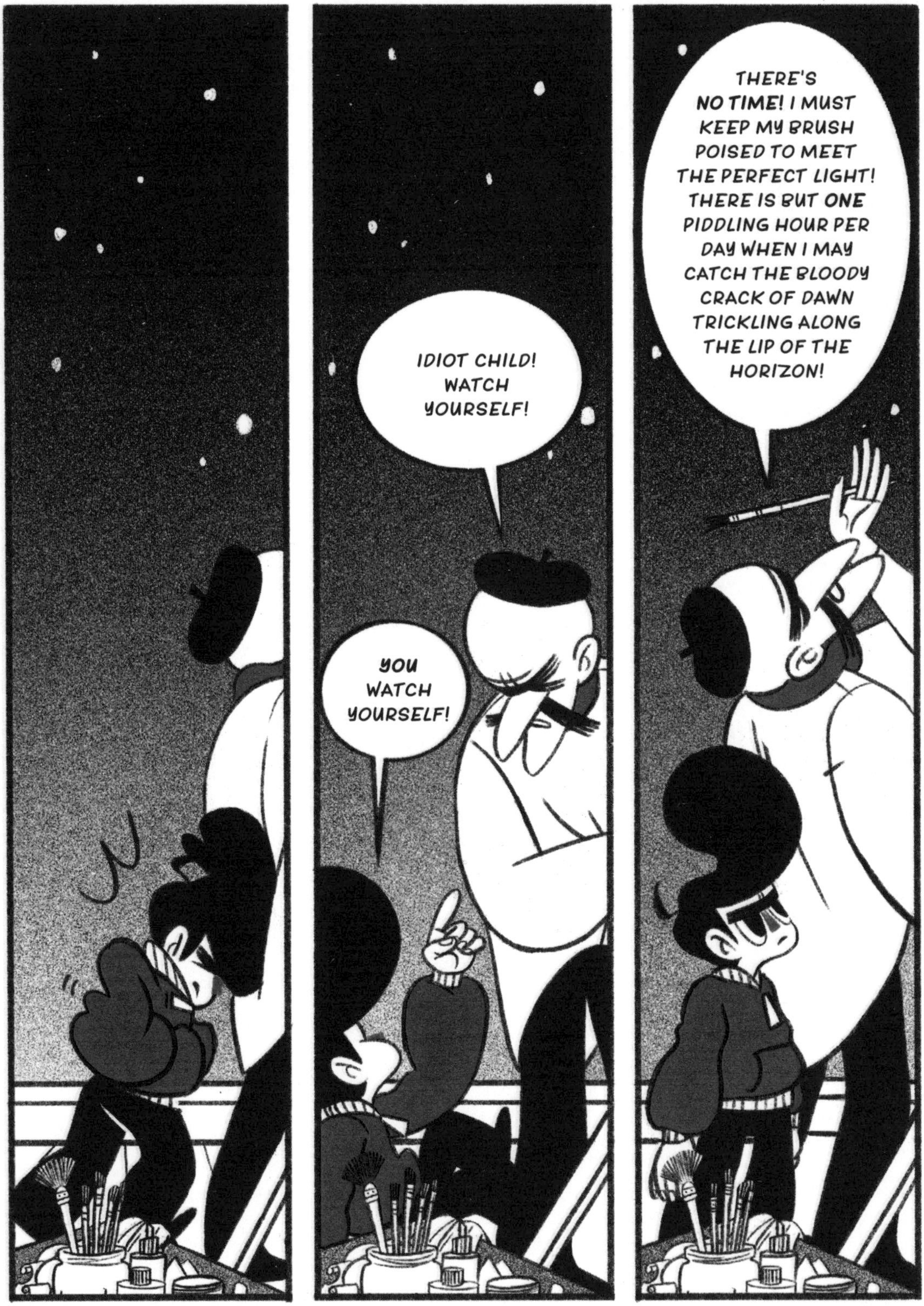
IDIOT CHILD! WATCH YOURSELF!
YOU WATCH YOURSELF!
THERE'S NO TIME! I MUST KEEP MY BRUSH POISED TO MEET THE PERFECT LIGHT! THERE IS BUT ONE PIDDLING HOUR PER DAY WHEN I MAY CATCH THE BLOODY CRACK OF DAWN TRICKLING ALONG THE LIP OF THE HORIZON!

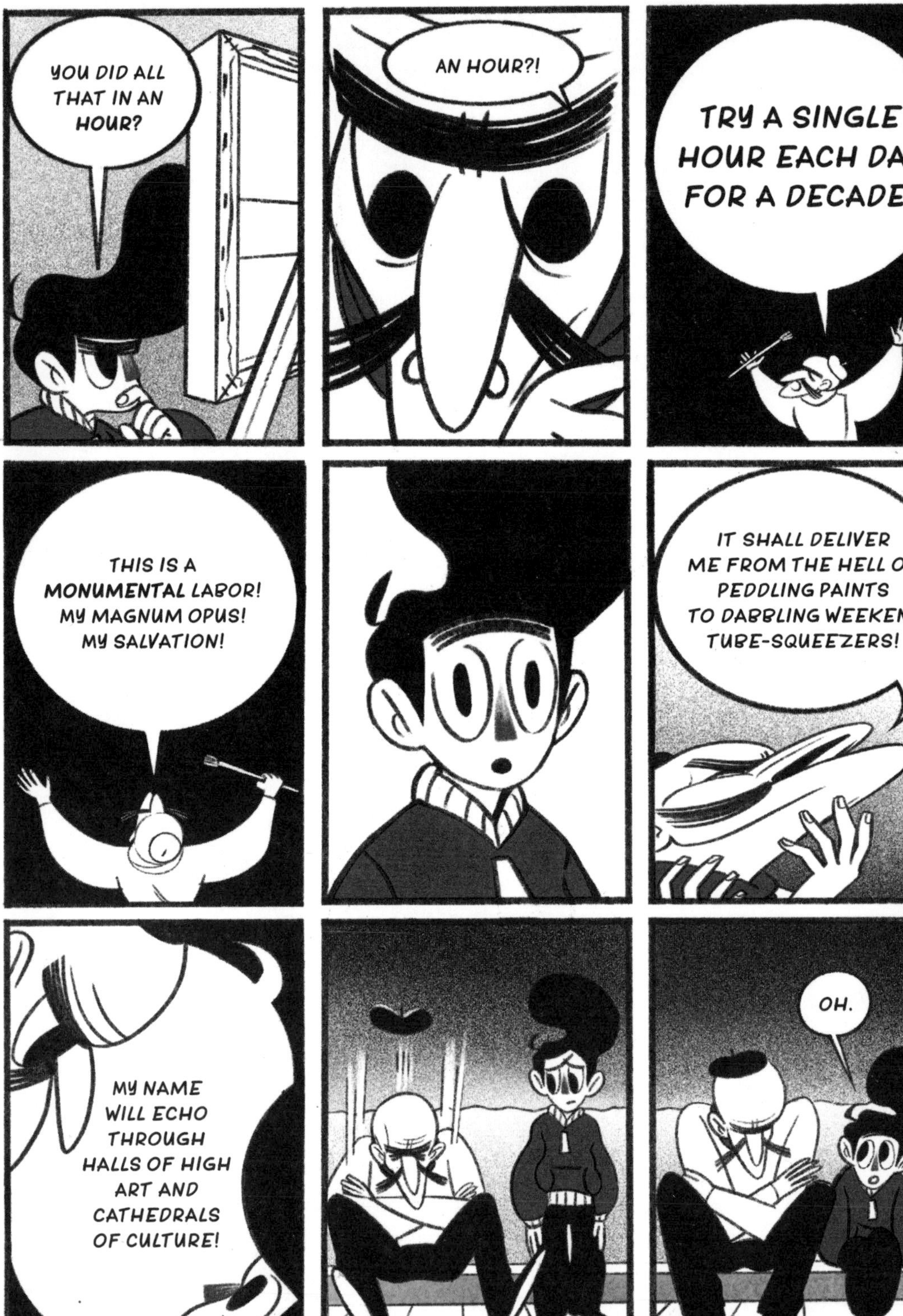
YOU DID ALL THAT IN AN HOUR?
AN HOUR?!
TRY A SINGLE HOUR EACH DAY FOR A DECADE!
THIS IS A MONUMENTAL LABOR! MY MAGNUM OPUS! MY SALVATION!
IT SHALL DELIVER ME FROM THE HELL OF PEDDLING PAINTS TO DABBLING WEEKEND TUBE-SQUEEZERS!
MY NAME WILL ECHO THROUGH HALLS OF HIGH ART AND CATHEDRALS OF CULTURE!
OH.

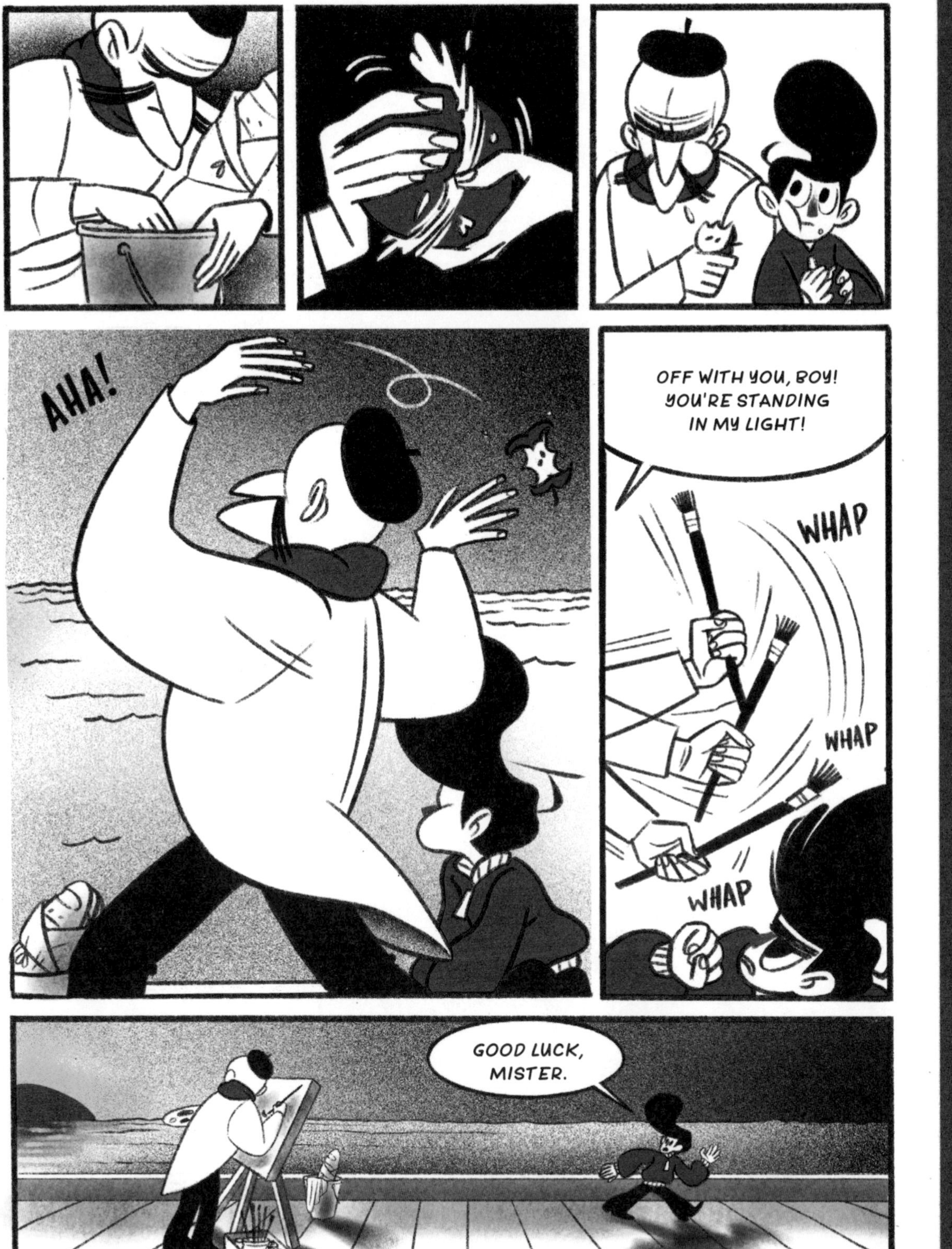
AHA!
OFF WITH YOU, BOY! YOU'RE STANDING IN MY LIGHT!
WHAP
WHAP
WHAP
GOOD LUCK, MISTER.

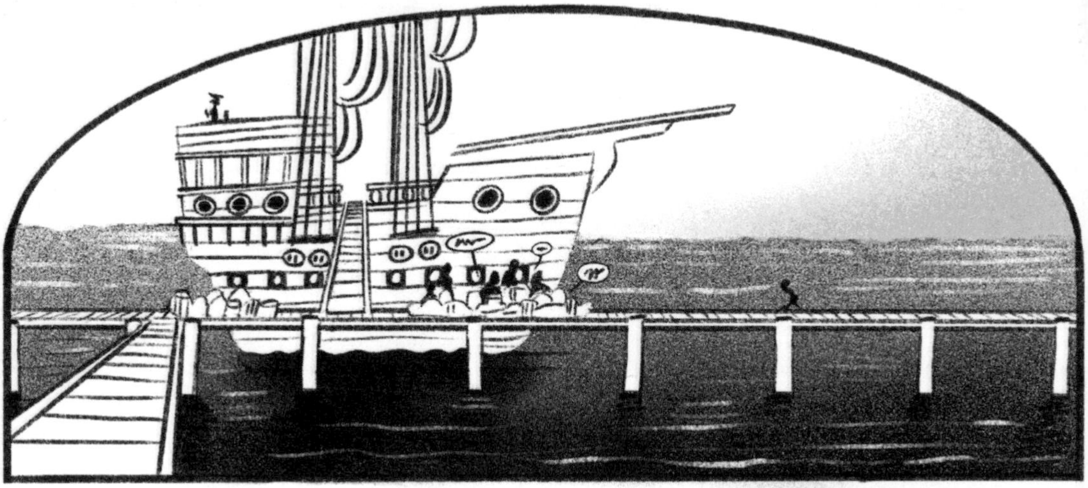

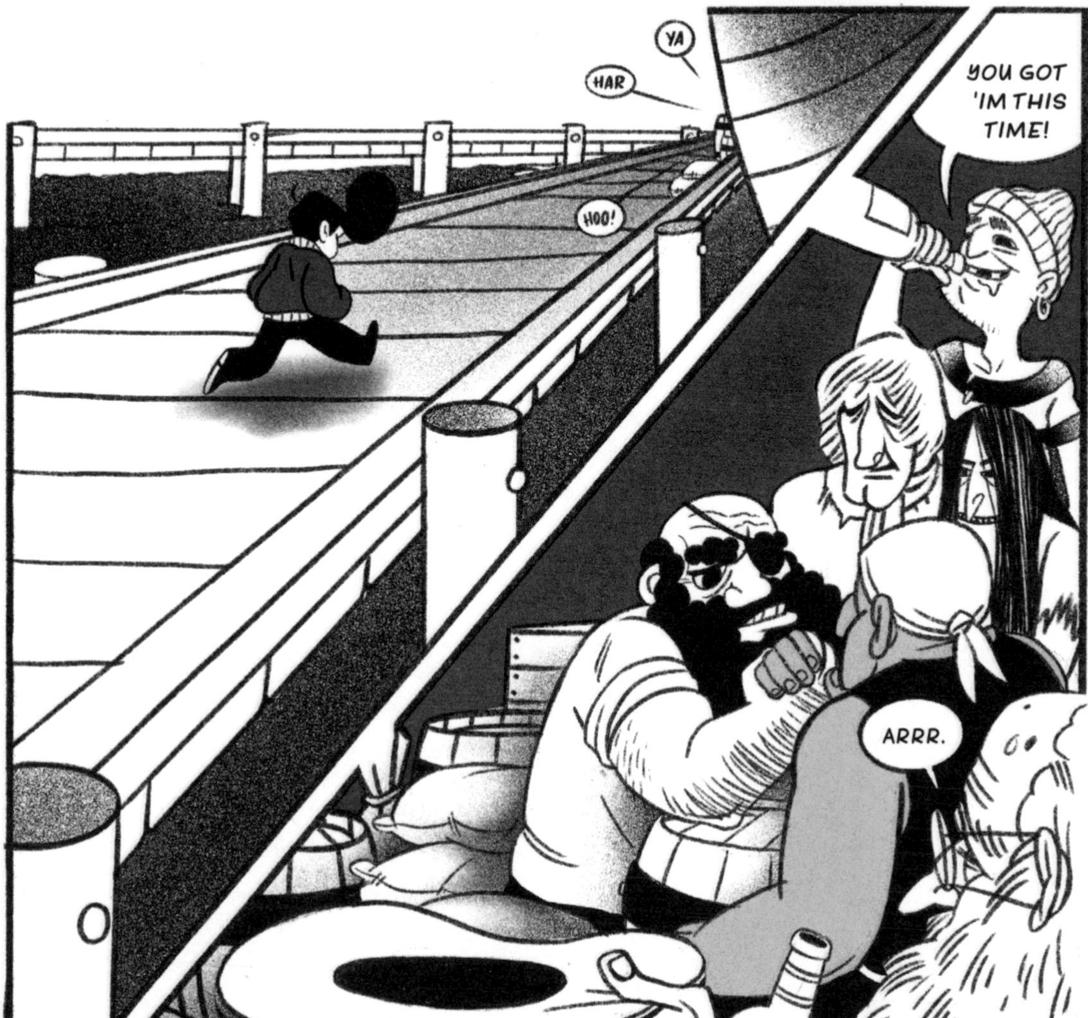
YA
HAR
HOO!
YOU GOT 'IM THIS TIME!
ARRR.

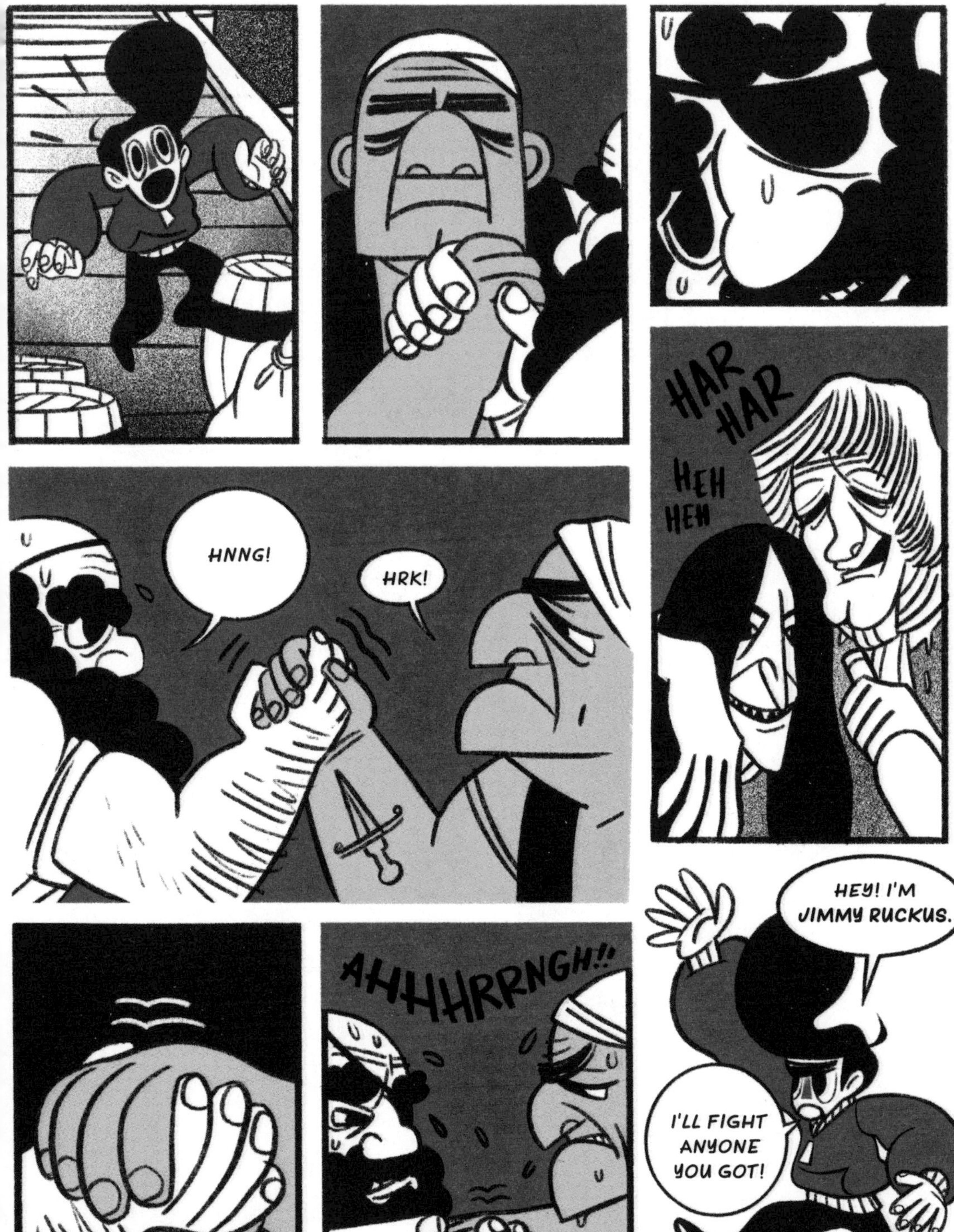
HAR HAR
HEH HEH
HNNG!
HRK!
HEY! I'M JIMMY RUCKUS.
AHHHRRNGH!!
I'LL FIGHT ANYONE YOU GOT!

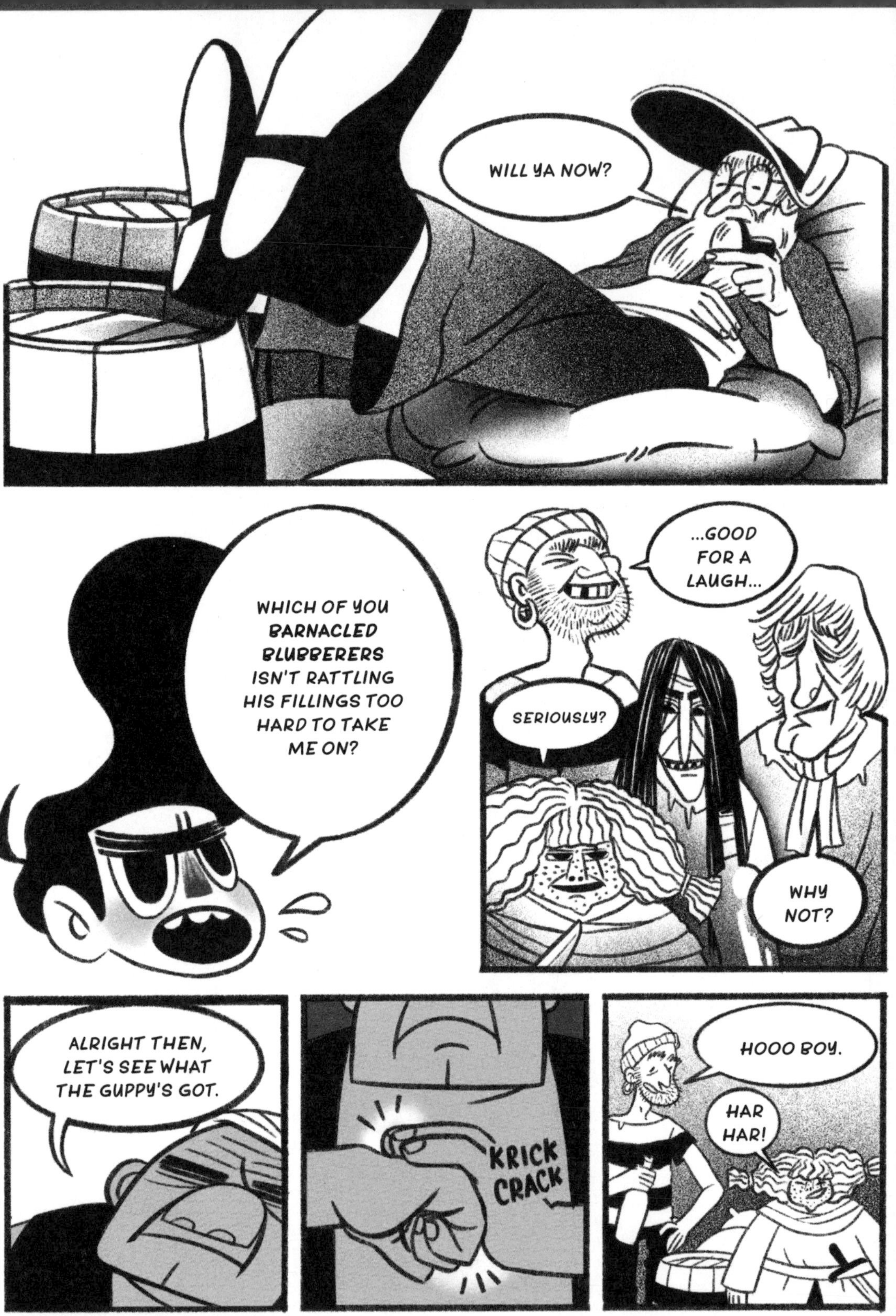
WILL YA NOW?
WHICH OF YOU BARNACLED BLUBBERERS ISN'T RATTLING HIS FILLINGS TOO HARD TO TAKE ME ON?
...GOOD FOR A LAUGH...
SERIOUSLY?
WHY NOT?
ALRIGHT THEN, LET'S SEE WHAT THE GUPPY'S GOT.
KRICK CRACK
HOOO BOY.
HAR HAR!

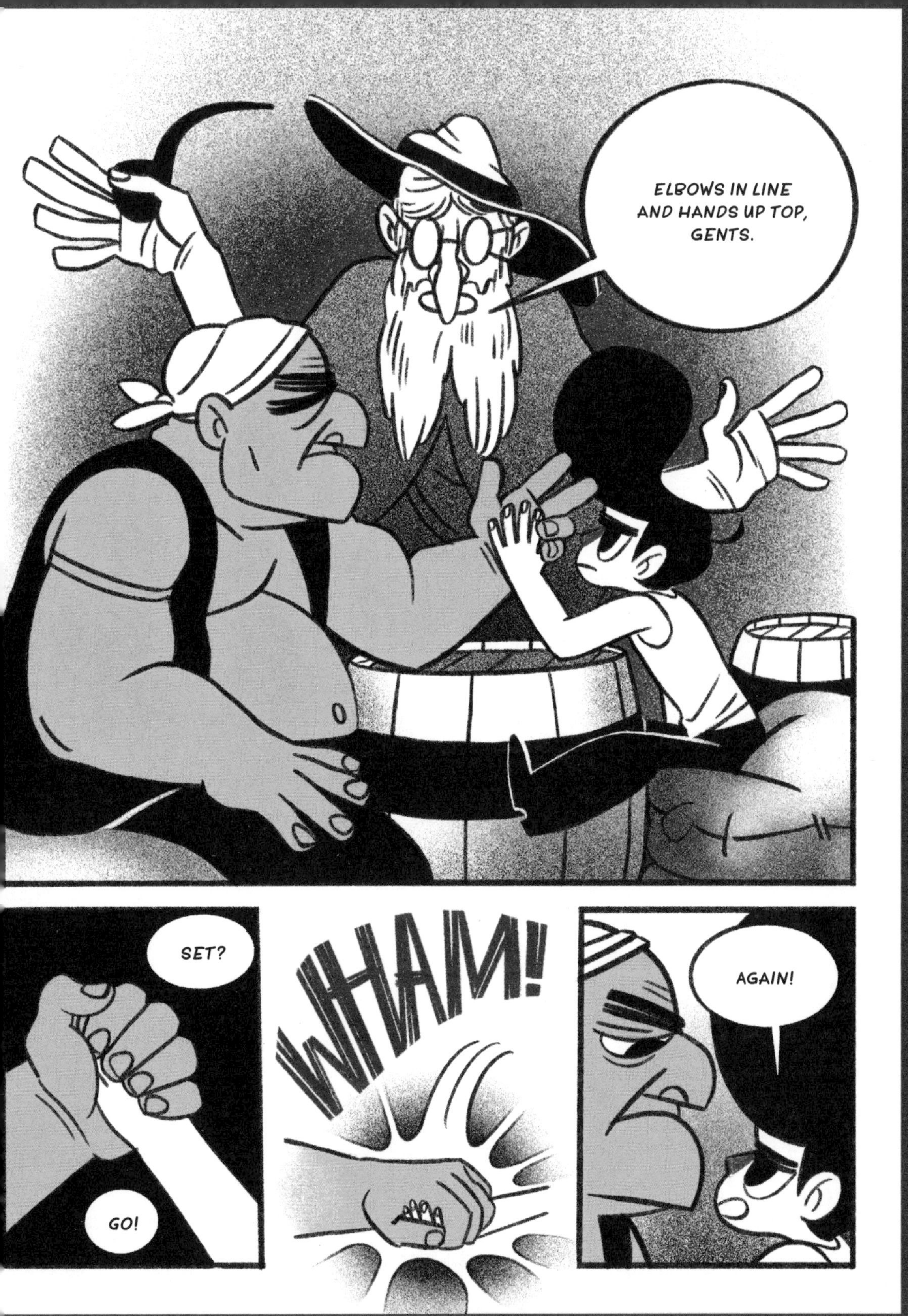
ELBOWS IN LINE AND HANDS UP TOP, GENTS.
SET?
GO!
WHAM!
AGAIN!

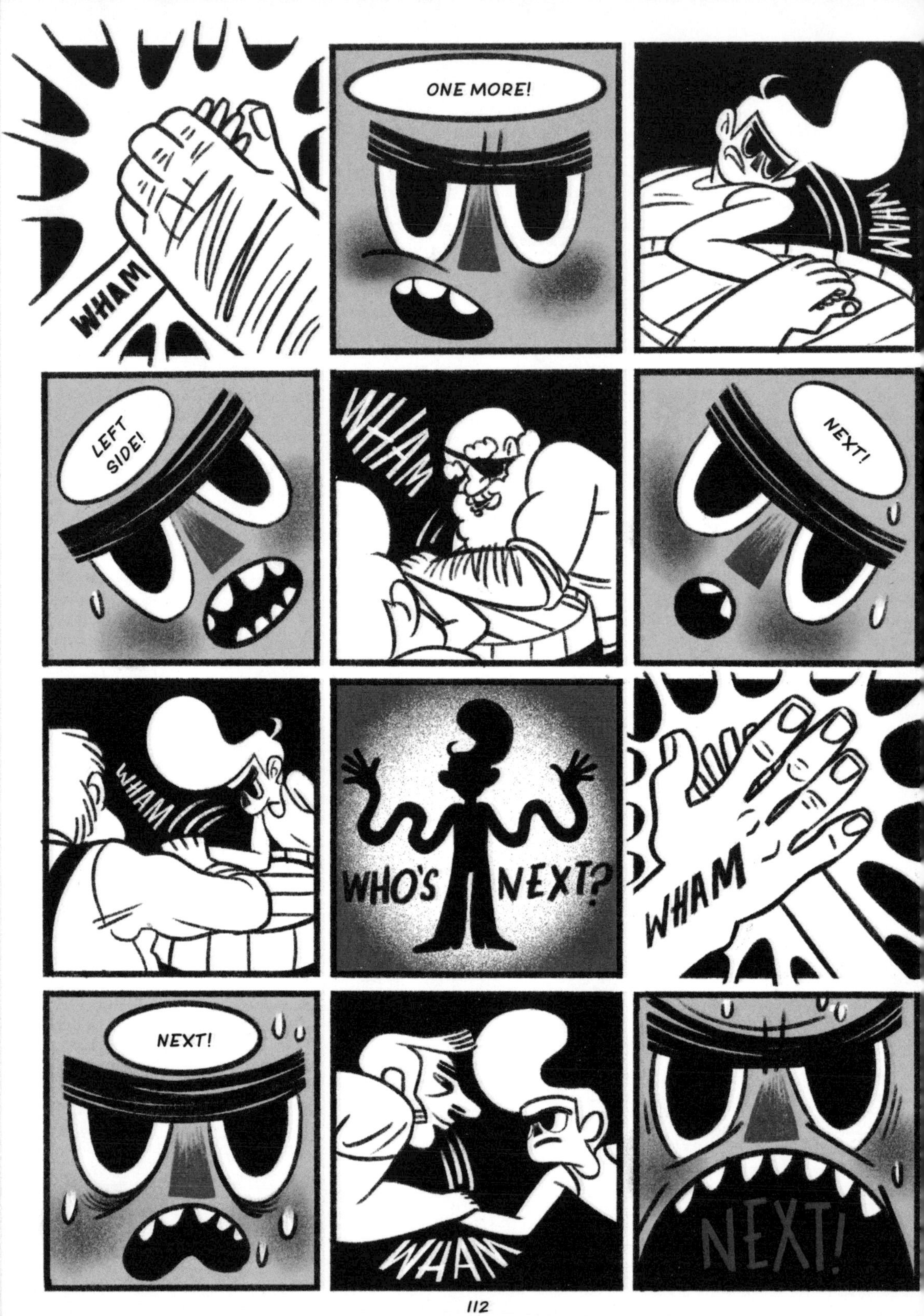

WHAM
ONE MORE!
WHAM
LEFT SIDE!
WHAM
NEXT!
WHAM
WHO'S NEXT?
WHAM
NEXT!
WHAM
NEXT!

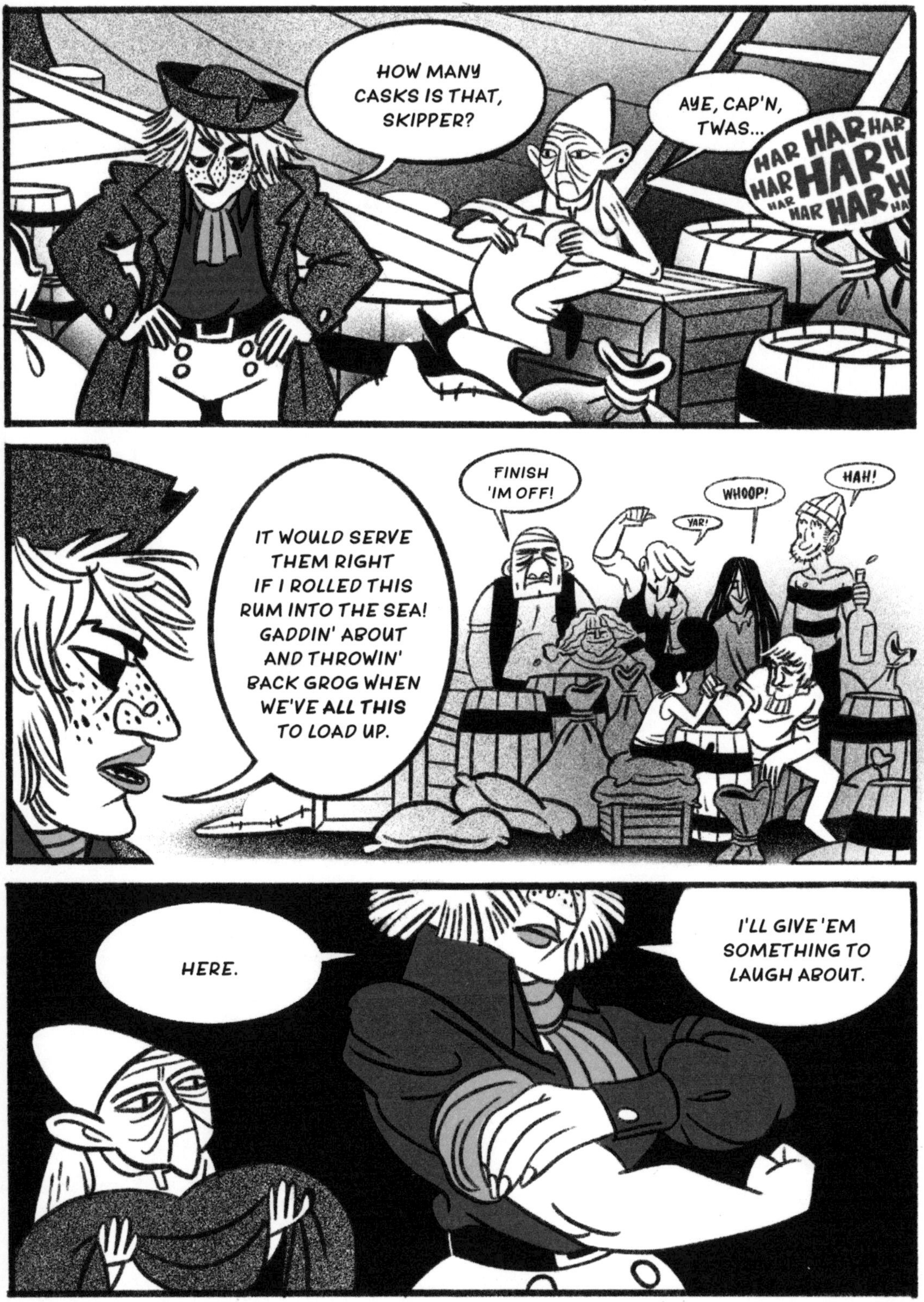
HOW MANY CASKS IS THAT, SKIPPER?
AYE, CAP'N, TWAS...
HAR HAR HAR HAR HAR HAR HAR HAR HAR HAR
IT WOULD SERVE THEM RIGHT IF I ROLLED THIS RUM INTO THE SEA! GADDIN' ABOUT AND THROWIN' BACK GROG WHEN WE'VE ALL THIS TO LOAD UP.
FINISH 'IM OFF!
YAR!
WHOOP!
HAH!
HERE.
I'LL GIVE 'EM SOMETHING TO LAUGH ABOUT.

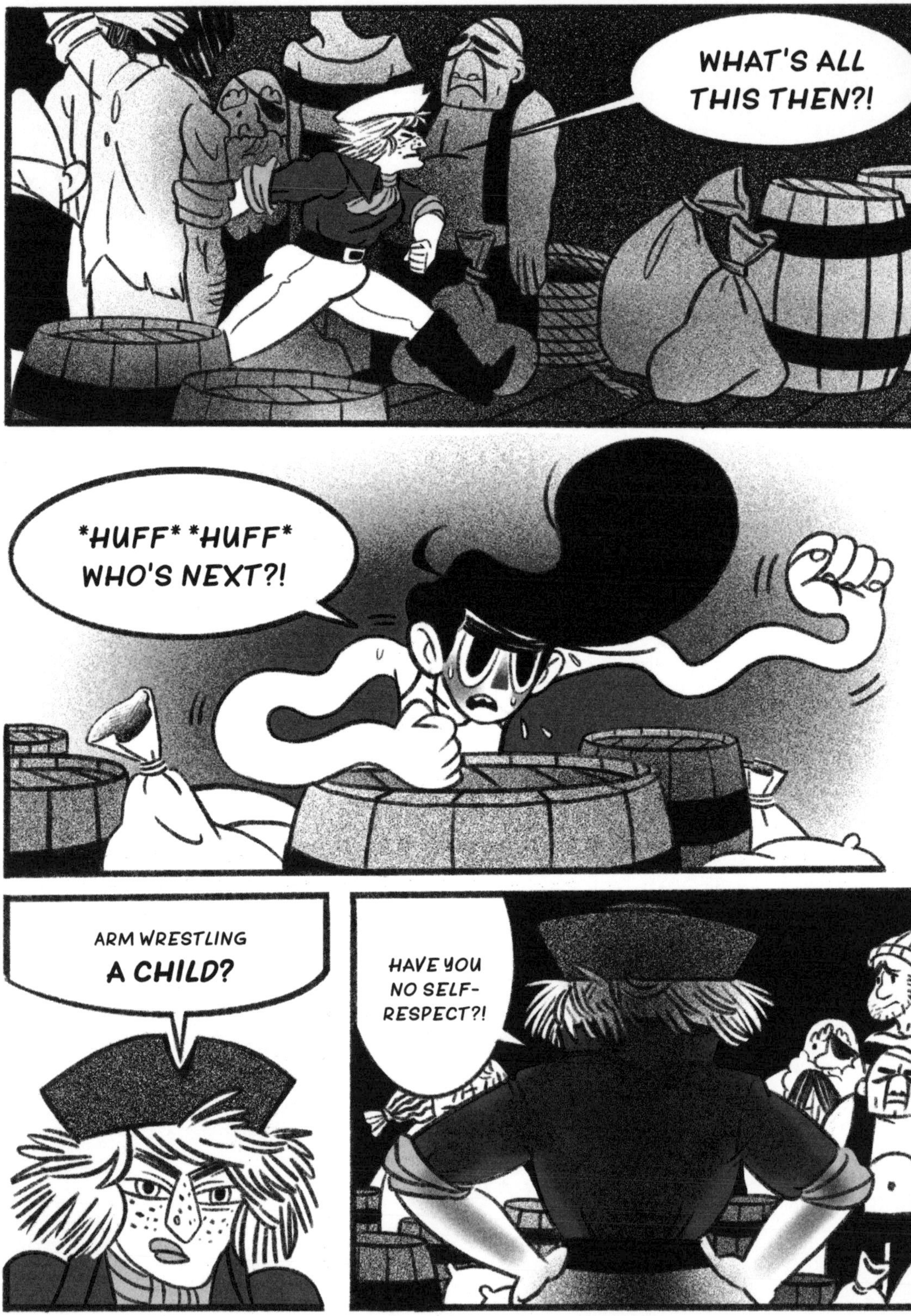
WHAT'S ALL THIS THEN?!
HUFF *HUFF* WHO'S NEXT?!
ARM WRESTLING A CHILD?
HAVE YOU NO SELF-RESPECT?!

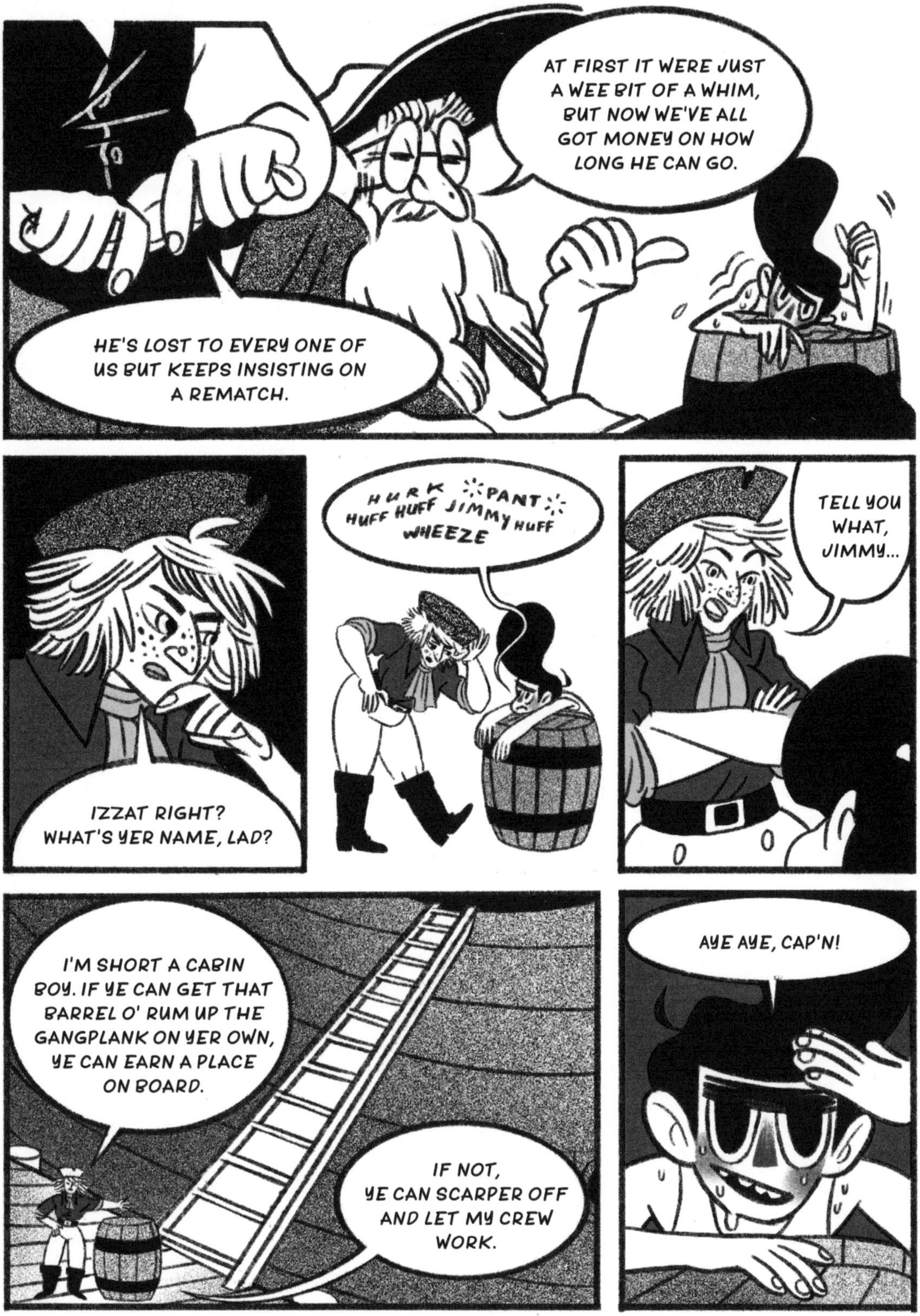
AT FIRST IT WERE JUST A WEE BIT OF A WHIM, BUT NOW WE'VE ALL GOT MONEY ON HOW LONG HE CAN GO.
HE'S LOST TO EVERY ONE OF US BUT KEEPS INSISTING ON A REMATCH.
IZZAT RIGHT? WHAT'S YER NAME, LAD?
HURK PANT HUFF HUFF JIMMY HUFF WHEEZE
TELL YOU WHAT, JIMMY...
I'M SHORT A CABIN BOY. IF YE CAN GET THAT BARREL O' RUM UP THE GANGPLANK ON YER OWN, YE CAN EARN A PLACE ON BOARD.
IF NOT, YE CAN SCARPER OFF AND LET MY CREW WORK.
AYE AYE, CAP'N!

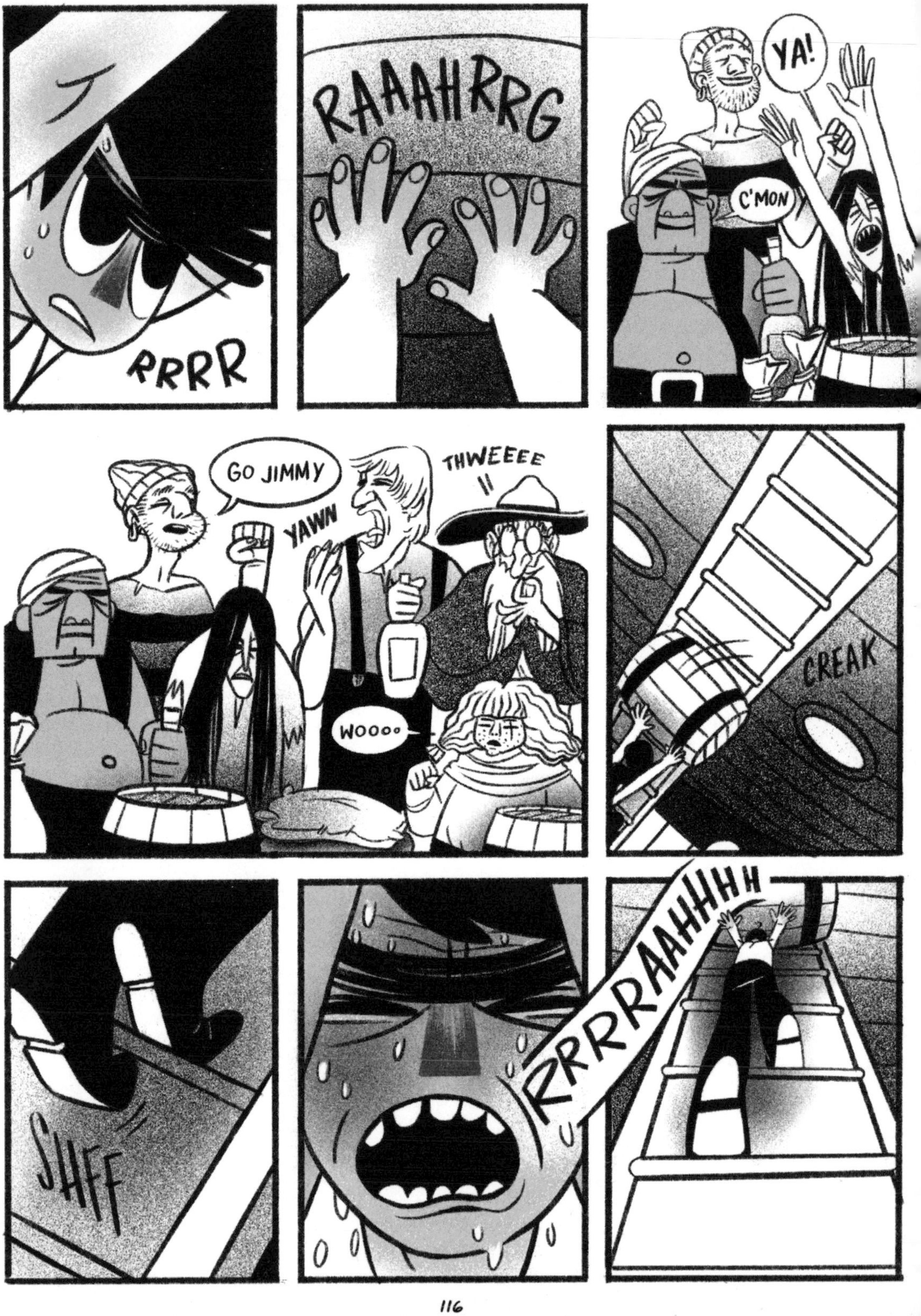
RRRR
RAAAHRRG
YA!
C'MON
GO JIMMY
THWEEEE
YAWN
WOOOo
CREAK
SHFF
RRRRAAHHHH

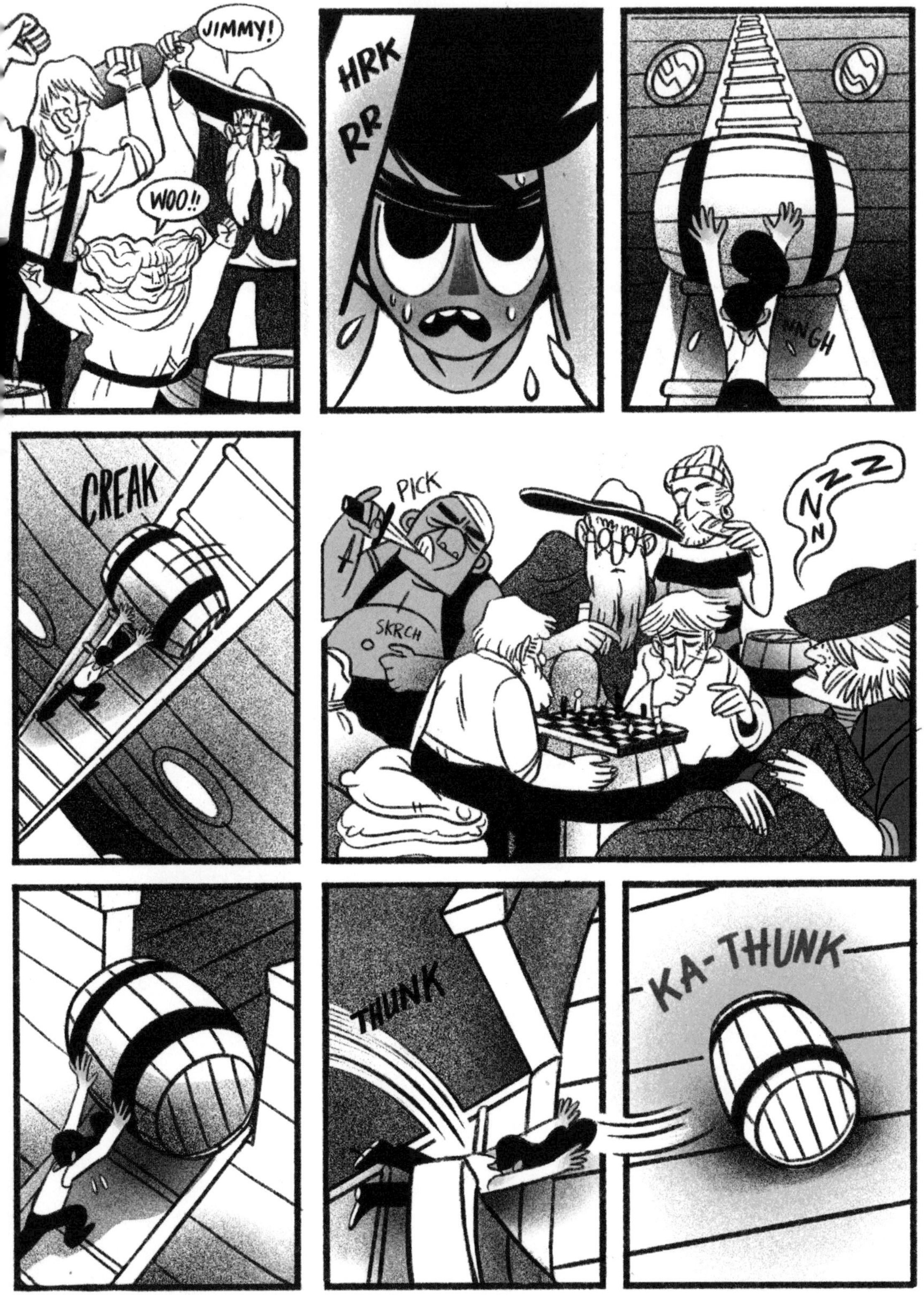
JIMMY!
WOO!!
HRK
RR
NNGH
CREAK
PICK
SKRCH
NNZZZ
THUNK
KA-THUNK

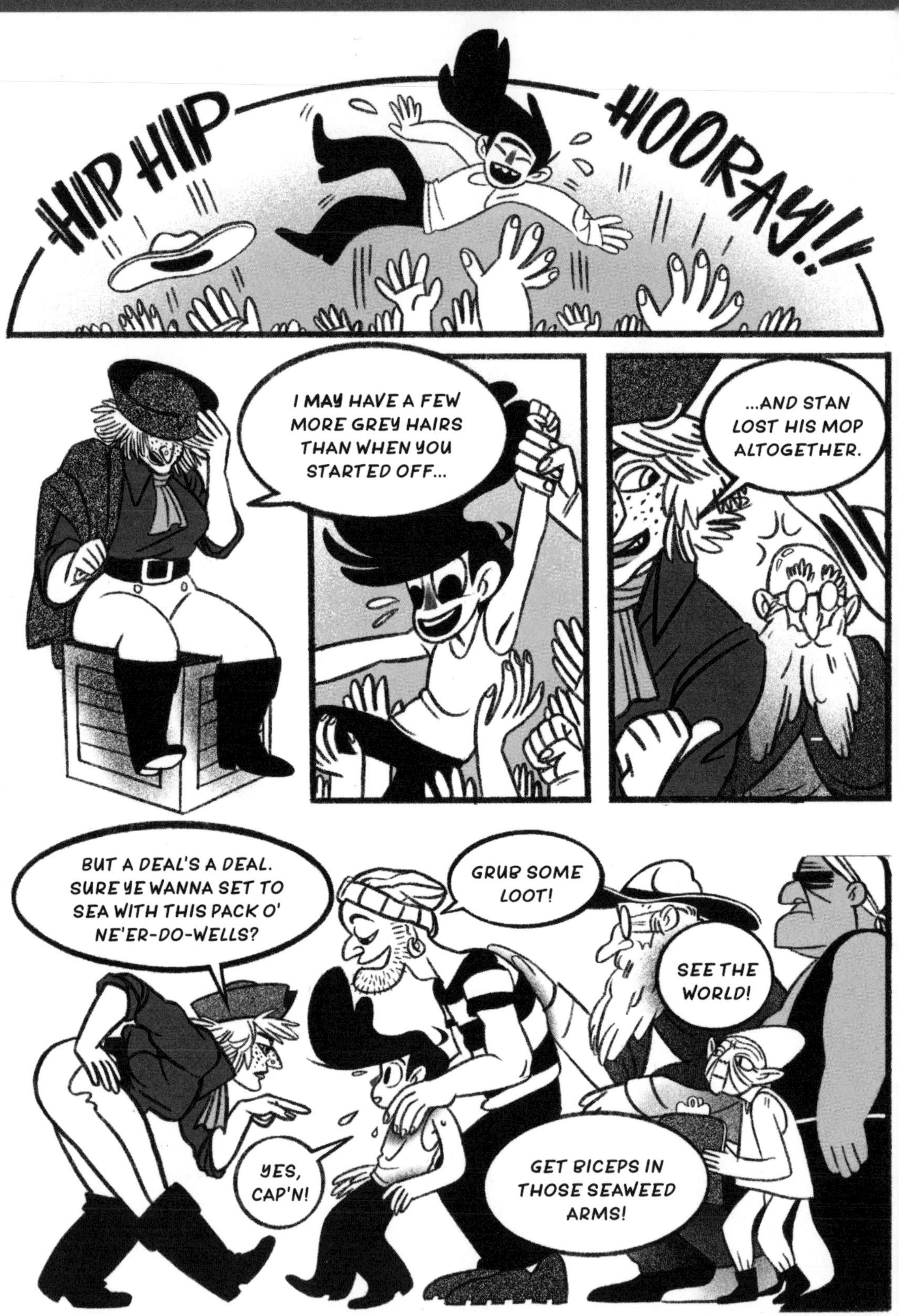
HIP HIP HOORAY!!!
I MAY HAVE A FEW MORE GREY HAIRS THAN WHEN YOU STARTED OFF...
...AND STAN LOST HIS MOP ALTOGETHER.
BUT A DEAL'S A DEAL. SURE YE WANNA SET TO SEA WITH THIS PACK O' NE'ER-DO-WELLS?
YES, CAP'N!
GRUB SOME LOOT!
SEE THE WORLD!
GET BICEPS IN THOSE SEAWEED ARMS!

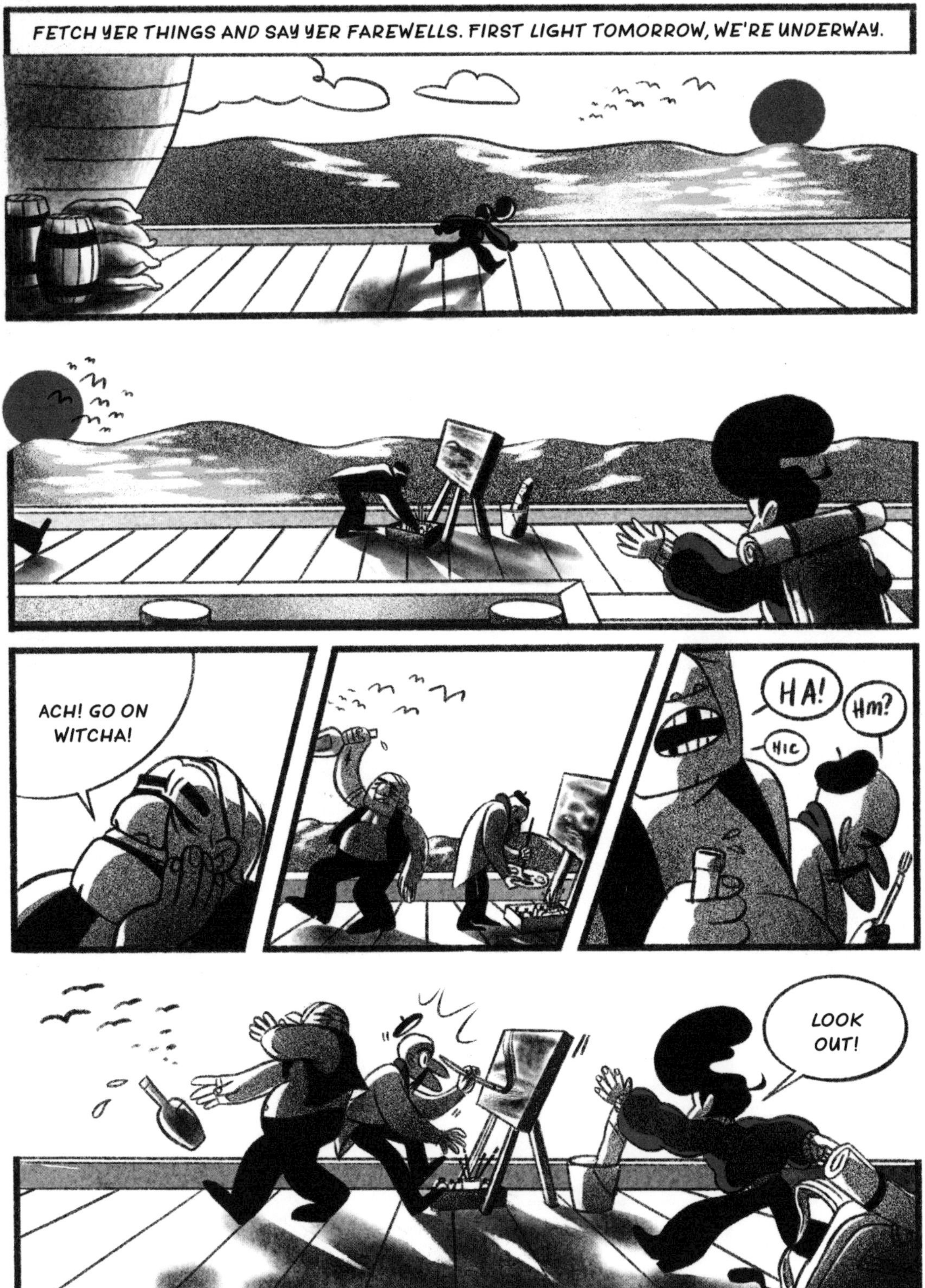
FETCH YER THINGS AND SAY YER FAREWELLS. FIRST LIGHT TOMORROW, WE'RE UNDERWAY.
ACH! GO ON WITCHA!
HA!
Hm?
HIC
LOOK OUT!

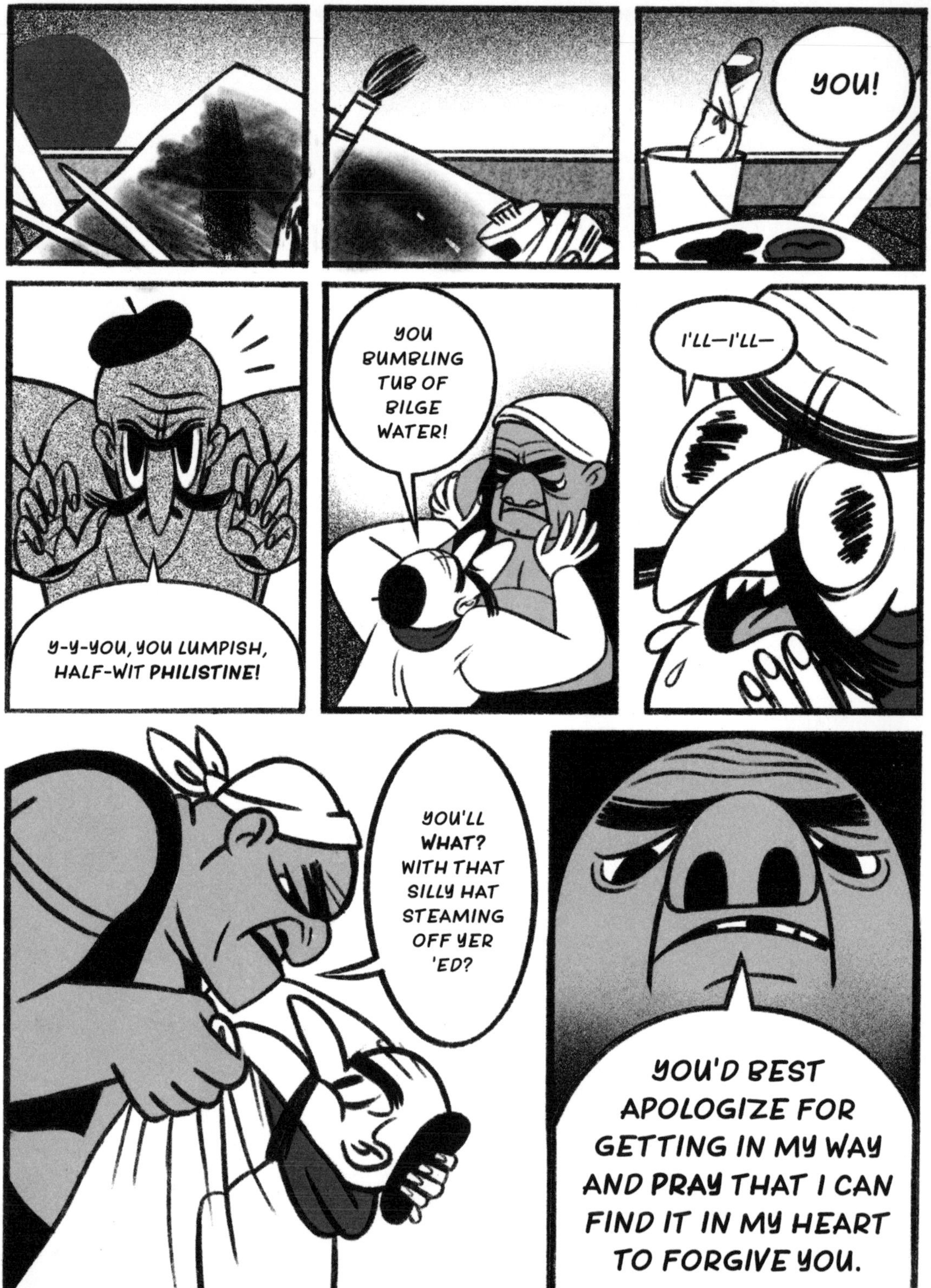
YOU!
Y-Y-YOU, YOU LUMPISH, HALF-WIT PHILISTINE!
YOU BUMBLING TUB OF BILGE WATER!
I'LL—I'LL—
YOU'LL WHAT? WITH THAT SILLY HAT STEAMING OFF YER 'ED?
YOU'D BEST APOLOGIZE FOR GETTING IN MY WAY AND PRAY THAT I CAN FIND IT IN MY HEART TO FORGIVE YOU.

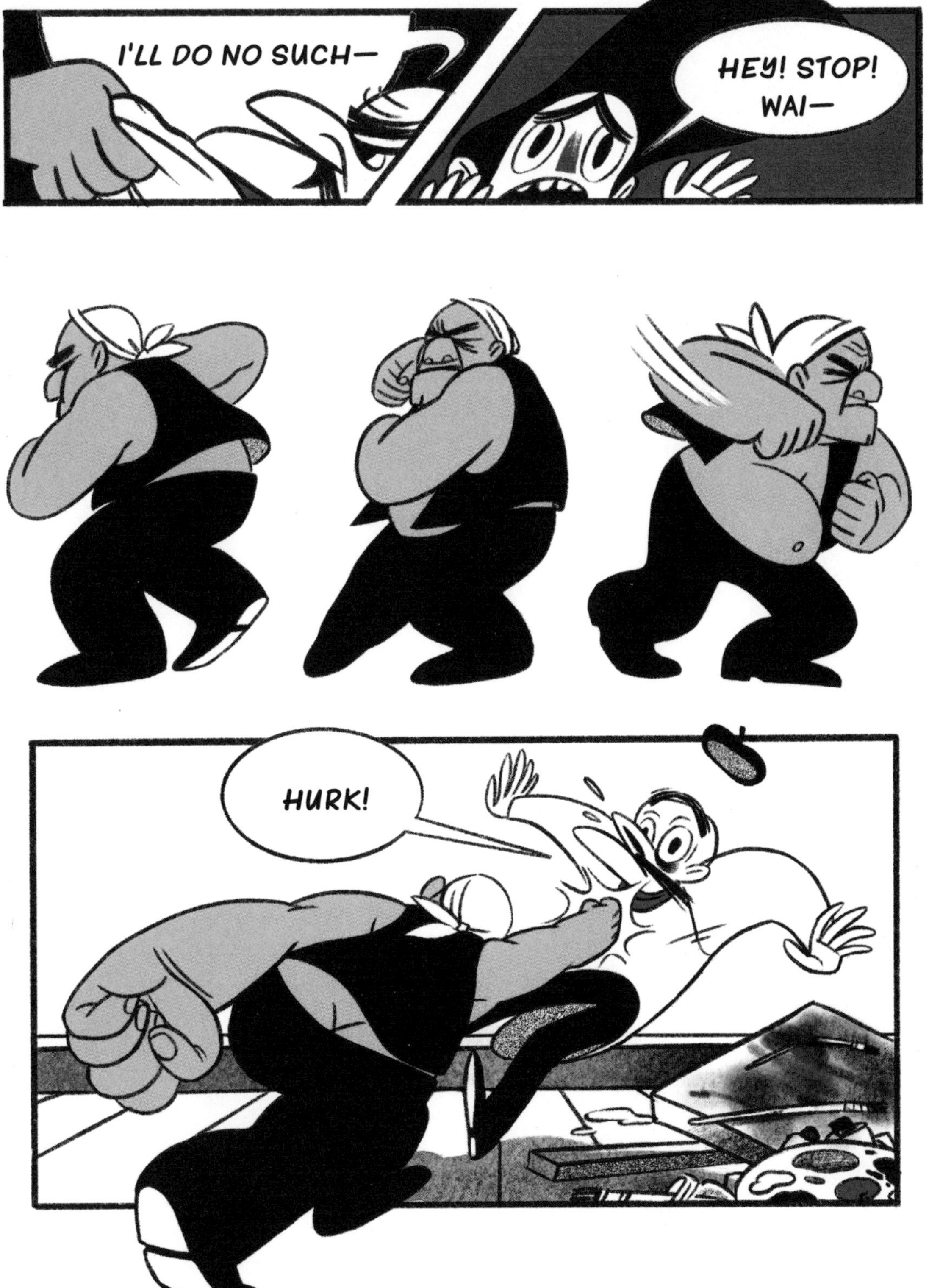
I'LL DO NO SUCH—
HEY! STOP! WAI—
HURK!

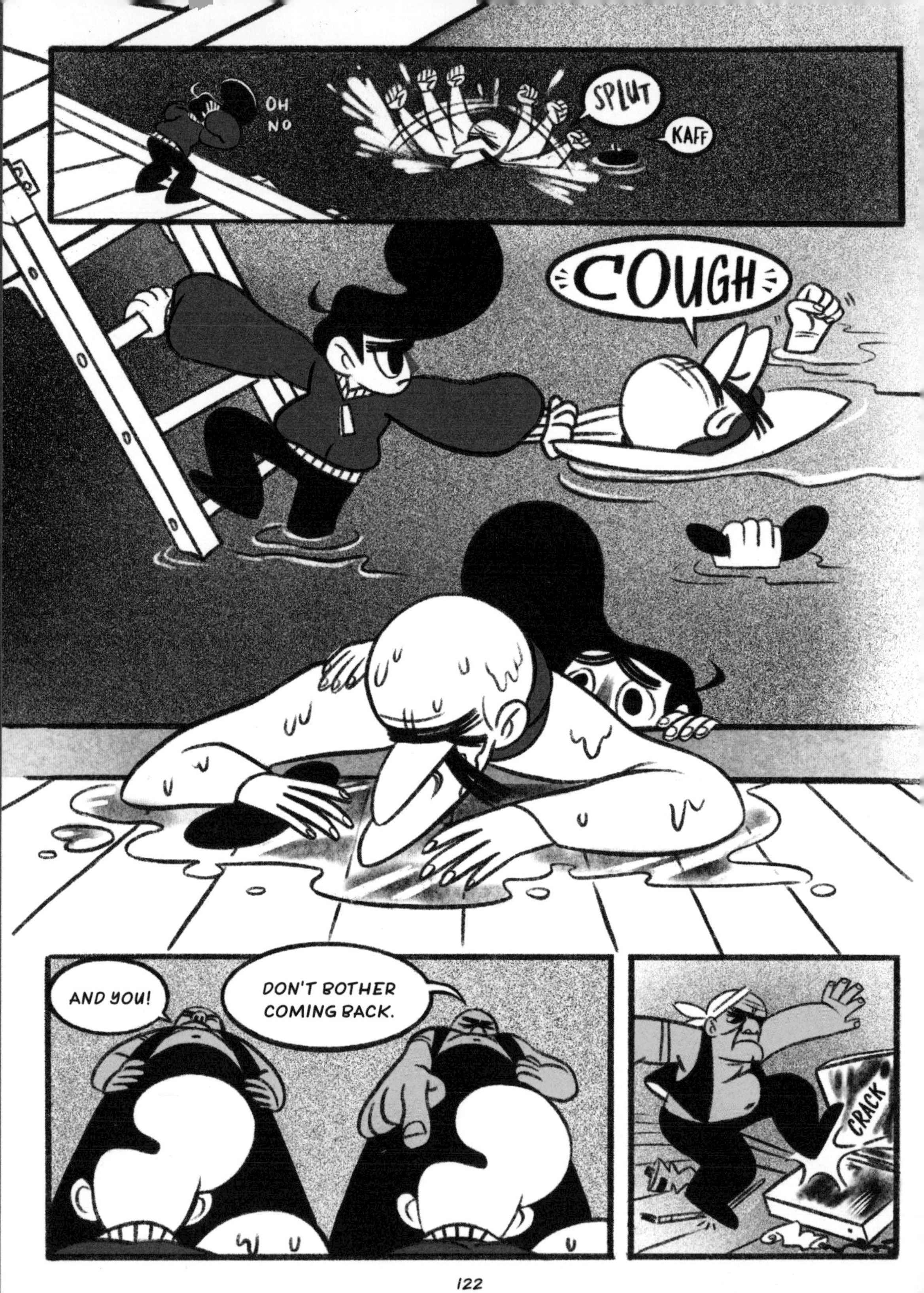

OH NO
SPLUT
KAFF
COUGH
AND YOU!
DON'T BOTHER COMING BACK.
CRACK

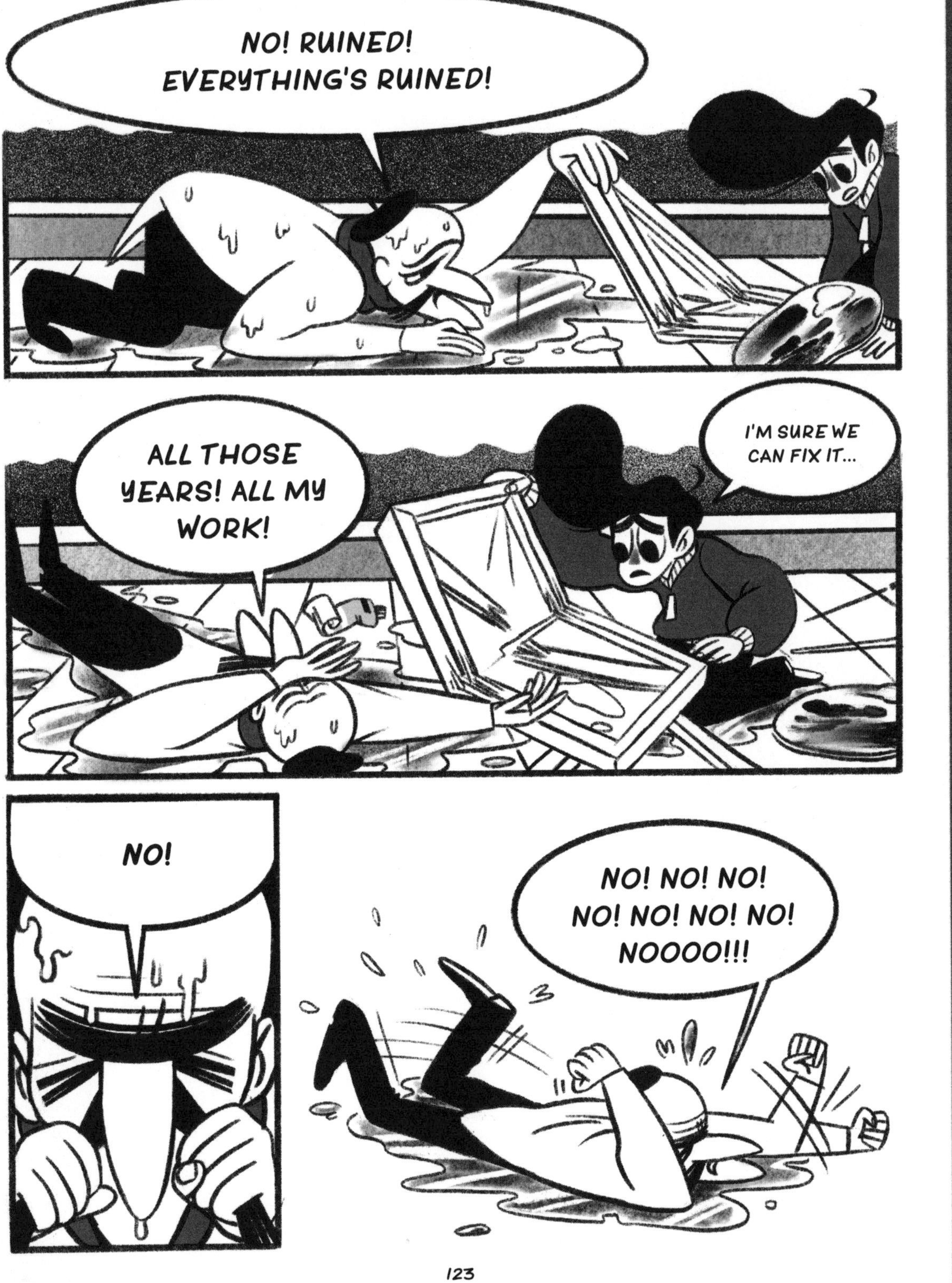
NO! RUINED!
EVERYTHING'S RUINED!
ALL THOSE YEARS! ALL MY WORK!
I'M SURE WE CAN FIX IT...
NO!
NO! NO! NO!
NO! NO! NO! NO!
NOOOO!!!

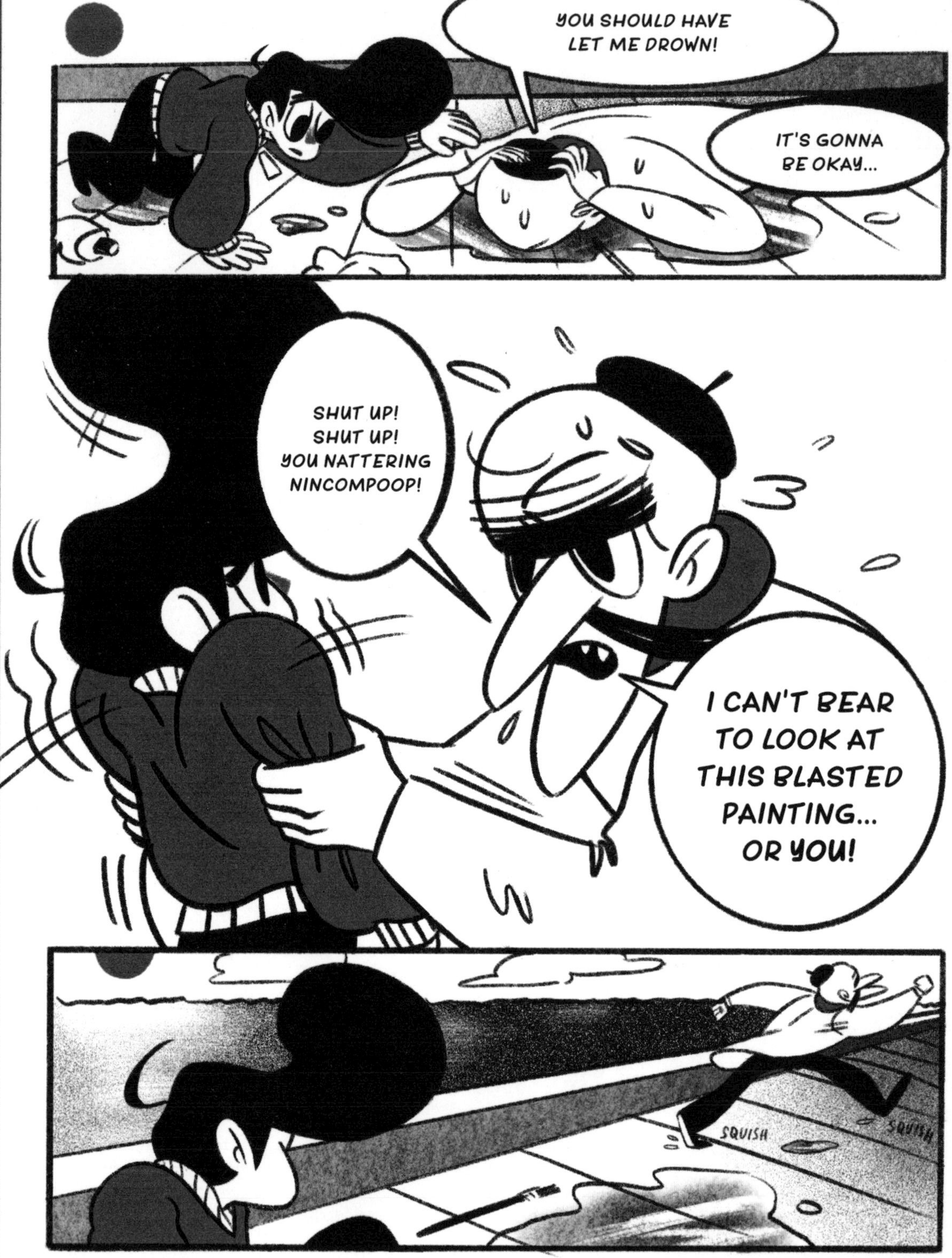

YOU SHOULD HAVE LET ME DROWN!
IT'S GONNA BE OKAY...
SHUT UP! SHUT UP! YOU NATTERING NINCOMPOOP!
I CAN'T BEAR TO LOOK AT THIS BLASTED PAINTING... OR YOU!
SQUISH
SQUISH

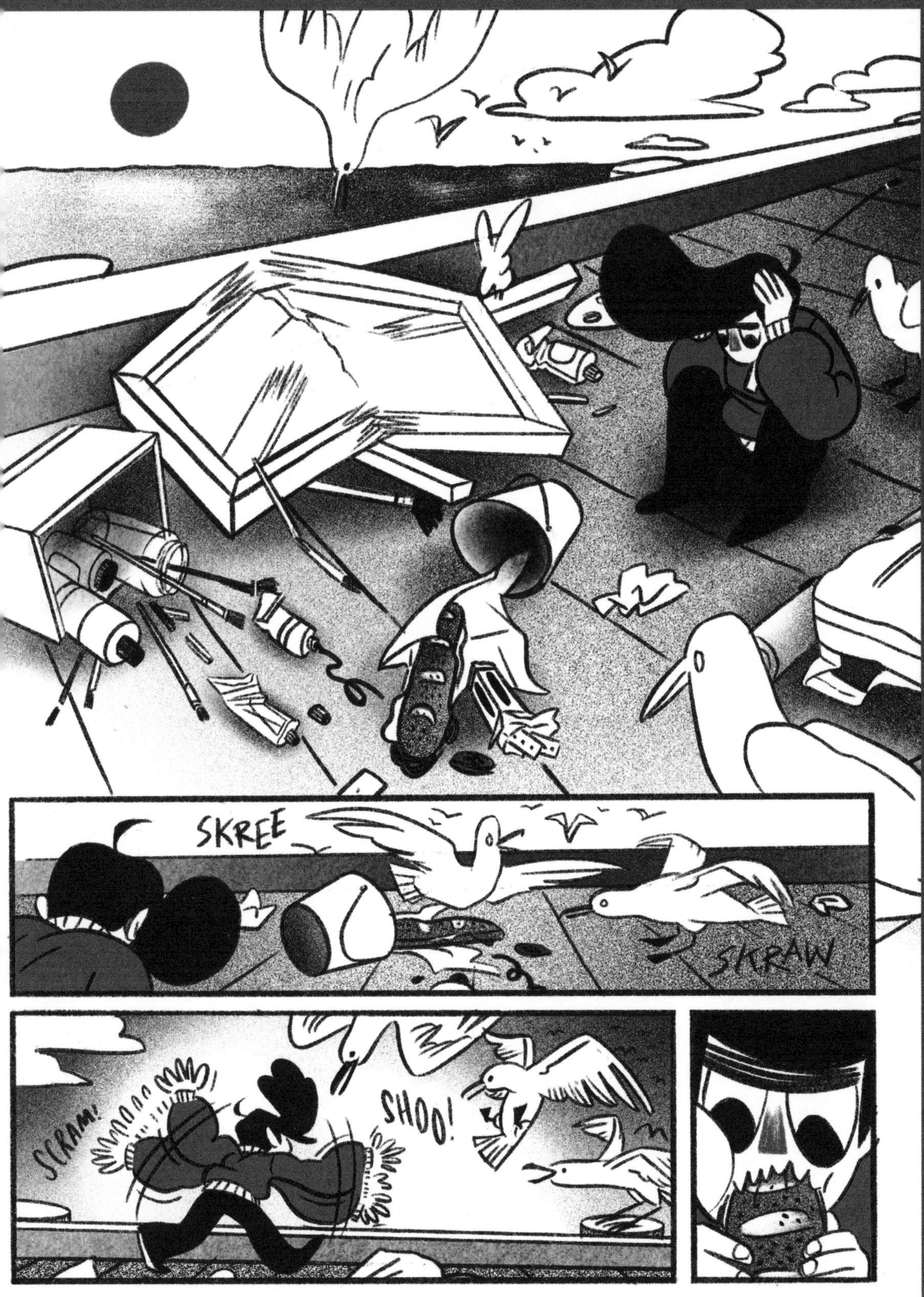
SKREE
SKRAW
SCRAM!
SHOO!

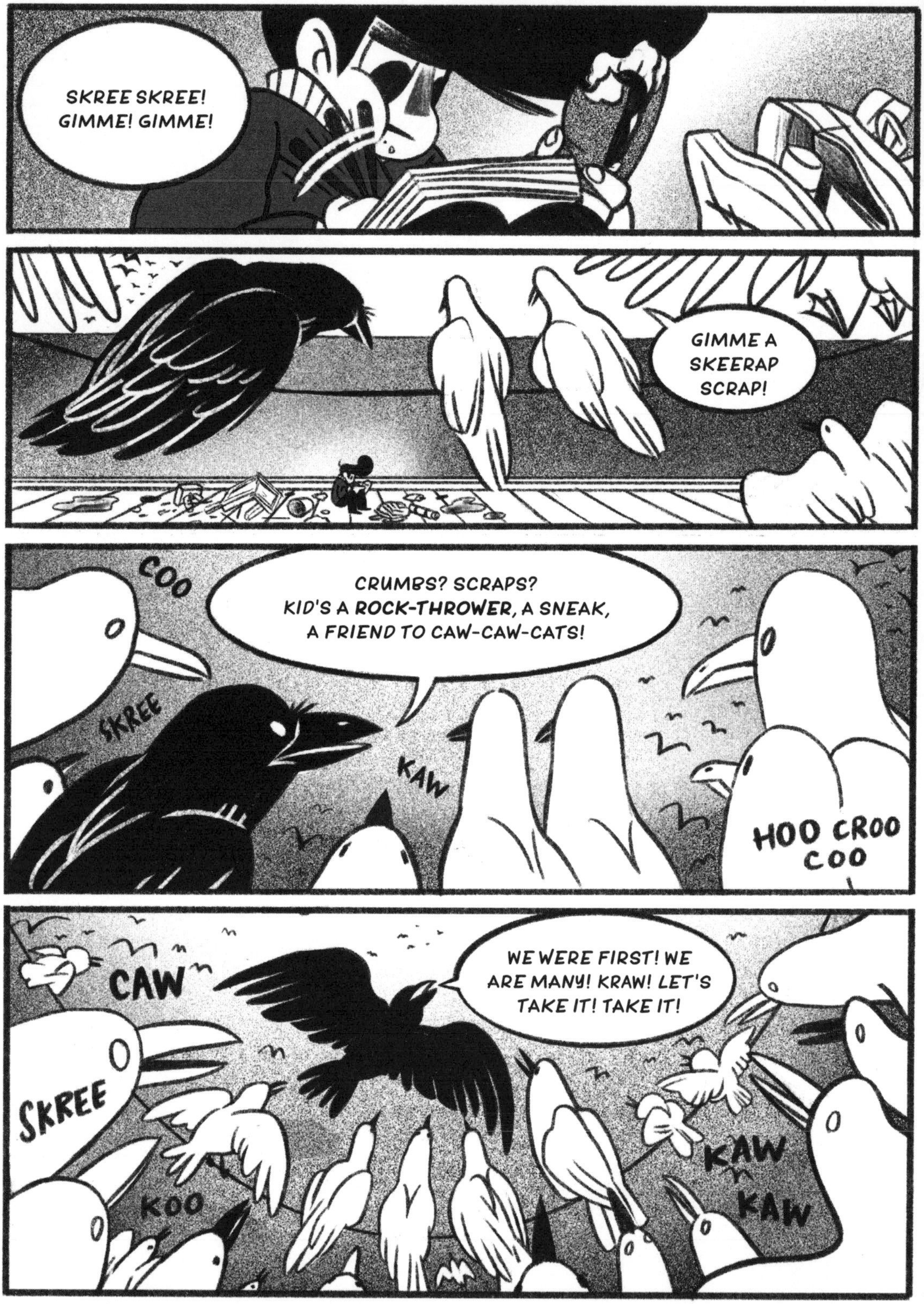
SKREE SKREE! GIMME! GIMME!
GIMME A SKEERAP SCRAP!
COO
CRUMBS? SCRAPS? KID'S A **ROCK-THROWER**, A SNEAK, A FRIEND TO CAW-CAW-CATS!
SKREE
KAW
HOO CROO COO
CAW
WE WERE FIRST! WE ARE MANY! KRAW! LET'S TAKE IT! TAKE IT!
SKREE
KOO
KAW
KAW

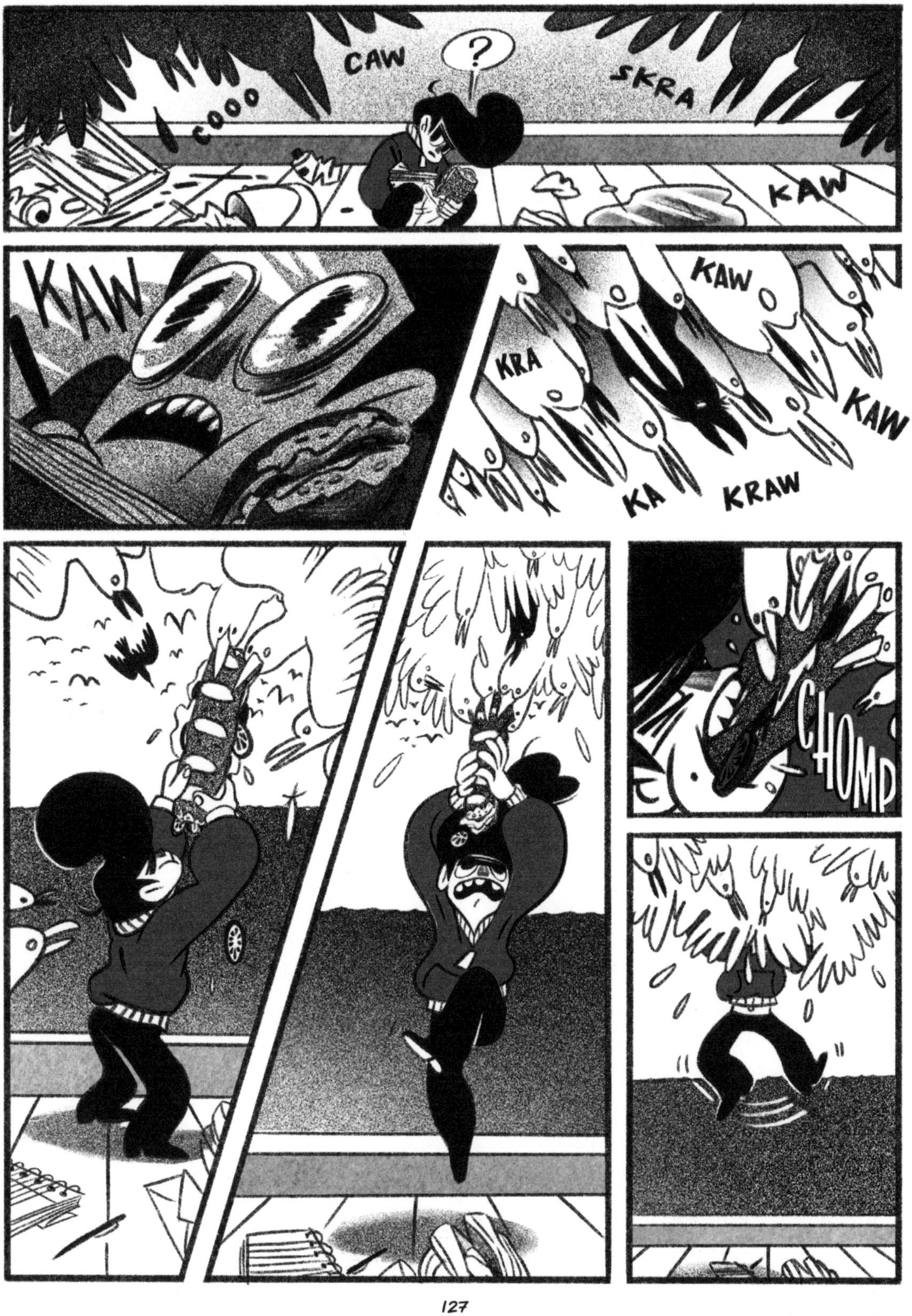
?
CAW
SKRA
COOO
KAW
KAW
KAW
KRA
KAW
KA
KRAW
CHOMP

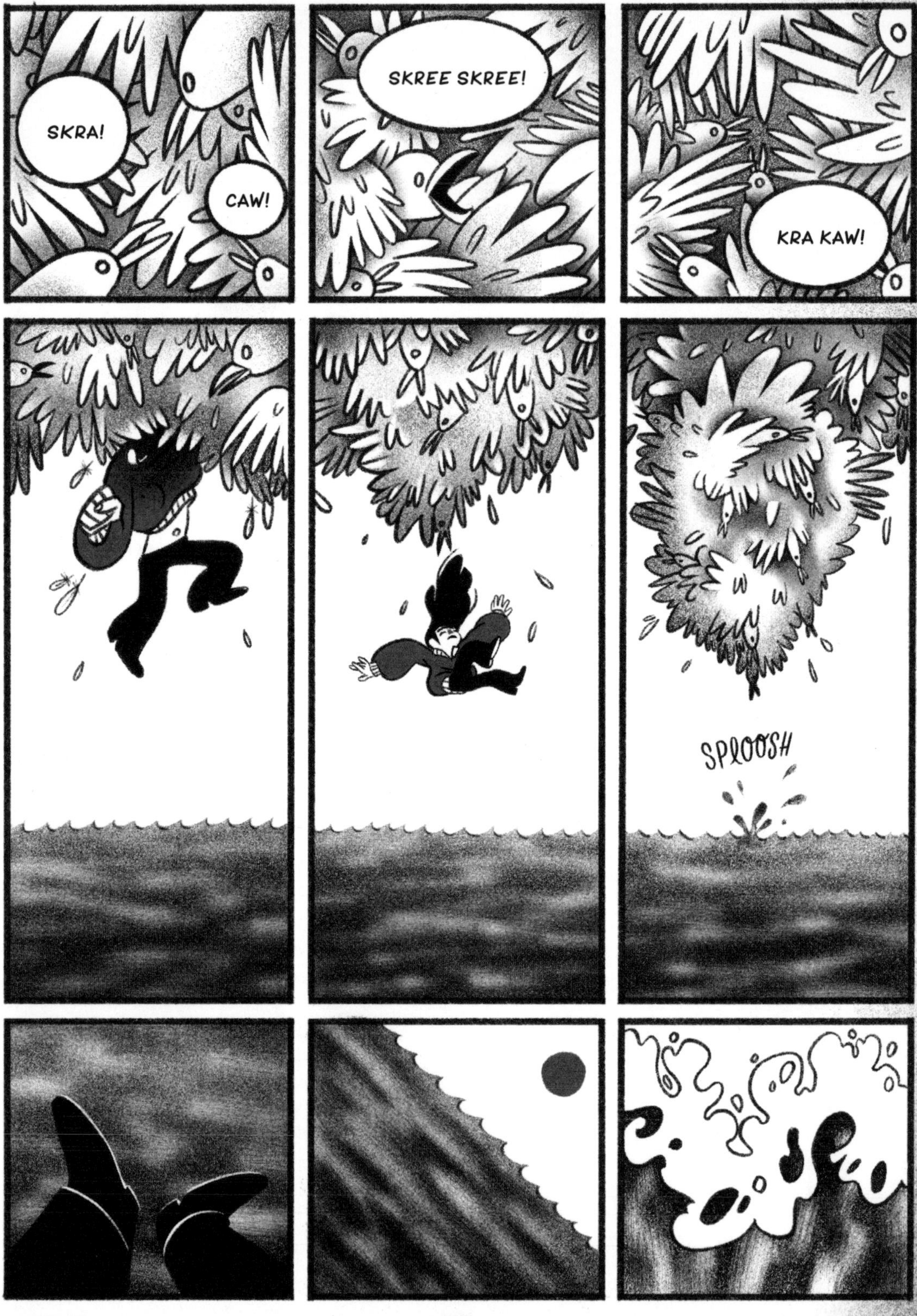
SKRA!
CAW!
SKREE SKREE!
KRA KAW!
SPLOOSH

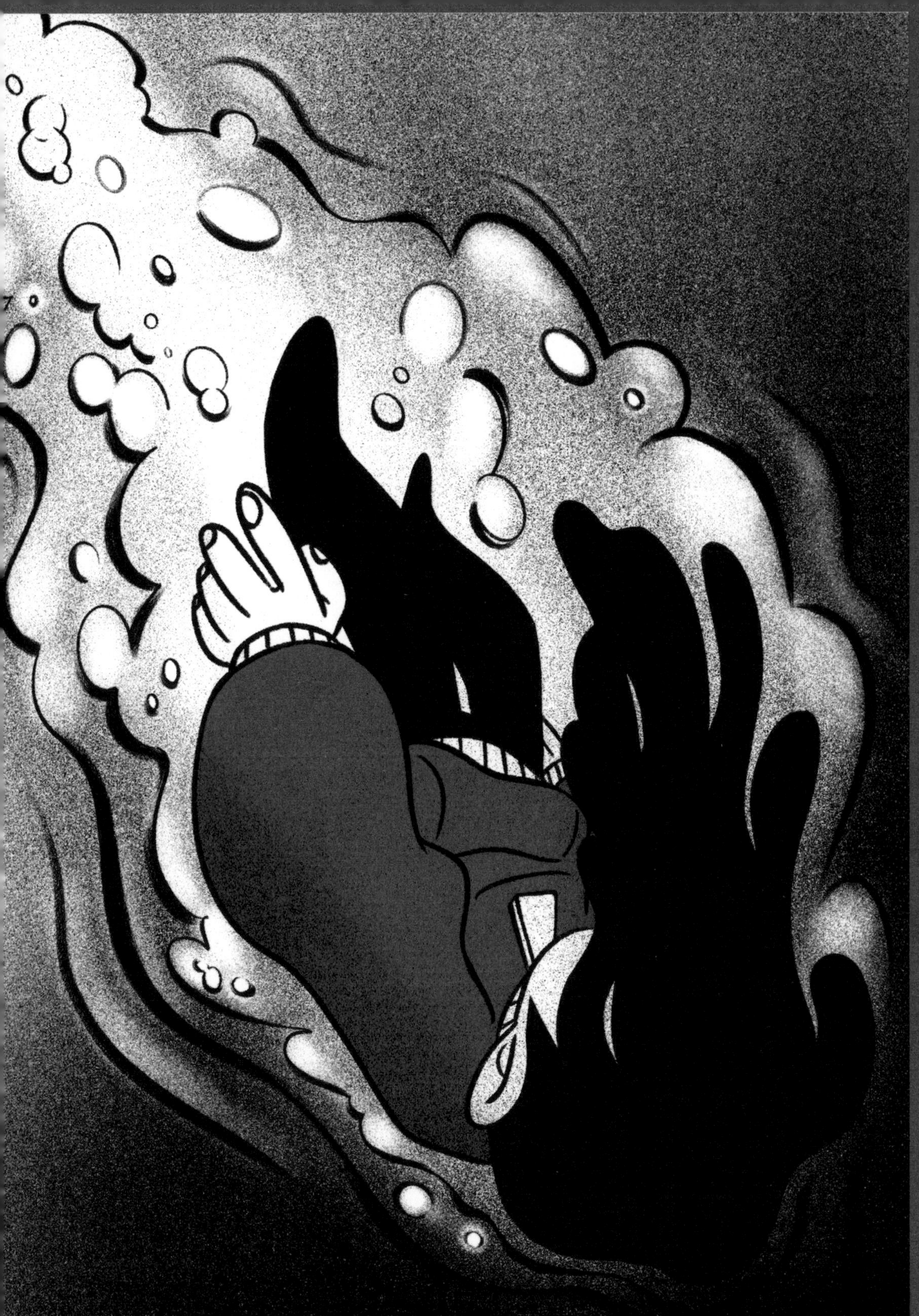

CHAPTER 5

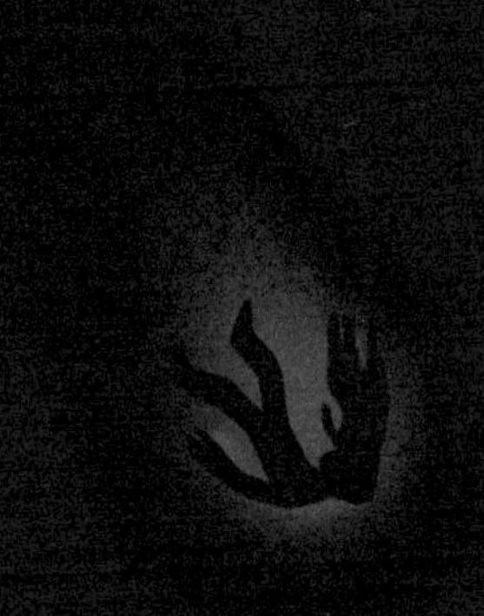

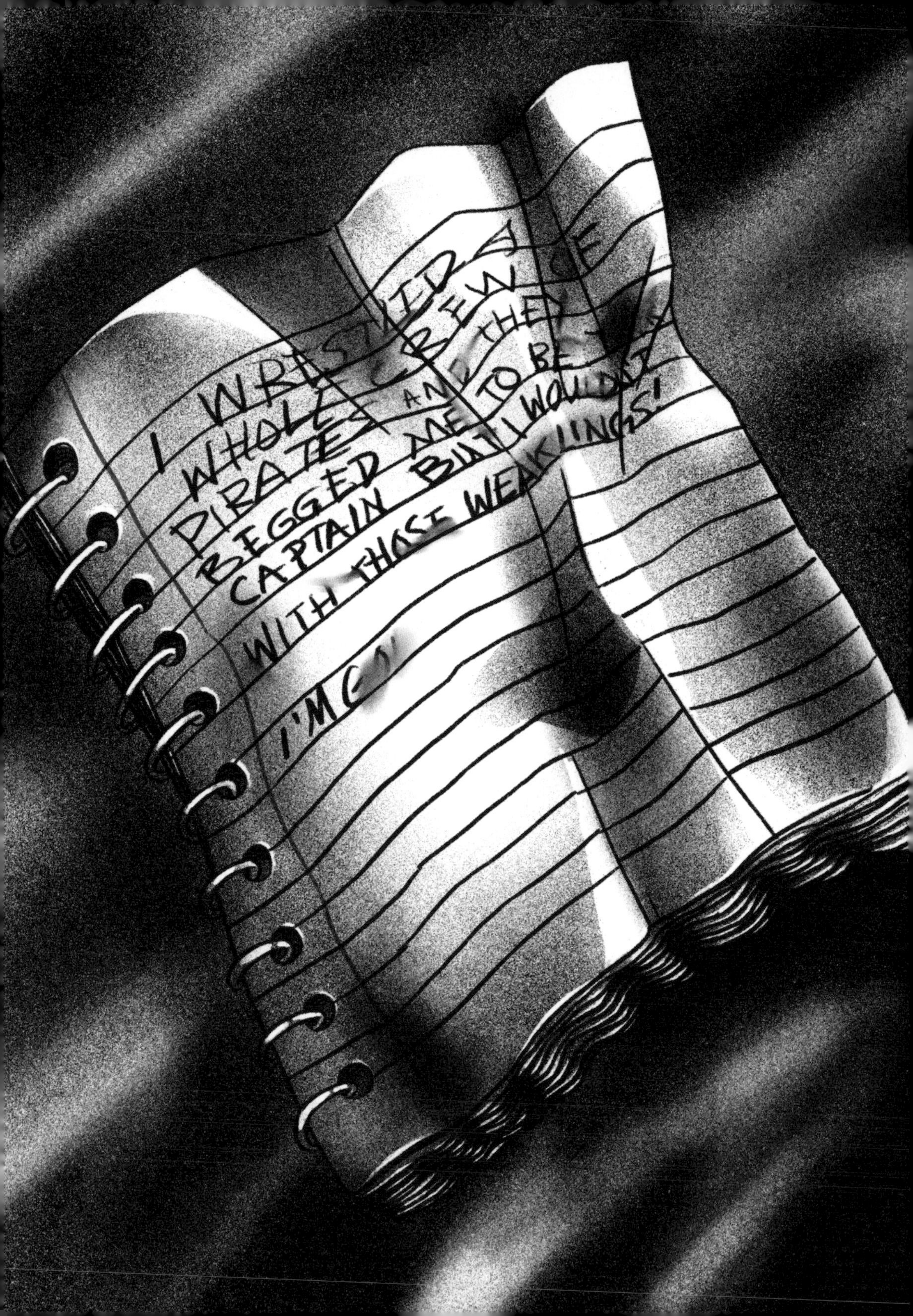
I WRESTLED A
WHOLE CREW
PIRATES AND THEY
BEGGED ME TO BE
CAPTAIN BUT I WOULDN'T
WITH THOSE WEAKLINGS!

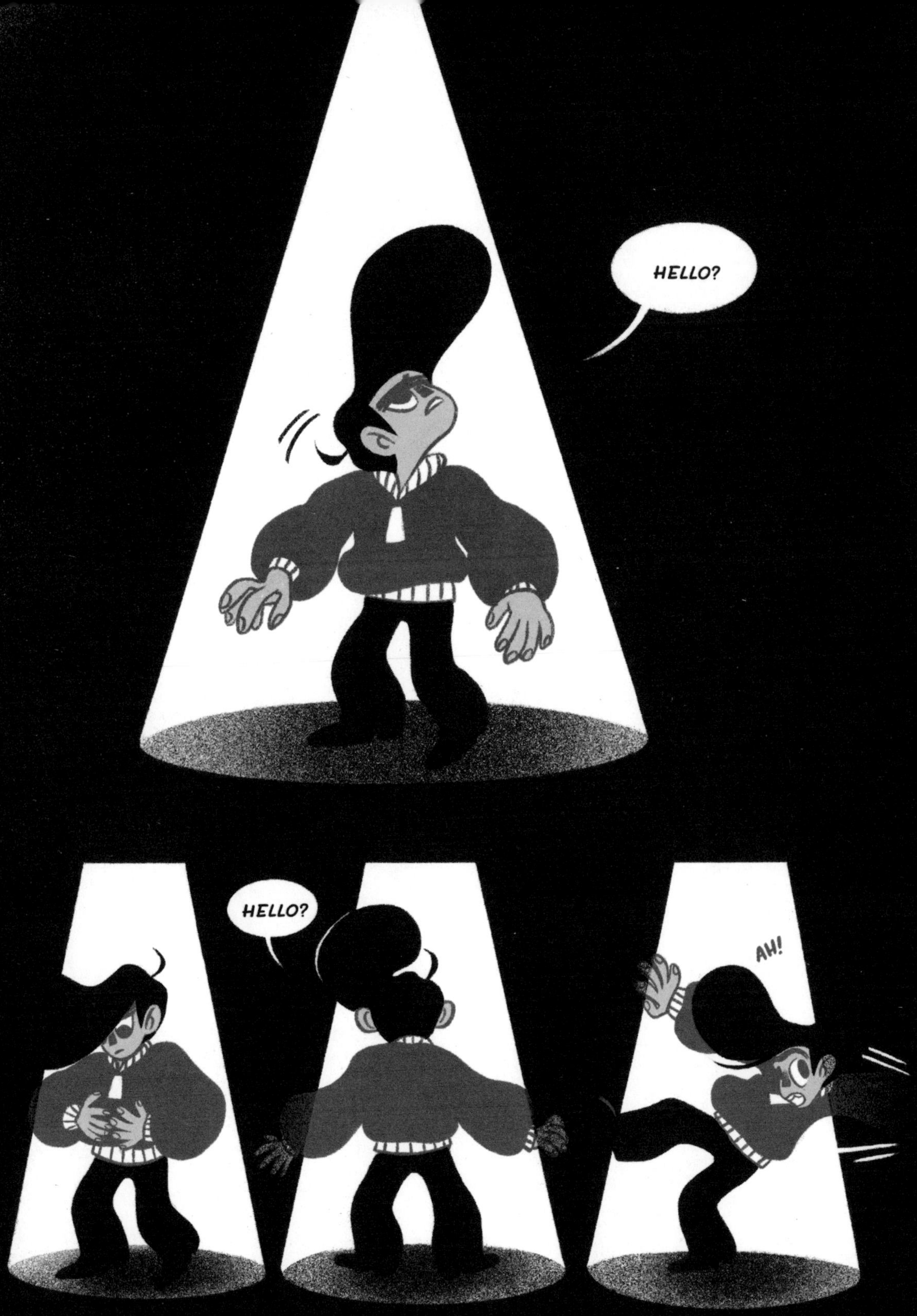
HELLO?
HELLO?
AH!

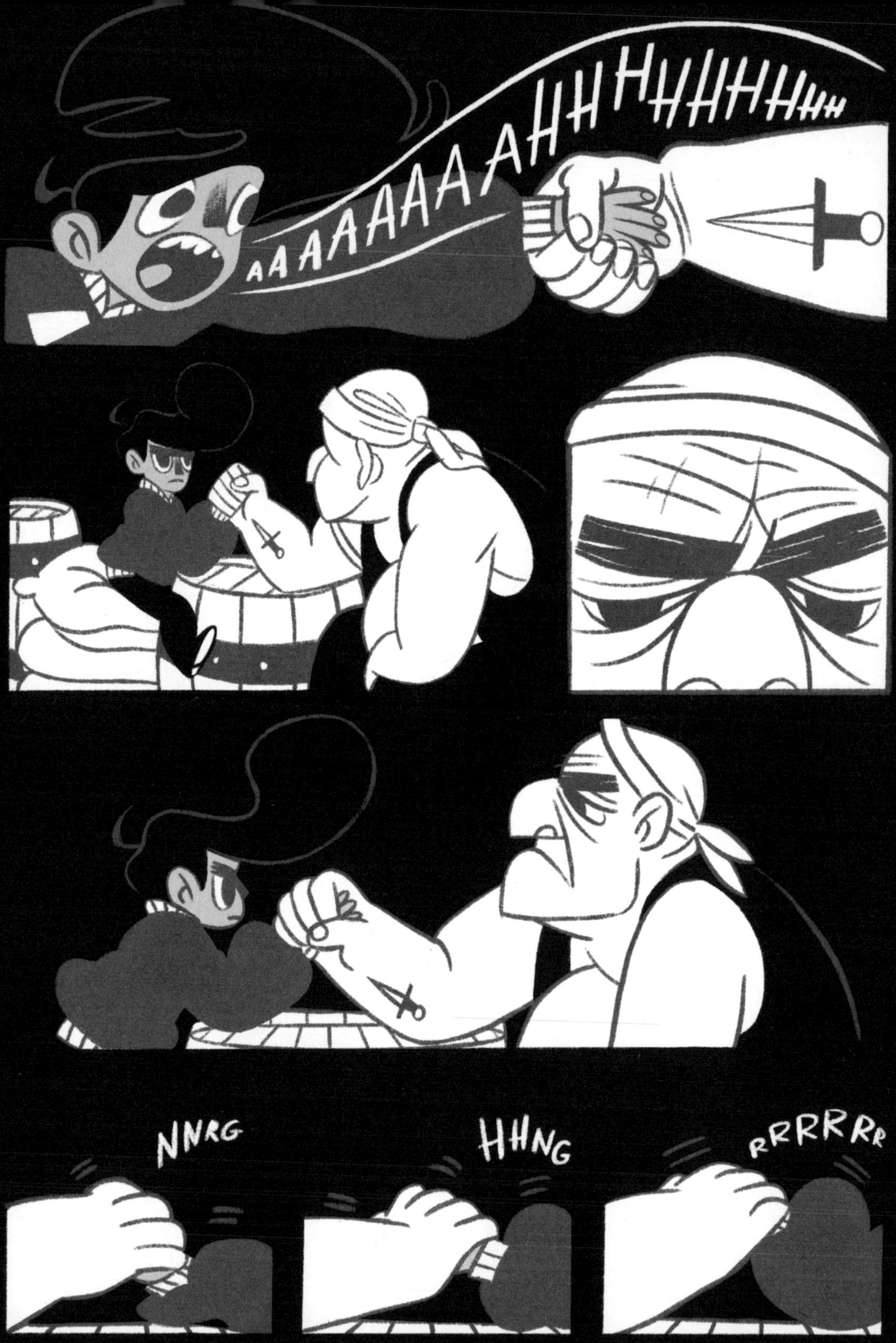
AAAAAAAAAAAHHHHHHHHHH
NNRG
HHNG
RRRRRR

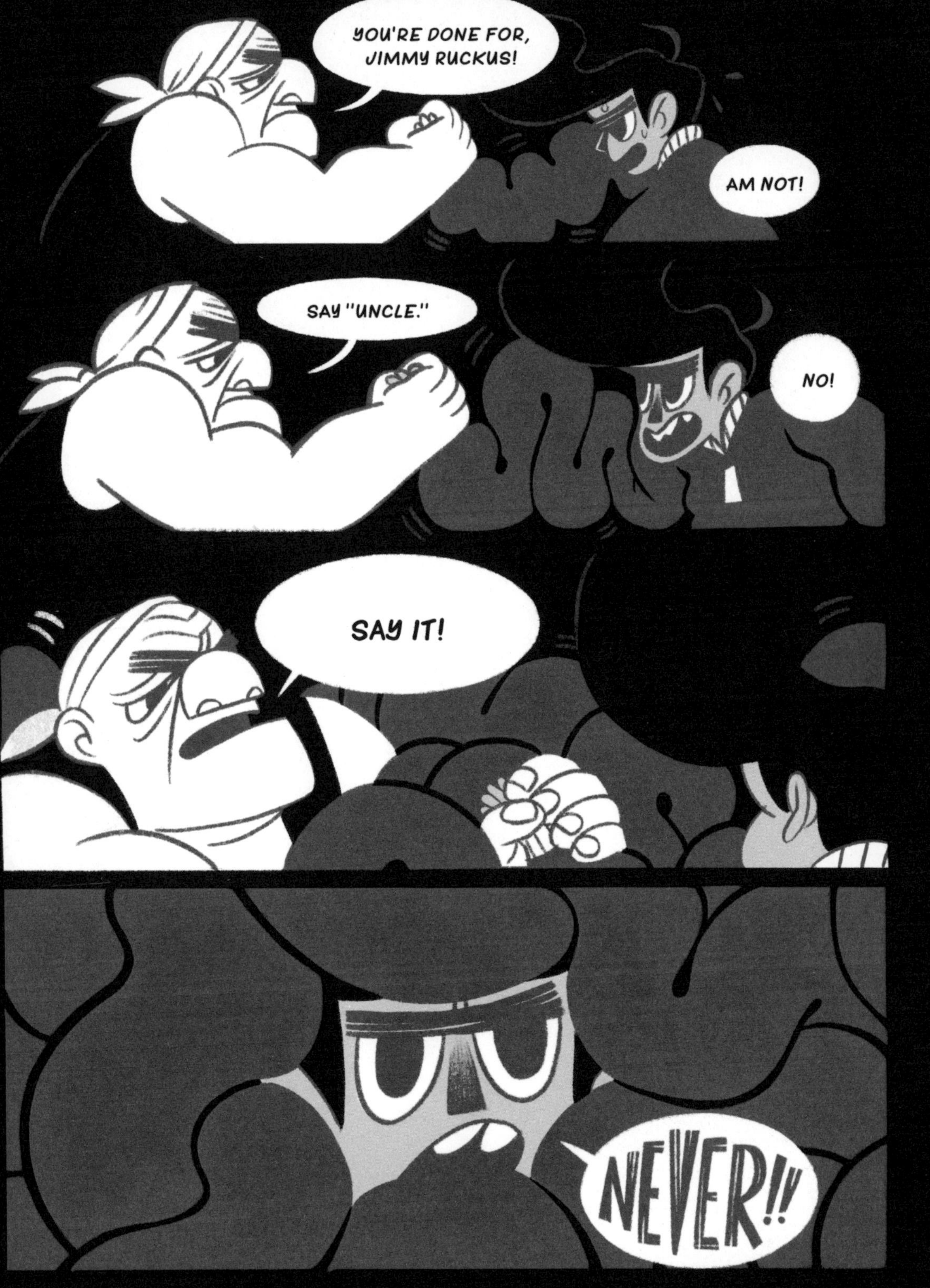
YOU'RE DONE FOR, JIMMY RUCKUS!
AM NOT!
SAY "UNCLE."
NO!
SAY IT!
NEVER!!

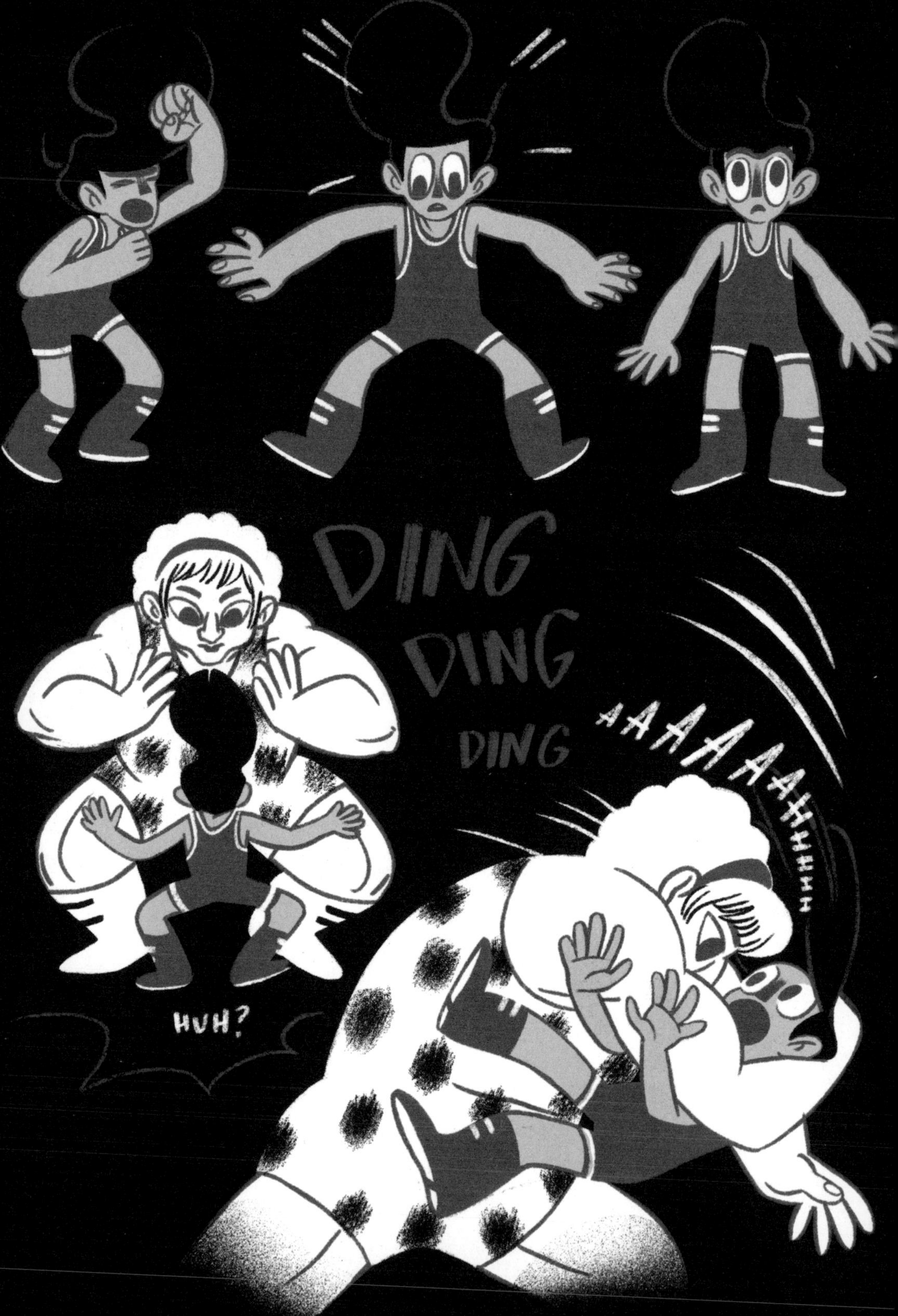
DING
DING
DING
AAAAAAAHHHHHH
HUH?

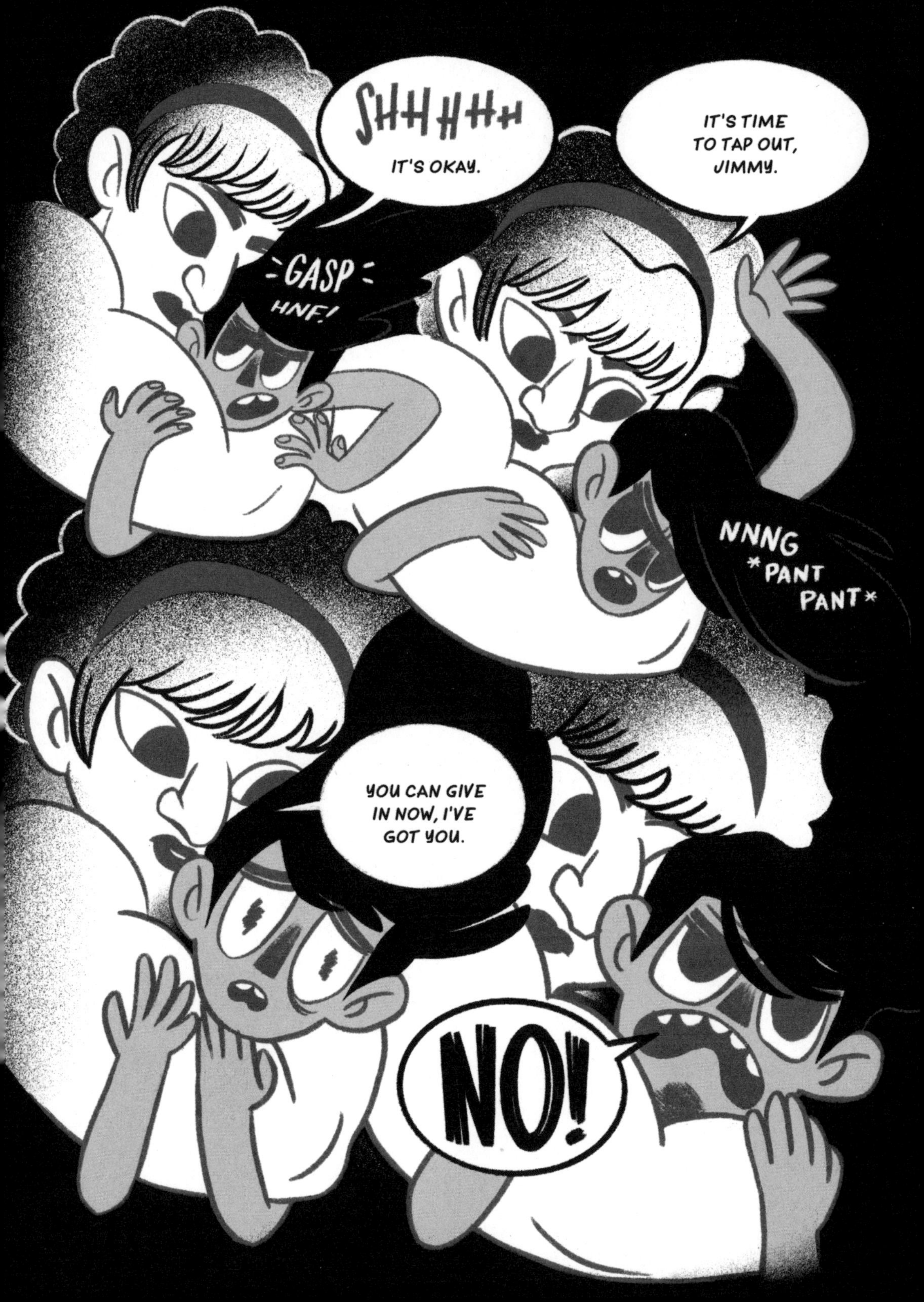
SHHHHH
IT'S OKAY.
IT'S TIME TO TAP OUT, JIMMY.
GASP
HNF!
NNNG
PANT PANT
YOU CAN GIVE IN NOW, I'VE GOT YOU.
NO!

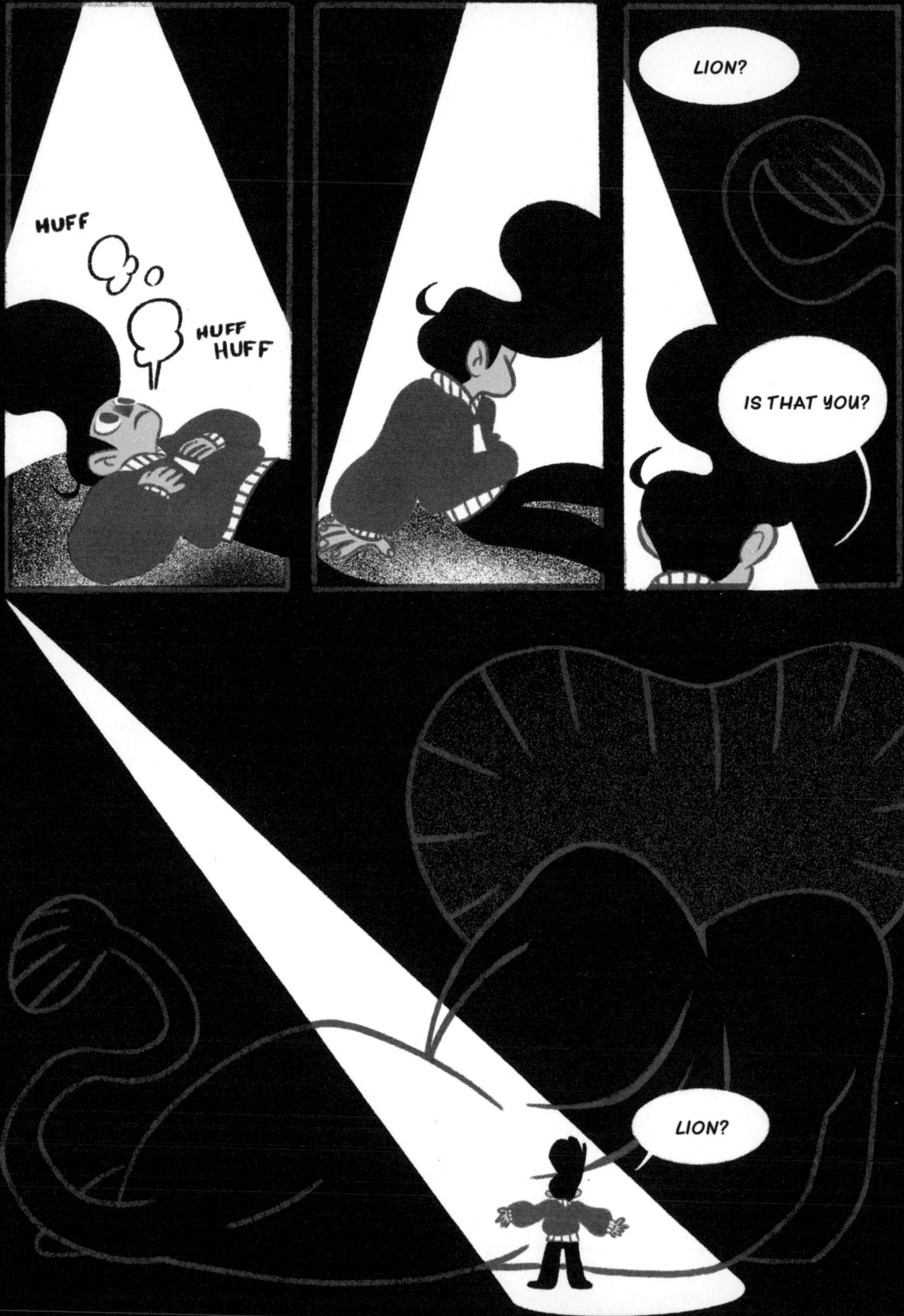
HUFF
HUFF
HUFF
LION?
IS THAT YOU?
LION?

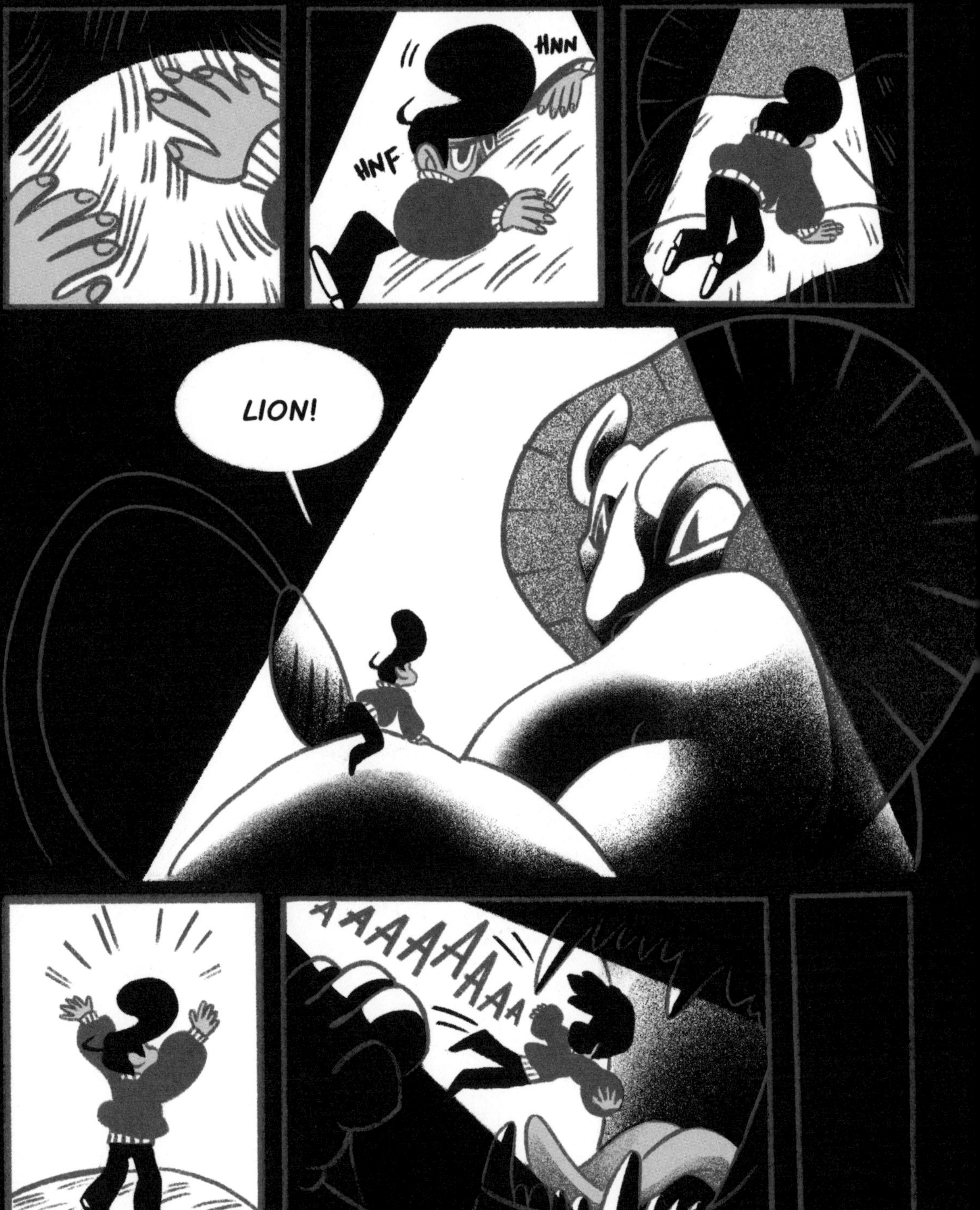
HNN
HNF
LION!
AAAAAAAAAAA

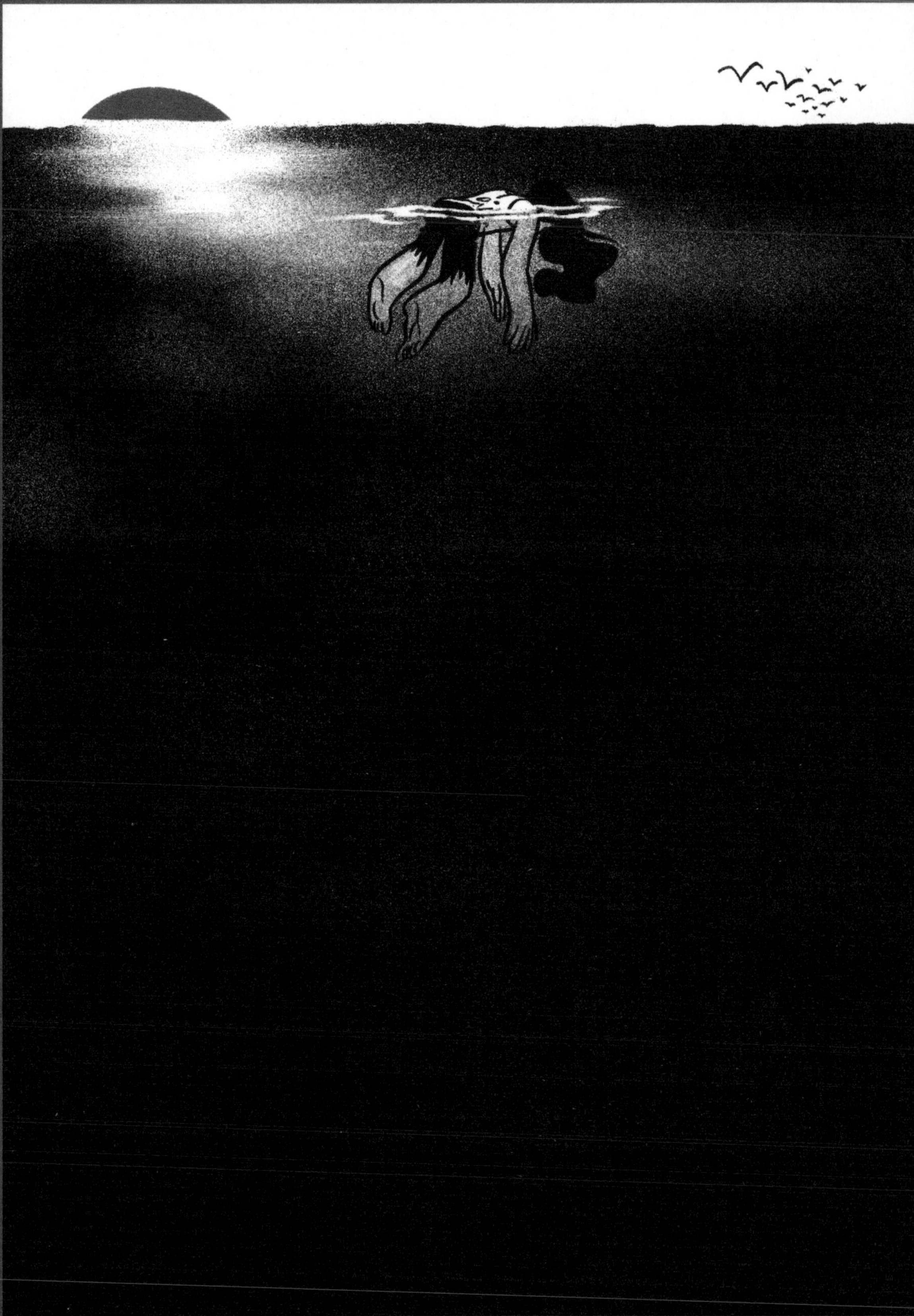

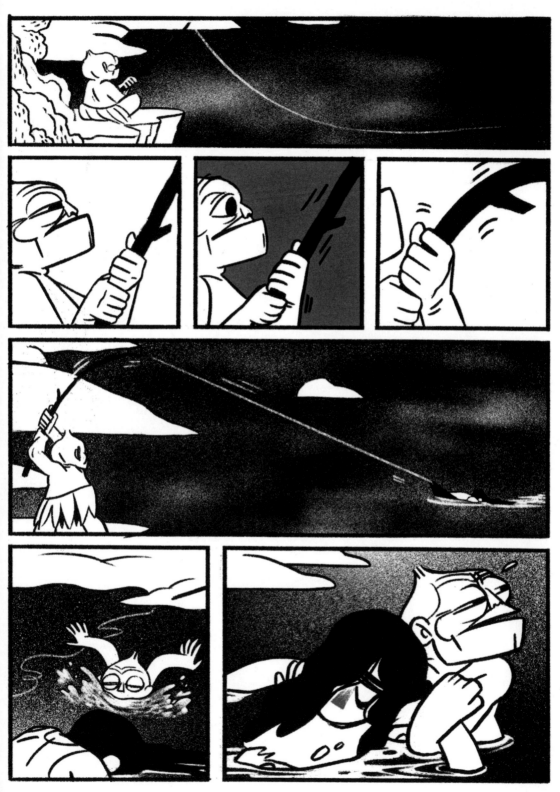

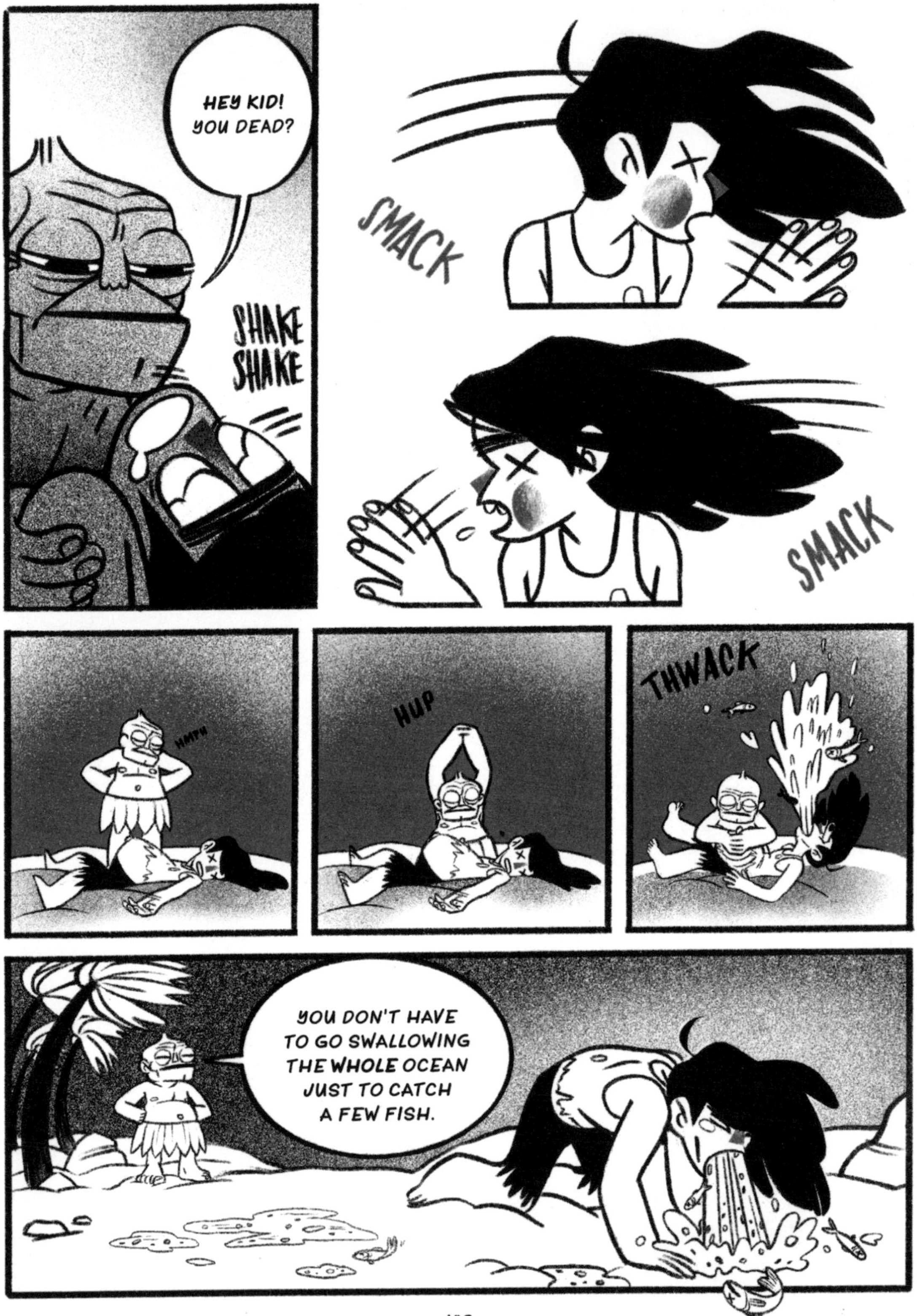
HEY KID! YOU DEAD?
SHAKE SHAKE
SMACK
SMACK
HMPH
HUP
THWACK
YOU DON'T HAVE TO GO SWALLOWING THE WHOLE OCEAN JUST TO CATCH A FEW FISH.

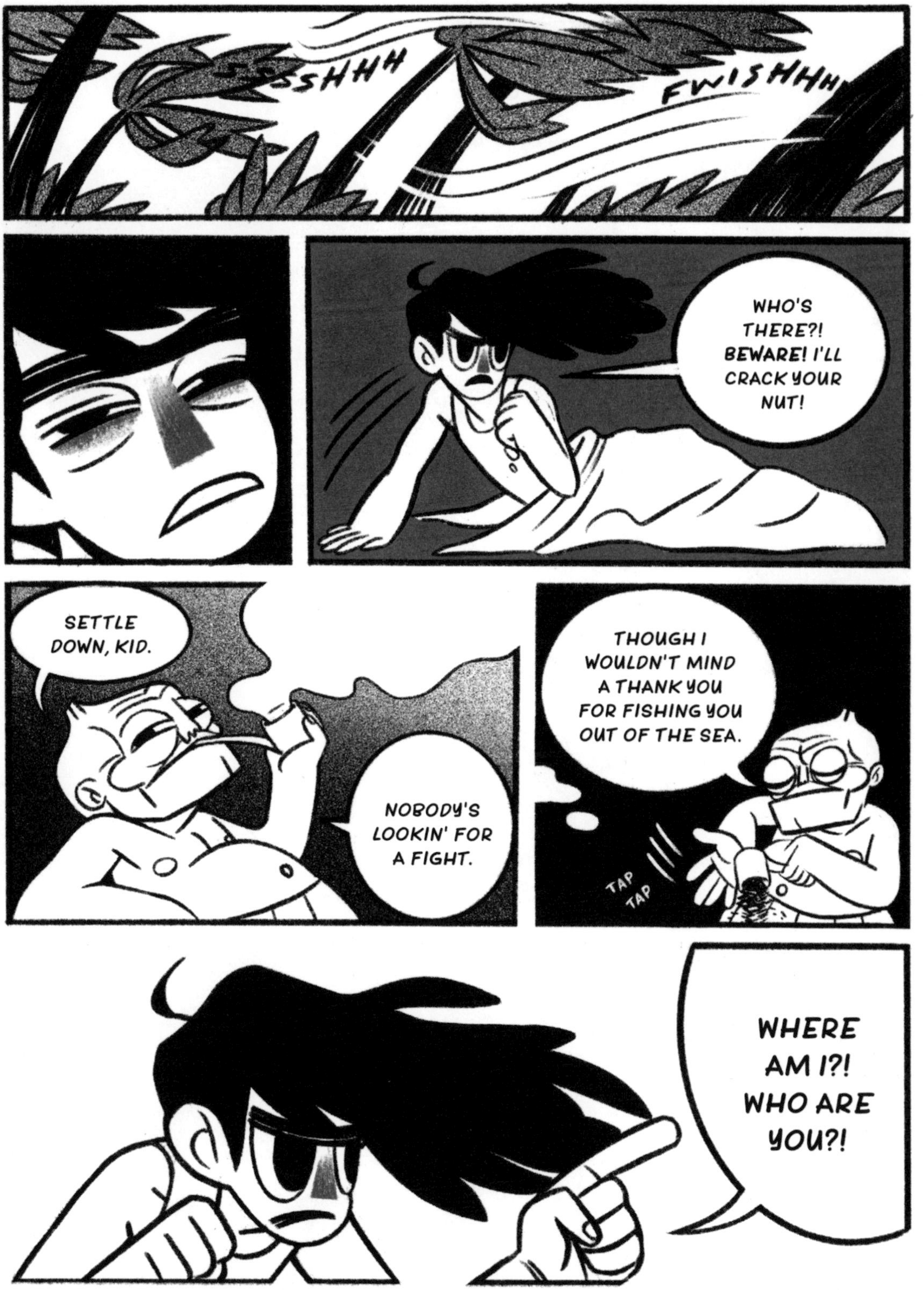
SSSSHHH
FWISHHH
WHO'S THERE?! BEWARE! I'LL CRACK YOUR NUT!
SETTLE DOWN, KID.
NOBODY'S LOOKIN' FOR A FIGHT.
THOUGH I WOULDN'T MIND A THANK YOU FOR FISHING YOU OUT OF THE SEA.
TAP TAP
WHERE AM I?! WHO ARE YOU?!

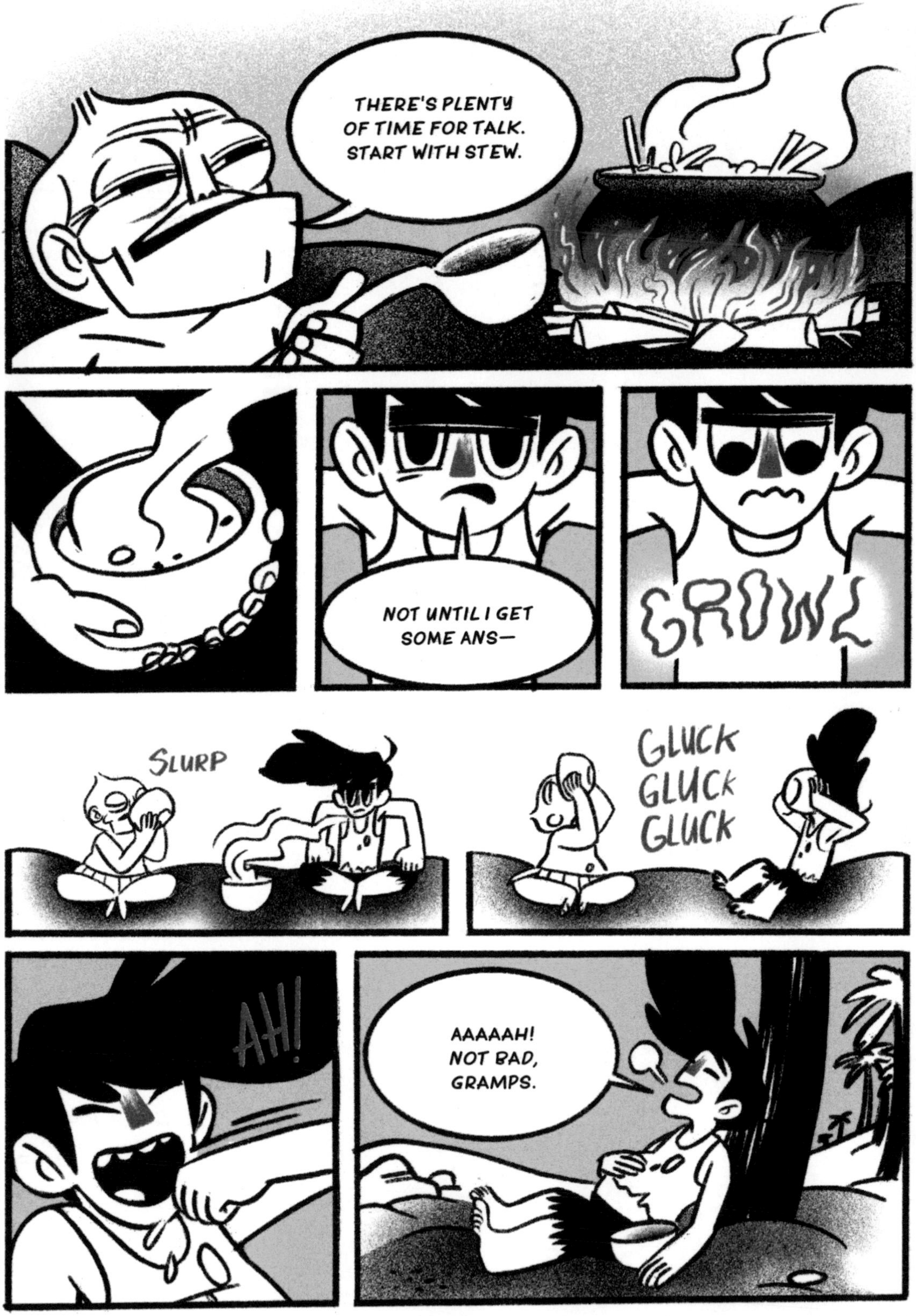
THERE'S PLENTY OF TIME FOR TALK. START WITH STEW.
NOT UNTIL I GET SOME ANS—
GROWL
SLURP
GLUCK
GLUCK
GLUCK
AH!
AAAAAH! NOT BAD, GRAMPS.

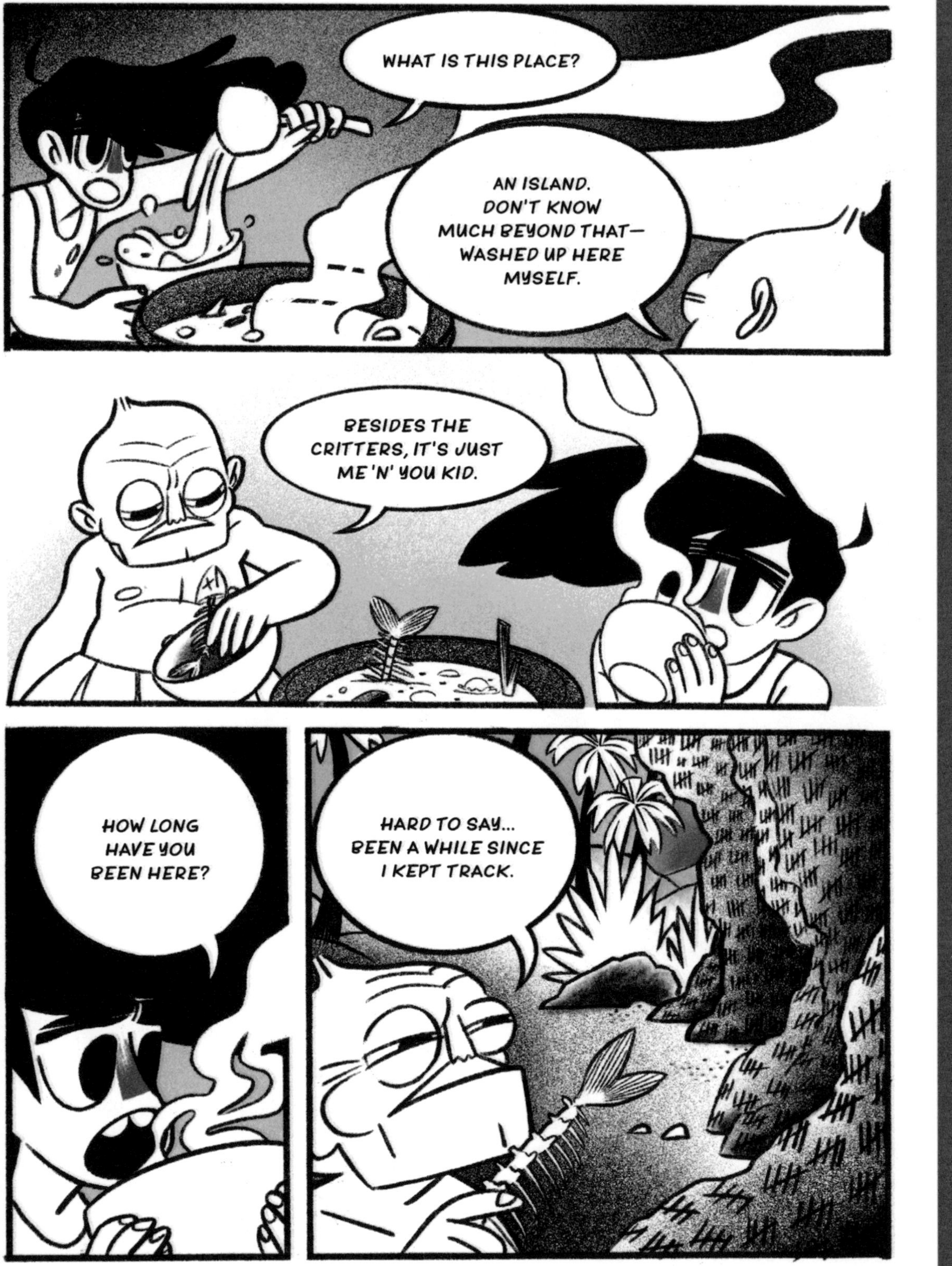
WHAT IS THIS PLACE?
AN ISLAND. DON'T KNOW MUCH BEYOND THAT— WASHED UP HERE MYSELF.
BESIDES THE CRITTERS, IT'S JUST ME 'N' YOU KID.
HOW LONG HAVE YOU BEEN HERE?
HARD TO SAY... BEEN A WHILE SINCE I KEPT TRACK.

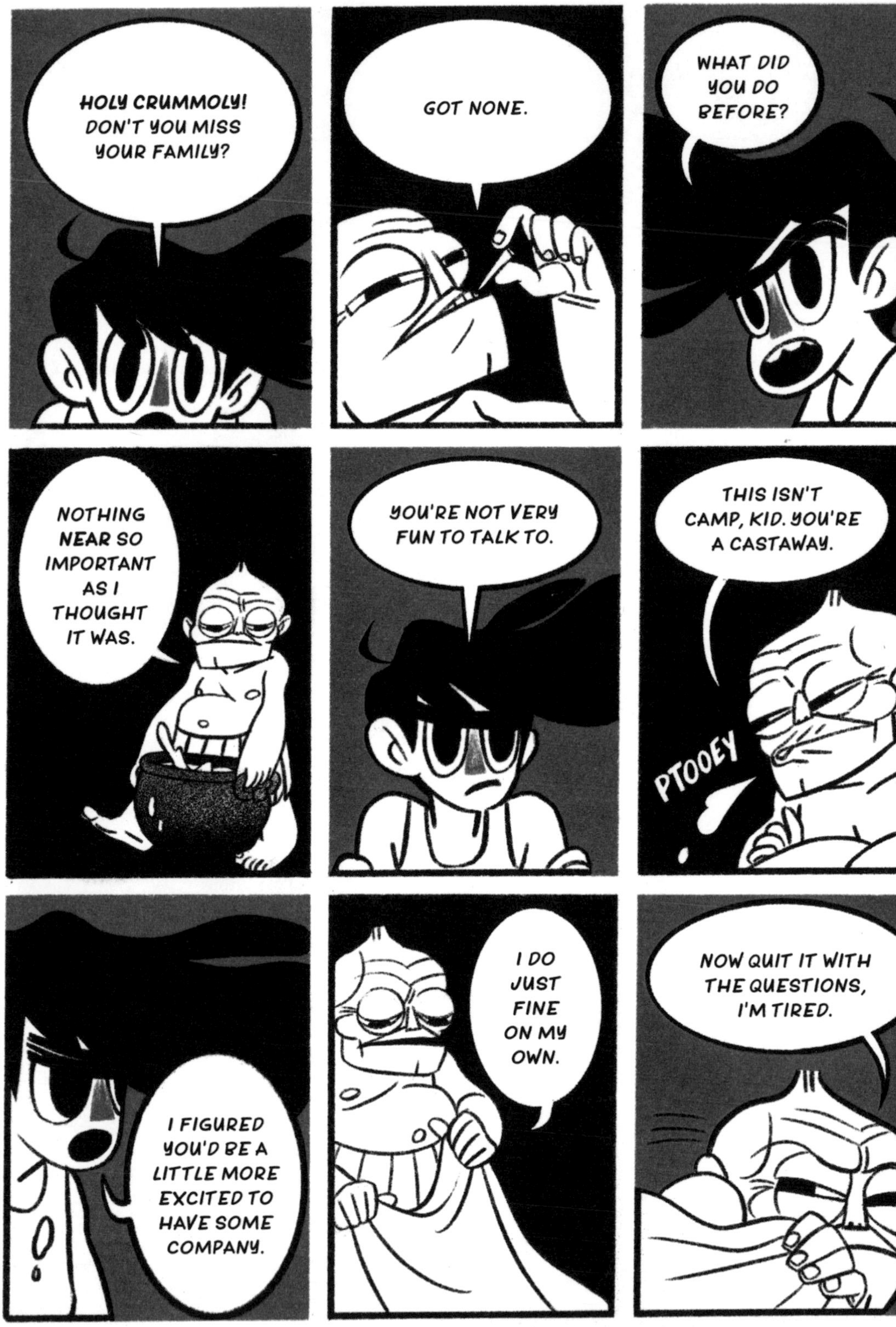

HOLY CRUMMOLY! DON'T YOU MISS YOUR FAMILY?
GOT NONE.
WHAT DID YOU DO BEFORE?
NOTHING NEAR SO IMPORTANT AS I THOUGHT IT WAS.
YOU'RE NOT VERY FUN TO TALK TO.
THIS ISN'T CAMP, KID. YOU'RE A CASTAWAY.
PTOOEY
I FIGURED YOU'D BE A LITTLE MORE EXCITED TO HAVE SOME COMPANY.
I DO JUST FINE ON MY OWN.
NOW QUIT IT WITH THE QUESTIONS, I'M TIRED.

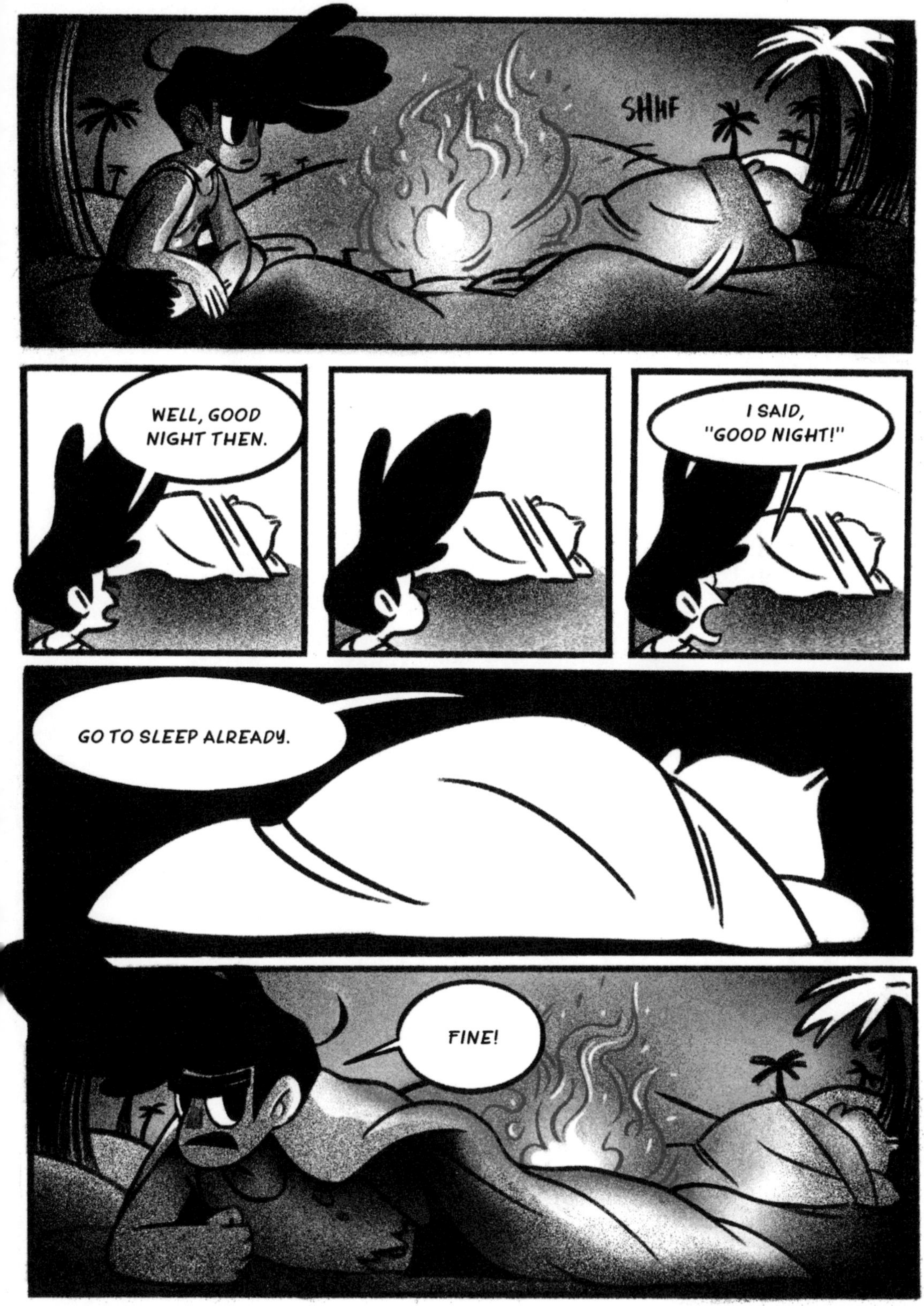
SHHF
WELL, GOOD NIGHT THEN.
I SAID, "GOOD NIGHT!"
GO TO SLEEP ALREADY.
FINE!

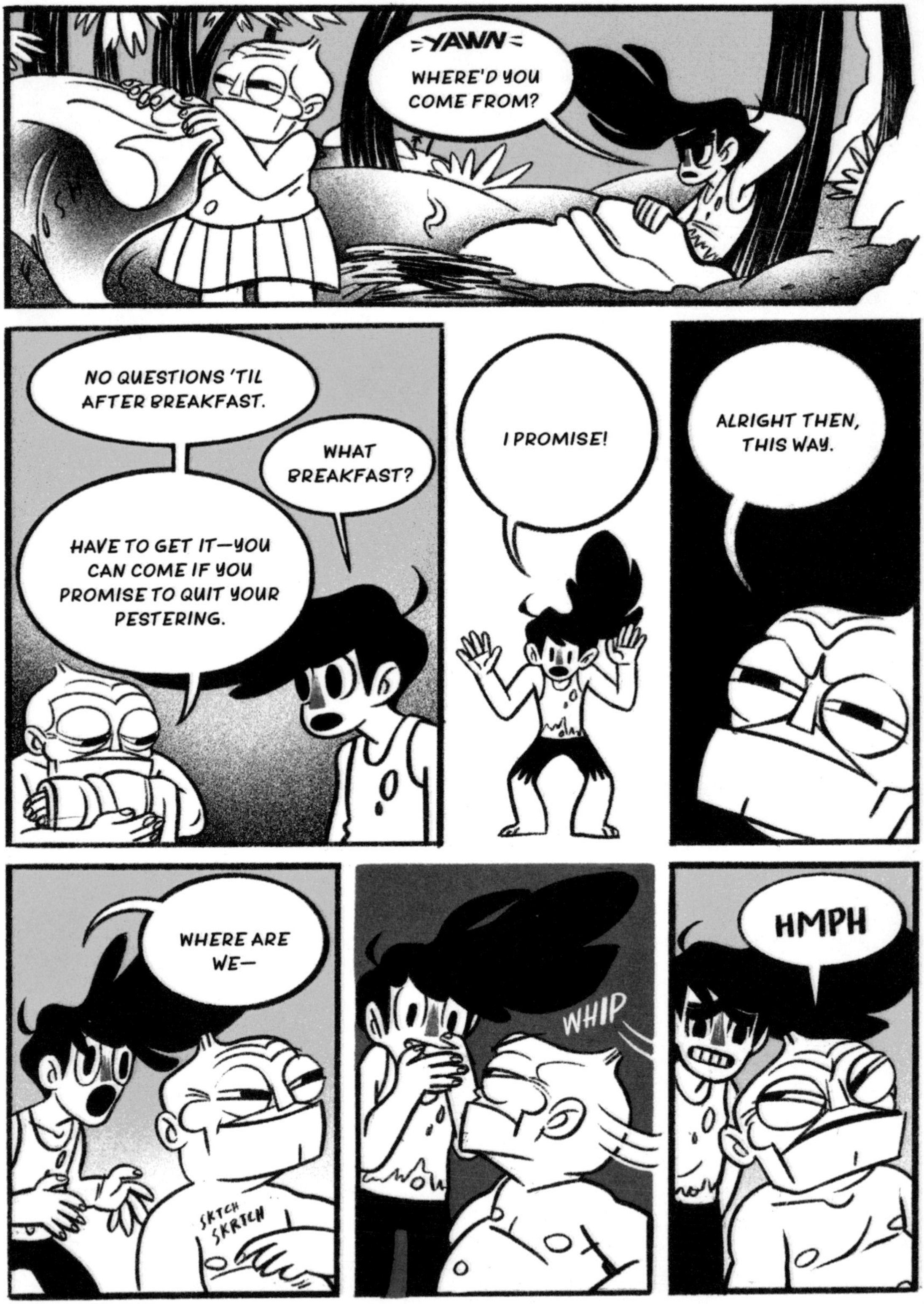
YAWN
WHERE'D YOU COME FROM?
NO QUESTIONS 'TIL AFTER BREAKFAST.
WHAT BREAKFAST?
HAVE TO GET IT—YOU CAN COME IF YOU PROMISE TO QUIT YOUR PESTERING.
I PROMISE!
ALRIGHT THEN, THIS WAY.
WHERE ARE WE—
SKTCH SKRTCH
WHIP
HMPH

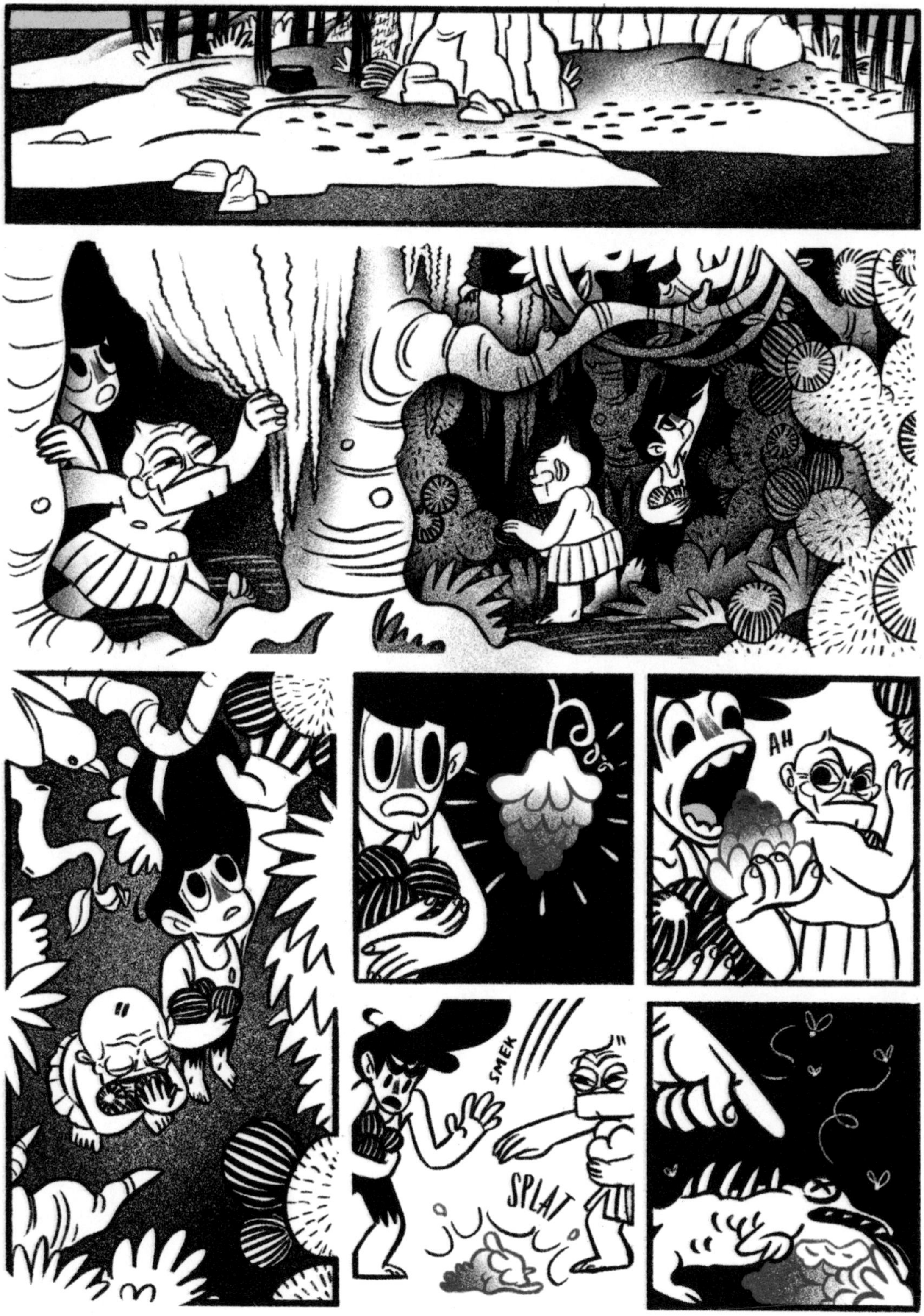
AH
SMEK
SPLAT

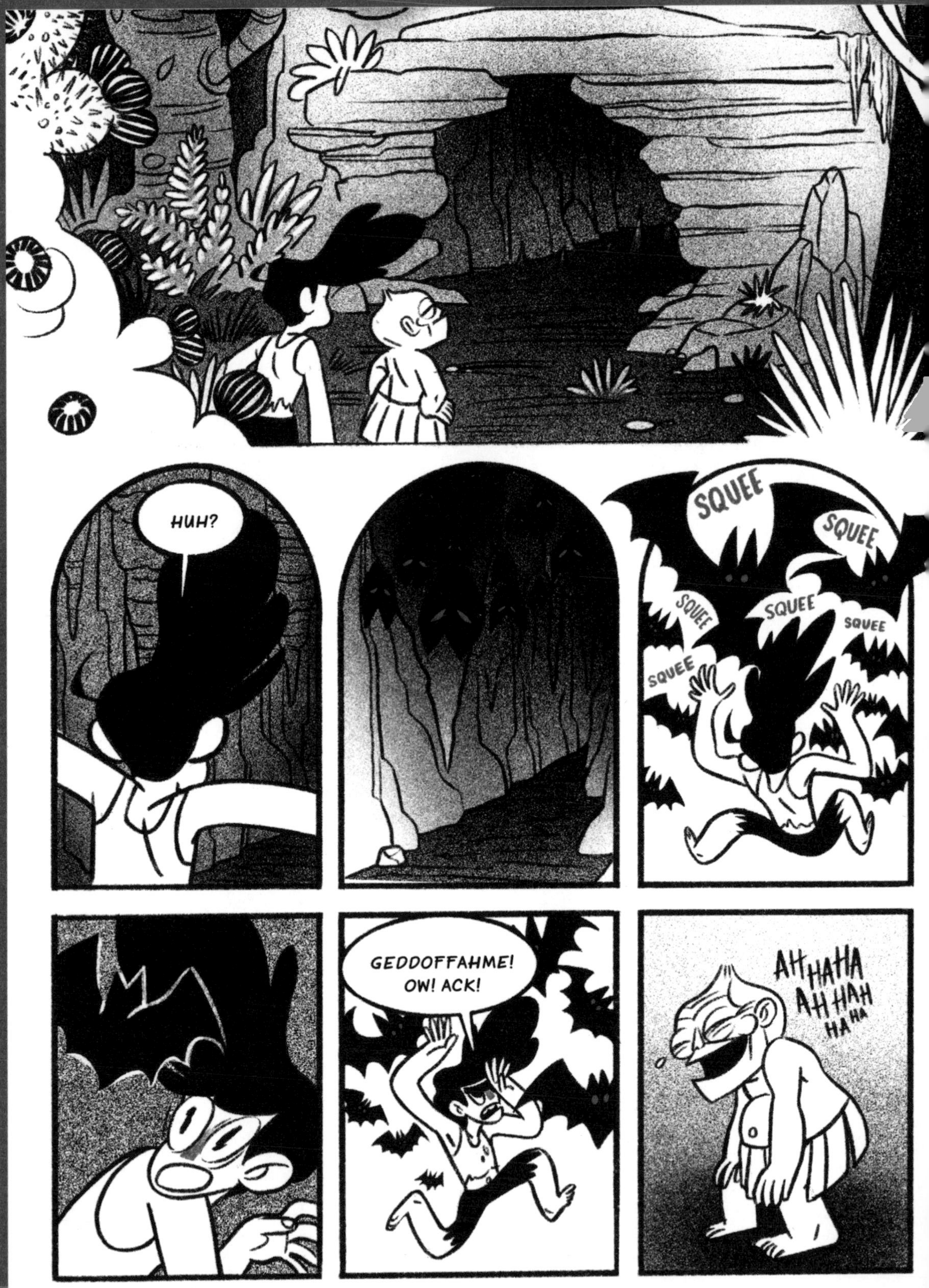
HUH?
SQUEE
SQUEE
SQUEE
SQUEE
SQUEE
SQUEE
GEDDOFFAHME! OW! ACK!
AH HAHA AH HAH HA HA

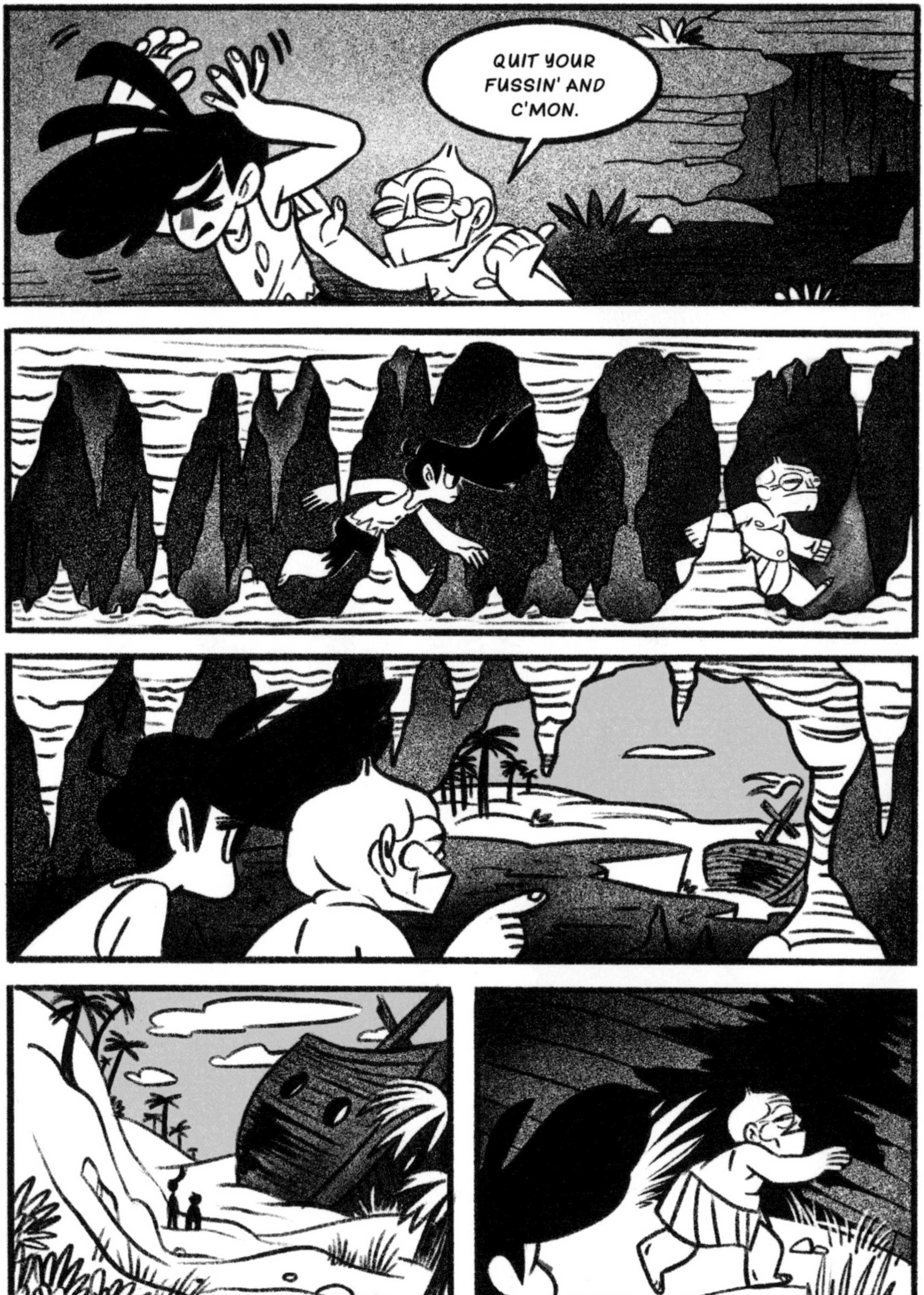
QUIT YOUR FUSSIN' AND C'MON.

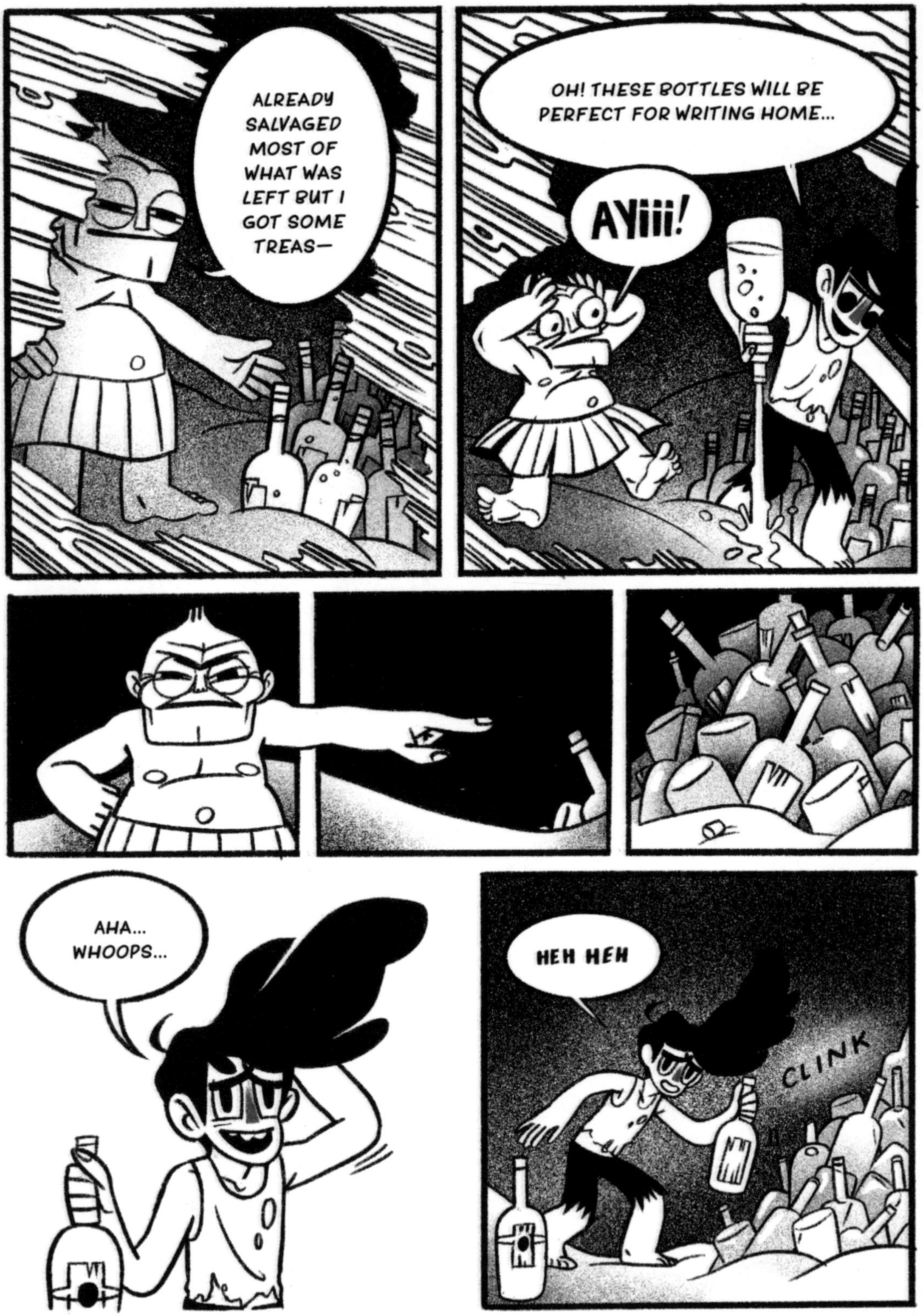
ALREADY SALVAGED MOST OF WHAT WAS LEFT BUT I GOT SOME TREAS—
OH! THESE BOTTLES WILL BE PERFECT FOR WRITING HOME...
AYiii!
AHA... WHOOPS...
HEH HEH
CLINK

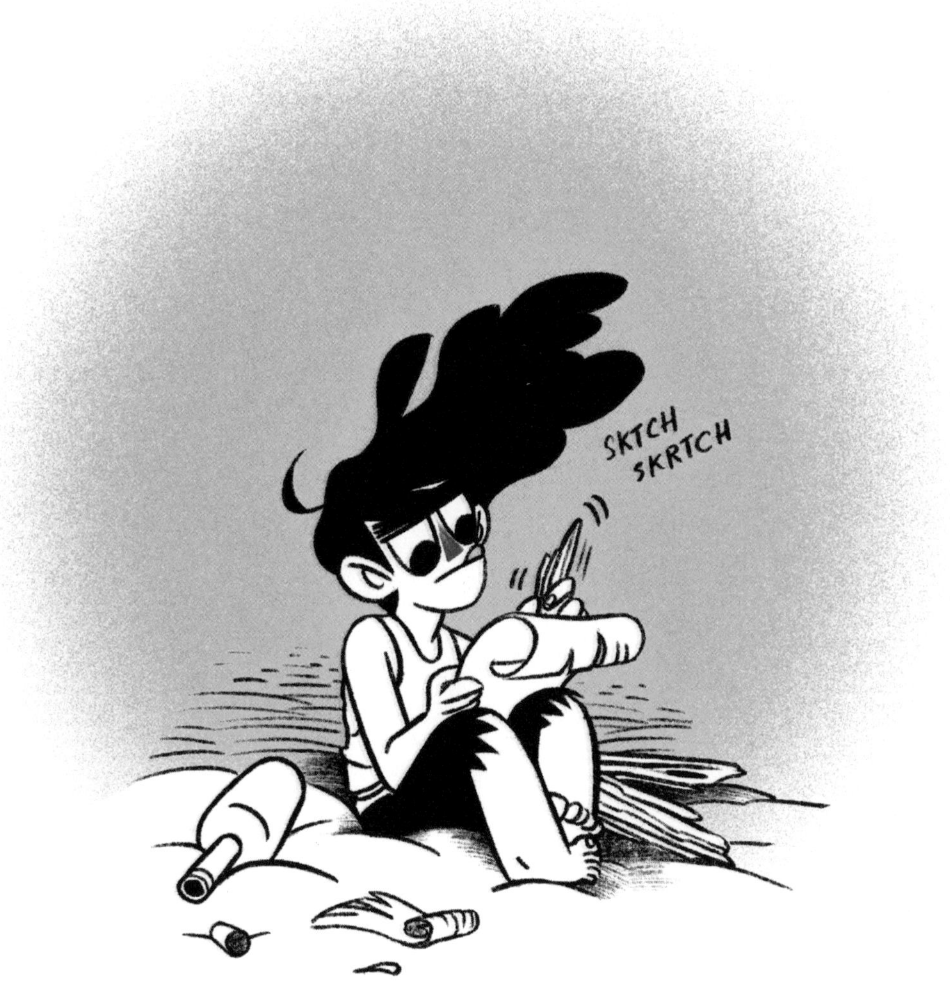
SKTCH
SKRTCH

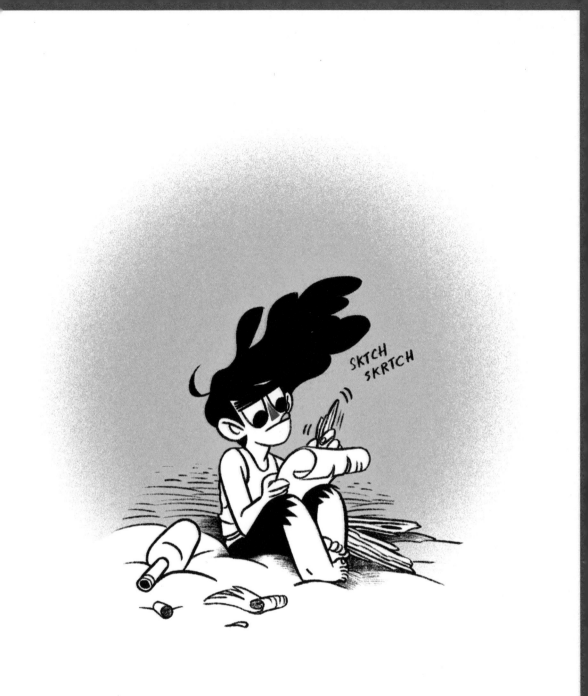

CHAPTER 6

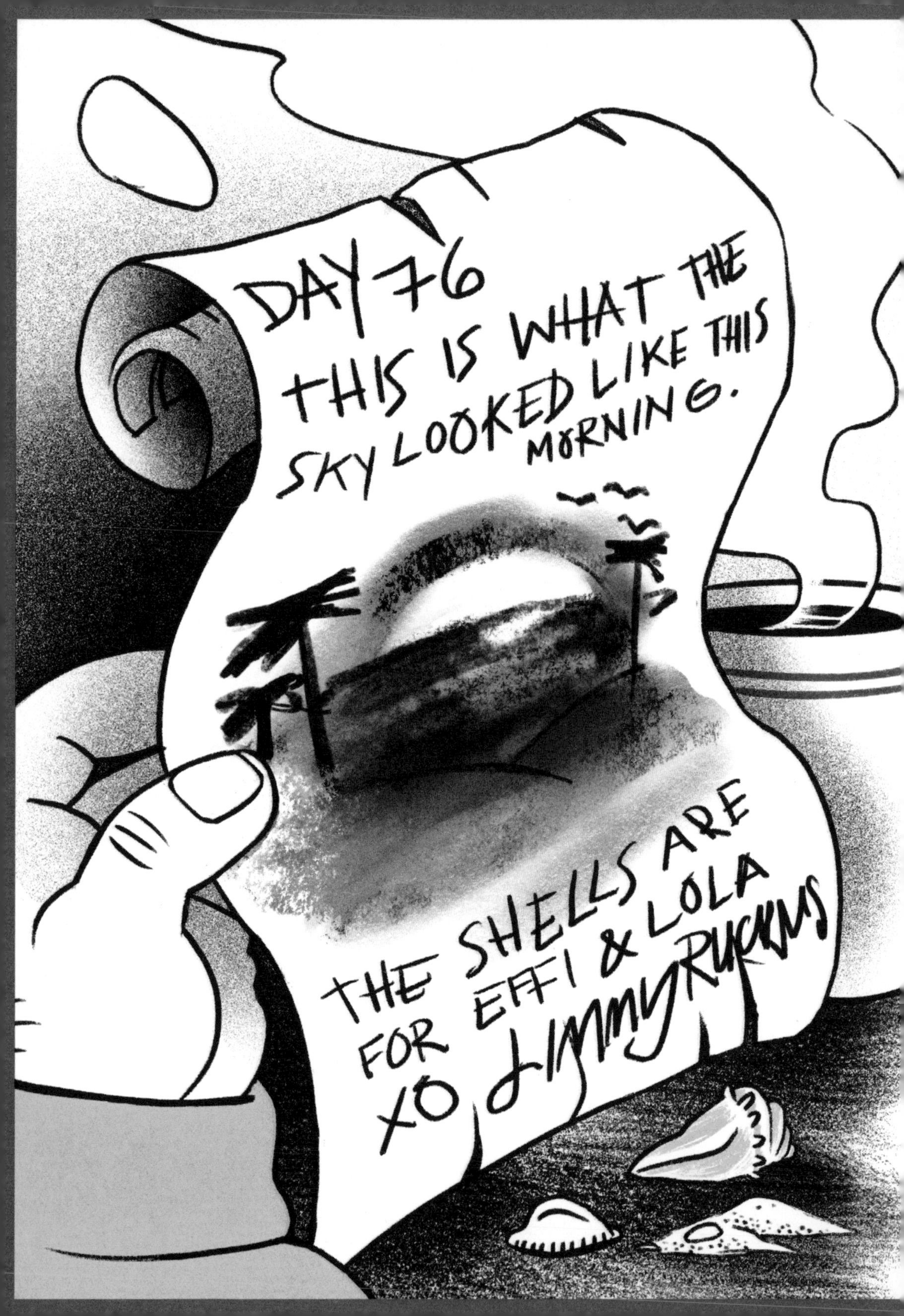
DAY 76
THIS IS WHAT THE
SKY LOOKED LIKE THIS
MORNING.
THE SHELLS ARE
FOR EFFI & LOLA
XO JIMMY RUCKUS

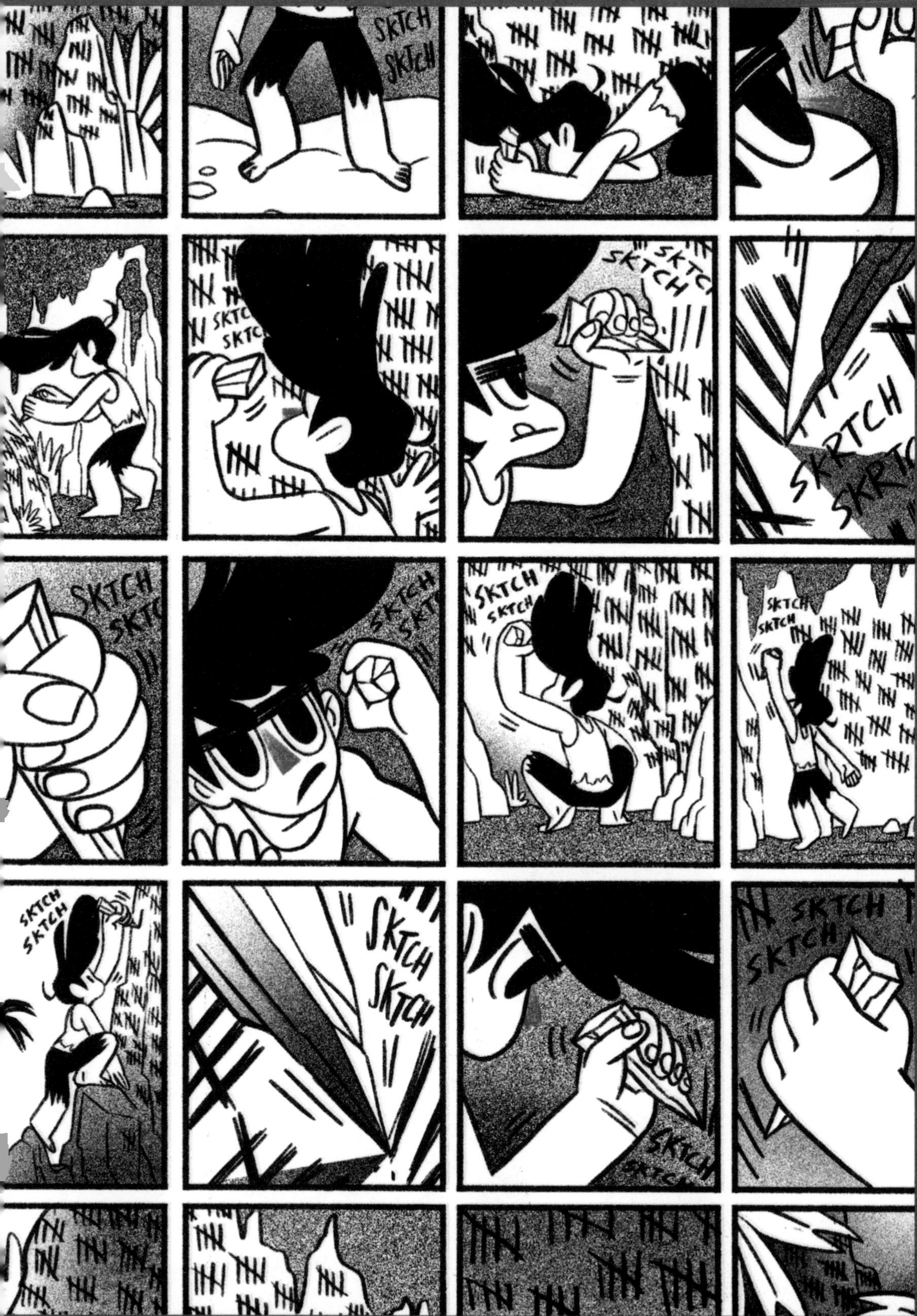
SKTCH SKTCH
SKTCH SKTCH
SKTCH
SKRTCH
SKTCH
SKTCH SKTCH
SKTCH SKTCH
SKTCH SKTCH
SKTCH SKTCH
SKTCH
SKTCH SKTCH

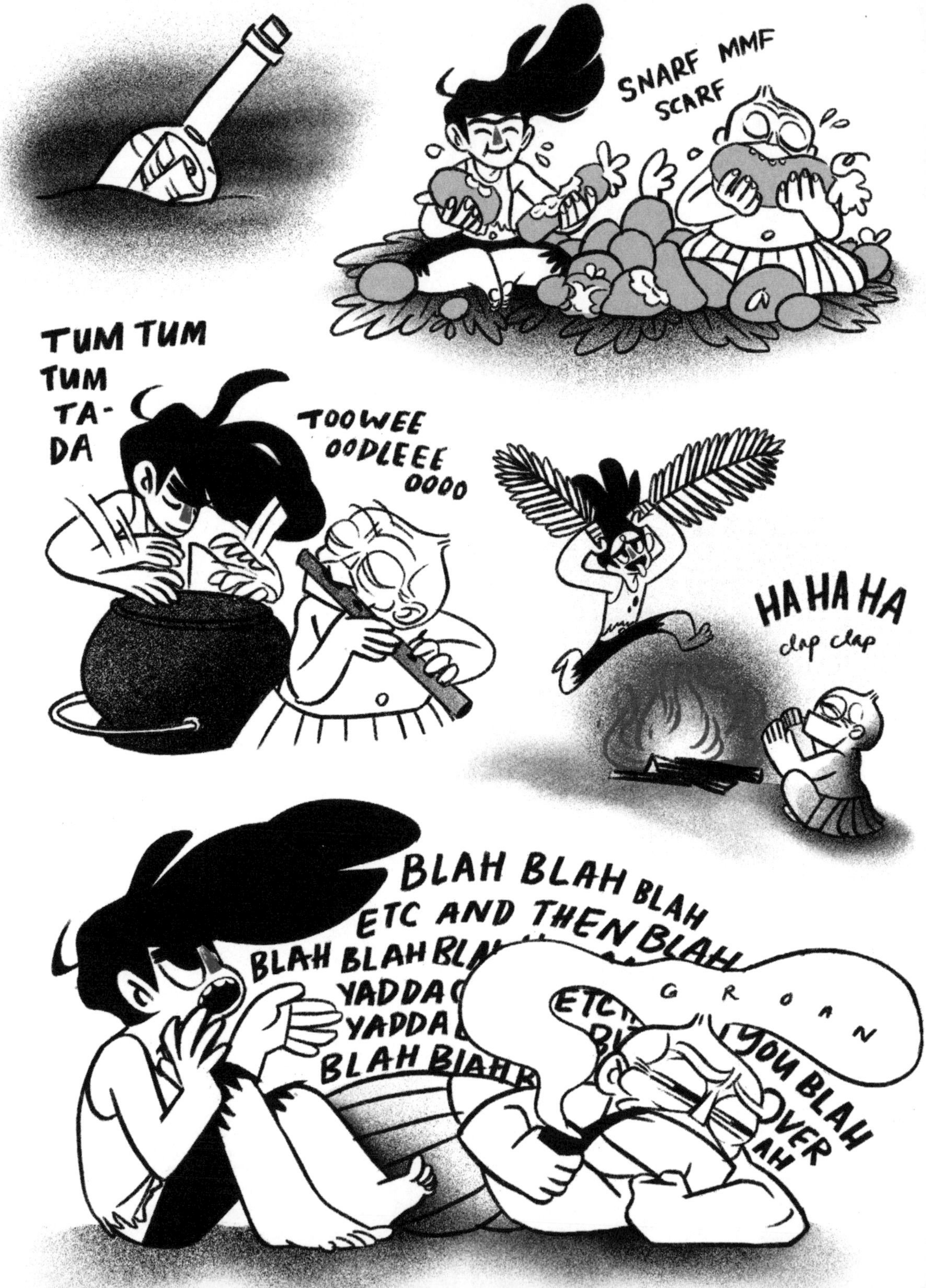

SNARF MMF
SCARF
TUM TUM
TUM
TA-
DA
TOOWEE
OODLEEE
OOOO
HA HA HA
clap clap
BLAH BLAH BLAH
ETC AND THEN BLAH
BLAH BLAH
YOU BLAH
OVER
GROAN

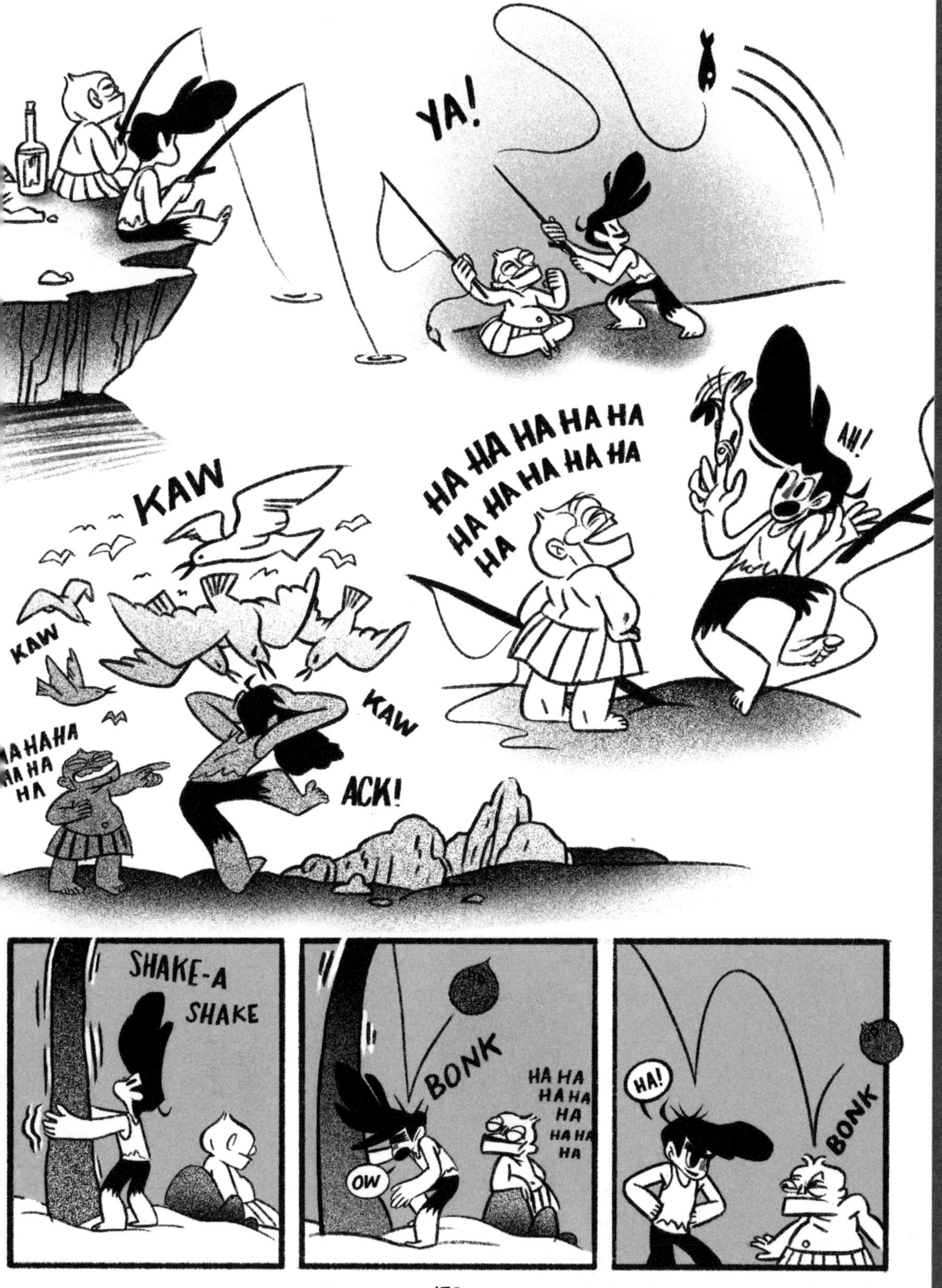
YA!
AH!
HA HA HA HA HA
HA HA HA HA HA
HA HA HA HA HA
HA
KAW
KAW
KAW
HA HA HA
HA HA
HA
ACK!
SHAKE-A
SHAKE
BONK
HA HA
HA HA
HA
HA HA
HA
OW
HA!
BONK

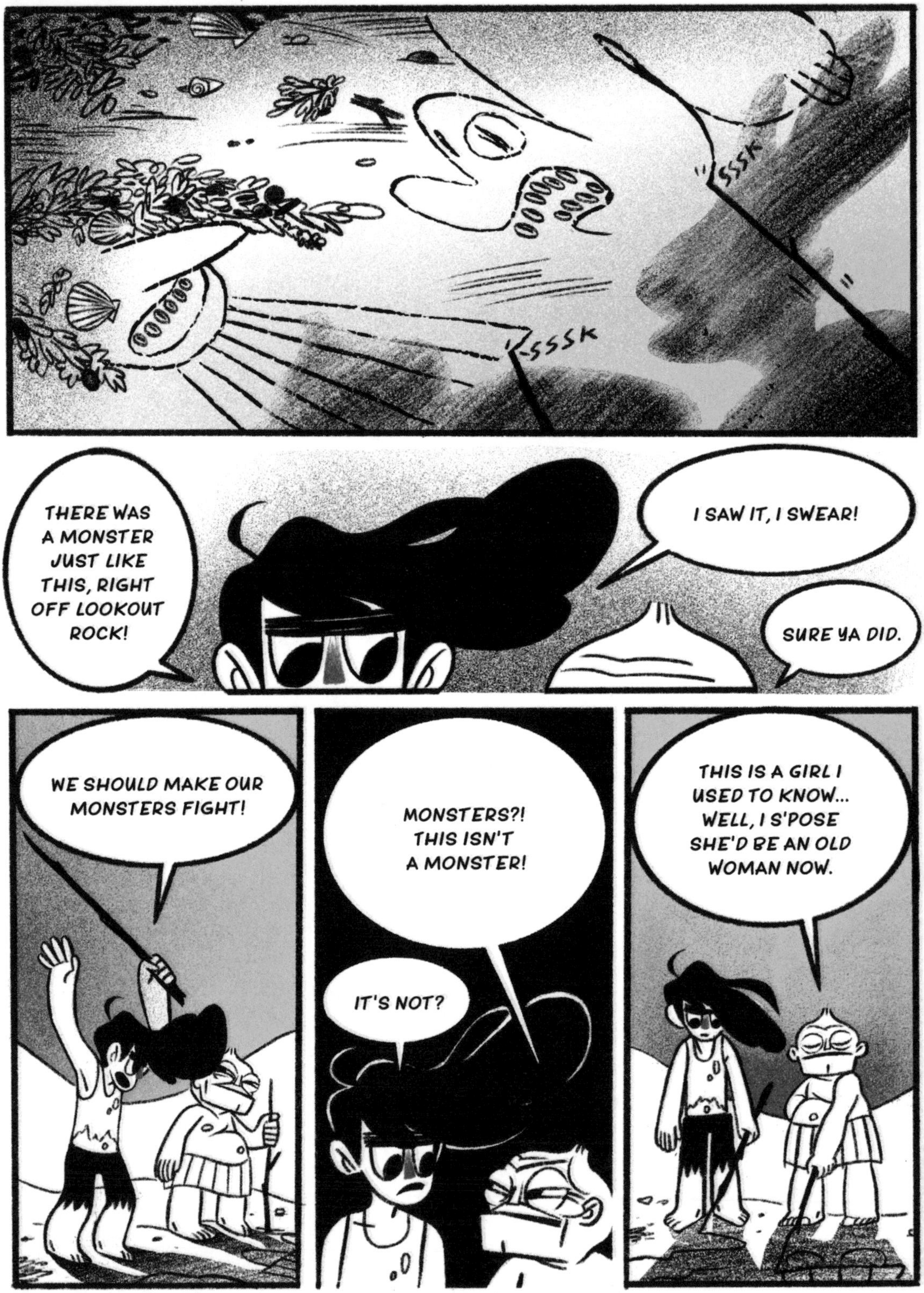
SSSK
SSSSK
THERE WAS A MONSTER JUST LIKE THIS, RIGHT OFF LOOKOUT ROCK!
I SAW IT, I SWEAR!
SURE YA DID.
WE SHOULD MAKE OUR MONSTERS FIGHT!
MONSTERS?! THIS ISN'T A MONSTER!
IT'S NOT?
THIS IS A GIRL I USED TO KNOW... WELL, I S'POSE SHE'D BE AN OLD WOMAN NOW.

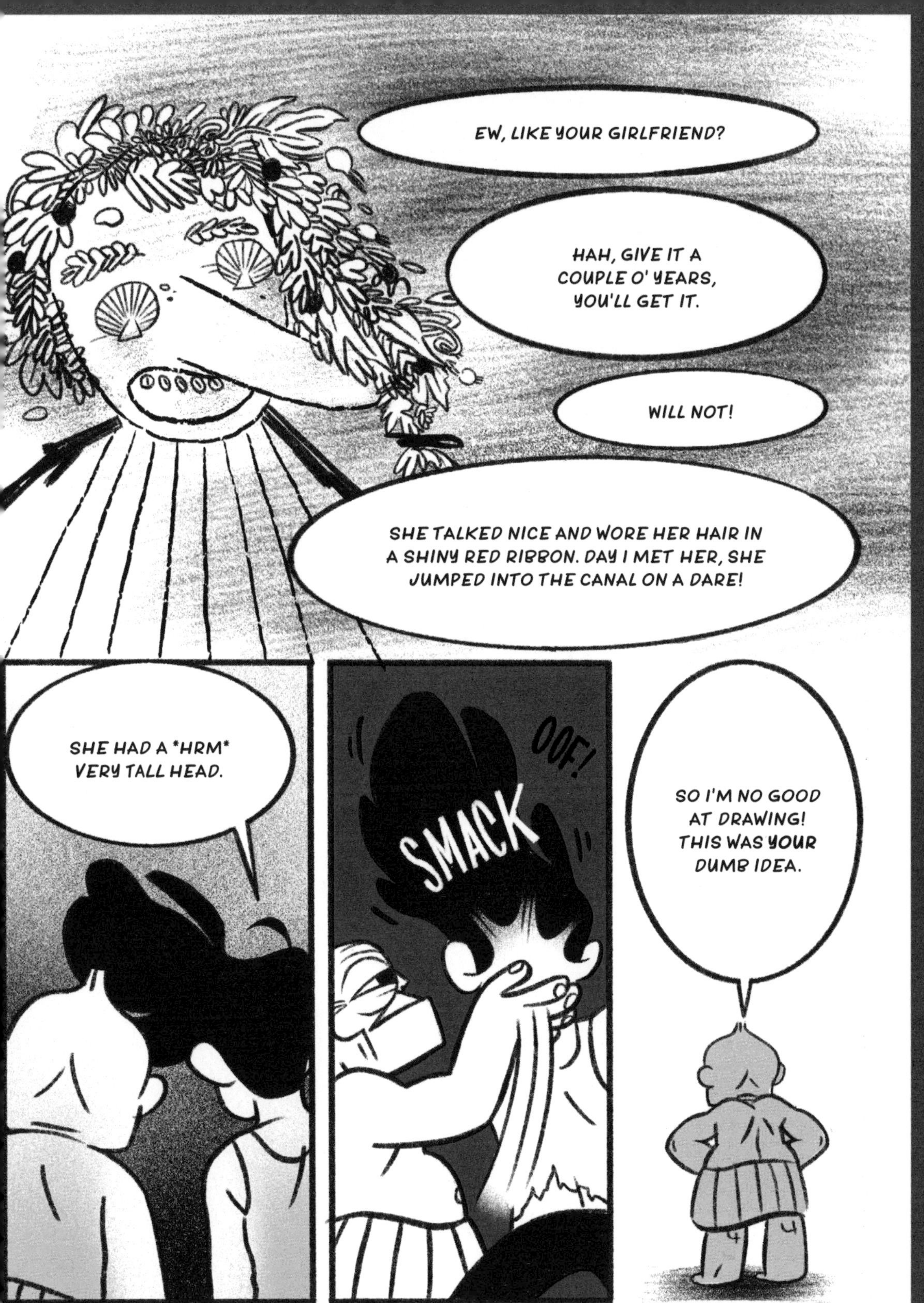
EW, LIKE YOUR GIRLFRIEND?
HAH, GIVE IT A COUPLE O' YEARS, YOU'LL GET IT.
WILL NOT!
SHE TALKED NICE AND WORE HER HAIR IN A SHINY RED RIBBON. DAY I MET HER, SHE JUMPED INTO THE CANAL ON A DARE!
SHE HAD A *HRM* VERY TALL HEAD.
OOF!
SMACK
SO I'M NO GOOD AT DRAWING! THIS WAS YOUR DUMB IDEA.

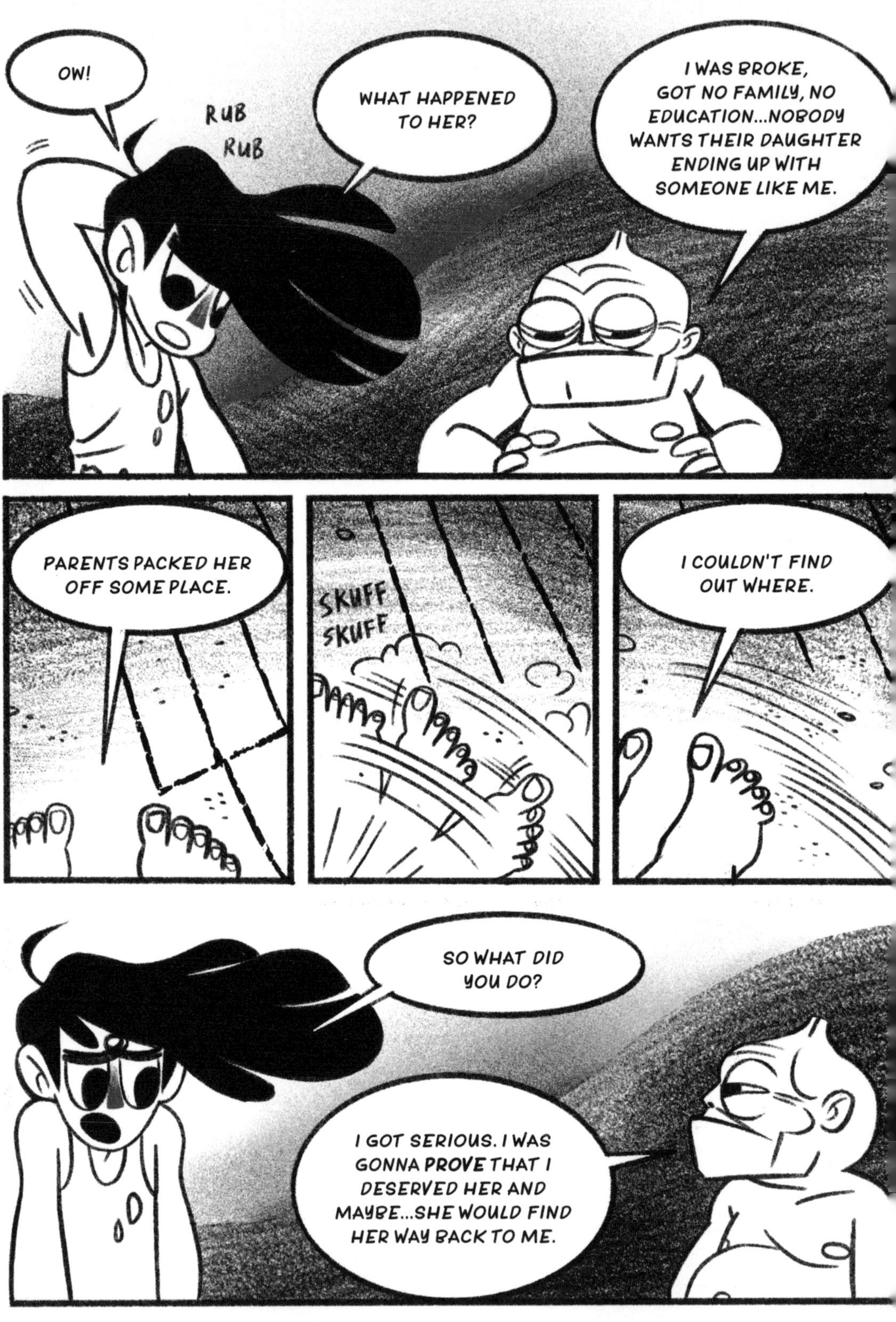
OW!
RUB
RUB
WHAT HAPPENED TO HER?
I WAS BROKE, GOT NO FAMILY, NO EDUCATION...NOBODY WANTS THEIR DAUGHTER ENDING UP WITH SOMEONE LIKE ME.
PARENTS PACKED HER OFF SOME PLACE.
SKUFF
SKUFF
I COULDN'T FIND OUT WHERE.
SO WHAT DID YOU DO?
I GOT SERIOUS. I WAS GONNA **PROVE** THAT I DESERVED HER AND MAYBE...SHE WOULD FIND HER WAY BACK TO ME.

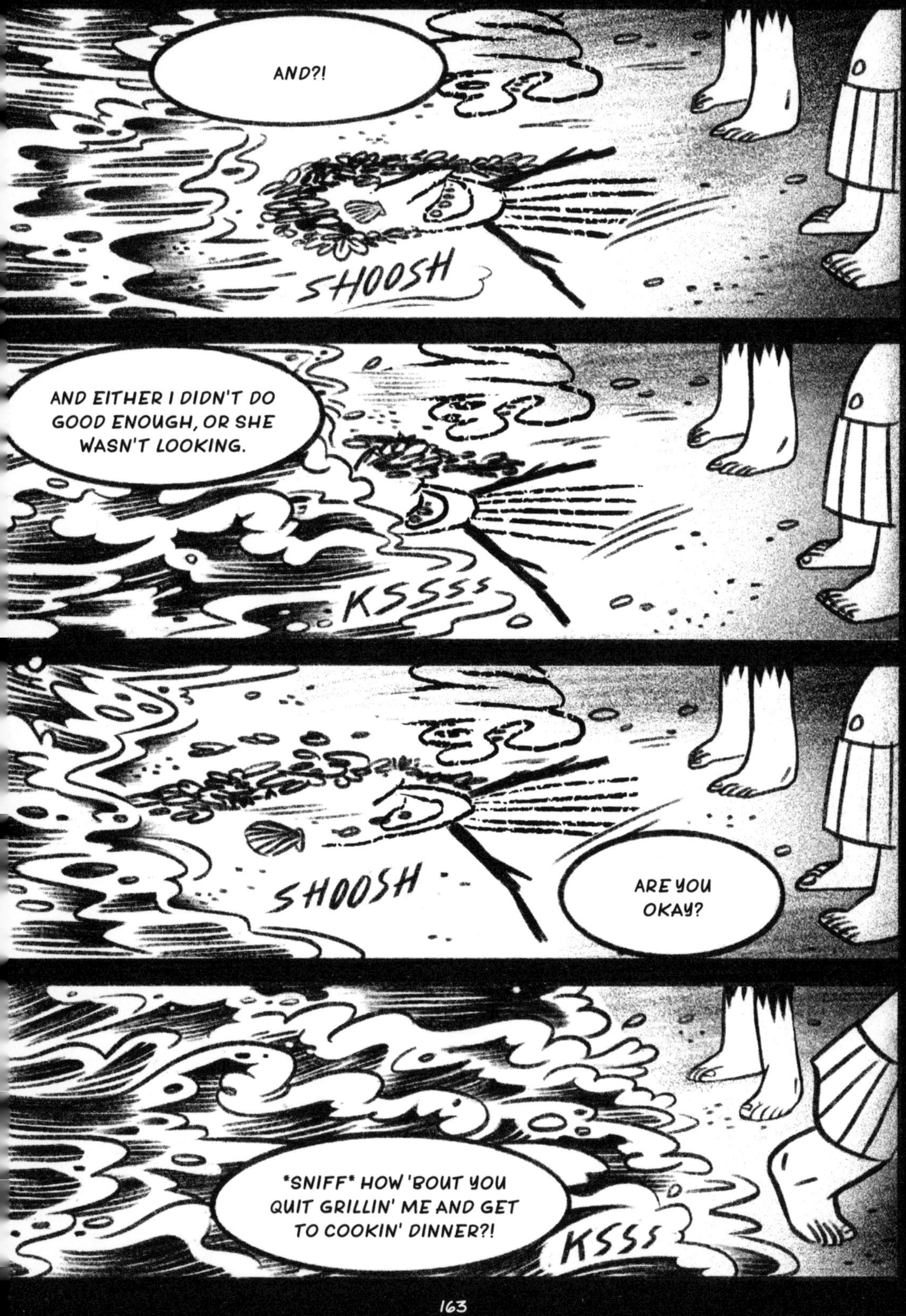
AND?!
SHOOSH
AND EITHER I DIDN'T DO GOOD ENOUGH, OR SHE WASN'T LOOKING.
KSSSS
SHOOSH
ARE YOU OKAY?
SNIFF HOW 'BOUT YOU QUIT GRILLIN' ME AND GET TO COOKIN' DINNER?!
KSSS

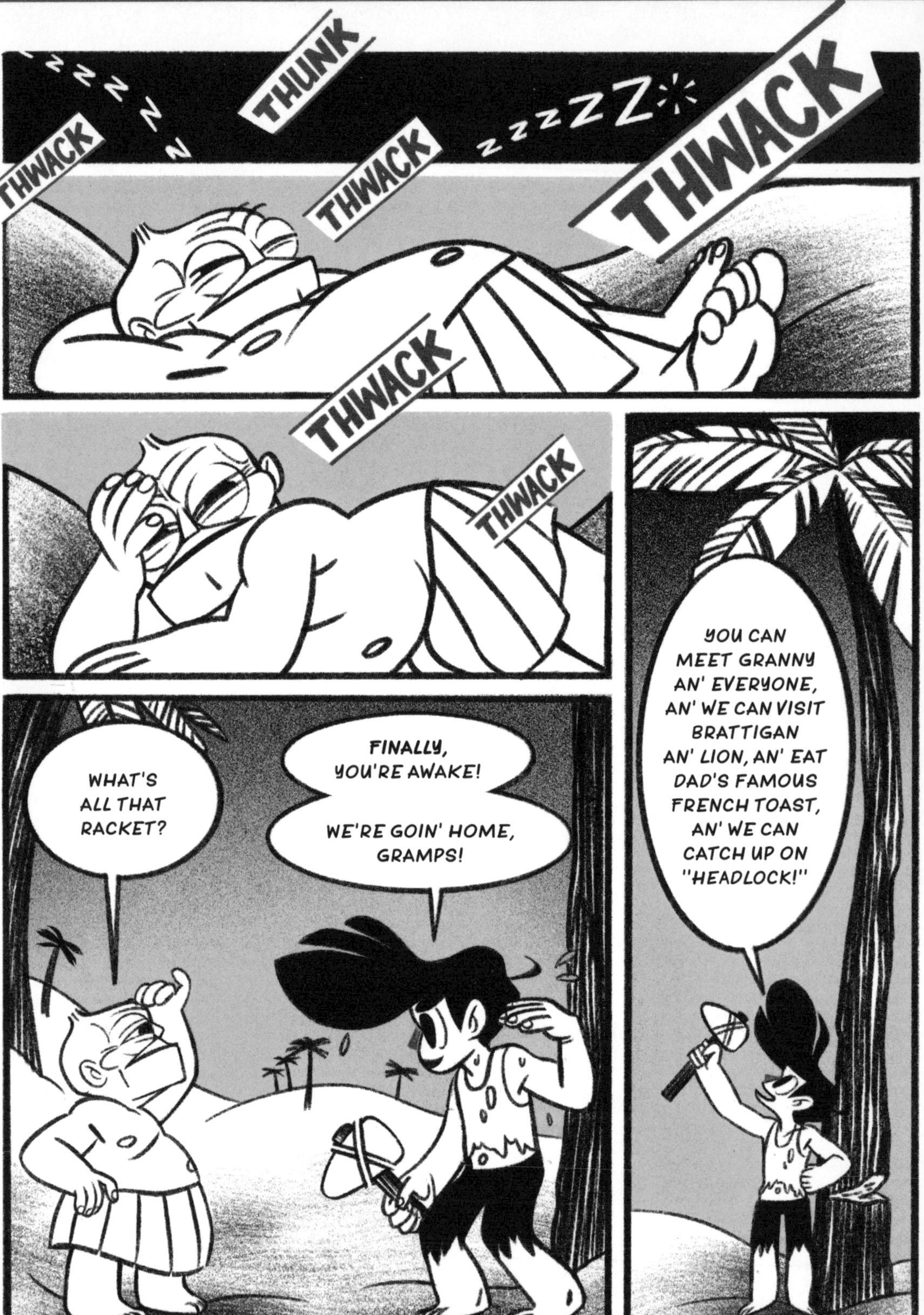

z z z z z z z
THWACK
THUNK
THWACK
z z z Z Z Z
THWACK
THWACK
THWACK
THWACK
WHAT'S ALL THAT RACKET?
FINALLY, YOU'RE AWAKE!
WE'RE GOIN' HOME, GRAMPS!
YOU CAN MEET GRANNY AN' EVERYONE, AN' WE CAN VISIT BRATTIGAN AN' LION, AN' EAT DAD'S FAMOUS FRENCH TOAST, AN' WE CAN CATCH UP ON "HEADLOCK!"

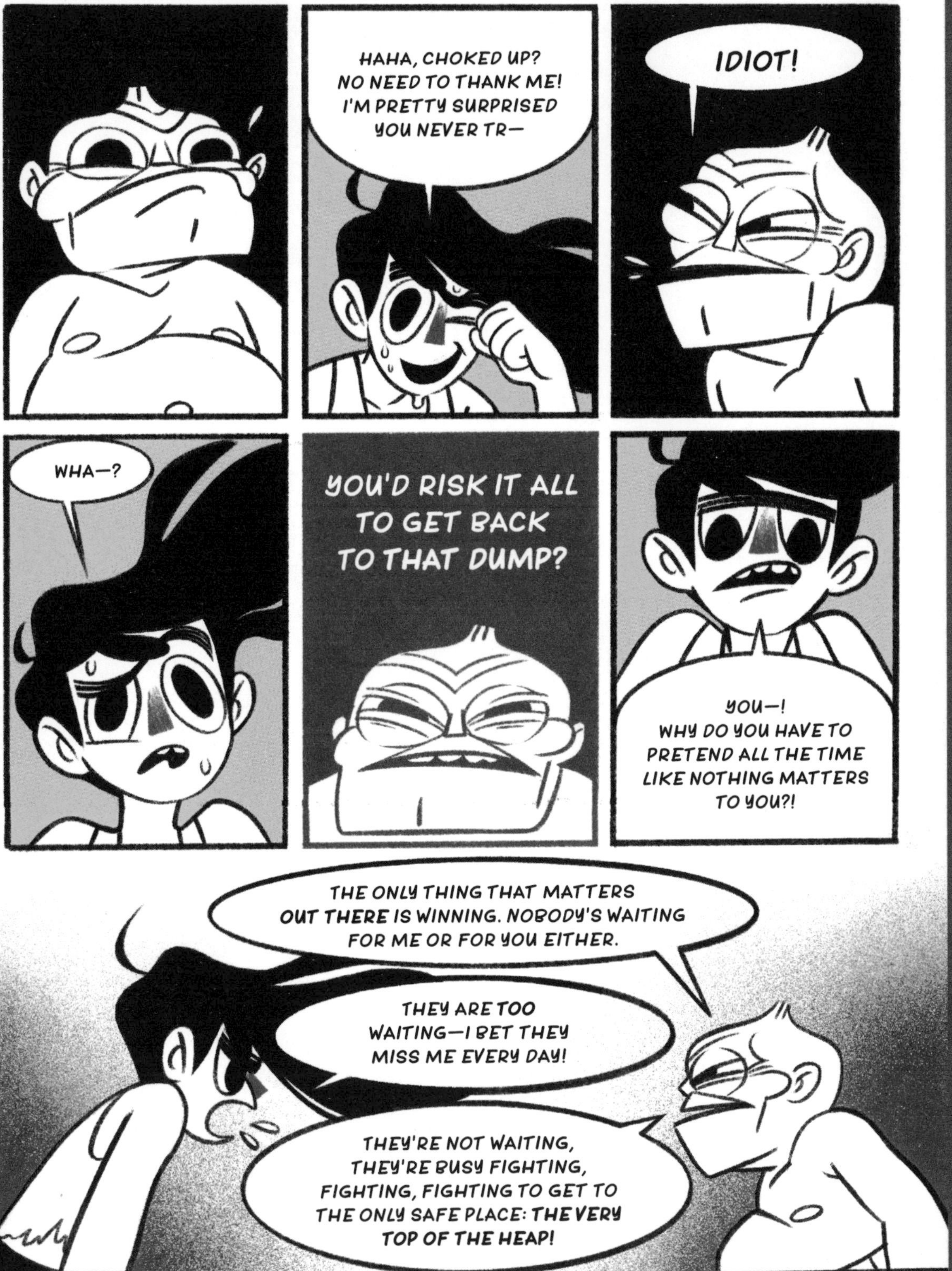
HAHA, CHOKED UP? NO NEED TO THANK ME! I'M PRETTY SURPRISED YOU NEVER TR—
IDIOT!
WHA—?
YOU'D RISK IT ALL TO GET BACK TO THAT DUMP?
YOU—! WHY DO YOU HAVE TO PRETEND ALL THE TIME LIKE NOTHING MATTERS TO YOU?!
THE ONLY THING THAT MATTERS OUT THERE IS WINNING. NOBODY'S WAITING FOR ME OR FOR YOU EITHER.
THEY ARE TOO WAITING—I BET THEY MISS ME EVERY DAY!
THEY'RE NOT WAITING, THEY'RE BUSY FIGHTING, FIGHTING, FIGHTING TO GET TO THE ONLY SAFE PLACE: THE VERY TOP OF THE HEAP!

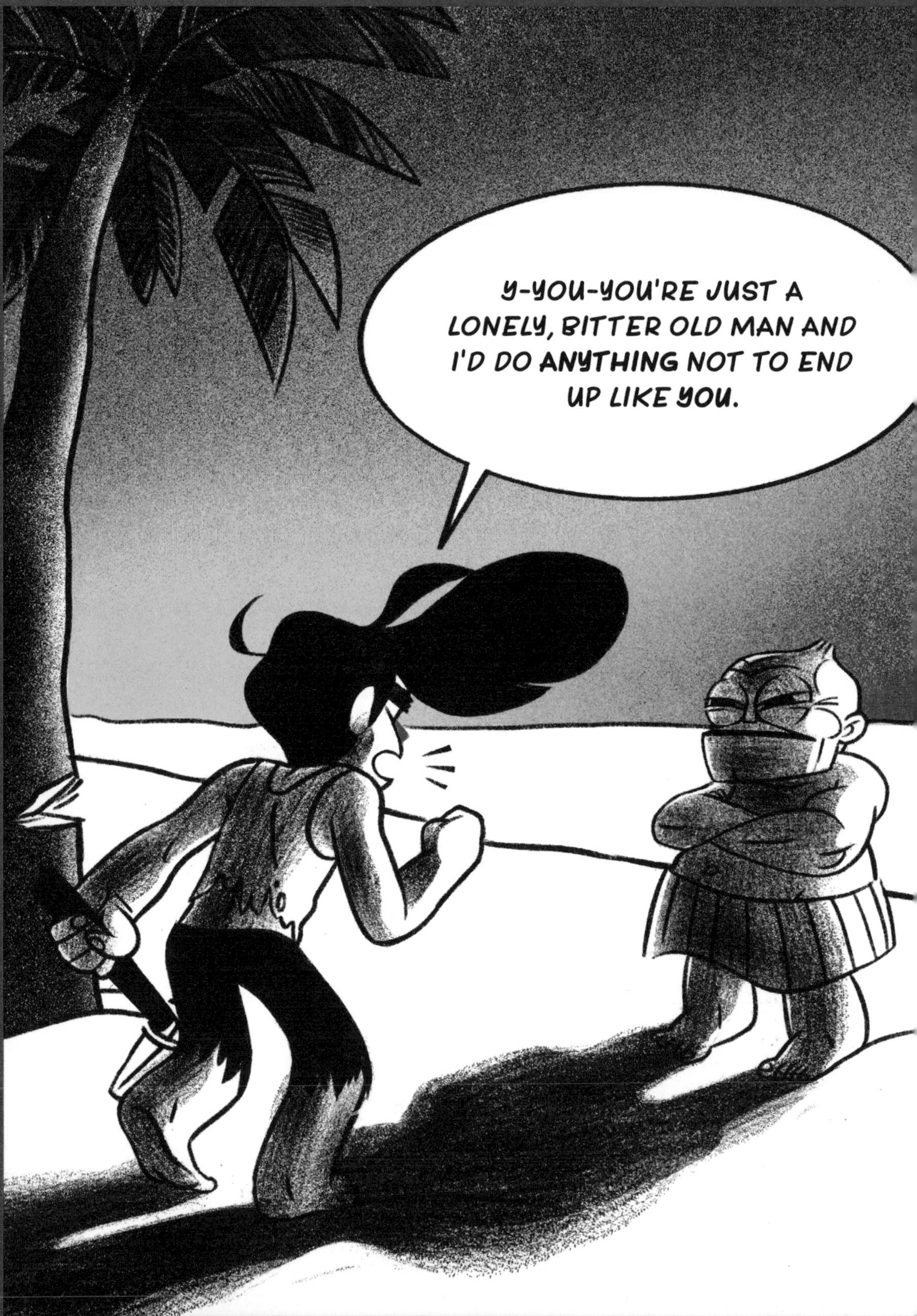
Y-YOU-YOU'RE JUST A LONELY, BITTER OLD MAN AND I'D DO ANYTHING NOT TO END UP LIKE YOU.

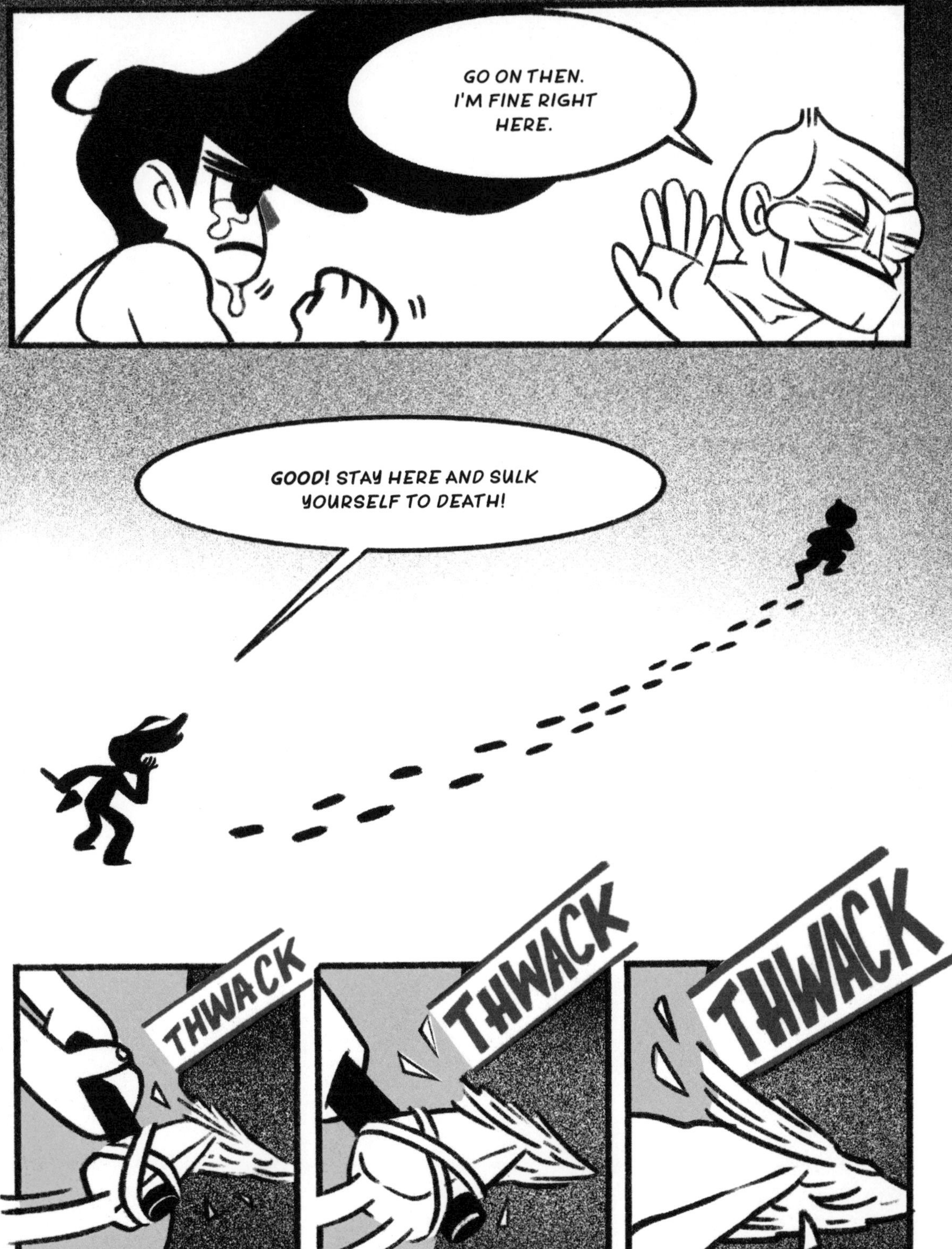
GO ON THEN. I'M FINE RIGHT HERE.
GOOD! STAY HERE AND SULK YOURSELF TO DEATH!
THWACK
THWACK
THWACK

CHAPTER 7

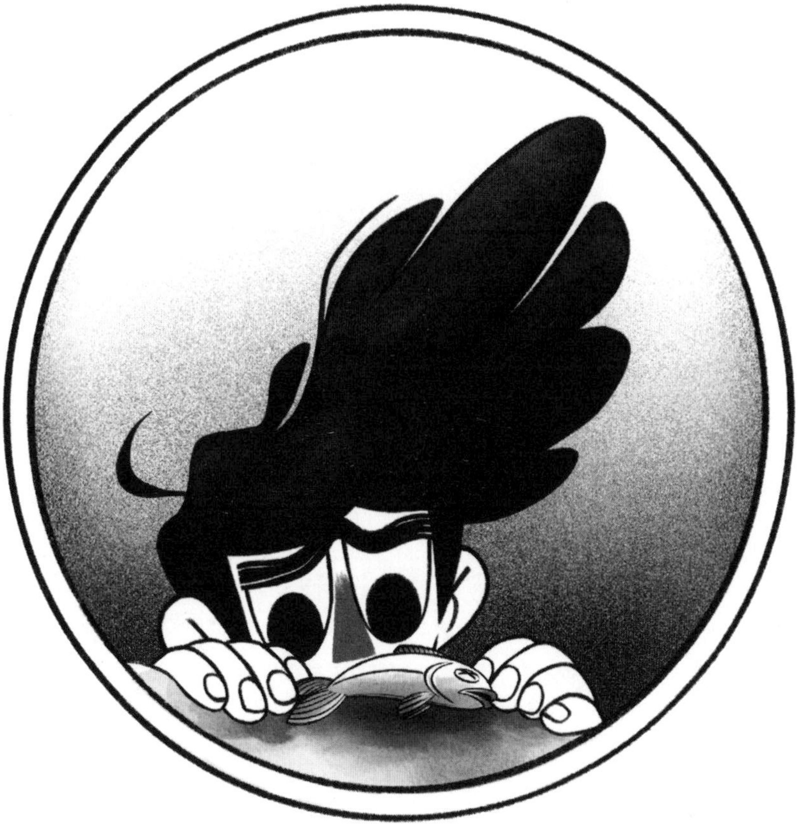

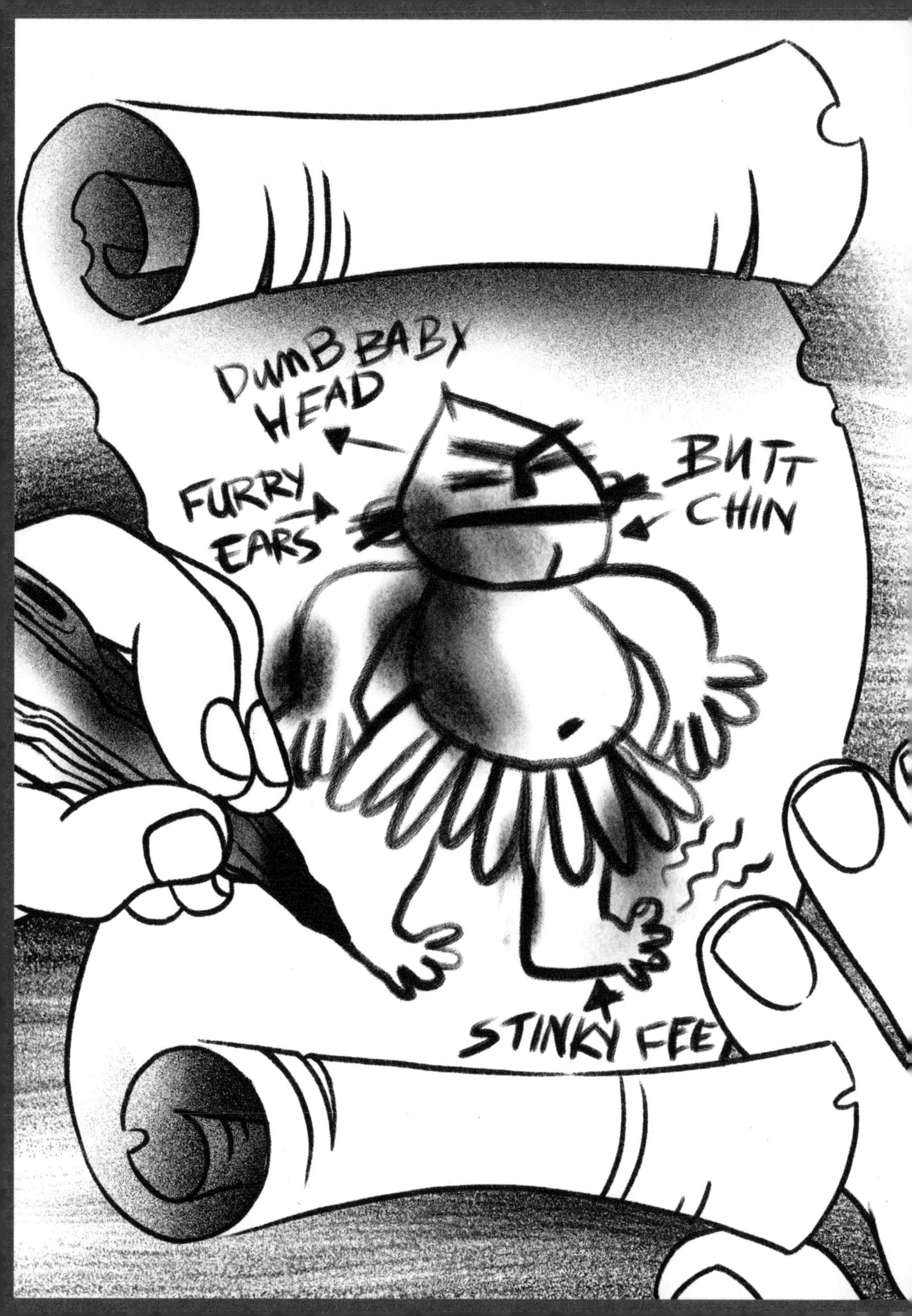
DumB BABY
HEAD
FURRY
EARS
BUTT
CHIN
STINKY FEE

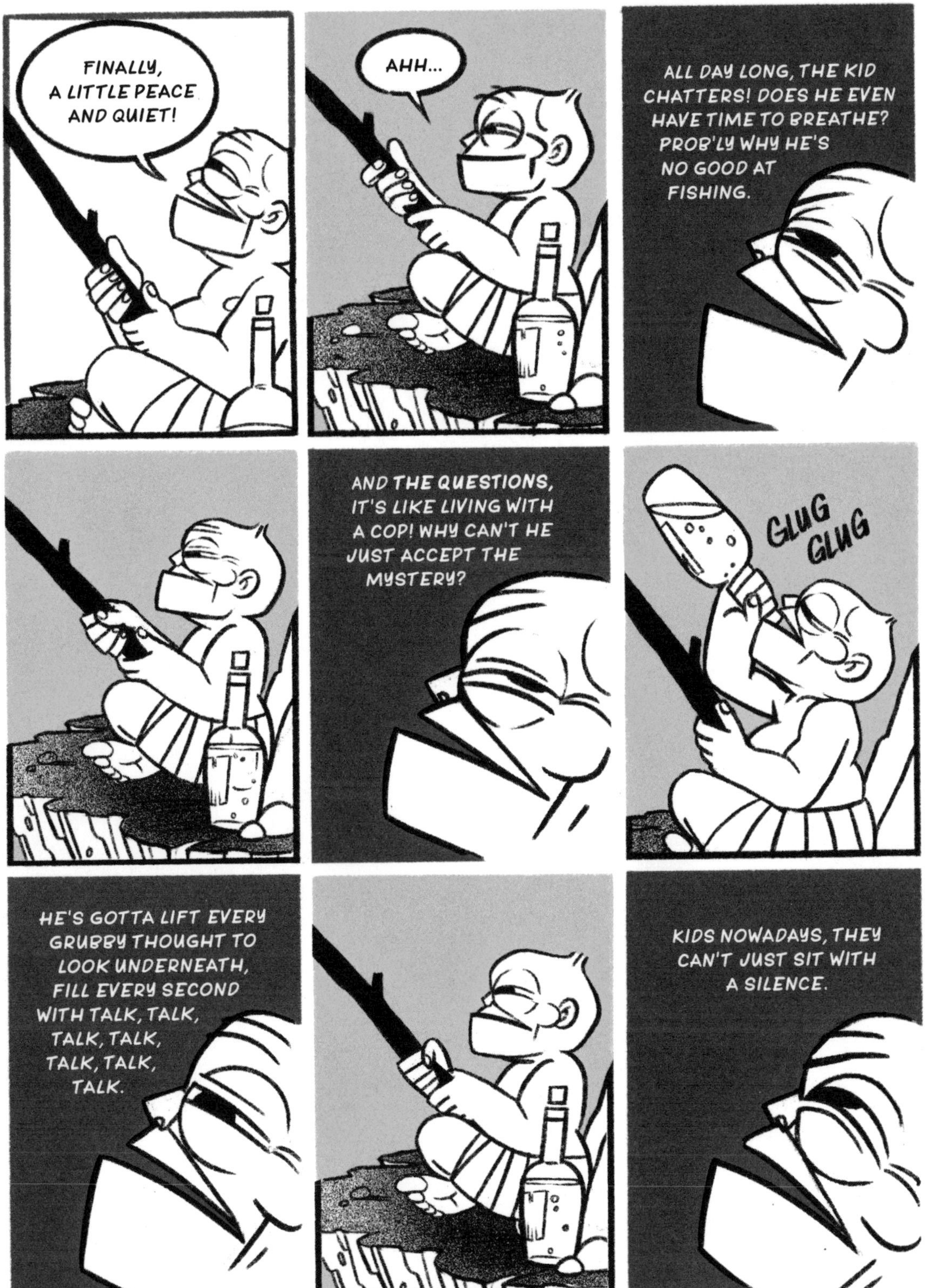
FINALLY, A LITTLE PEACE AND QUIET!
AHH...
ALL DAY LONG, THE KID CHATTERS! DOES HE EVEN HAVE TIME TO BREATHE? PROB'LY WHY HE'S NO GOOD AT FISHING.
AND THE QUESTIONS, IT'S LIKE LIVING WITH A COP! WHY CAN'T HE JUST ACCEPT THE MYSTERY?
GLUG GLUG
HE'S GOTTA LIFT EVERY GRUBBY THOUGHT TO LOOK UNDERNEATH, FILL EVERY SECOND WITH TALK, TALK, TALK, TALK, TALK, TALK, TALK.
KIDS NOWADAYS, THEY CAN'T JUST SIT WITH A SILENCE.

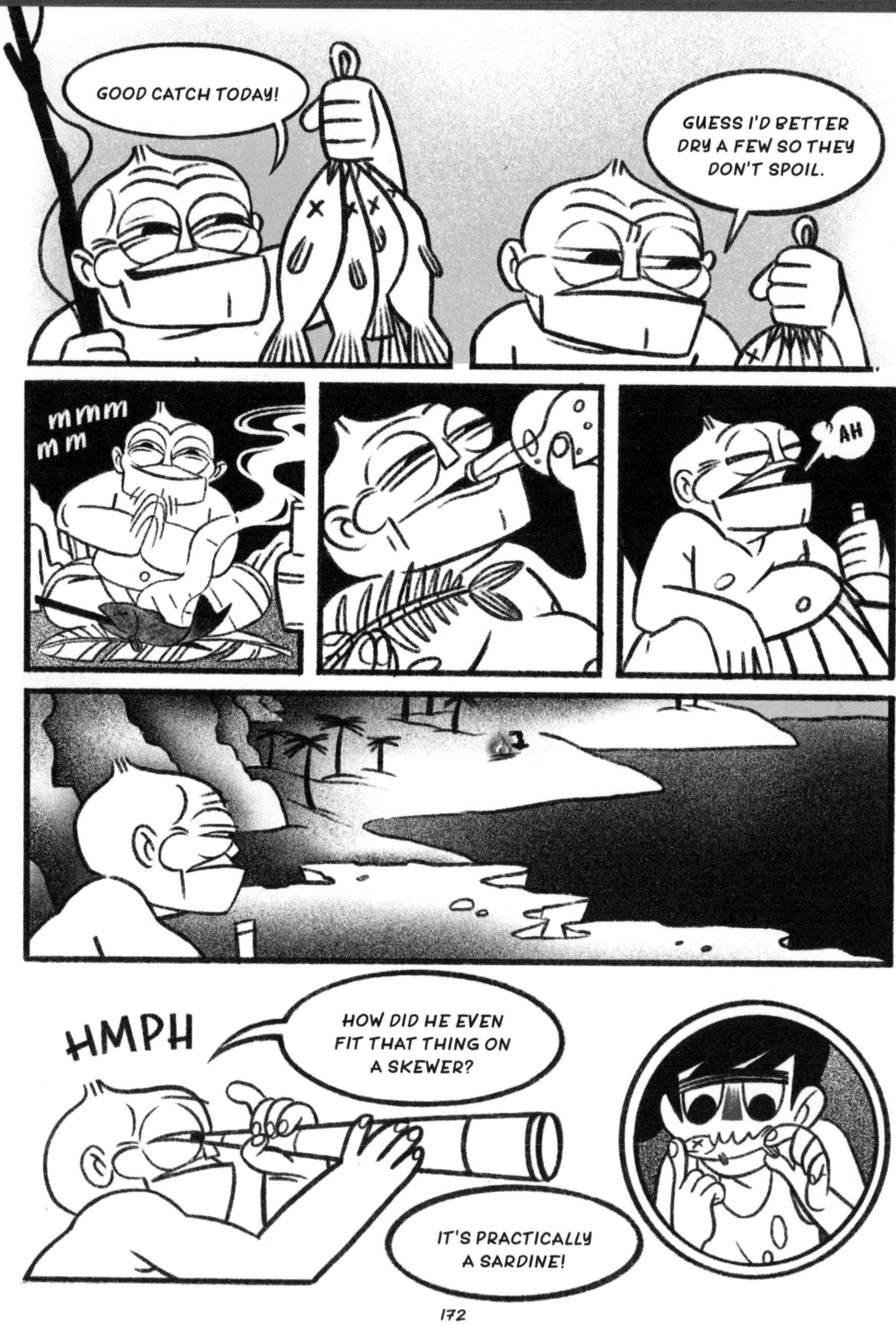
GOOD CATCH TODAY!
GUESS I'D BETTER DRY A FEW SO THEY DON'T SPOIL.
mmm mm
AH
HMPH
HOW DID HE EVEN FIT THAT THING ON A SKEWER?
IT'S PRACTICALLY A SARDINE!

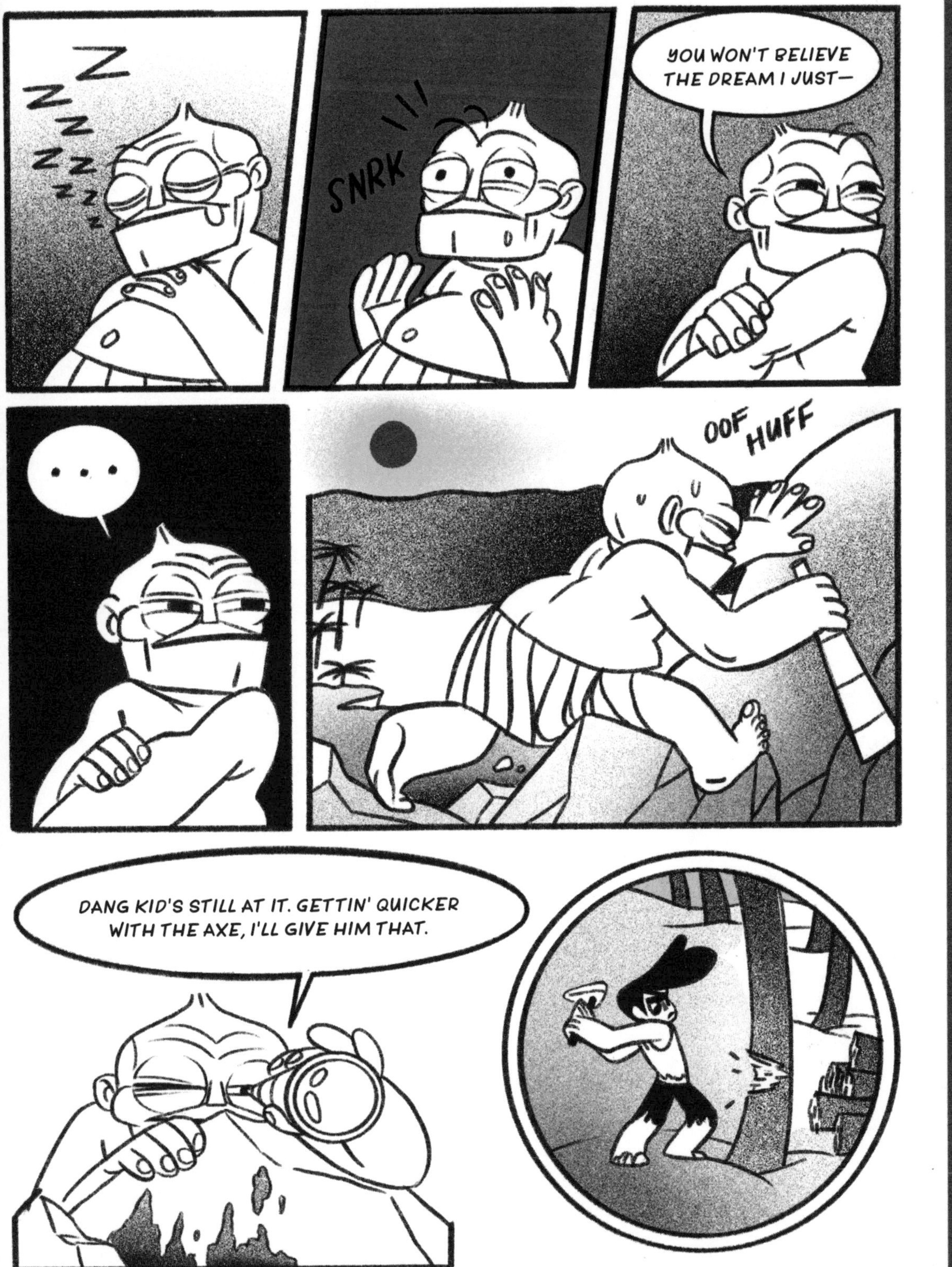
Z Z Z Z Z Z Z Z Z
SNRK
YOU WON'T BELIEVE THE DREAM I JUST—
. . .
OOF HUFF
DANG KID'S STILL AT IT. GETTIN' QUICKER WITH THE AXE, I'LL GIVE HIM THAT.

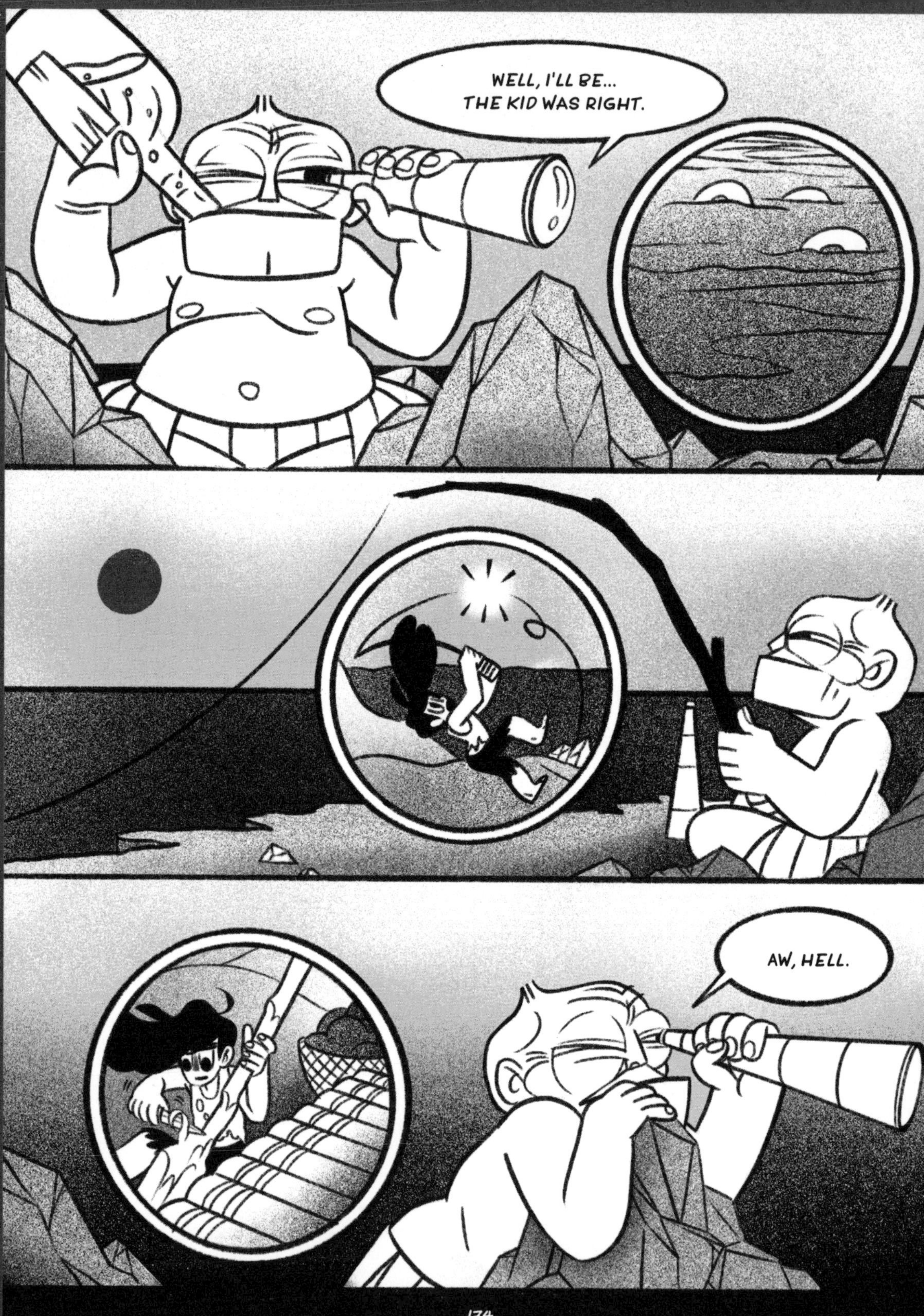
WELL, I'LL BE...
THE KID WAS RIGHT.
AW, HELL.

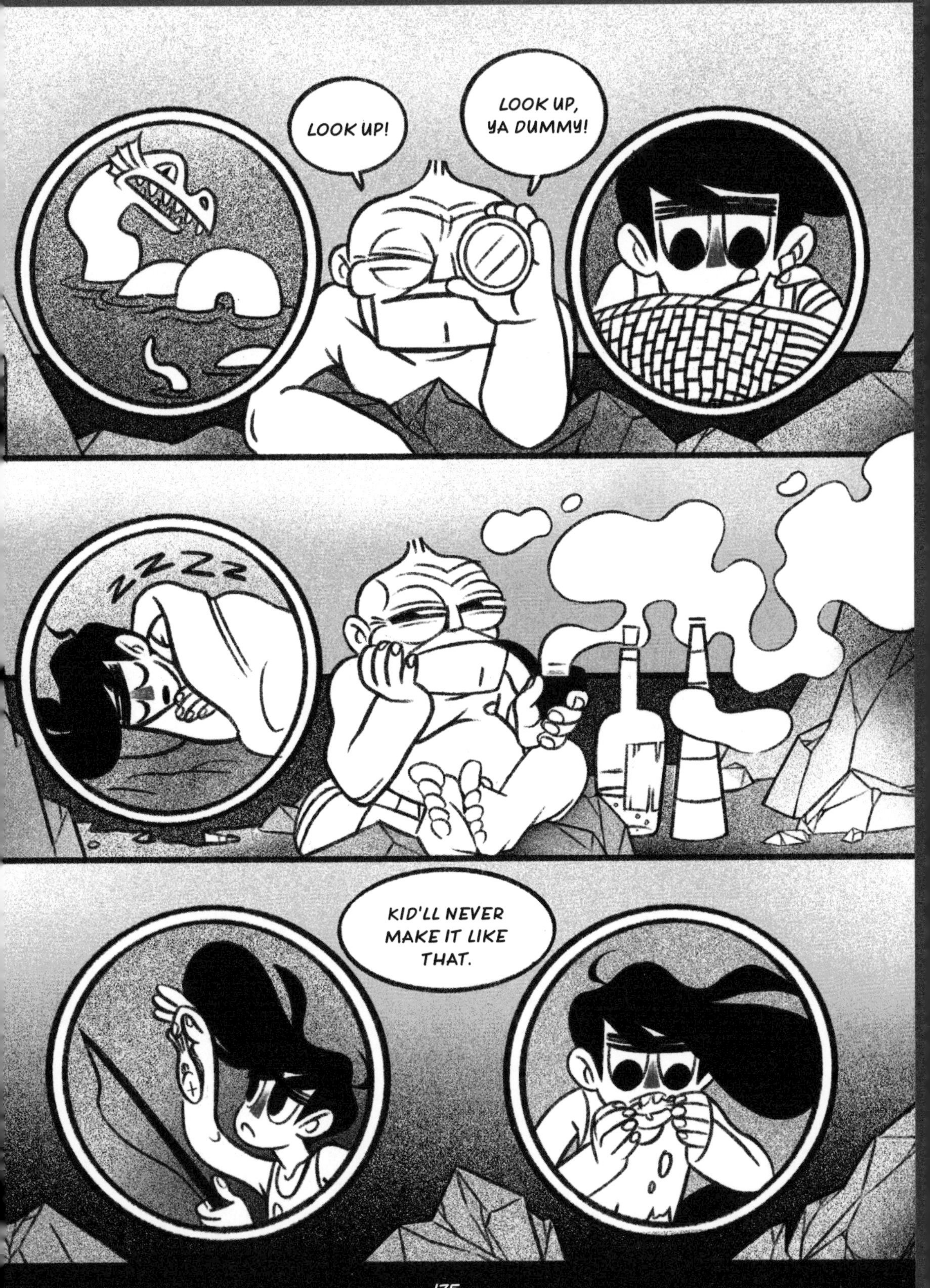
LOOK UP!
LOOK UP, YA DUMMY!
KID'LL NEVER MAKE IT LIKE THAT.

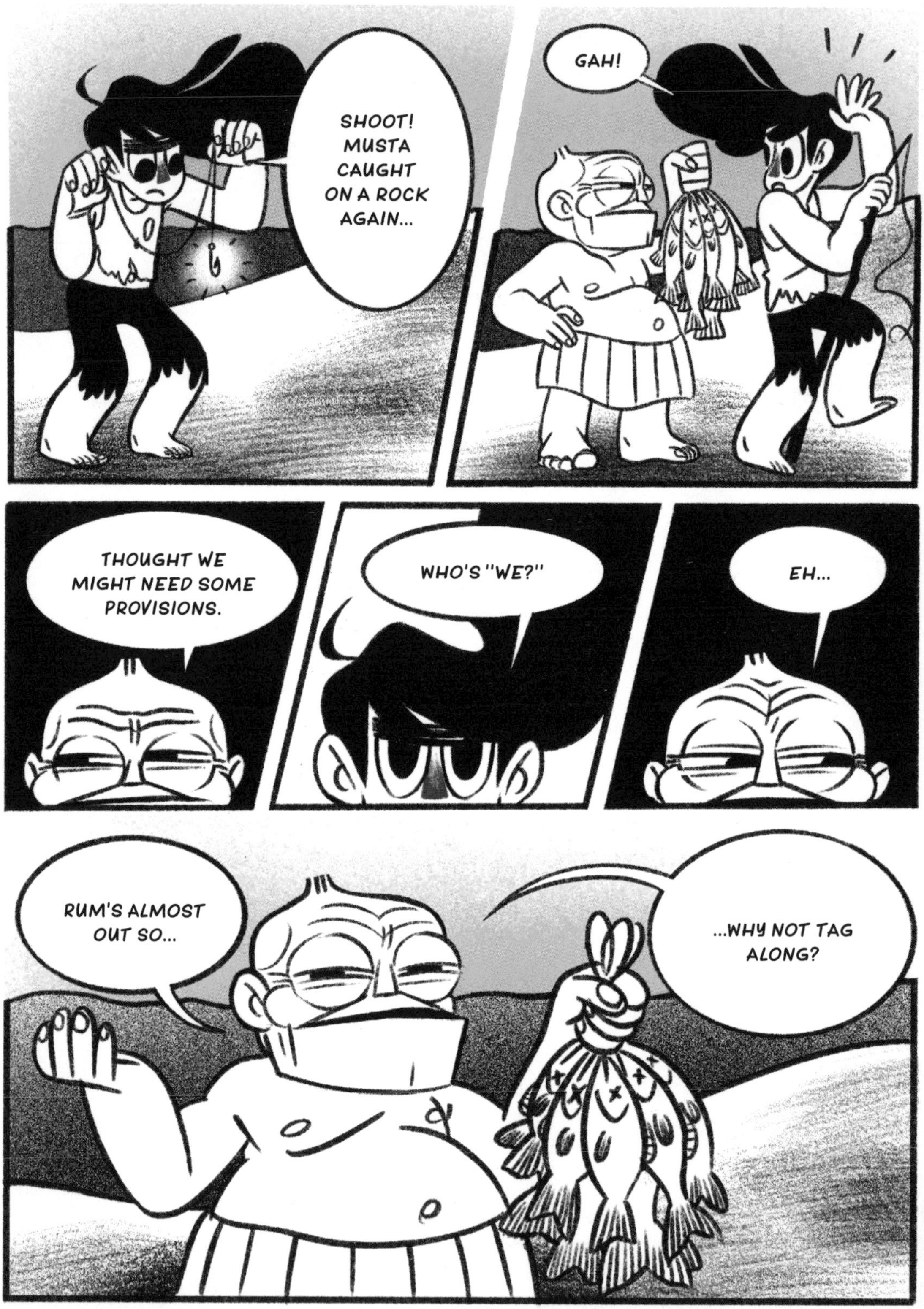
SHOOT! MUSTA CAUGHT ON A ROCK AGAIN...
GAH!
THOUGHT WE MIGHT NEED SOME PROVISIONS.
WHO'S "WE?"
EH...
RUM'S ALMOST OUT SO...
...WHY NOT TAG ALONG?

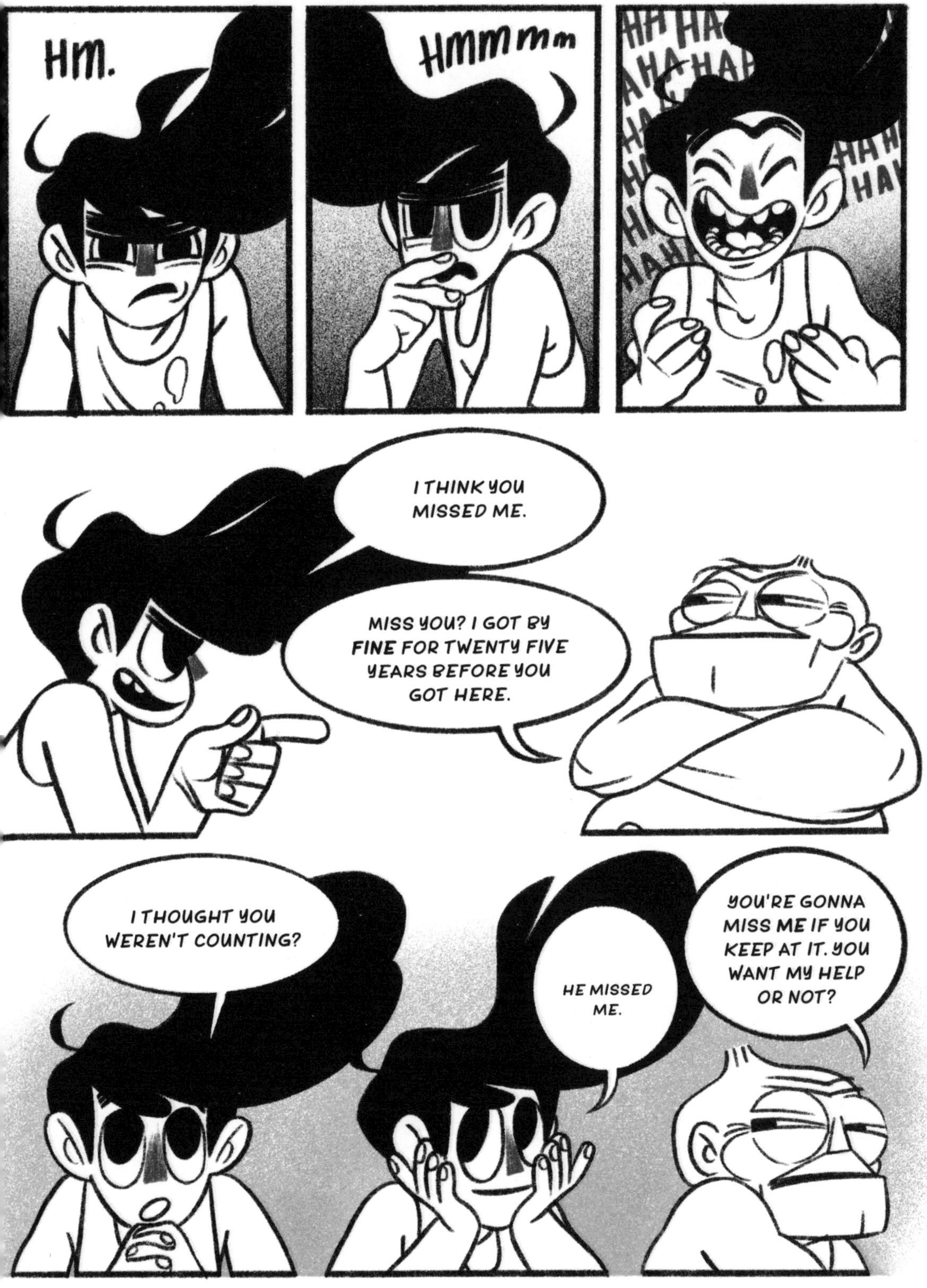

HM.
HMMMMM
HAHAHAHAHAHAHAHAHA
I THINK YOU MISSED ME.
MISS YOU? I GOT BY FINE FOR TWENTY FIVE YEARS BEFORE YOU GOT HERE.
I THOUGHT YOU WEREN'T COUNTING?
HE MISSED ME.
YOU'RE GONNA MISS ME IF YOU KEEP AT IT. YOU WANT MY HELP OR NOT?

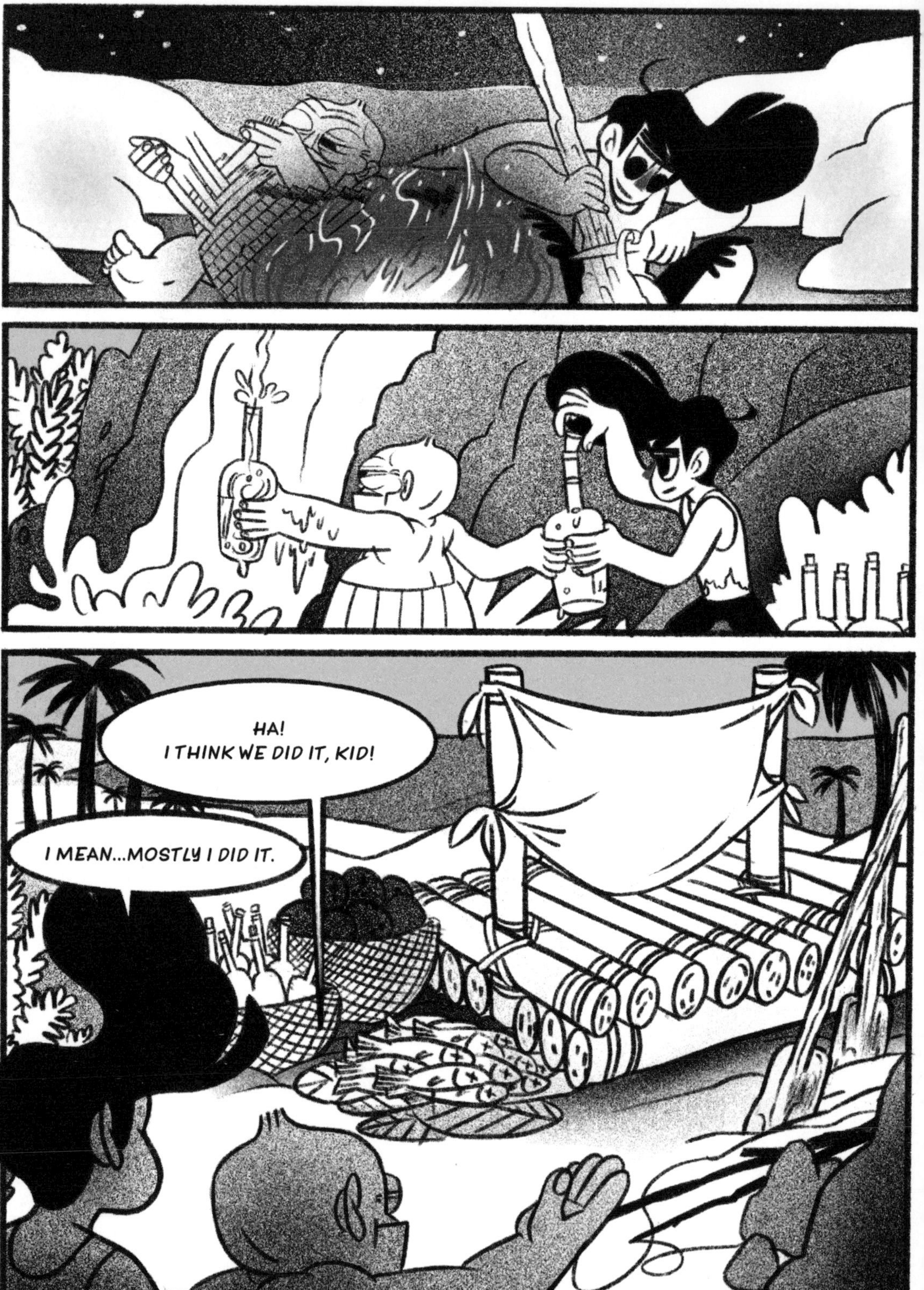
HA!
I THINK WE DID IT, KID!
I MEAN...MOSTLY I DID IT.

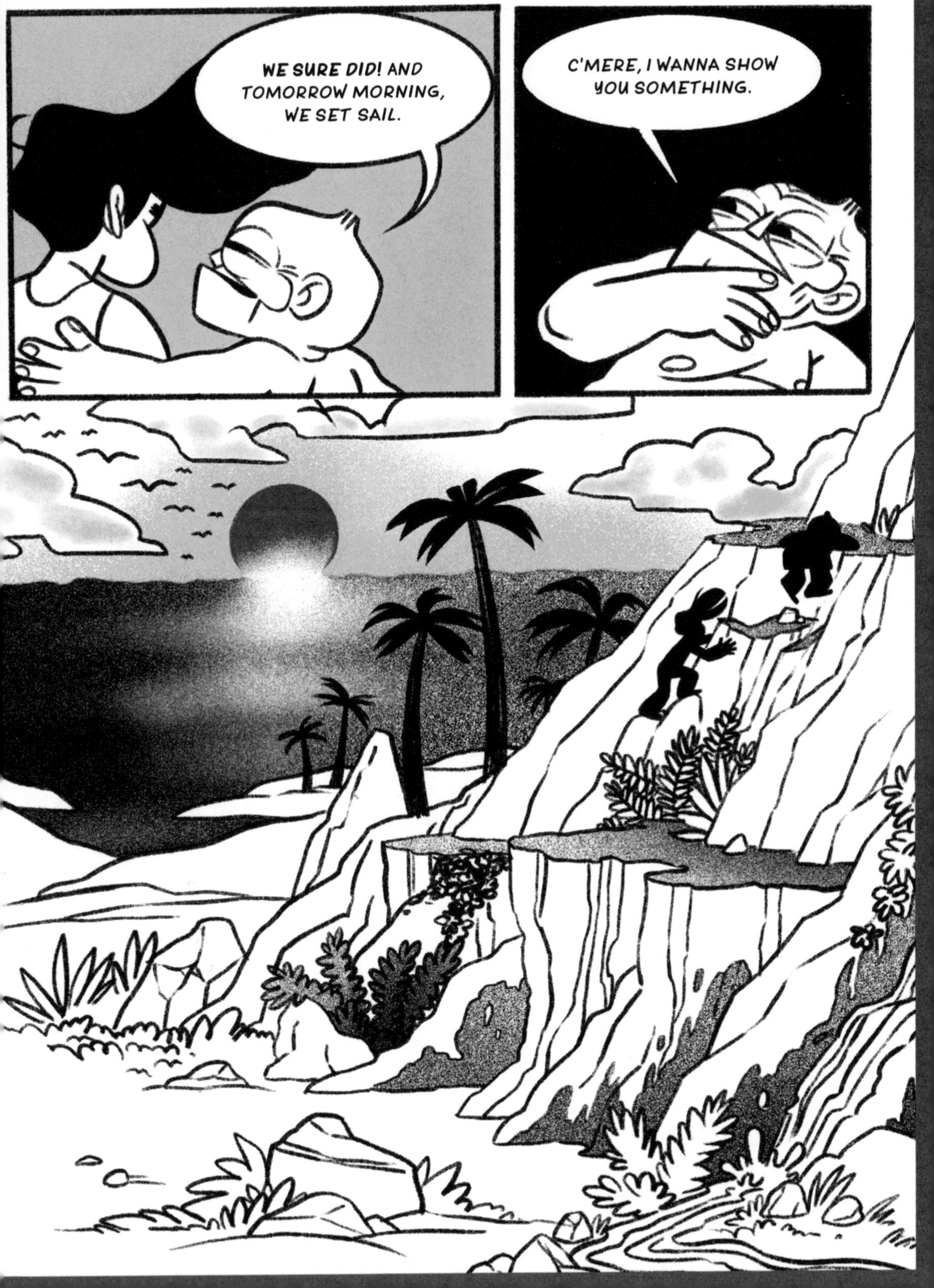
WE SURE DID! AND TOMORROW MORNING, WE SET SAIL.
C'MERE, I WANNA SHOW YOU SOMETHING.

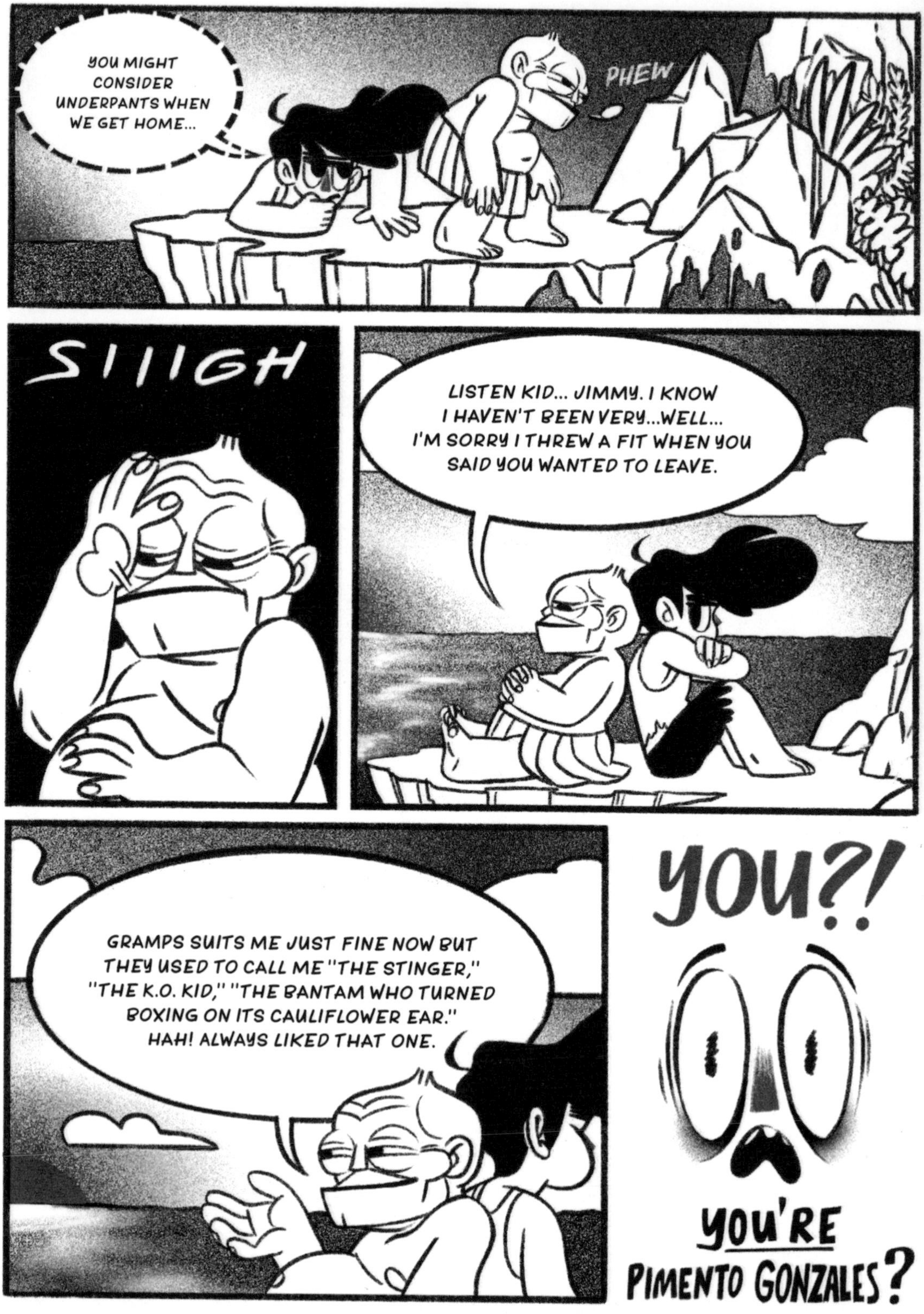
YOU MIGHT CONSIDER UNDERPANTS WHEN WE GET HOME...
PHEW
SIIIGH
LISTEN KID... JIMMY. I KNOW I HAVEN'T BEEN VERY...WELL... I'M SORRY I THREW A FIT WHEN YOU SAID YOU WANTED TO LEAVE.
GRAMPS SUITS ME JUST FINE NOW BUT THEY USED TO CALL ME "THE STINGER," "THE K.O. KID," "THE BANTAM WHO TURNED BOXING ON ITS CAULIFLOWER EAR." HAH! ALWAYS LIKED THAT ONE.
YOU?!
YOU'RE PIMENTO GONZALES?

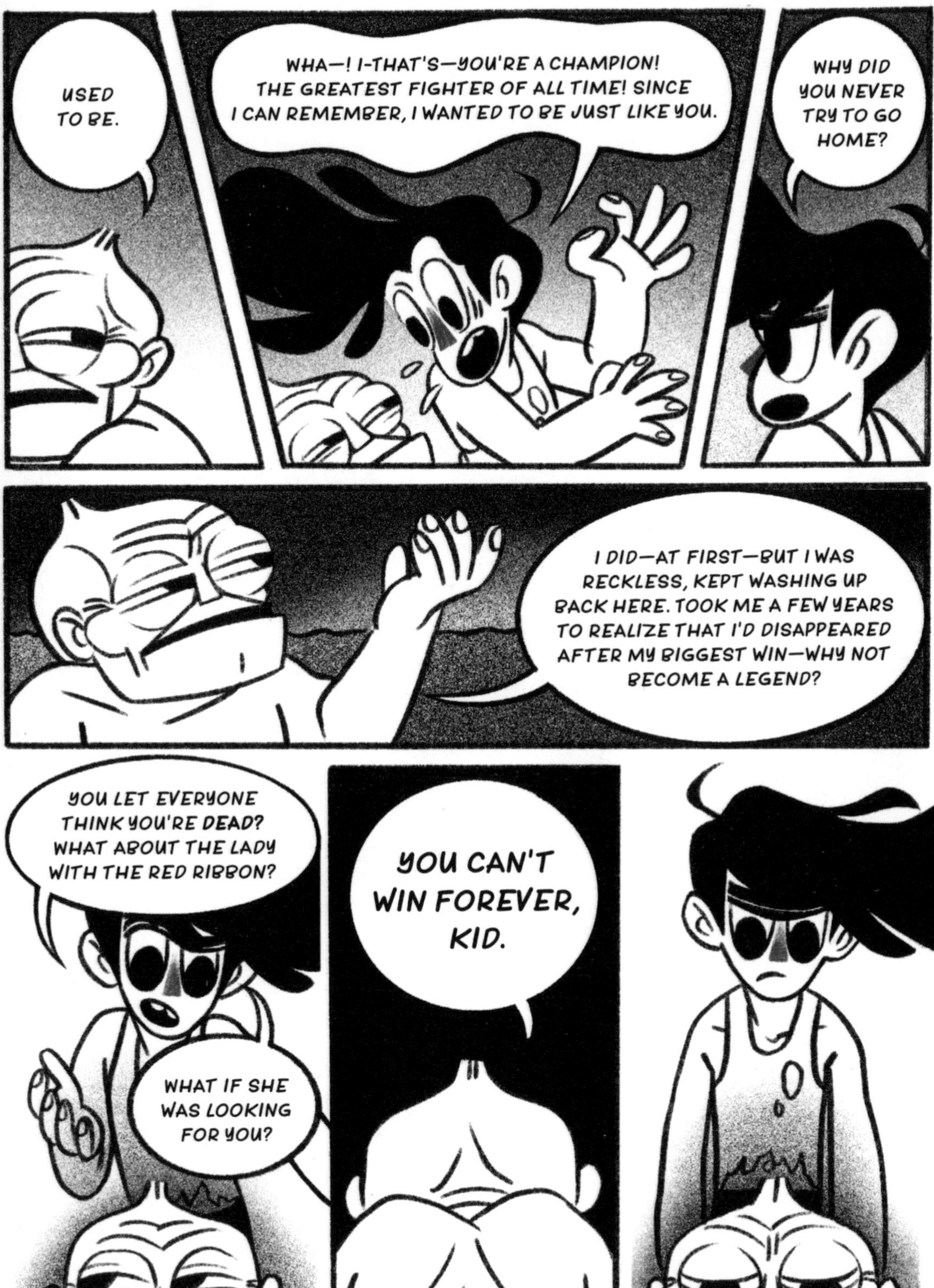
USED TO BE.
WHA—! I-THAT'S—YOU'RE A CHAMPION! THE GREATEST FIGHTER OF ALL TIME! SINCE I CAN REMEMBER, I WANTED TO BE JUST LIKE YOU.
WHY DID YOU NEVER TRY TO GO HOME?
I DID—AT FIRST—BUT I WAS RECKLESS, KEPT WASHING UP BACK HERE. TOOK ME A FEW YEARS TO REALIZE THAT I'D DISAPPEARED AFTER MY BIGGEST WIN—WHY NOT BECOME A LEGEND?
YOU LET EVERYONE THINK YOU'RE *DEAD*? WHAT ABOUT THE LADY WITH THE RED RIBBON?
WHAT IF SHE WAS LOOKING FOR YOU?
YOU CAN'T WIN FOREVER, KID.

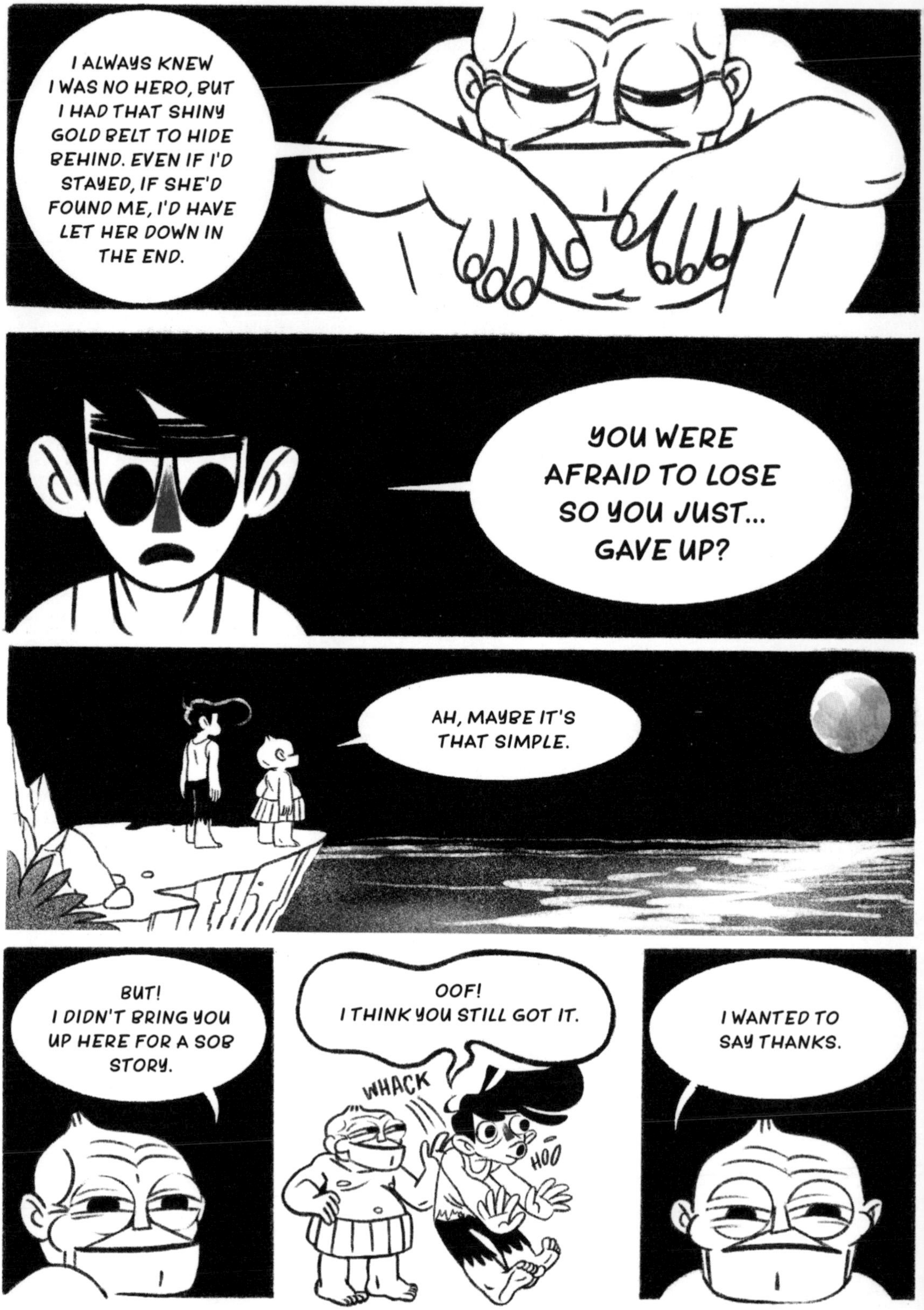
I ALWAYS KNEW I WAS NO HERO, BUT I HAD THAT SHINY GOLD BELT TO HIDE BEHIND. EVEN IF I'D STAYED, IF SHE'D FOUND ME, I'D HAVE LET HER DOWN IN THE END.
YOU WERE AFRAID TO LOSE SO YOU JUST... GAVE UP?
AH, MAYBE IT'S THAT SIMPLE.
BUT! I DIDN'T BRING YOU UP HERE FOR A SOB STORY.
OOF! I THINK YOU STILL GOT IT.
WHACK
HOO
I WANTED TO SAY THANKS.

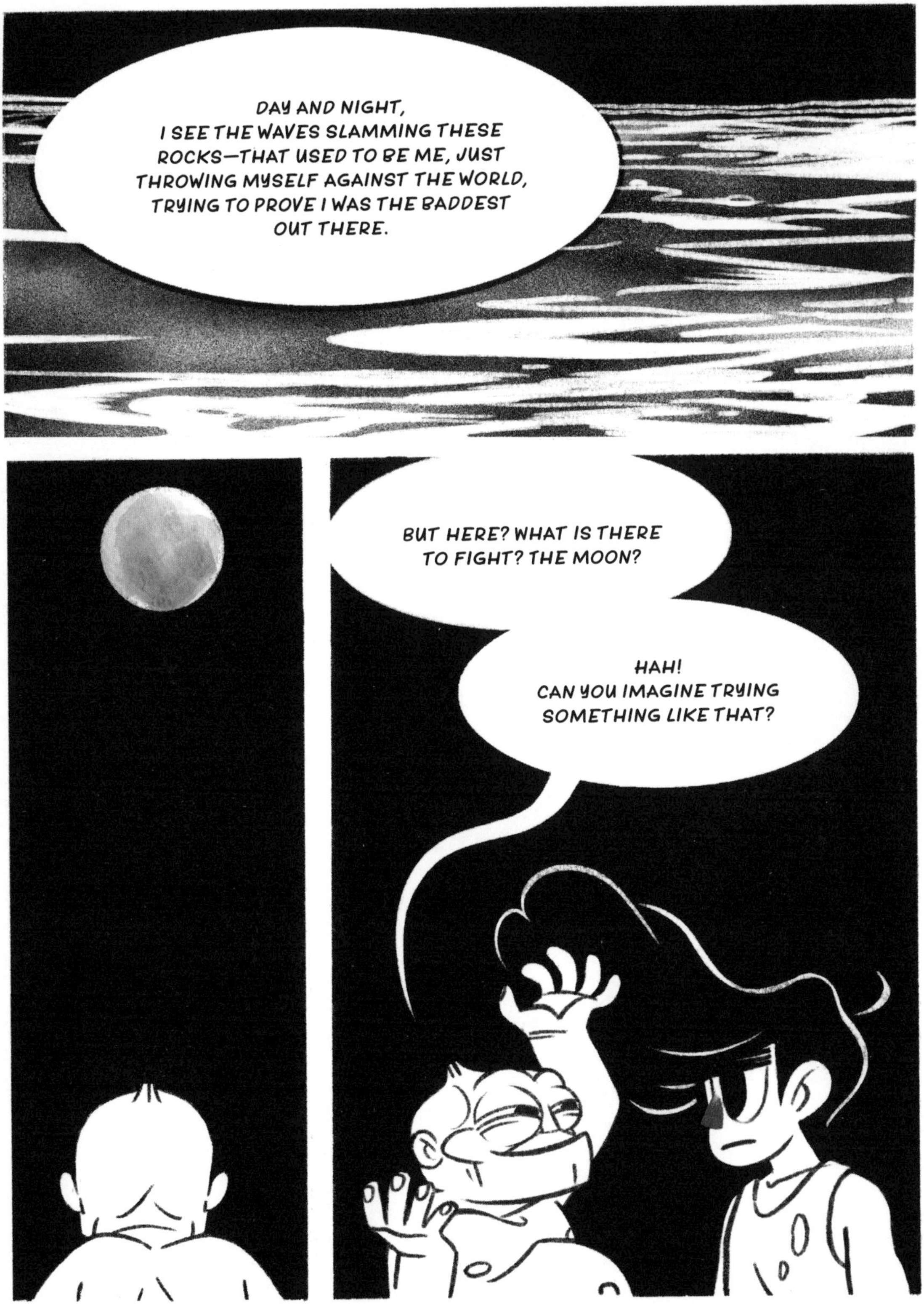
DAY AND NIGHT, I SEE THE WAVES SLAMMING THESE ROCKS—THAT USED TO BE ME, JUST THROWING MYSELF AGAINST THE WORLD, TRYING TO PROVE I WAS THE BADDEST OUT THERE.
BUT HERE? WHAT IS THERE TO FIGHT? THE MOON?
HAH! CAN YOU IMAGINE TRYING SOMETHING LIKE THAT?

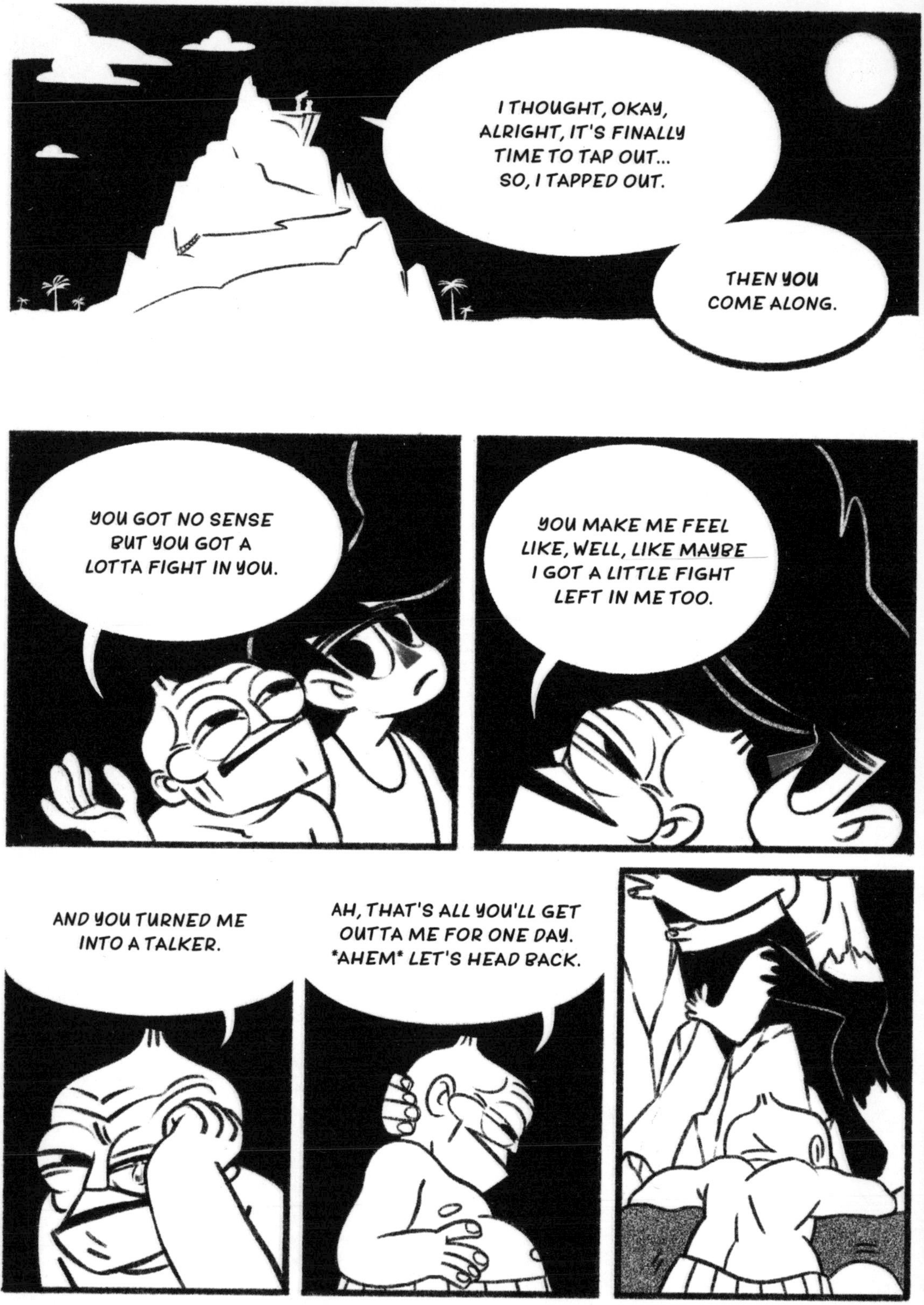
I THOUGHT, OKAY, ALRIGHT, IT'S FINALLY TIME TO TAP OUT... SO, I TAPPED OUT.
THEN YOU COME ALONG.
YOU GOT NO SENSE BUT YOU GOT A LOTTA FIGHT IN YOU.
YOU MAKE ME FEEL LIKE, WELL, LIKE MAYBE I GOT A LITTLE FIGHT LEFT IN ME TOO.
AND YOU TURNED ME INTO A TALKER.
AH, THAT'S ALL YOU'LL GET OUTTA ME FOR ONE DAY. *AHEM* LET'S HEAD BACK.

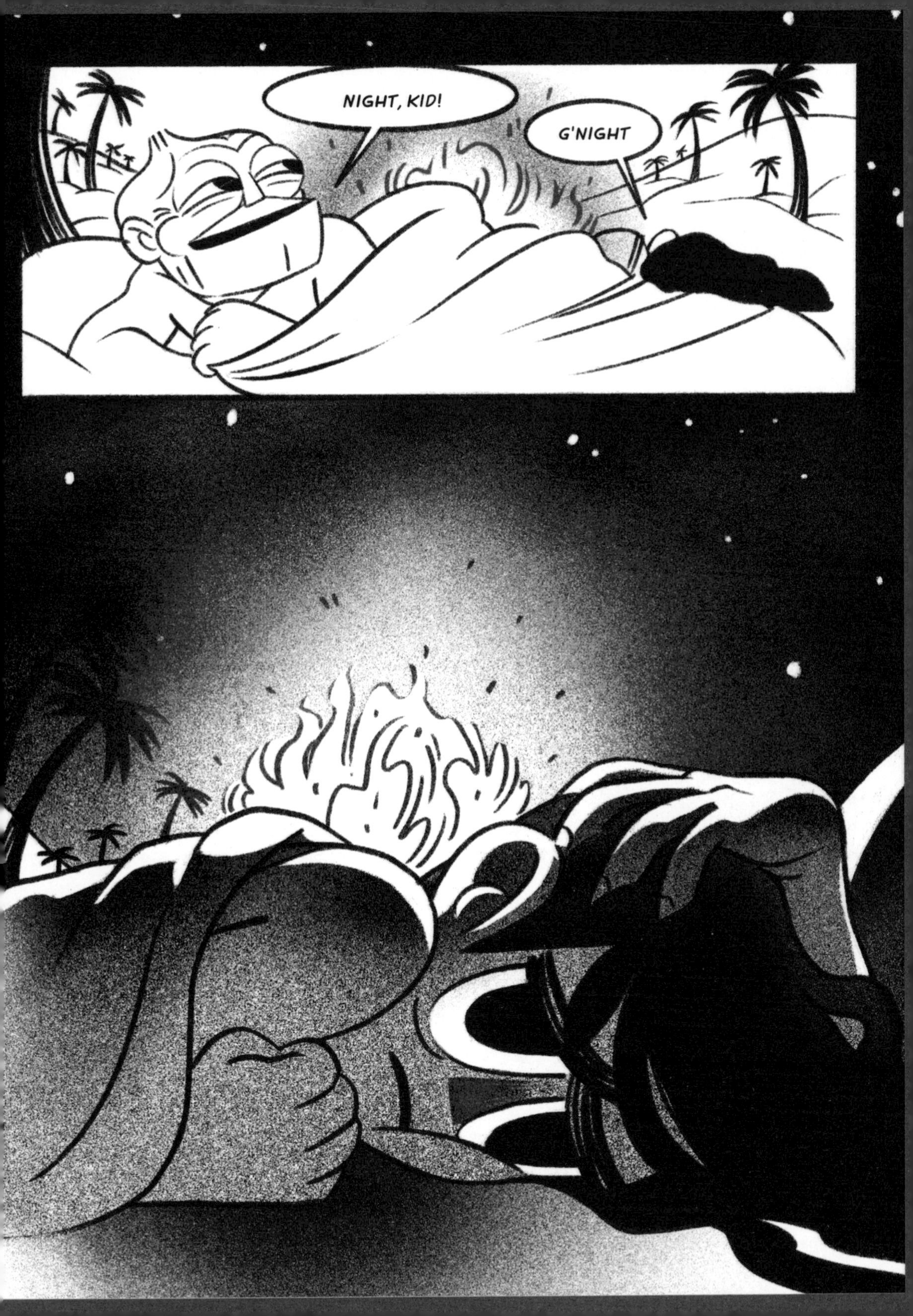
NIGHT, KID!
G'NIGHT

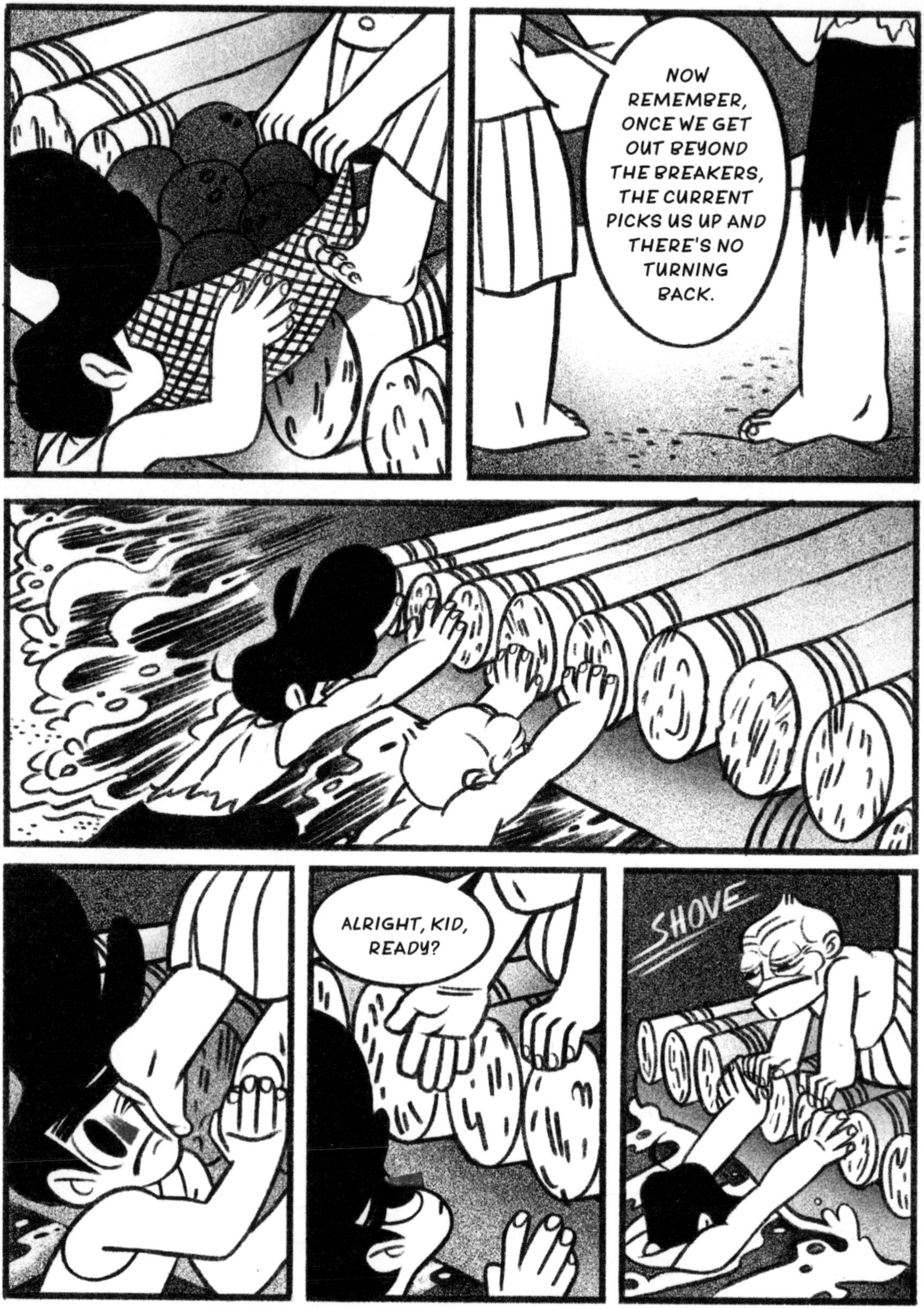
NOW REMEMBER, ONCE WE GET OUT BEYOND THE BREAKERS, THE CURRENT PICKS US UP AND THERE'S NO TURNING BACK.
ALRIGHT, KID, READY?
SHOVE

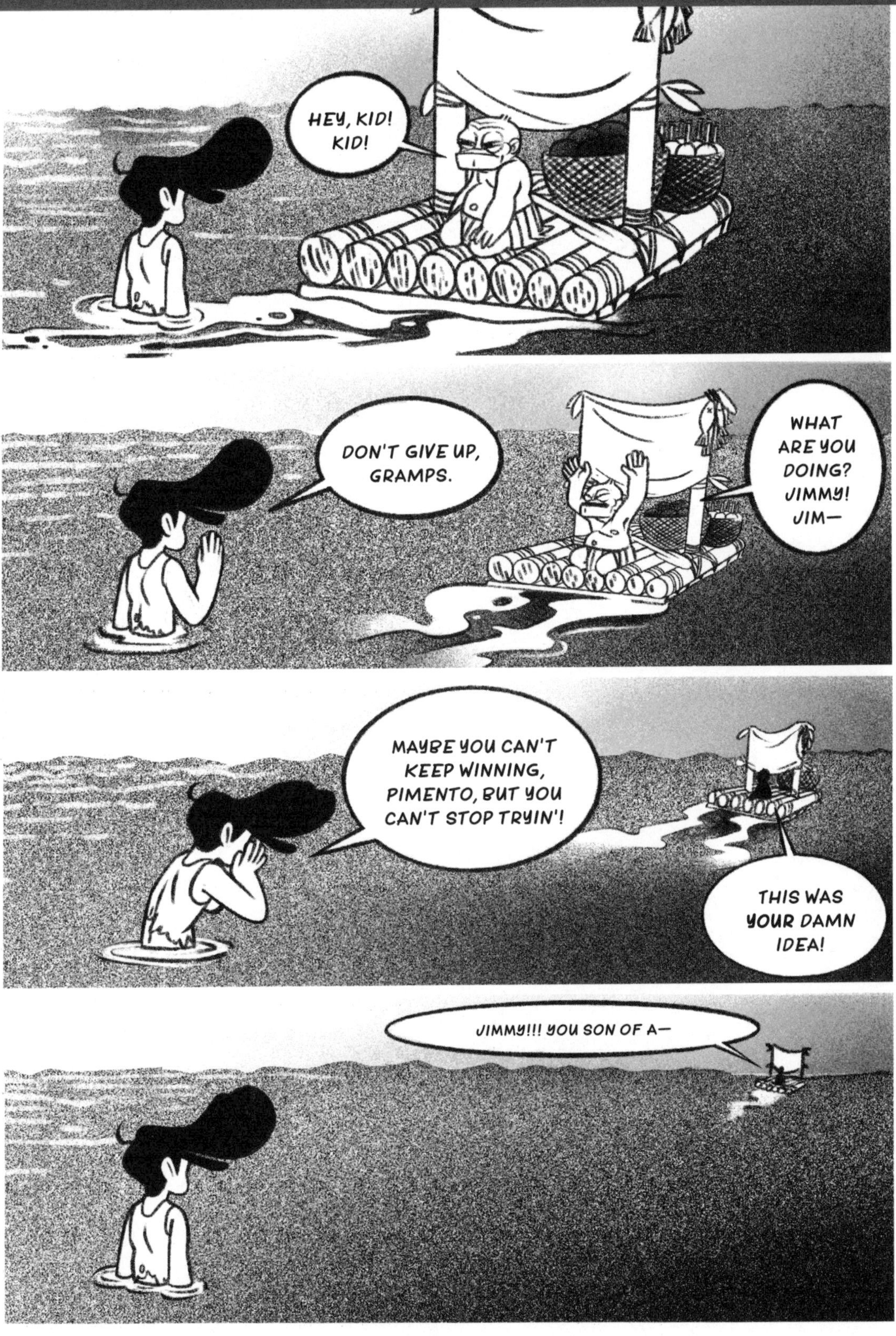
HEY, KID!
KID!
DON'T GIVE UP, GRAMPS.
WHAT ARE YOU DOING? JIMMY! JIM—
MAYBE YOU CAN'T KEEP WINNING, PIMENTO, BUT YOU CAN'T STOP TRYIN'!
THIS WAS YOUR DAMN IDEA!
JIMMY!!! YOU SON OF A—

CHAPTER 8

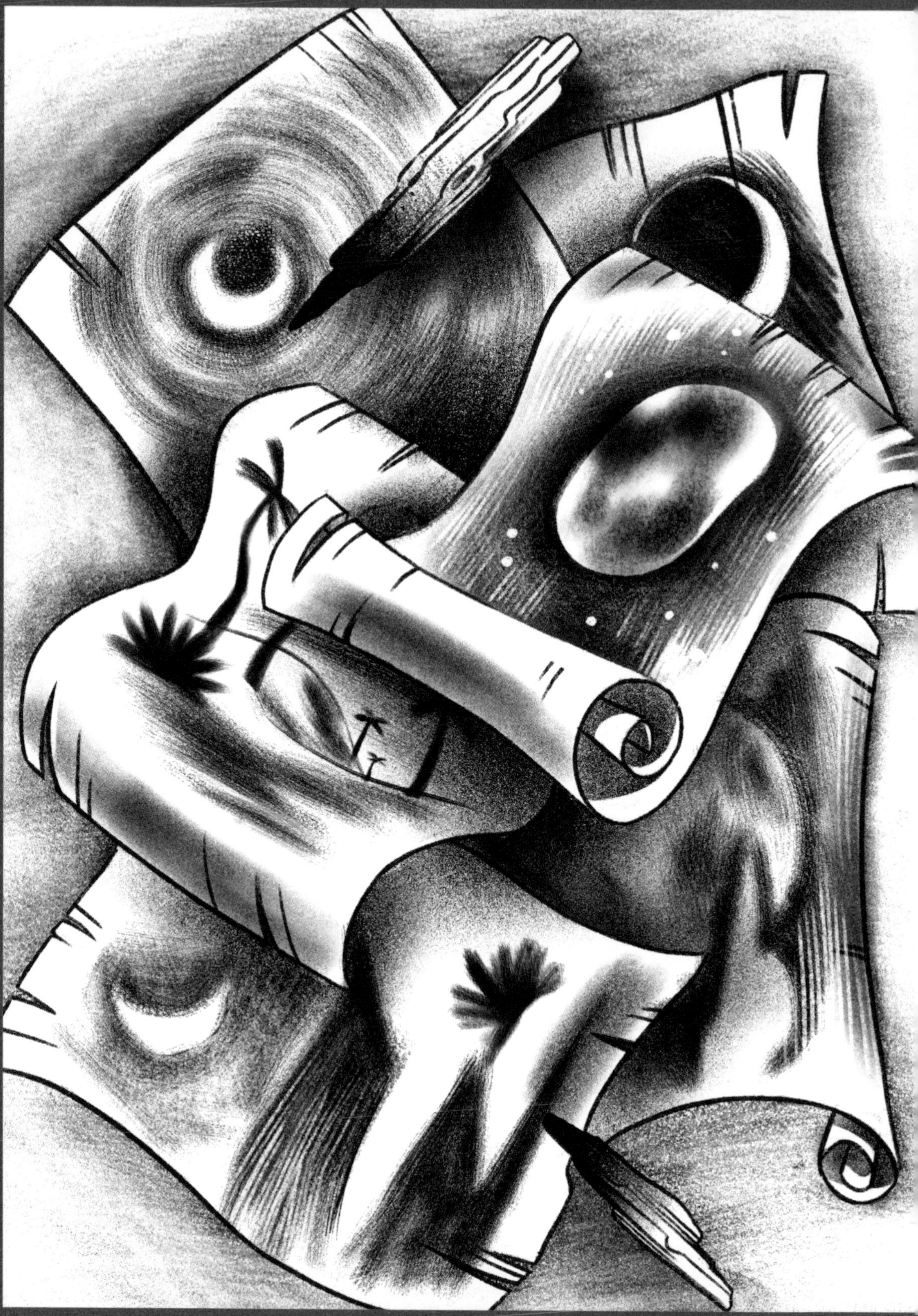

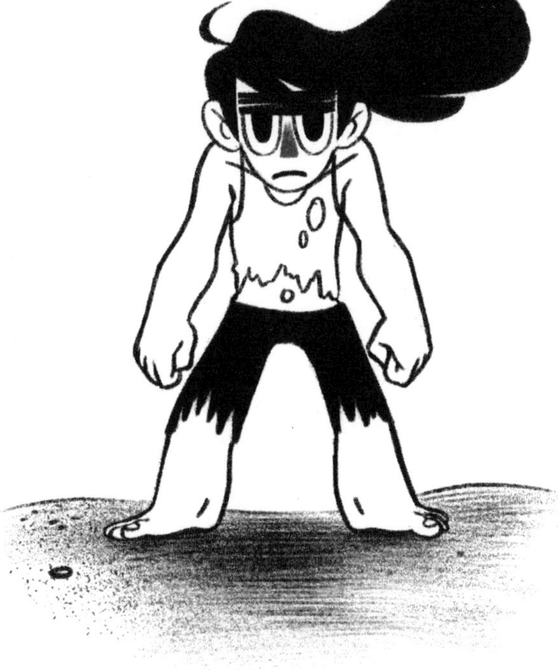

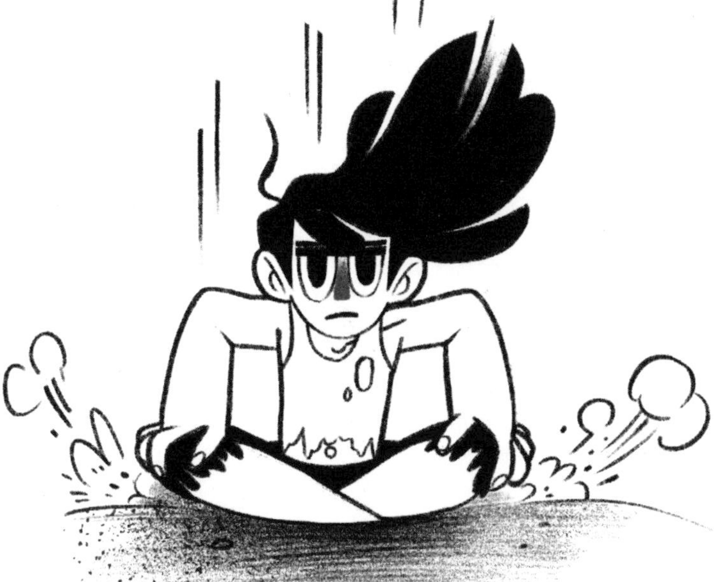

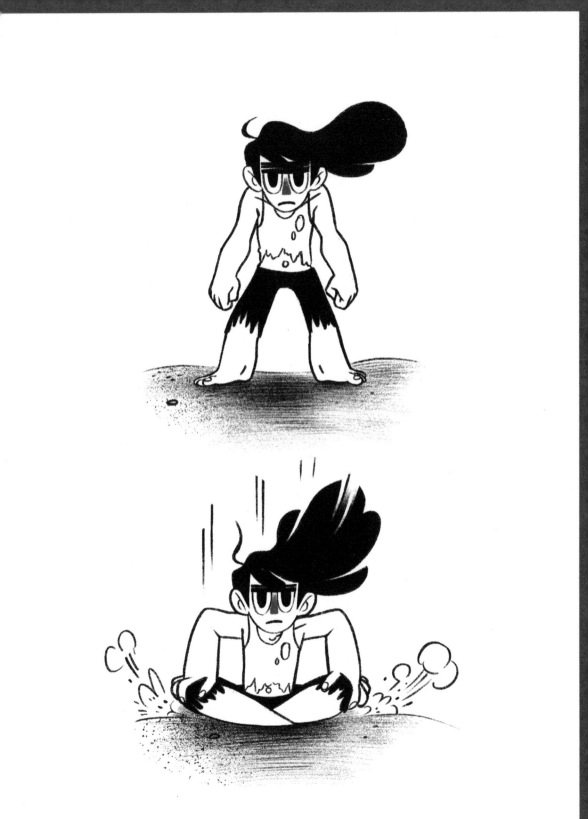

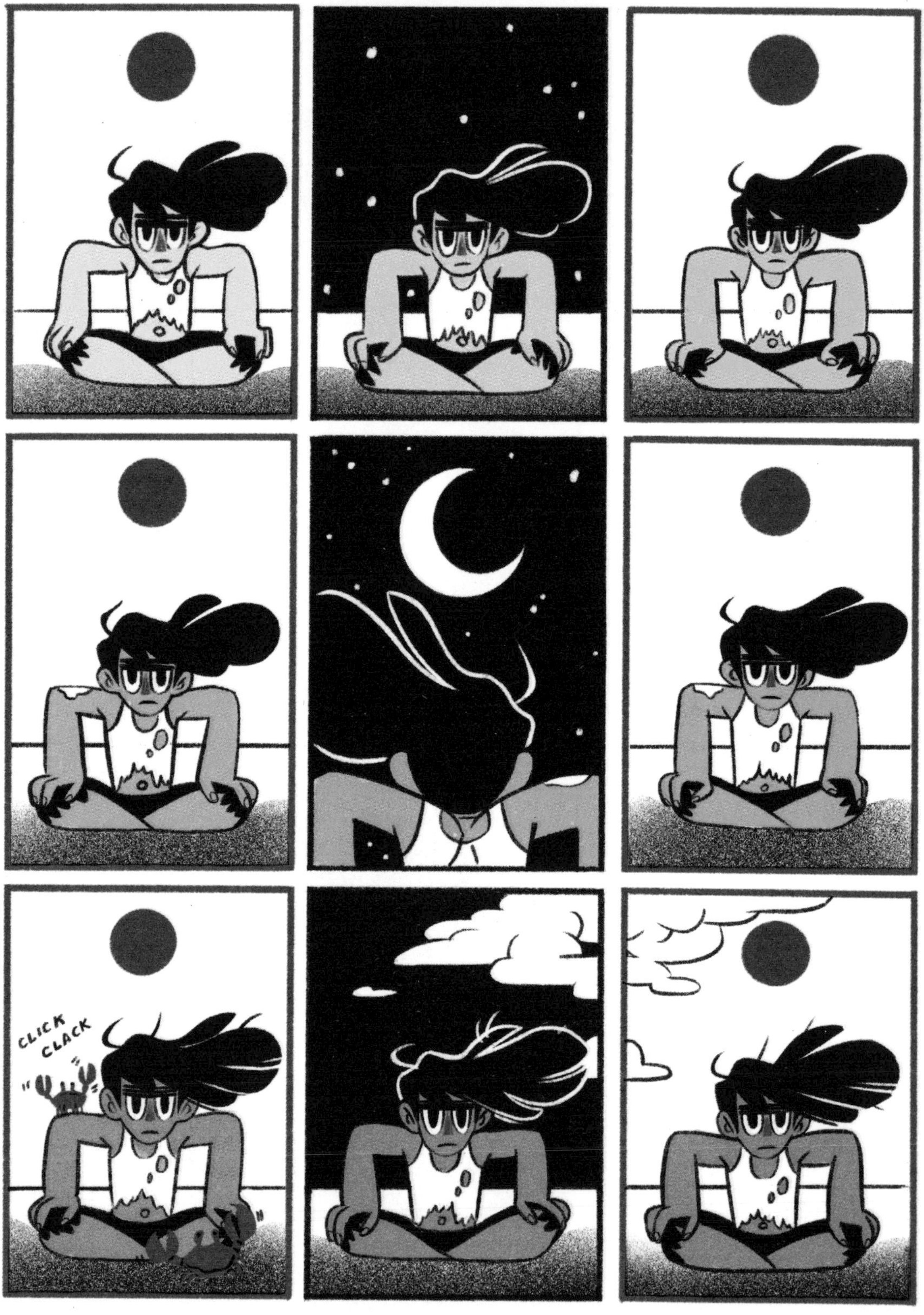
CLICK
CLACK

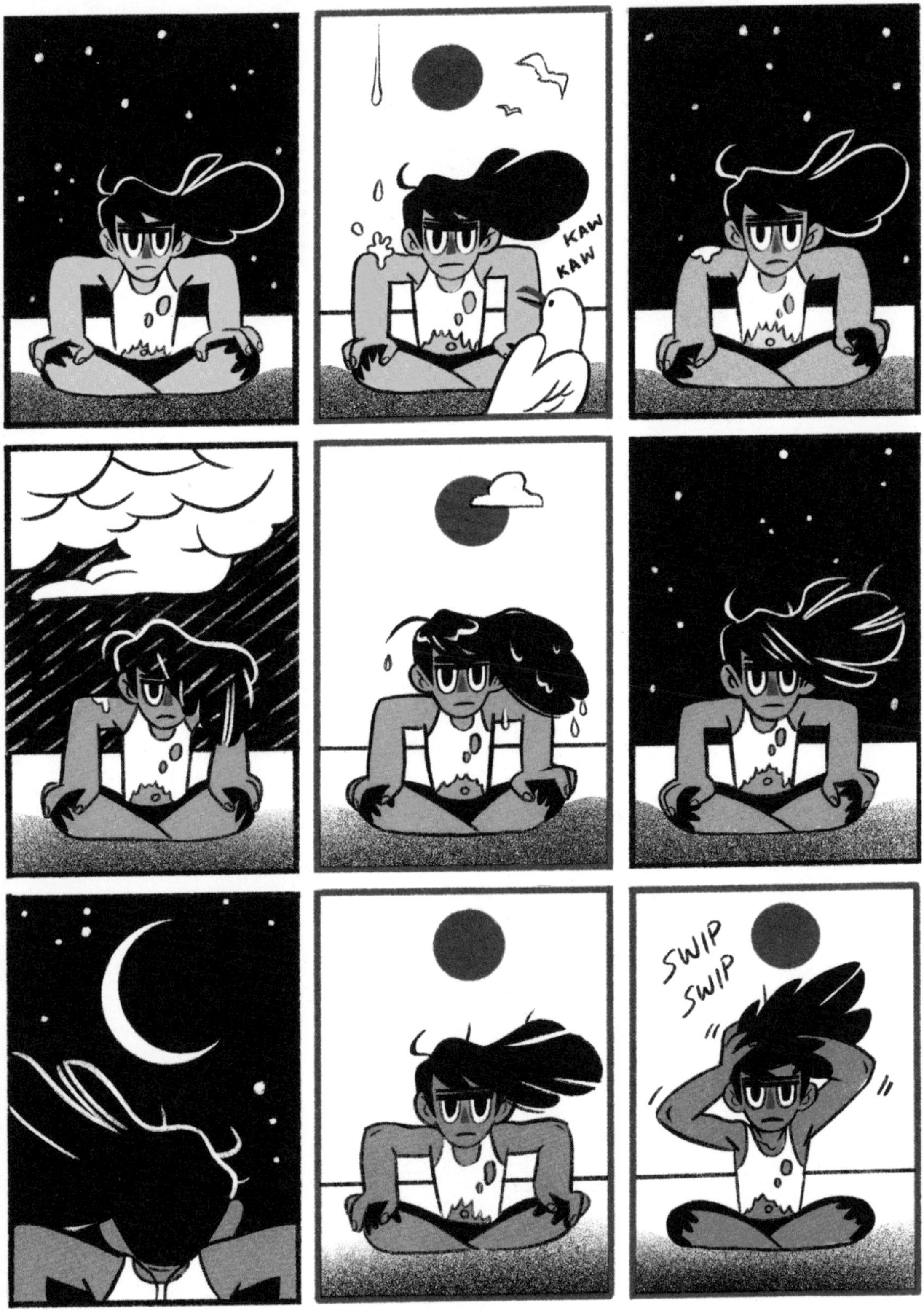
KAW KAW
SWIP SWIP

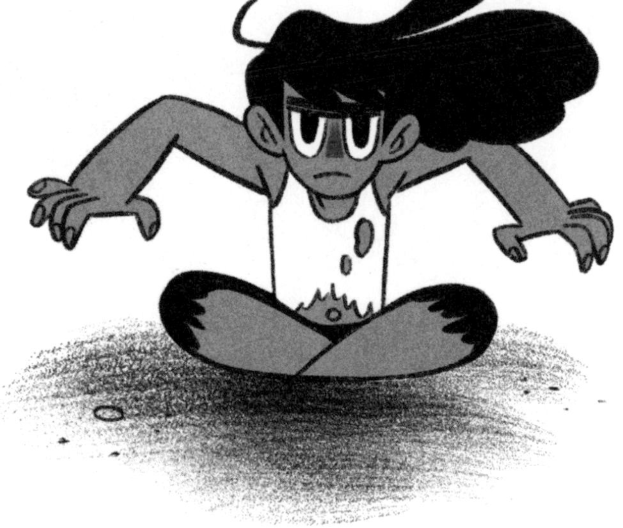

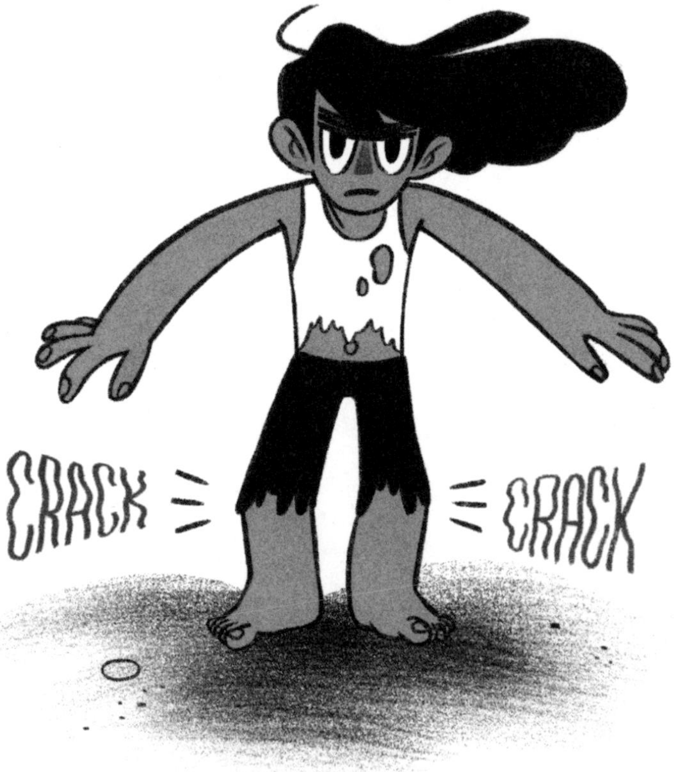
CRACK
CRACK

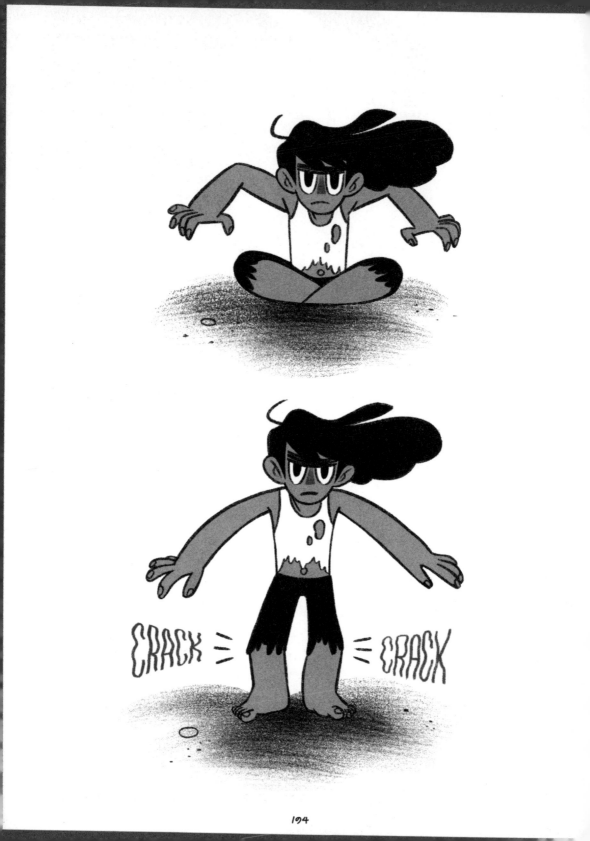

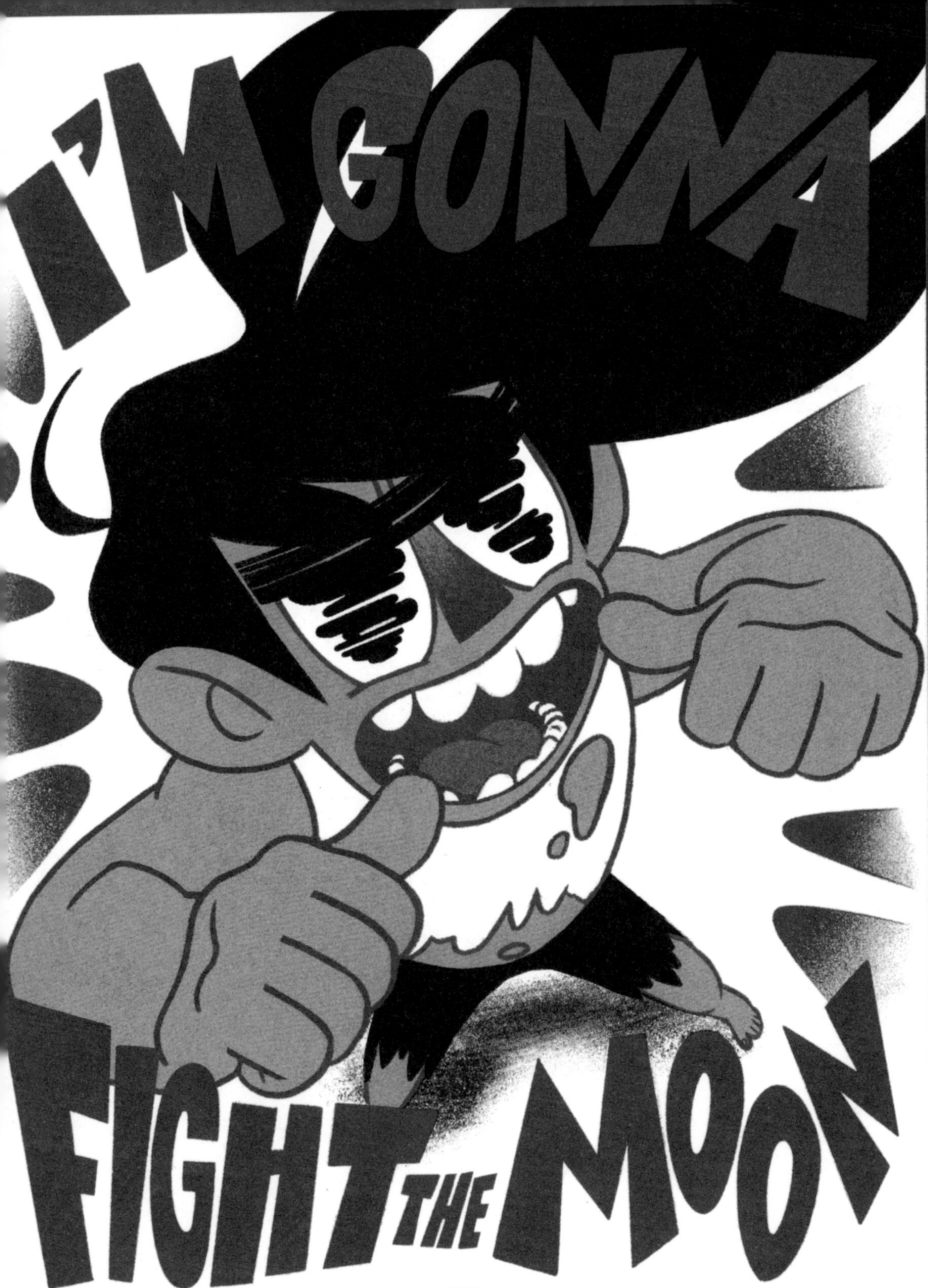
I'M GONNA
FIGHT THE MOON

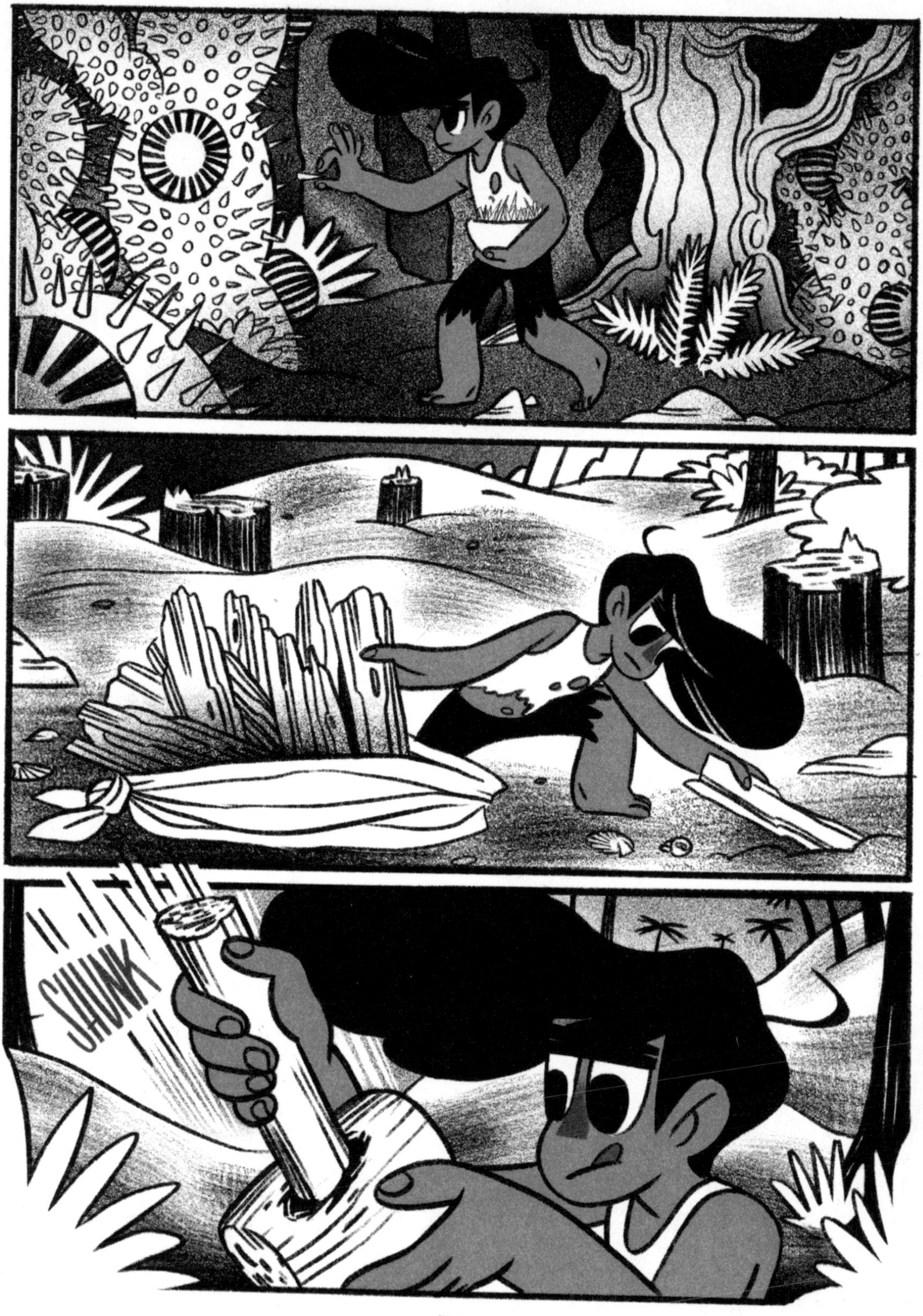
SHUNK

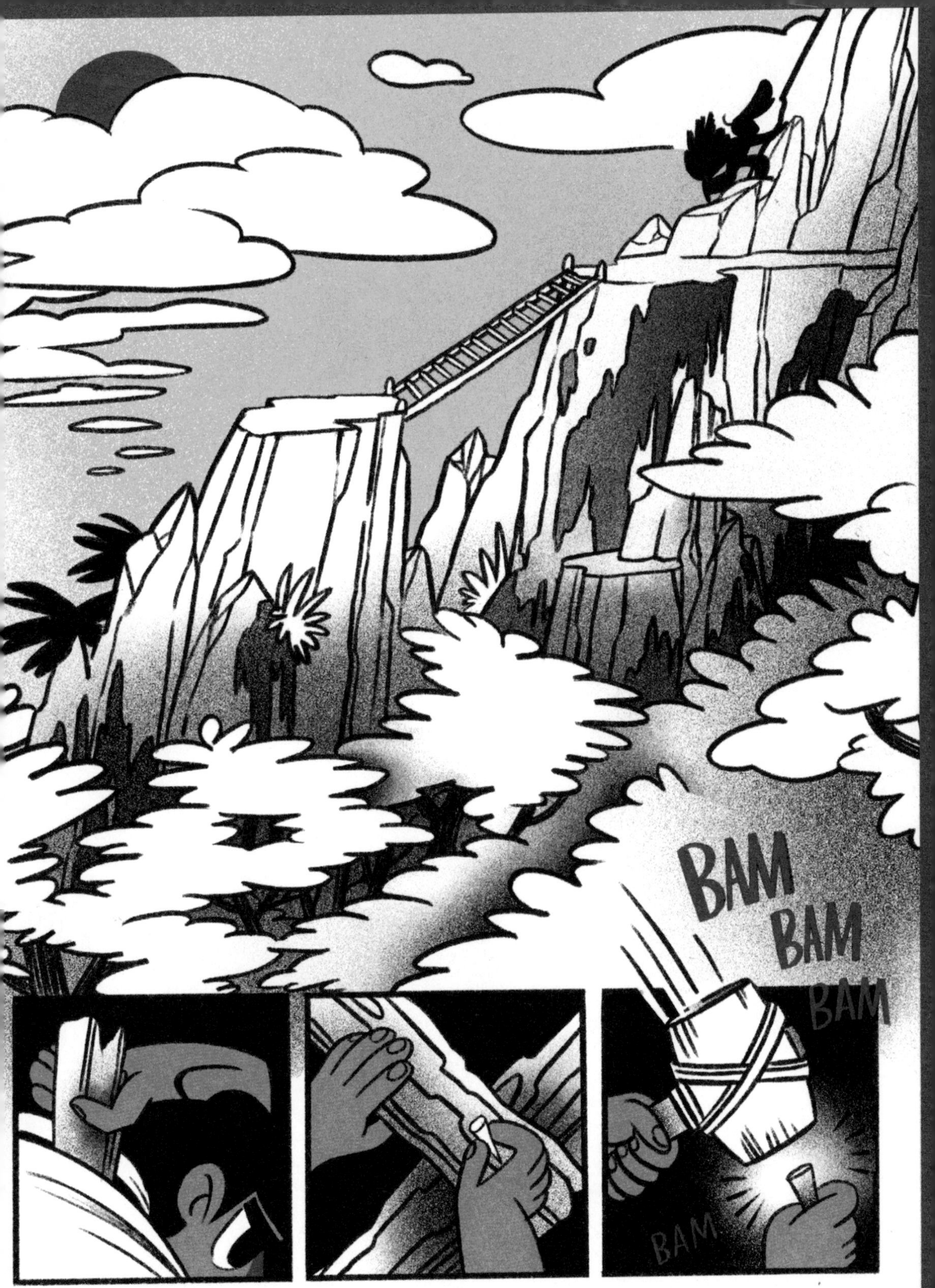
BAM
BAM
BAM
BAM

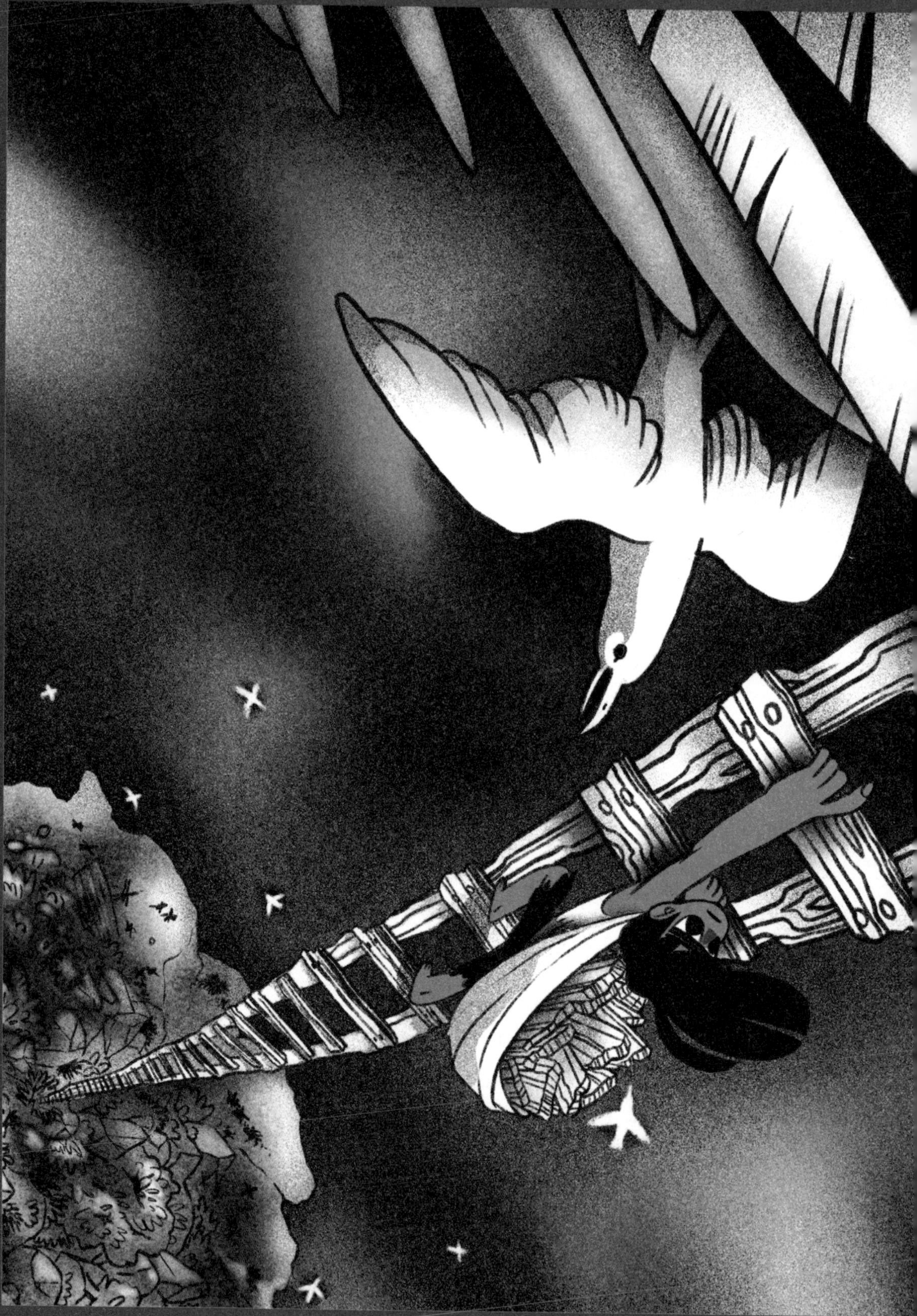

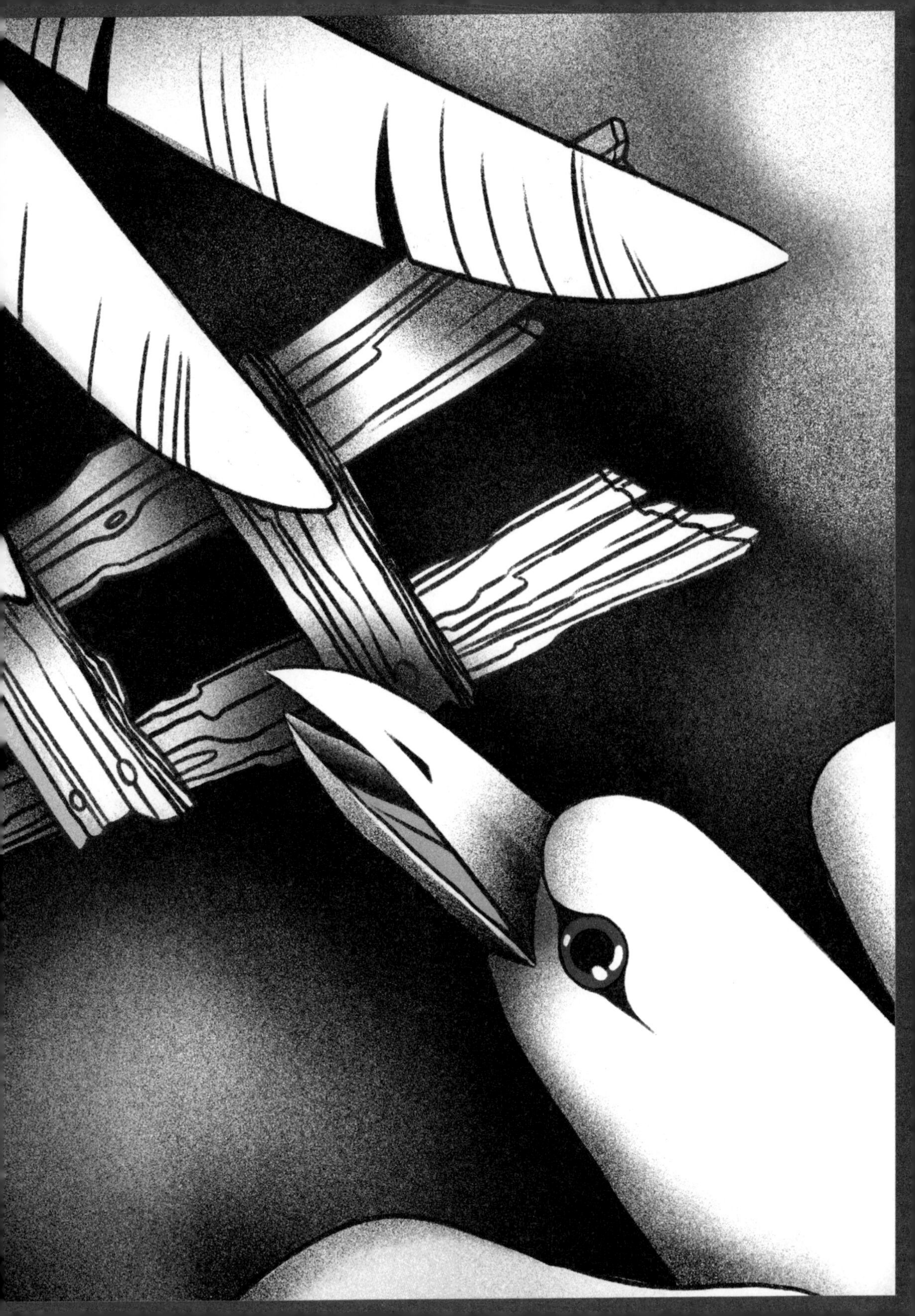

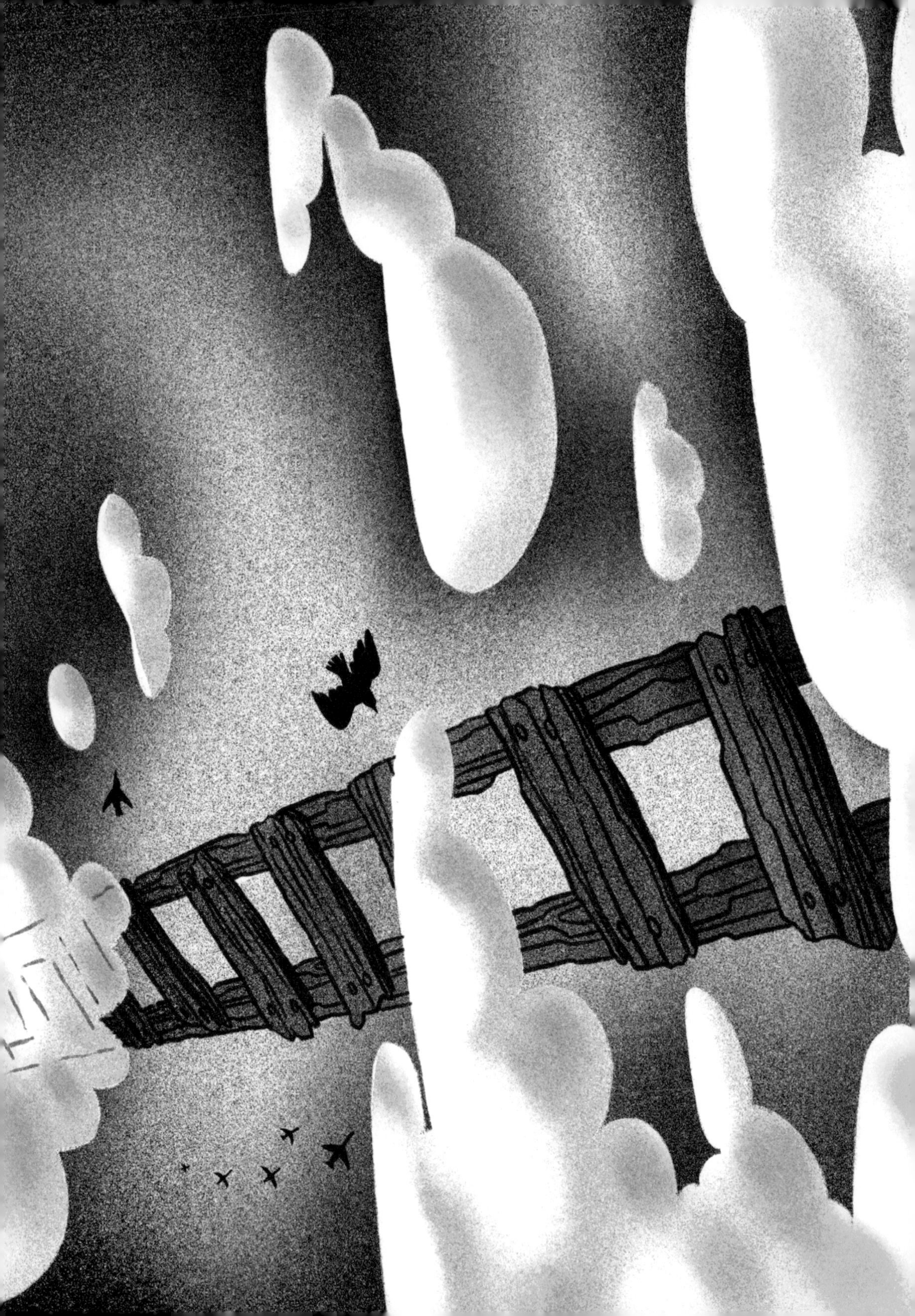

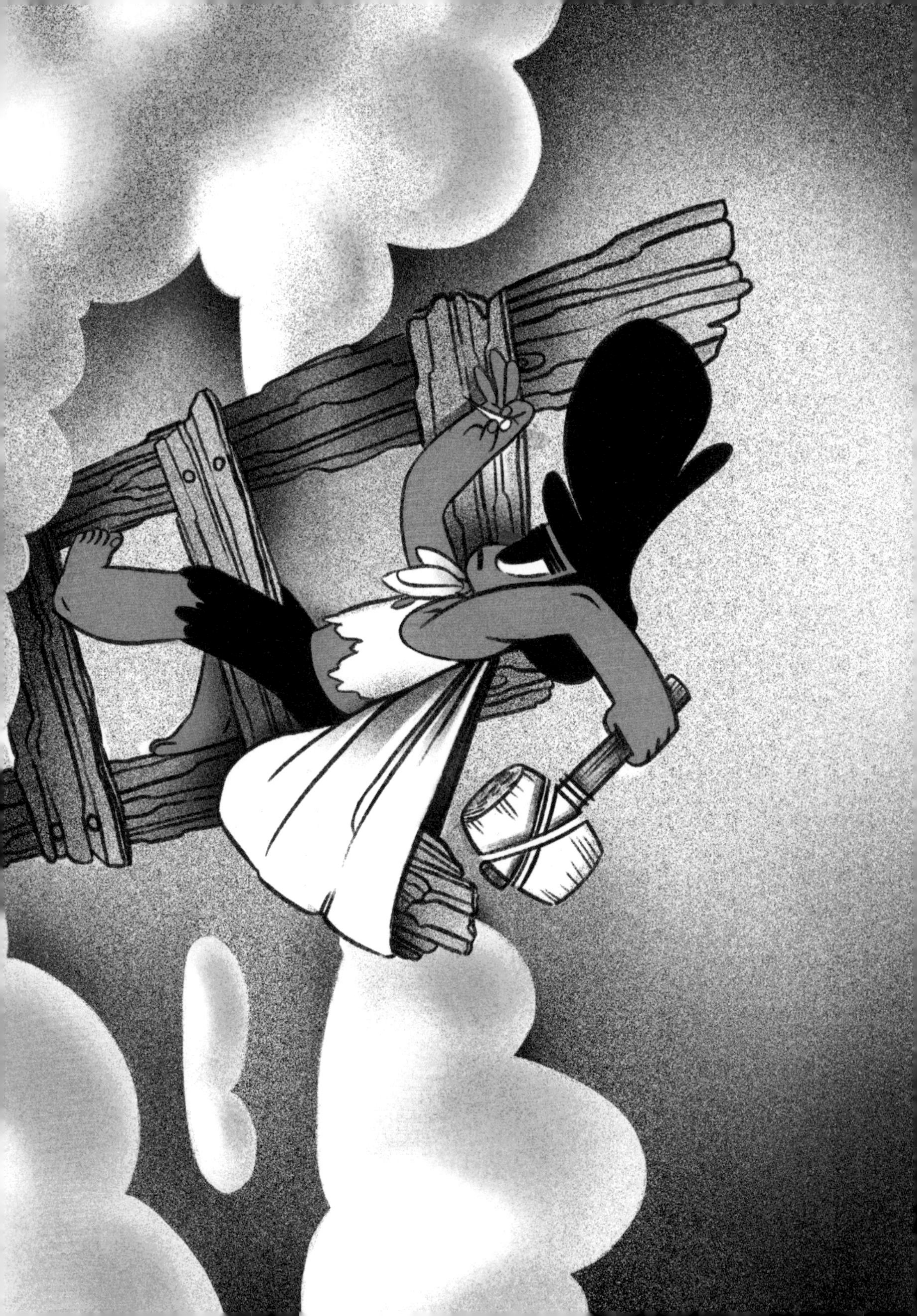

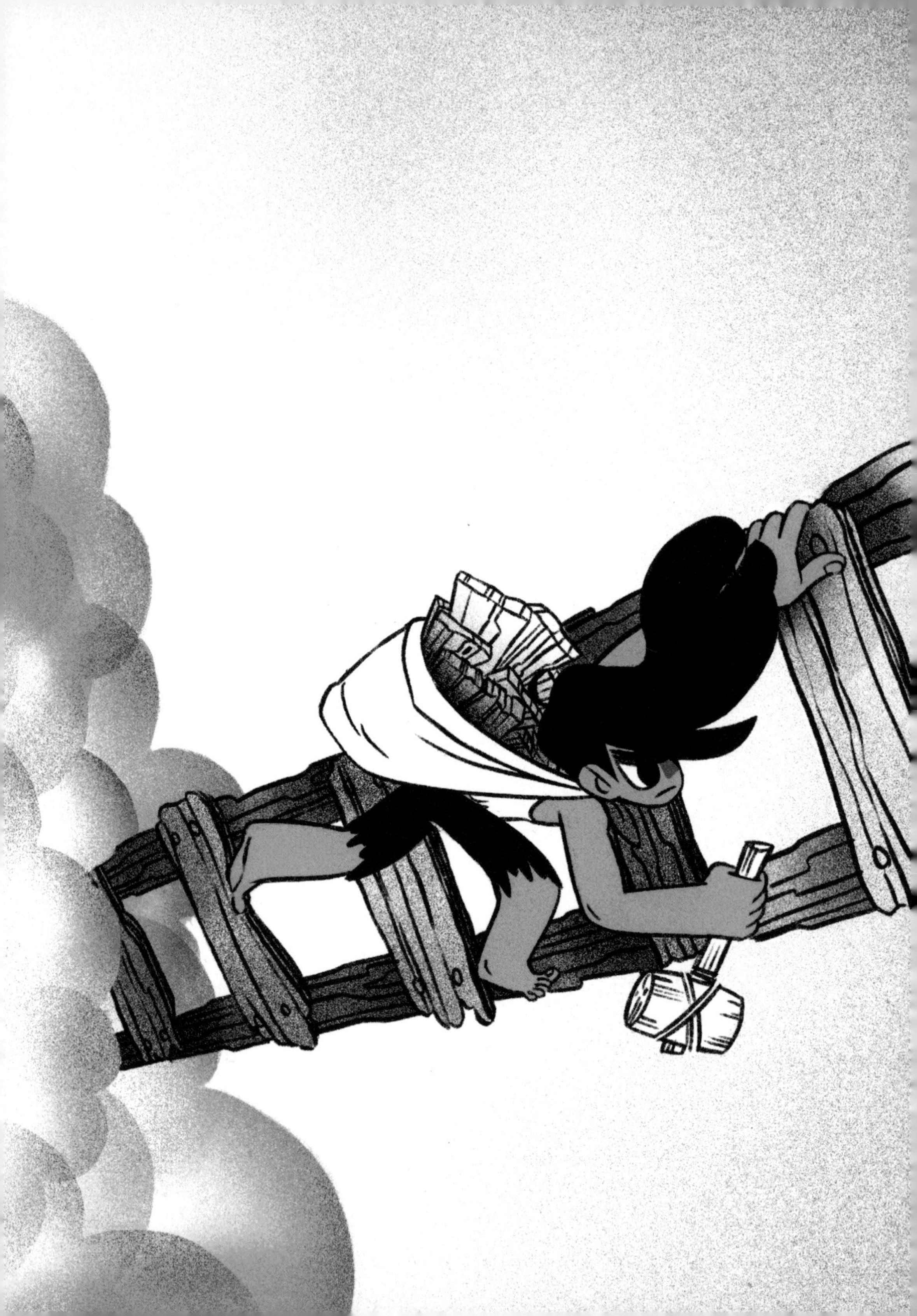

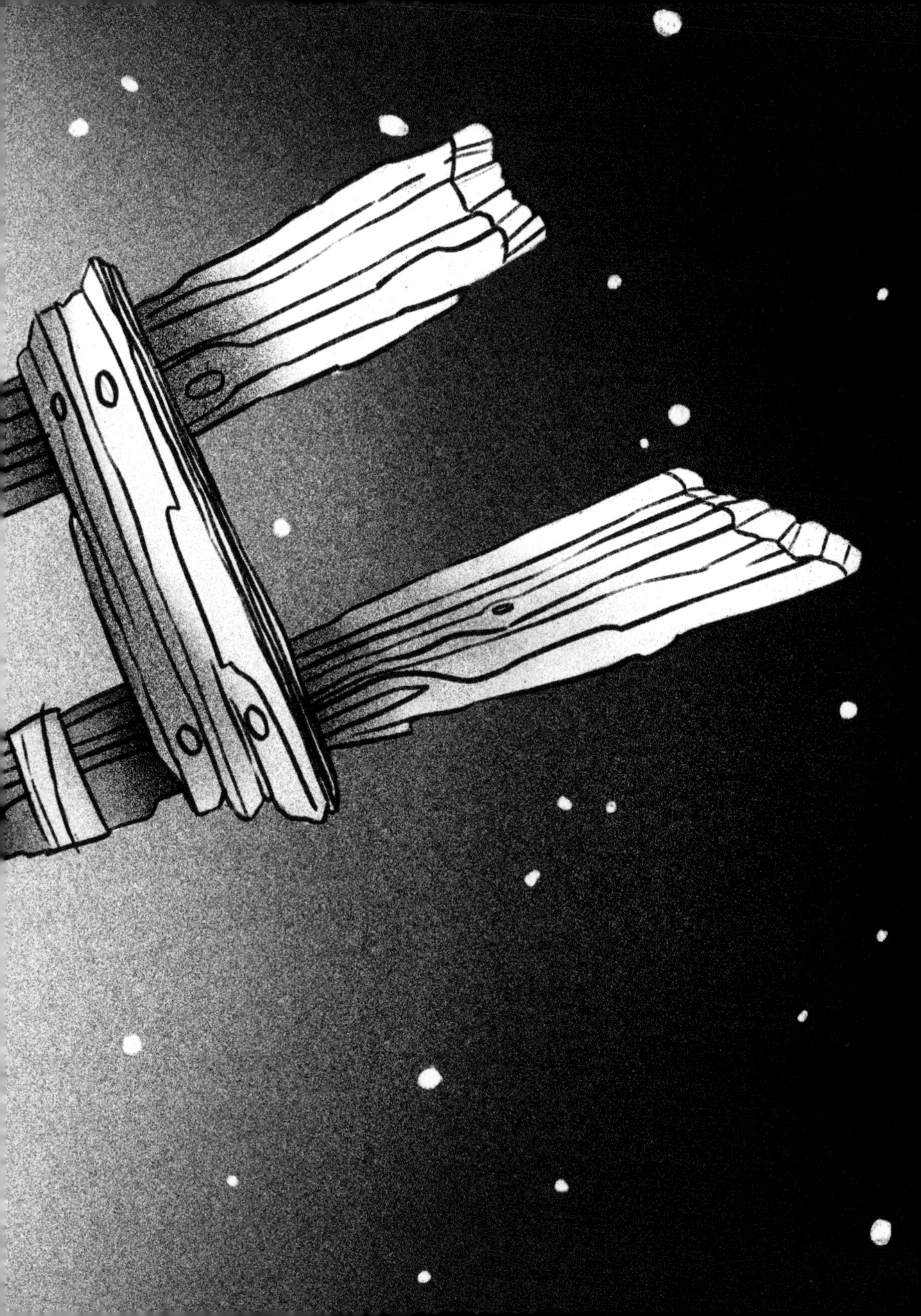

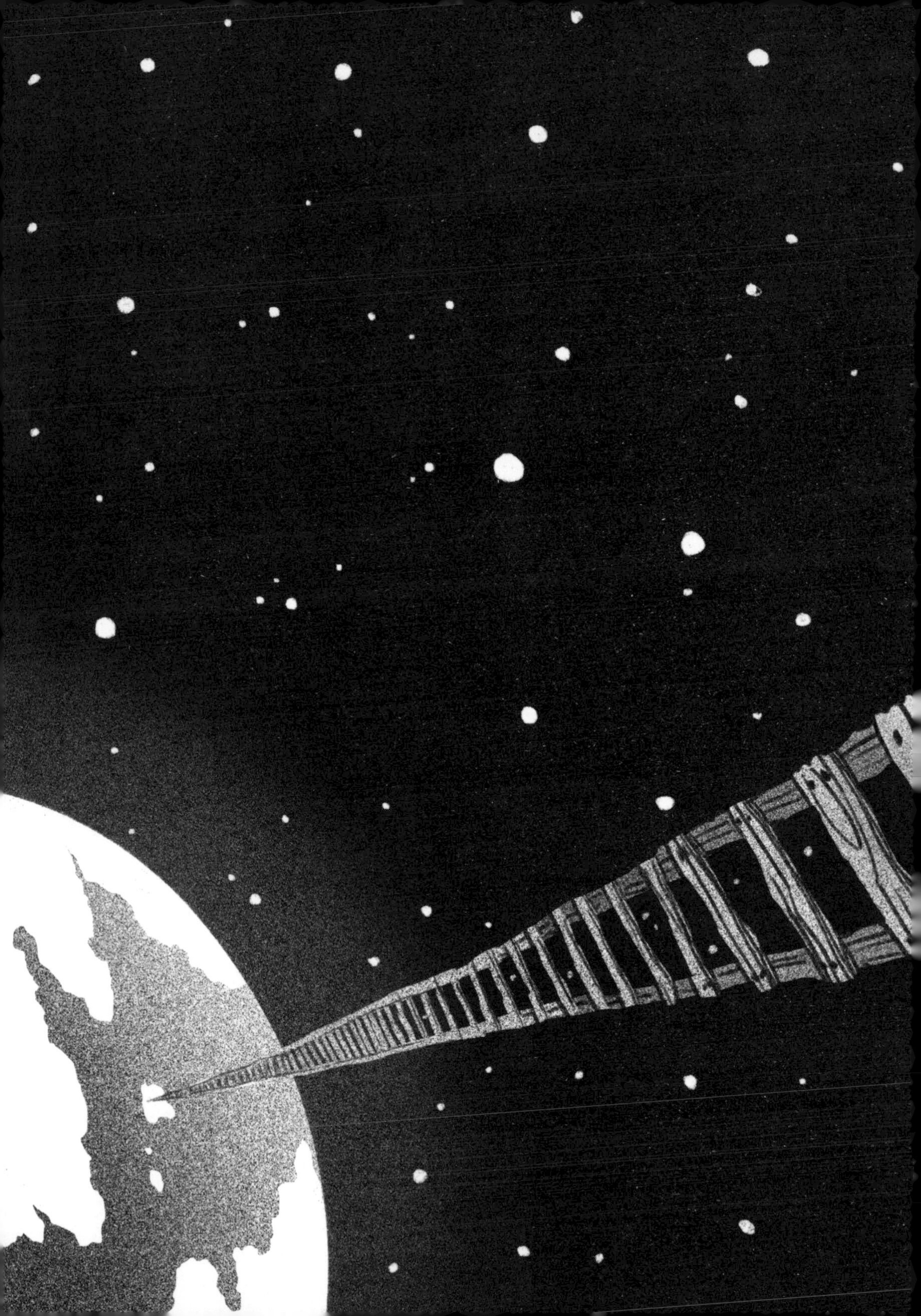

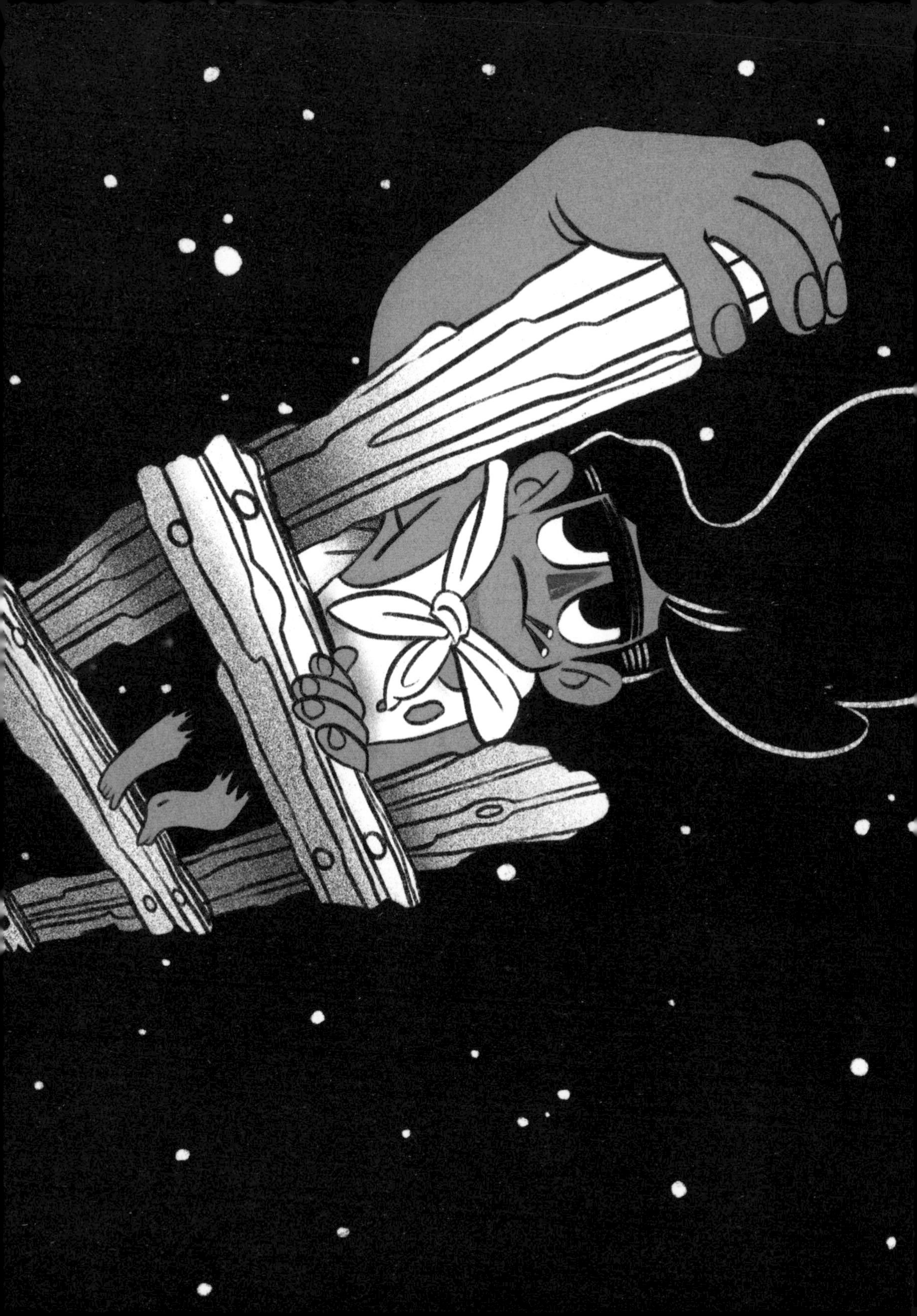

EPILOGUE

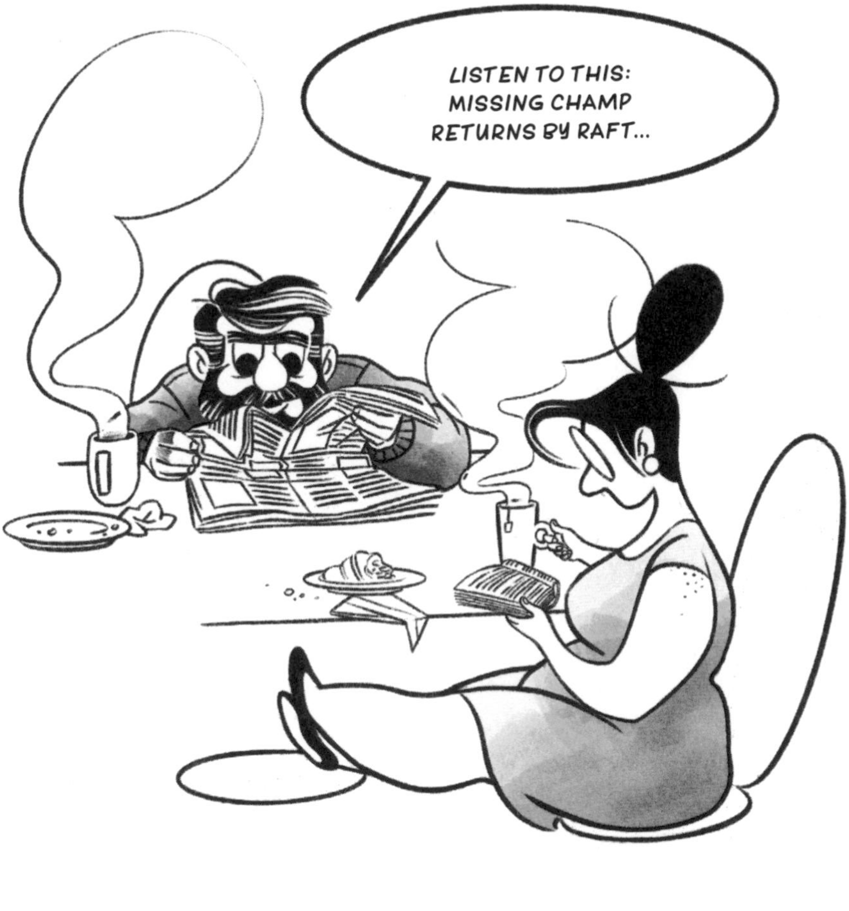
LISTEN TO THIS:
MISSING CHAMP
RETURNS BY RAFT...

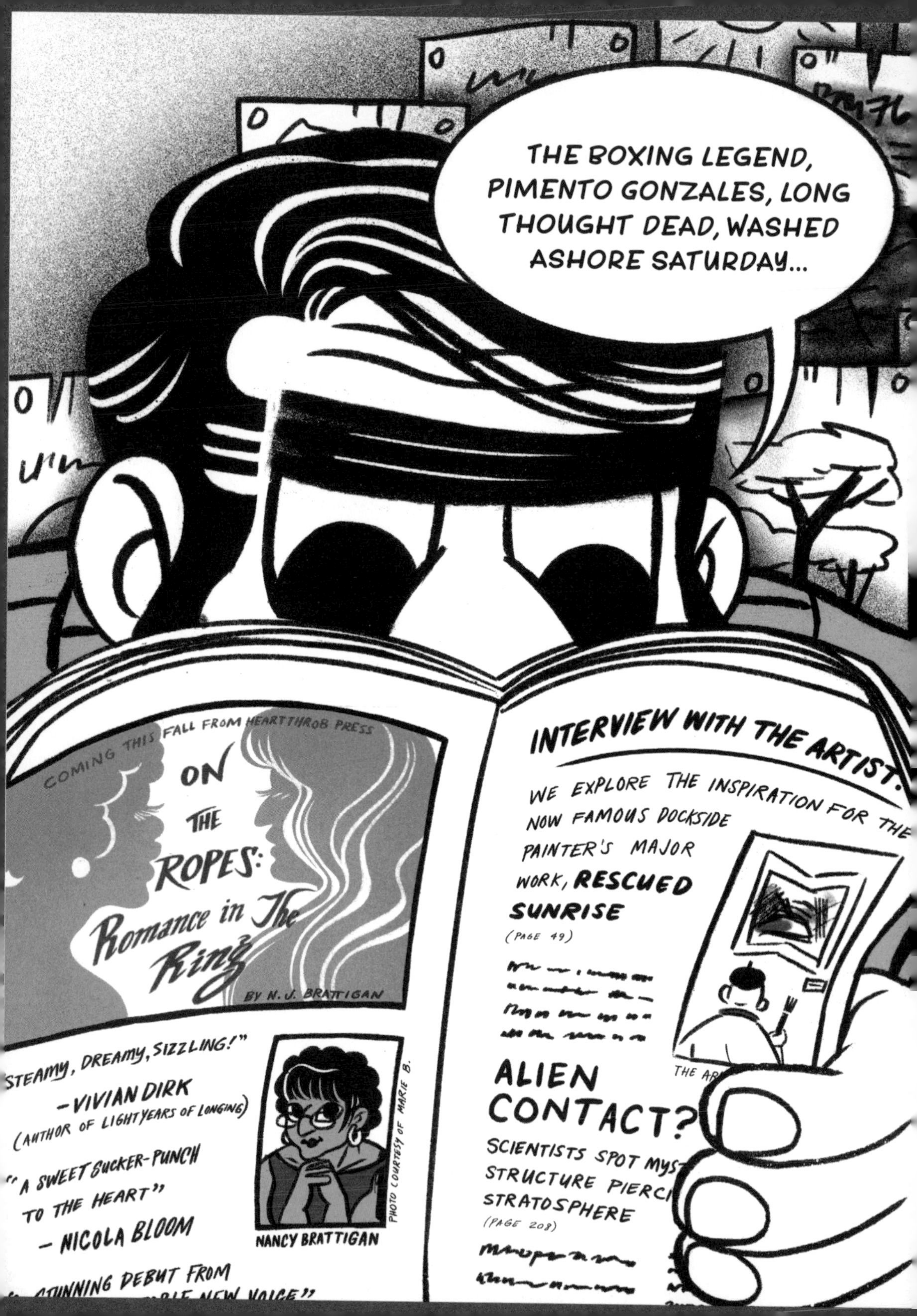
THE BOXING LEGEND, PIMENTO GONZALES, LONG THOUGHT DEAD, WASHED ASHORE SATURDAY...
COMING THIS FALL FROM HEARTTHROB PRESS
ON THE ROPES: Romance in The Ring
BY N. J. BRATTIGAN
STEAMY, DREAMY, SIZZLING!"
–VIVIAN DIRK
(AUTHOR OF LIGHTYEARS OF LONGING)
"A SWEET SUCKER-PUNCH TO THE HEART"
– NICOLA BLOOM
PHOTO COURTESY OF MARIE B.
NANCY BRATTIGAN
STUNNING DEBUT FROM
INTERVIEW WITH THE ARTIST.
WE EXPLORE THE INSPIRATION FOR THE NOW FAMOUS DOCKSIDE PAINTER'S MAJOR WORK, RESCUED SUNRISE
(PAGE 49)
ALIEN CONTACT?
SCIENTISTS SPOT MYS
STRUCTURE PIERC
STRATOSPHERE
(PAGE 208)

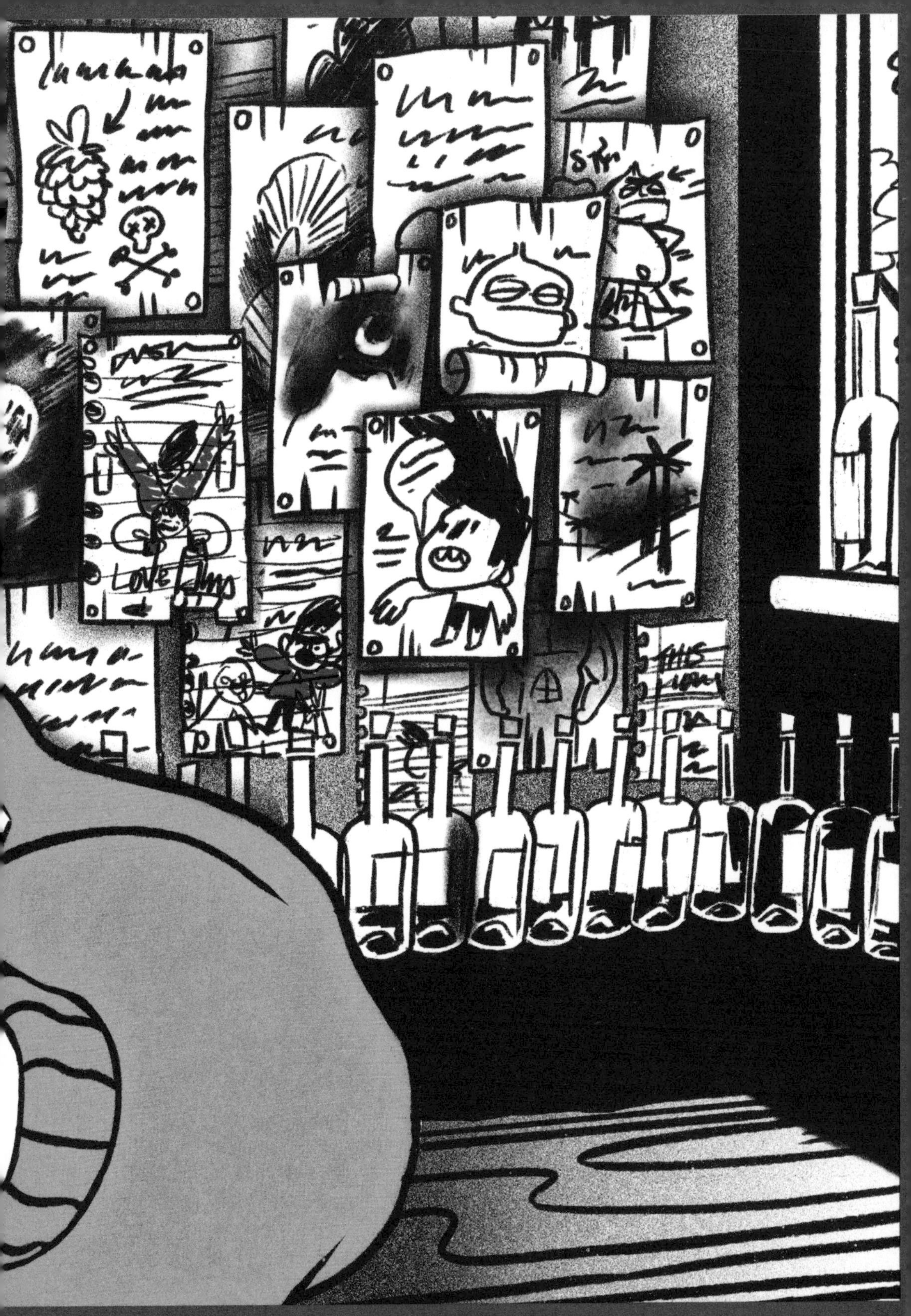
LOVE

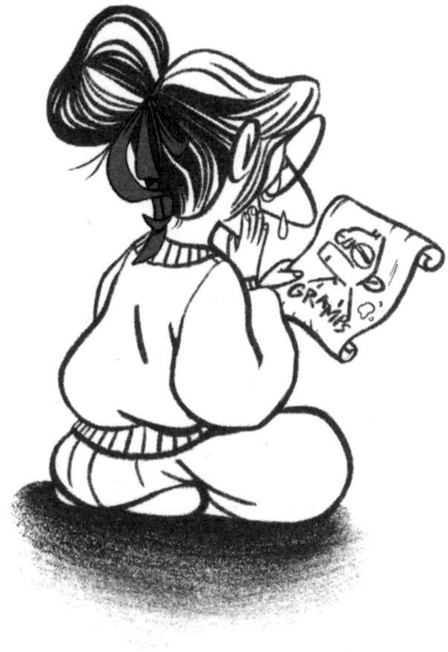
GRAMPS

ABOUT LARA

Lara Kaminoff is a cartoonist and book-slinger living in Seattle with her beloved and their cat, Creeper. She's inspired by an endless parade of podcasts, the magical world of fungi, brilliant friends, climbable trees, and danceable floors. Right now she's probably talking too fast, thinking too hard, or trying to fix something that ain't broke.

ACKNOWLEDGEMENTS:

This book has been a wild ride up a real steep learning curve, full of swerving delights and creaky wheels, and I have so many people to thank for its existence:

Many thanks to **Ayoola Solarin** for plucking Jimmy from the "maybe" pile and helping to get his little heart pumping; **Ivanna Khomyak** for her keen eye, perfectionism, and patience (a clink of the coffee mug from across the pond!); **Niamh Jones** for her humor, sweetness, and hand-holding (I owe you the coziest sweater); **Alessandra Sternfeld of Am-Book** for advocating for artists and fighting for this book; **Jacq Cohen** for helping me navigate the choppy waters of publishing; **Avi Ehrlich of Silver Sprocket** and **Kelly Froh of Short Run** for their snappy responses and solid advice.

I owe a great debt to the Seattle arts community: to **4Culture** for funding Jimmy's first gouache-painted foray onto the page, to **Push/Pull Underground Art & Comics** for reeling in a new generation of sequential art degenerates, to **Short Run Comix & Arts Festival** for giving me a seat at the table, and to **The Elliott Bay Book Company** and my book-slinging sibs in the **Book Workers Union** for making me a home among the stacks and cedar, and bringing incredible stories to the people of Seattle everyday.

My deep gratitude and eternal affection to: Mountain woman, perfect peach, and purveyor of fine soups and vistas, **Marie Bouassi**; early reader and incorrigible encourager, **Shawn Cecil**; art-talkin', long-walkin' straight shooter, **Sage Cruser**; cabin comrade and protest pal, **Jacob Schear**; my number one peanut forever and always, **Ariel Sayre**; and the dear laughter-rattled and wave-kissed **Harrops** for their tireless love and support.

Finally, I am profoundly grateful to **Susan Kaminoff** for sharing your page-turning passion and fighting fiercely for understanding above all things; **Pepper Kaminoff** for insisting I know how to take a good fall (go down easy and protect your head); **Alex Kaminoff** for teaching me it's better to suffer defeat among friends than be the lonely victor; and **Travis Rommereim**, for feeding and petting and soothing and chatting and joking and dreaming and generally tolerating the long nights, early mornings, and quiet madness of book-making. Iloveyoulloveyoulloveyou. From the back porch, xoxo, L

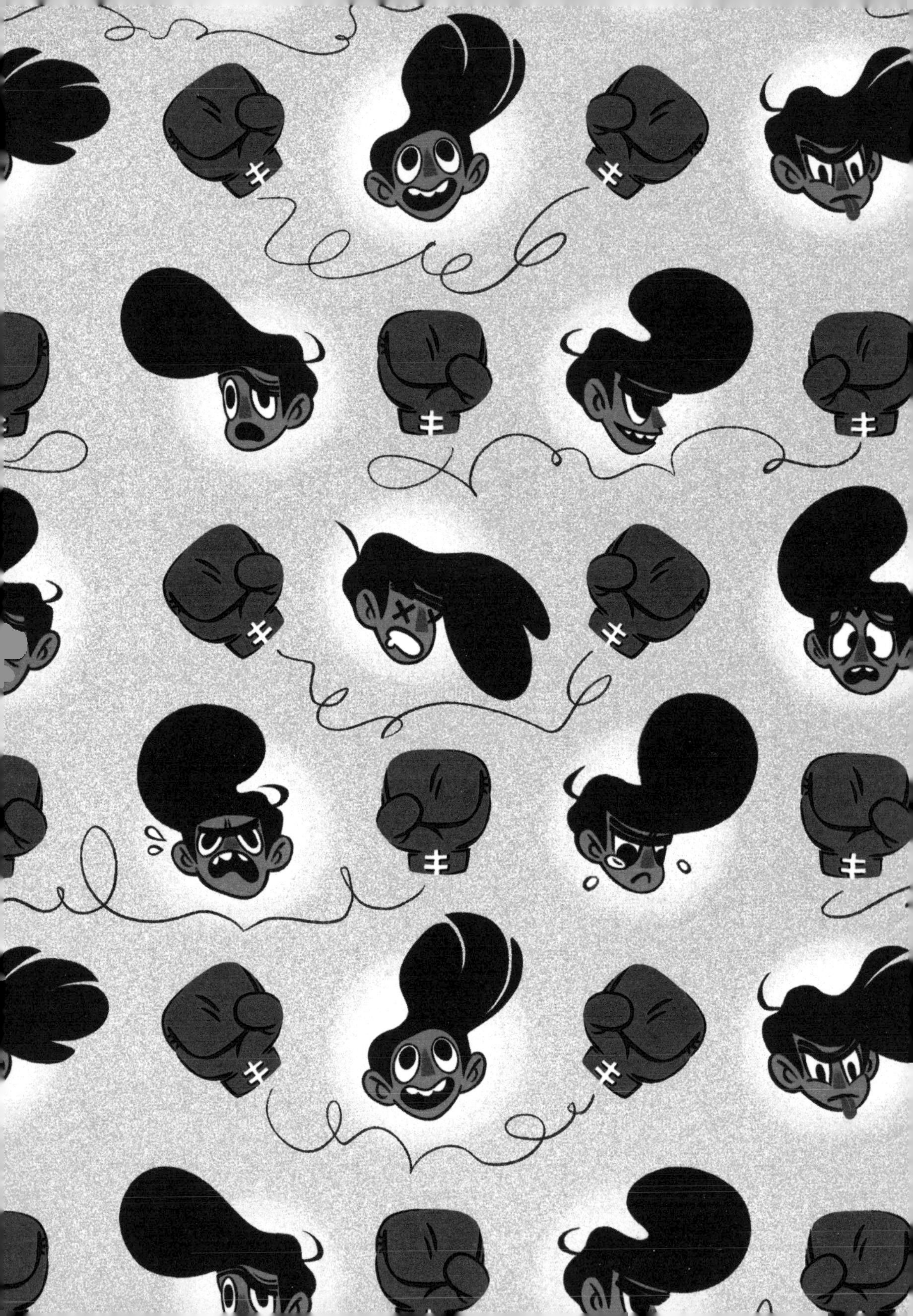